NEE HEMISH

This is a composite picture by Jose Rey Toledo of the history, heritage, and culture of Jemez Pueblo today. (Description of this illustration is found on page iv.)

NEE HEMISH

A History of Jemez Pueblo

Joe S. Sando

FOREWORD BY ALFONSO ORTIZ

UNIVERSITY OF NEW MEXICO PRESS : ALBUQUERQUE

Description of Frontispiece

This is a composite picture by Jose Rey Toledo of the history, heritage, and culture of Jemez Pueblo today. In the first row are Friar Marcus de Niza and his guide, Esteban, as they are portrayed at Jemez annually on November 12. At the bottom on the right is the Pecos bull, seen at Jemez on August 2, a contribution of the Pecos Pueblo people who migrated to Jemez in 1838. Above the bull is the dancing horse, a parody or representation of the Spanish conquistadores who first entered the Pueblo world in the sixteenth century. On both sides of the horse are the *abuelos* who accompany the dancing horse as well as the veiled dancing figures known as *matachines* who perform at Jemez on December 12.

In the left lower corner is the Christian cross, with the *tabo* or clown behind it, who is followed by a row of "fiesta day" corn dancers. They in turn are followed by the choir or singers for the corn dancers.

In the middle left margin a man waves the sacred pueblo standard or flag over the dancers. Above him stands the pueblo governor with the Spanish cane in his hand, which is the governor's sign of office and authority. Next to the governor is the Franciscan padre, who played a large part in the ancient drama. Next to the padre is the conquistador with his sword and helmet.

The scene is in the Christian church yard with the Pueblo Indian kiva shown above the choir. The pueblo homes are in the background beneath billowing New Mexico clouds, with rain falling in the distance.

Library of Congress Cataloging in Publication Data

Sando, Joe S., 1923–
    Nee Hemish, the history of Jemez Pueblo.

    Bibliograpy: p.
    Includes index.
    1. Jemez Indians—History.   2. Jemez Pueblo (N.M.)—History.   I. Title.
    E99.J4S26   1982   978.9'00497   82-16110
    ISBN 0-8263-0629-2

Dedicated to
the women of Jemez Pueblo;
the hardworking, patient women of Jemez.
Through their perseverence
they have kept our culture alive.

Contents

Illustrations

NOTE: Ornaments on the chapter-title pages are taken from old Pecos pottery decorations.

Lucas Toledo
Al Waquie
1965 New Mexico state AAU cross-country champions from Jemez
    Pueblo
Lupe M. Romero
Stone sculpture by Clifford Fragua
Stella Loretto
Evelyn Mora Vigil
Lucy Y. Lowden
Jose Rey Toledo
Traditional Jemez nativity scene
Two ancient ceremonial dances
Jemez children learning the Dance of the Buffalo

Foreword

In this intimate account of Jemez Pueblo from distant times to the modern era, Joe Sando profiles the multi-faceted history of one of the most vital and enduring of the Pueblo Indian communities of New Mexico. It is intimate because it is a story told by an insider, one whose experiences and perceptions of Jemez span nearly six decades. Sando writes about many of the events he describes with the authority of a participant and a witness.

The story told here is multi-faceted; Sando is not content to rely on just a single discipline of scholarship or to filter Jemez knowledge through the sieve of a particular, externally imposed theory or methodology. He writes about what has concerned the Jemez people in the past, what they are concerned about in the present, and what they are likely to be concerned about far into the future. This is a view of Jemez life as seen from the inside looking out through time. And, because the fate of the Jemez people has long been inseparable from that of the other pueblo people, this volume can also be understood as giving voice to pueblo-wide concerns as well.

Lest the reader be left with the impression that no grand design or methodology is present in this book, let me hasten to add that there is a method here. It is one distinctive to the author himself, though—

to what he understands to be the story of the Jemez people from their remembered origins onward, of their struggles, accomplishments, and aspirations as seen from within the community. The sustained commitment with which this story is told will long be seen as one of the enduring contributions of this study, for it is not merely a contribution to knowledge. It is that, most assuredly, but it is more, a contribution to our understanding and appreciation of the Jemez way of life.

Right from the beginning the author tells us of the Jemez people:

The secret of their existence was simple: they came face to face with nature but did not exploit her. They became a part of the ecological balance instead of abusing and destroying it, accepting the terms of their environment and becoming a part of the land, utilizing what the land had to offer without changing it.

This message constitutes one theme running through this book, albeit implicitly most of the time. Yet it is a message that can be understood to summarize succinctly the story not only of Jemez but of the pueblos generally, and of most other native North American peoples as well.

By deepest instinct Joe Sando is a historian, and this book is a multi-faceted history of Jemez. In Chapter 2 Sando makes a careful historical case for the respect of the Jemez people for their land. He demonstrates that the Jemez people have held their land through time by a careful and continuous use and stewardship of it, rather than because it was granted to them and set aside for their use by some distant European monarch. The many evocative, vivid, and poetic names they have for particular places indicate that they believed that landscape to be sacred and knew it intimately.

Especially noteworthy in regard to the land is Chapter 3, which deals with the legal history and current status of the land that is Jemez, and of other lands once under the direct stewardship of the Jemez people. One ownership confrontation occurring in 1892–93 between the Jemez, Santa Ana, and Zia Pueblos on the one hand, and the presumed Spanish heirs of a portion of the Indian aboriginal homeland on the other, is typical of the threats the Jemez people have long had to battle in their efforts to survive. Attorney Thomas B. Catron, representing the Spanish heirs of the three pueblos' homeland, got up in the Court of Private Land Claims and denied there is such a body or person known as the Pueblo of Zia, Santa Ana, or Jemez, or that any such body, either jointly or separately, exists or has any right to exist in proceedings for the confirmation of any grant title whatever, or that any such body is or was an [sic] authorized, empowered or entitled to hold, take, possess or enjoy said real estate, either under the laws of the Kingdom of Spain, Mexico, or the United States. He denied such Indians can sue or bring suit by virtue of designation as Indians.

And this was not the first time that the Jemez people had to prove that they even existed, let alone that they had the right to continue existing. Nor, if more recent events surrounding Jemez life and land chronicled in later chapters can be taken as a guide, will that occasion in 1893 be the last time Jemez will be called upon to defend its right to exist. These long-standing and continuing threats to the Jemez land and its resources is another theme, an explicit one, of this book.

Yet another theme is an account of how the world of the Jemez people has been expanding even while their land base has been shrinking. This apparent paradox occurs because by increasing political awareness and participation, and through education, the arts, sports, and travel, among other things, the effective world in which Jemez people operate has vastly expanded over the last century. While chronicling the growing Jemez political participation and success at the local and county levels, Sando also resurrects numerous Jemez leaders from historical oblivion through a careful combing of archival sources. In this he not only recovers a meaningful and usable past for the Jemez people, one about which they can be proud, but he also corrects the historical record for its wholly negative treatment of some of the earlier Jemez leaders.

In Chapter 10, on education, we learn how the major issue of concern has changed in a century from that of whether Jemez children will get any education at all, to who shall control that education. Through most of the history of Western-style education at Jemez, it was all externally shaped and imposed. Jemez parents and officials had no say in what was being taught and how. Beginning in the late 1960s this began to change, as Jemez and other Indian leaders across the nation began to demand a voice in the operation of schools serving their children, from helping to determine overall educational policy to shaping curricula and hiring teachers. In this educational change Jemez has been but a microcosm of the spirit of self-determination in all important matters that pervaded Indian affairs through the 1970s.

No single example better exemplifies the fact that Jemez is part of a larger world than this matter of seeking educational self-determination. Another way of looking at the whole picture of changes in opportunities and aspirations through education is to note that early Jemez college graduates went into teaching for the most part, while more recent ones have professional degrees in law and public health, and other fields.

When discussing most of Jemez Pueblo's dealings with the federal government, Joe Sando has not isolated Jemez, since so much of that pueblo's land and water use history is bound up with Santa Ana and Zia. When we turn to consider Jemez' dealings with the surrounding municipalities, we have to bear in mind that it is in Sandoval County, along with five Keresan-speaking pueblos. And then there is the All-Indian Pueblo Council (AIPC), representing all nineteen pueblos of New Mexico. Jemez officials work closely with the AIPC in their most general and important policy dealings with both the state and federal governments, as Sando clearly demonstrates in several chapters. Hence, when he appears to weave in and out from a discussion of Jemez at one moment to a discussion of all three pueblos on the Jemez River watershed at the next moment, to a discussion of the pueblos in general, he is neither confused nor trying to confuse the reader. Most of Jemez' external relations cannot be seen in isolation from other pueblos, at the very least.

There is much more that I am tempted to mention or summarize from the diverse remaining chapters of this carefully crafted work, but I shall refrain from doing so, as this is an introduction, rather than a summary or review. I should, however, like to mention two further chapters and the Epilogue. In Chapter 11, a brief twentieth century history of running at Jemez, we come quickly to understand the original religious inspiration for the long-distance and high-altitude running for which several Jemez runners have become famous far beyond Jemez in this century. In his justifiably proud portrayal of several such individual runners and their individual achievements, we are also brought to understand that the original ceremonial basis for running has been carried over into modern athletic competition. Clearly what is an ancient and enduring tradition is, in Jemez at least, continuing and moving into new arenas.

In the chapter following, on the history of the twentieth century revival in pottery-making at Jemez and Pecos, Sando presents four profiles of active, living artists that could only have been done by a caring kinsman, friend, and neighbor. Three of the four individual profiles are of potters, and all four are original and insightful in different ways. That of Evelyn Mora Vigil is the story of how a sensitive and gifted potter used ancient and enduring signs and inspiration to locate the proper clay to revive the long-lost Pecos pottery-making traditions of her ancestors. This profile, and that on Estella Loretto, another potter, tells of their experiments with different clays until each gets it right, gets the clay to say the things each artist wanted it to say. In the sketch of Loretto, by far the youngest of the four, there is also much for reflection on the formative processes of inspiration, on the beginnings of an artistic career.

When all is said and done, the most intimate statement in the book is the Epilogue. In it, Sando discusses the seasonal round of festivals and ceremonies, again without betraying in the least the trust of the Jemez people. He manages to impart a good sense of the seasonal round, of the flavor of everyday life at Jemez, proving it can be done without revealing things which pueblo people feel have no place in print. When I finished reading this book I felt as if I had spent a couple of evenings with an old and good friend, as indeed I had. I hope other readers will share at least something of the same sense when they finish reading it. We would all be enriched if someone from each of the pueblos of New Mexico would produce as intimate and caring a portrait of each as Joe Sando has done for Jemez.

Alfonso Ortiz

University of New Mexico
October 1982

Preface

It became apparent to me early in my career as an educator that there was no history of American Indians written by a member of that American subculture. Through the years Indian students have asked me where relevant history such as they had heard from their parents and grandparents might be found. Fellow tribal members of mine from Jemez, in quest of information for school term papers, and out of their own curiosity, have called me, asking about their history. These experiences have motivated me to research Jemez history with the idea of writing another book as a sequel to *The Pueblo Indians*, which was published in 1976.

I am fortunate that I am one of that disappearing breed raised in an atmosphere of limited influence from the dominant society. I am also fortunate that I survived World War II to take advantage of the G.I. Bill, which opened up a new world to me. These experiences, along with the knowledge of my first language, are now producing fruit through my ability to relate to the older generation who are familiar with the oral tradition.

Researching and learning about our Jemez history from the older people and the archives was a dream come true. Although it was heartbreaking to watch the expressions of the older people as I talked with them concerning our former land holdings, I could imagine the same expressions on the faces of other older people as they told the ones who told me.

Although I will get the credit, this project has been a family affair. I cannot thank my wife, Louisa, enough, since she was instrumental in providing access to much of the resource material, and has done both editing and proofreading. As a realty specialist with the B.I.A., she is familiar with the enormous files at the Southern Pueblos Agency. Our son Parker was also of assistance, since he helped revise the Pueblo Land Status Reports for the bureau, while waiting to hear about his state bar examination. The land status booklet on Jemez was invaluable as a starting point in researching the pueblo's land history and status.

Throughout the book I have used as source material the files of the current Southern Pueblos Agency, the old Southern Pueblos Agency, and the United Pueblos Agency for the time period in which the Northern and Southern Pueblos were combined under one agency. References to documents in the Jemez files are meant to inform the reader they they are to be found *somewhere* in these materials; they do not refer to any specific location.

My thanks to Dr. Richard N. Ellis, historian, and Dr. Alfonso Ortiz, anthropologist, both of the University of New Mexico, for reviewing my work while in progress. David Margolin did a fine job of copy editing, and I thank him.

And without financial help from the National Endowment for the Humanities (contract number P.S. 297030-78-342), this work would not have been possible. The findings and conclusions presented here do not necessarily represent the views of N.E.H.

"Tsa-ba-no-pa" to the many Jemez people I talked with during interviews and casual conversations concerning Jemez history and personalities.

Finally, whatever errors this book may contain, the work that has gone into it has been a labor of love.

Paa Péh/Joe S. Sando

Echo From Beyond

We are the First Inhabitants
of Jemez Pueblo.
We are the ones
Who traveled South
From the mountains,
With bows in hand,
In the prime
of our youth.

It was we who
Broke the trails
To your hunting grounds,
Cleared the land
Which is your lifeline,
Harnessed the river
Which waters your fields.
We, who with sweat-streaked faces,
Saw in
Setting sun the
Promise of Tomorrow.

Here we lived
And loved,
Fought and drove the Spaniards,
The Apaches, the Navajos,
And the Comanches and Utes
From our fields
And homes.
Built the kivas
For your recreation
and education.

We served our turn.
We laid the
Strong foundations.
We are content.
Look not back
Too long,
Too often;
But build, like us.
Carry on
For your sons
For a better day
Tomorrow.

1

In the Beginning

It is commonly held by experts in American prehistory that bands of hunters, ancestors of some of the American Indians, crossed the Bering Straits sometime after one of the maximum glacial advances of the Pleistocene ice age, although many questions remain, such as exactly when and where this happened. The tools, weapons, and clothing of the first Americans remain unknown, but there is consensus among social scientists that these bands of hunters were of Asian stock. Research in biology, language, and archeology have supposedly supported this conclusion.

Nevertheless, among all the works that have been written, there is not one that explains where these original settlers of North America came from. Nor has any society or people ever been identified across the Straits with cultures, languages, or blood types similar to those of modern Native Americans.

Most American Indians do not believe that the continent of America was formed by the Creator and then left without people; we believe that we were created and then placed on this continent. Maybe there is a story to tell here after all, if there is any truth to oral history; for there appears to be as much doubt about the Christian theory of the creation of Adam and Eve in paradise as there is concerning Darwin's theory of evolution. Currently, discoveries and theories previously re-

1

jected are being examined, reexamined, and applied to the first New World natives, particularly the Pueblo Indians.

Dr. Jeffrey Goodman, director of Archeological Research Associates, Inc., of Tucson, Arizona, explains in *American Genesis* (1981) that some human remains and artifacts which have been tested date as far back as seventy thousand years ago. He maintains that professional archeologists no longer accept the traditional archeological version of American Indian origins, but rather that the first fully modern men made their world debut in North America.

Another recent idea is that of deciphering American inscriptions apparently written in various European and Mediterranean alphabets dating from over two thousand years ago. According to Dr. Barry Fell of Harvard University, a marine biologist, in his book *America, B.C.* (1976), the inscriptions speak not only of visits by ancient ships, but also of permanent colonies of Celts, Basques, Libyans, and even Egyptians. These apparent inscriptions have been found on buried temples, on tablets, on gravestones, and on cliff faces in nearly all parts of the United States, Canada, and Latin America.

From this we might infer that early colonists from Europe and the Mediterranean influenced ancient America through visitation, settlement, and no doubt intermarriage. To make the possibility more interesting, it has been suggested that American Indians have blood types similar to those of people of the Mediterranean area.

If we accept Native North American oral history and Goodman's theory, then we can start with the ancient people who have been in North America for many thousands of years and still allow for European and Mediterranean colonists to strengthen or boost the developing culture. This appears to be what the indigenous people have been saying in their oral history. But later Europeans with their "proof positive" and "show-me" attitudes have prevailed, and remain largely unwilling to consider, much less to confirm, native creation accounts.

Native oral history, then, leaves room for an American origin, as well as for the land-bridge theory, with later arrivals of other people via the Atlantic and subsequent dispersal, whether from the Caribbean or Yucatan. This latter probability arises from the number of loanwords in Pueblo Indian languages from native tribes to the south. Let us look at the land-bridge theory first.

It is conceivable that after centuries of pre-Columbian life, traditions and oral history were shared, exchanged, copied, adopted, and adapted throughout the continent. Consequently, almost every tribe has a creation story of coming from the underworld led by a bird, animal, or leader of some sort. Bear in mind that various groups of American Indians were not alike by any means, but important features common to them all were Asiatic characteristics such as black hair (usually straight), brown skin, dark eyes, and a broad face with prominent cheek bones.

If there was a crossing of the land bridge, or as Goodman calls it, "a recent return migration" (1981: 180), it probably took place during two periods (Driver 1969). Anthropologists, archeologists, climatologists, ethnologists, and linguists have assembled evidence that there were two land bridges between Siberia and Alaska during the late Pleistocene ice age. The first existed between approximately 50,000 and 40,000 B.C.; the second between approximately 20,000 and 8,000 B.C. The second bridge was evidently wider than the first, and reached its maximum width of one thousand miles in about 18,000 B.C. However, to increase the puzzle, the climate during the time of the first land bridge was probably milder and more favorable to humans than it is today.

An impediment to migration into North America over this second bridge was an ice barrier just south of Alaska, between approximately 21,000 and 11,000 B.C. But the sudden appearance of evidence of people in North America at many localities around 10,000 B.C., or soon after, appears to indicate that there may have been ice-free corridors through which human groups could travel.

If any groups did migrate, scientists believe that they were the Athapascans, Eskimos, and Aleuts. The time they crossed is uncertain, but these groups are apparently the only ones to show a true affinity with Asian populations.

The theory that all Indians migrated persists, however, because Native Americans have a closer physical resemblance to Asians than they do to any other major physical type in the Old World. Scholars go further, to say that the resemblance is closer to the marginal Mongoloids of Indonesia, west-central Asia, and Tibet. This means that Native Americans do not as closely resemble the central Asians of Mongolia, China, or Japan.

But the mystery of the first Americans' origin remains, since today their descendants' cultures, religions, languages, and diets are unlike those of Asians. Genetic traits indicate to us in no uncertain terms the differences between Native North Americans and Asians. Traits such as blood types, ear wax, and fingerprint patterns give evidence of the uniqueness of Native North Americans (Goodman 1981:180).

Another theory that is gaining momentum is that of Thor Heyerdahl. Some time ago he sailed in a reed raft from the Persian Gulf to a point in South America, proving that another group of people may have crossed the Atlantic to begin a society of Native Americans, or at least to influence the natives.

As time goes by and additional research is carried out this theory may become as popular as the land-bridge theory, since not only is there much similarity in food and language among North, Central, and South America, but some religious practices also appear to be similar; even ancient legends appear to coincide. Most Native Americans, like the Pueblo Indians, have creation stories of emerging from the underworld. A most comprehensive compilation of native creation stories, foreign discoveries and voyages, and biblical episodes was made by Bill Coffer (1978), of Choctaw-Cherokee ancestry. These creation stories, however, do not mention crossing the land bridge.

The Jemez Pueblo people, or Hemish, the subject of this book, have creation stories of emerging from the underworld. The legends speak of the beginning, when they were under the direct guidance of the Creator after emerging from the underworld, known to them as Hua-vu-na-tota, via a lake called Hoa-sjela, now known as Stone or Boulder Lake, on the Jicarilla Apache reservation, in Rio Arriba County, in northwestern New Mexico.

Other Pueblos, like the Tewas, speak of a lake in the San Juan Mountain Range, north of Alamosa, Colorado, as the place of their emergence. For the Taos Pueblo people it is their sacred Blue Lake. As more American Indians write down what they can of their oral history, the culture, religious beliefs, and ceremonies of their ancestors may be compared, to interpret the already voluminous literature on ethnology and archeology.

Undocumented as they are, traditions concerning the existence of the ancestors of Native Americans persist, as they have for thousands of years. It may be vague, mythical, remote, and clouded by the romantic mists of antiquity, but tribal oral history is valuable and sacred for those raised within its confines.

But to return to our study of the beginning, and in order to give the reader some perspective of time in Pueblo prehistory, a simplified explanation of the different archeological eras is presented. This classification is called the Pecos Classification, and was established as the result of a meeting called in 1927 by Alfred Vincent Kidder, to set a time frame for each of the Basket Maker periods. The Basket Makers are generally taken to be the ancestors of the present-day Pueblo Indians. The different eras of the Pecos Classification are as follows:

Basket Maker I Period—10,000 B.C. *to the Birth of Christ*
    Nomadic hunters and seed gatherers
    Cave dwellings without rock and mud masonry work
    Wooden clubs or rabbit sticks, as used today
Basket Maker II Period—A.D. 1 *to* A.D. 450
    Sedentary
    Baskets but no pottery; sandals; bags
    Raising squash and flint-type corn; no beans
    Pit houses with central fire pits
    Fur-string blankets
    Metates
    Spears and atlatls
Basket Maker III Period—A.D. 450 *to* A.D. 700
    Organized communities of pit houses
    Bows and arrows
    New varieties of corn; beans
    Turkeys
Pueblo I Period—A.D. 700 *to* A.D. 900
    First true pottery—corrugated utility vessels
    Loom weaving
    Turkey-feather cord
    Turquoise jewelry
    Cotton introduced
    Surface dwellings—first true pueblos
    Kivas developed
Pueblo II Period—A.D. 900 *to* A.D. 1150
    Cliff dwellings where caves existed
    Ring baskets
    Painted designs on pottery
    Spindles
    Cotton blankets start to replace fur and feather blankets
    Dance courts (plazas) in center of pueblos
Pueblo III Period—A.D. 1150 *to* A.D. 1300 (*also known as Great Pueblo, or Classic Age*)
    Flowering of architecture
    Pottery reaches peak technical, artistic quality
    Arts and crafts

Great terraced houses
Great kivas developed
Spectacular ceremonial life
Period of great drought (1276–99)
Movement south and southeast
   Pueblo IV Period—A.D. *1300 to* A.D. *1600*
   Masonry deteriorates, following migration(?)
   Corrugated pottery disappears
   Lead glaze and polychrome appear
   Spanish enter Southwest, 1539–40
   Spanish explorations
Pueblo V Period—A.D. *1600 to Present*
   Pueblo Revolt, 1680–92
   Mexican Period (1821–48)
   American Period (1848–present)

The Hemish Move On

It is uncertain whether the Hemish were in their ancestral home area as long ago as the Pueblo III period (1150–1300). According to Hemish legends, following their emergence from the lake the Hemish lived for untold centuries within sixty or seventy miles of Hoa-sjela. For the greater part of this time they lived in a simple, primitive condition, dominated by the physical forces of climate and geography. Barren as the landscape may appear, and rugged as the huge canyons and mountains may seem, they provided the people with a hard-won livelihood. Indeed, the Hemish struggled for a bare existence in their wandering search for food and shelter. This is what Morgan (1877) referred to as humans beginning their career "at the bottom of the scale and working their way up from savagery to civilization through the slow accumulation of experimental knowledge."

The secret of their existence was simple: they came face to face with nature but did not exploit her. They became a part of the ecological balance instead of abusing and destroying it, accepting the terms of their environment and becoming a part of the land, utilizing what the land had to offer without changing it.

Very likely their first shelters were caves, followed by enclosures within the caves made of rock and mud, and lastly, pit houses. They divided their time between open-air shelters and caves in the sandstone cliffs. The cave dwellings were not deep caves as such, but rock shelters, relatively shallow, well lighted recesses at or near the bases of cliffs. The last vestige of pit-house architecture remains in the pueblos today: the kiva entrance, with the ladder separated from the smoke hole only by the ceiling crossbeam.

Legends tell us that the initial family living arrangements were by clans in certain defined areas. The clans were further broken down into extended families, essentially self-sufficient economic units co-operating in growing and collecting food, hunting, and farming. As raiding tribes burst onto the scene about the time of the Pueblo I and II periods, dwellings began to be built alongside cliffs in some of the most inaccessible areas high above Gy'a-wahmu ("boulder canyon"), known today as Largo Canyon, and other neighboring areas south of the San Juan River.

The Hemish were not alone, for to the north and northeast were the Tewas, and to the west and northwest were the Keresans. The Tewas today are known by their Spanish-named villages—San Juan, Santa Clara, San Ildefonso, Nambe, Pojoaque, and Tesuque. Five of the Keresan villages are Cochiti, Santo Domingo, San Felipe, and several villages of the Laguna Pueblos. Legends describe their migration routes as coming from the Aztec area and going east to enter the Rio Grande area from the north, via Chama and El Rito. The other three Keresan villages are Acoma, Santa Ana, and Zia. Traditional legends define their migration route as straight south from Chaco Canyon, with the latter two stopping along the Rio Puerco for a time, before moving east to the banks of the Jemez Creek, where they are today.

The Lagunas were a part of the eastern Keresans, until they fled the Rio Grande in the troubled years after the great Pueblo revolution of 1680.

With these neighbors the Hemish traded and exchanged ideas. Most importantly, they formed an alliance for mutual benefit and protection against the common enemy, the raiders. The other two groups probably served as buffers for the Hemish from the Yuta-ongs (Utes) and K'e-latosh (Navajos). Except for language, the Keresans and the Tewas had similar cultures in terms of food, costumes, religious beliefs, and practices. They supplemented their diet of game animals with cultivated produce such as squash and a type of corn, as well as with berries and other wild products from the land and the forest.

The ancient Hemish homeland was a vast wilderness of sparsely peopled, piñon-covered rolling hills, flat-topped mesas, and deep desert canyons. From their homes they could see the snow-covered San Juan mountain range about forty miles to the north, in present-day Colorado.

Today when the opng-soma (war chief) recites the prayer-oratory, he includes

the mountain range which the sun follows from east to west, the mountain range to the north, white with snow, the mountain range visible daily from the place of the origin of the Hemish people, that mountain range which is hallowed by the spirits of our grandfathers.

Ignorant at first of the origins of natural phenomena, yet their awareness of an obvious pattern in nature led to a search for cause and responsibility. And from this the first real forms of religion emerged. Since then, the tradition of religious beliefs has permeated every aspect of the people's lives; it determines their relation with the natural world and with their fellows. The basic concern of their religion is continuity of the harmonious relationship with the world in which they live. "To maintain such a relationship between the people and the spiritual world, various societies exist, with particular responsibilities for weather, fertility, curing, hunting, and pleasure or entertainment of the people" (Sando 1976:22).

Two religious organizations for the protection of people and property are the men's Arrow and Eagle societies, which grew out of the need for protection against raiders. To this day they exist as highly military organizations, with leadership similar to that of any modern-day military unit.

These two societies protected the people from outside harm, and in the late eighteenth and nineteenth centuries were heavily depended upon by the Spaniards and Mexicans in their struggles against the raiding Apaches, Comanches, Navajos, and Utes. Because these societies performed so well as deterrants against raiding tribes, to this day the former enemies, the Navajos, call the ancestors of the Pueblo Indian people Anaazaja. It is probable that Anaazaja comes from two words: *anaa*, meaning enemy, enmity, and discord (Wall-Morgan 1958) and *zaja*, meaning ancestors. The word Anaazaja, then, means "enemies of our ancestors." However, anthropologists have created a word, Anasazi, to mean "the ancient ones"—describing the ancestors of the Pueblo Indians, among whom were the Hemish, who started the Arrow and Eagle societies to fight Navajos and other enemies. As more native speakers of Indian languages reach the universities, they find many strange words created by social scientists; these they accept, as a prerequisite for communication in the classroom. However, these words are often unknown by the Indian tribes of whose language they are supposed to be a part.

Likewise, to the chagrin of the Pueblo Indians, many of their aboriginal ruins now bear Navajo names like Tsegi, Betatakin, and Kiet Siel in northern Arizona, and Navajo Reservoir in northern New Mexico. The ancestors of the Ashiwish (Zunis) have been called the Mogollon and Mimbres cultures; a Zuni ruin in Arizona is known as Grasshopper Village.

Today, when descendants of the former enemies meet, they often exchange versions of incidents handed down by word of mouth through the generations. The Navajos tell the Pueblos how their ancestors described ancient Pueblo warriors as being of small stature, but with unlimited endurance to run and fight. They would outflank the fleeing Navajos by running around a mountain, then lying in wait to attack as the Navajos approached nonchalantly. The small size of the ancient Pueblo people is deducible from the size of the ancient shelters or cliff dwellings on top of boulders around Largo Canyon and in the Gallina area, ancient homeland of the Hemish.

The Navajos arrived in the Southwest from the Northwest toward the end of the Pueblo IV period. Different in culture as the K'ela-tosh were, and being newcomers in a strange land, they relied heavily upon the Hemish and other Pueblo tribes for food and other necessities of life. No doubt for many years there existed negative memories of the rude and abrasive invasion, and the subsequent hostile relationship with the raiding tribes, or "bárbaros," as the Spanish called them; but the hardship resulting from the Navajo and Apache invasion from the northwest is not felt today. What is known is that it led to the concentration of population, with marked progress and strong local specialization in material traits such as basketry, pottery, and weaving. Necessity was truly the mother of invention for the Pueblos at this time; besides functional tools, they developed religious-social activities as a result of close living, which became their recreation.

For many years the Hemish lived in the Largo Canyon–Jicarilla area of today. But the good years did not compensate for the dry years, which brought little rainfall and many raiders. So it may have occurred to the leaders that they would have to move to another area in search of crop-producing water and tranquility.

Consequently, during a winter solstice ceremony, the high priests (of the *cacique* society) and the "fathers" called upon the guiding spirits (Tia-saish) to announce to them their intentions of moving. Having informed the dieties, they tied prayer feathers to Ma'sewi and She'oyewi, the twin war gods, for assistance and protection during the approaching days of uncertainty and the journey to the next homeland.

So the Hemish moved from west of Stone Lake to south of Stone Lake, creating a land base that now extended from the lake to the Gallina-Cuba area (Ford, Peckham, and Schroeder 1972:25). Here they built stone-and-mud shelters on top of large boulders and at points of mesas that offered commanding views of large areas, in order to be able to spot unfriendly intruders at a distance—and the shelters could also be defended against the same intruders.

In the Gallina area the Hemish scattered as far south as Pae'-holer-sele-kwa ("yellow mountain place") and Paa-voda-sha-nu ("hidden spring place"), both west of today's Cuba. West of La Ventana is Ona-'gya-nu ("petrified footprint") and Wachu-paa-wa ("rainbow springs"). A complete ceremonial altar was still visible on the cliffs by the spring in the recent past. Besides shrines left and refurbished occasionally, the area continues to contribute to Jemez culture through a mineral used by the people for painting dance costumes. Permission now has to be granted by the new, non-Indian owner before the people can go in to obtain the needed mineral.

Not having escaped the danger of raiders, and with the attraction of a new land of "milk and honey," after at least three hundred years in the Gallina area the Hemish moved again, perhaps prompted entirely by the great drought of A.D. 1276–99. Since communications were always open with other Pueblo tribes, even over great distances, the Hemish were aware of the Te-wesh (Tiwas) over the mountains to the southeast, along a great river that flowed all year long.

In that direction they journeyed, again after informing the dieties during the winter solstice. After a short trip south on relatively flat land, they climbed the Nacimiento range to the east. Well over the range are the Rio de las Vacas and the Rio Cebolla. Here they established themselves at places like Pe-fwo-wa ("sun flower place") and Tuva-kwa (?). The latter is very important to the Jemez people today, but was obviously never visited by the Spaniards, since it has never been mentioned in print before. Judging from their oral traditions, Hemish culture blossomed after they arrived in the Jemez high country, during the Pueblo III period.

Before the Hemish left the Gallina area, they placed shrines along their way as a sign of identification for ownership, to be protected by the twin gods from the vicissitudes of nature—floods, lightning, tornadoes, and drought. Thus there are shrines at Pau-wa-s'ta-wa ("holy ghost spring"), Sae-yu-shun-kio-kwa ("bird peak"), Pe-pen-huni-kwa ("mountain's end"), Da-'ash-te-kwa ("petrified stone place"), Pe-kwile-gi ("sunbeam place"), also known as Peñasco Spring, and the last and most southern point of Jemez spiritual land today, Pe-paa-kwa ("sun spring"), west of San Ysidro.

In the new home area shrines were also placed at Tsung-paa-gi ("sad spring"), Wa-ha-bela-wa ("butterfly place"), both below Tu-va-kwa, and along the two creeks mentioned above. The others were farther east, in San Diego Canyon: Guisewa ("soda dam"), Daha-enu ("battleship rock"), at the Jemez Falls, and on top of Wa-ve-ma (Redondo Peak), and the northeast-corner boundary mark at Pa-shum-mu ("flower mountain"), now known as Chicoma Peak. Unfortunately, most of these places, though in use today, are no longer in Jemez ownership so, again, permission has to be obtained before visiting these places ceremonially. The only known spot owned by Jemez is on top of Redondo Peak, where a "generous" area, four feet by four feet, is set aside by the "benevolent" owner of the surrounding timber and grazing area. The only reason it is set aside is that it contains a visible shrine. The most important shrines in use currently are Tu-va-kwa, Wa-ve-ma, and Pe-kwile-gi.

Other than the Valle Grande, Jemez lost its forested areas in 1905, when President Theodore Roosevelt, without consulting the owners, declared much of the area government forest land, although there is documentation showing that the tribe continued to use the area as late as 1927. Up until that time the young men went to these areas to herd horses during the months of June and July, before the herd was returned to the village to be used in threshing wheat. The dates are visible today on the aspen trees, where herders carved their initials and the date.

There are many stories of the experiences of young Jemez men while they were out herding horses. In a particularly popular story told to the grandchildren, during the late 1800s a raiding Navajo group was discovered unaware in the Valle Grande, camped on the west edge near a thick growth of scrub oak. The Jemez men were camped on the southeast side of the large, grassy meadow of Valle Grande. Since the Jemez men had spotted the Navajos first, they had the advantage; individual assignments and instructions were given, including the method

of communications (whistling in different tones and length, plus im-
itating different bird calls for different situations). Cristobal Sando,
grandfather and great-grandfather of the present-day Sandos, was selected to shoot the Navajo purported to be the leader. With their bows
and arrows three men penetrated the thick brush surrounding the
Navajo camp; the others were stationed at different distances, to prevent
the raiders from reaching the herd and from inflicting damage to the
men. After patiently waiting for the right situation and position of the
Navajo leader, Grandpa Cristobal let fly an arrow. The fatal shot
reached its mark and caused great excitement, confusion, and furor
among the raiders. They took off toward the west, with more Jemez
arrows flying after them—intended more as scare tactics than to kill
the raiders. In their haste the raiders left twisted strips of cowhide and
some strips of tanned deerhide.

To return to the former tribal homeland, other Jemez villages on
top of Mun-stia-shun-qkio-kwa ("big thumb hilltop place," or San
Diego Mesa) are the two visited by de Vargas and other Spaniards—
A-stio-le-kwa ("grinding-stone lowering place") toward the point of the
mesa, and Amu-shun-kwa ("anthill place") on Holiday Mesa, to the
northwest. Rarely mentioned in print are Wa-han-kwa ("pumpkin place"),
on the ridge overlooking present-day Jemez Springs, and its neighbor
to the south, Ko-le-wa-han-anu ("small pumpkin"). It is very probable
that Guisewa developed as a result of the arrival of Padre Alonzo de
Lugo, the first missionary to the Hemish, who came in with Oñate
in 1598.

The reason behind this deduction is that traveling the trail up to
Wa-han-kwa from Jemez Springs takes a person in good physical shape
at least an hour and a half, on a very steep, barely visible trail. It takes
the same amount of time to slide back down from the top. Thus, it
is probable that Padre de Lugo decided to build the first Hemish mission
church down below, at Guisewa, Jemez Springs today. The San Jose
Mission Church there is now a state monument.

Other early sites along San Diego Canyon are north of Soda Dam.
The one nearest to it is Noni-shagi ("aspen growing place") and Unshagi
("cedar growing place"), below Battleship Rock and Camp Shafer. East
of Battleship Rock, along the East Fork, is Ho-kin-ti-le-ta ("white hole
place"), listed as Hot Springs Pueblo on some maps.

Then there is Pa-to-kwa ("turquoise moiety place"), at the south
base of Mun-stia-shun-qkio-kwa. Until recently the land on which the
ruins of Pa-to-kwa are located was in private ownership, and the land

was unmercifully vandalized with a front-end loader, while someone was searching for a "golden church bell." The location is now under federal ownership, supervised by the Forest Service. Northwest from here, on Virgin Canyon, is Bule-tza-kwa ("shell eye place").

The other area to which the Hemish spread is the eastern highlands of the San Juan Mesa and Paliza Canyon. Some were permanent homesites, while others were summer farming homes. The raiding tribes searched so thoroughly for food that the Hemish tried to remain as inaccessible and hidden as possible, as we shall see in later chapters. The two larger villages of importance were Sesho-kwa ("eagle living place"), which is remembered as a place where drying venison was always hanging; and Wa-han-cha-nu-kwa ("pumpkin moiety place"). The other, smaller settlements might very well have been farming areas: Wabaa-kwa (?) and Wa-cak-kwa ("wide open place"). These locations seem rather remote from the four-corners region of today, but oral history has it that the raiders still came to these farming areas.

In due time some of the people from the eastern highlands, under pressure from de Lugo or Padre Salmeron, who replaced him in 1618, began to filter to areas near present-day Walatowa (Jemez Pueblo). Shelters were erected by two natural springs near Jemez Creek: Guila-wemu ("value ridge"), north of Jemez, and Kia-stya-shun-kwa ("man-ure hill place"), south of the government day school. Later, Seto-kwa ("eagle cage place") sprang up, as a wandering band returned to the Hemish community.

Once the eastern highlanders from Seshokwa and Wahanchanukwa came to Walatowa, they probably never returned to their old homes, in contrast to the westerners, who returned to their own homes during times of conflict with the Spaniards. This deduction is based on the nearly complete disappearance of the ruins in the San Juan and Paliza areas, while signs of ancient sites were still identifiable in the west until at least the 1940s.

Certainly the dawning years vanish into the mists of legends, but after thousands of years of searching for prosperity, peace, and freedom, the permanent home of the Hemish became Walatowa, or Jemez Pueblo. Much remains to be said about the history made there during the Spanish and Mexican eras.

2

Mother Earth

The Jemez people have traditionally addressed the land on which they lived as No-wa-mu, or "Mother Earth." Since it is the source of their existence, it is sacrosanct—for thousands of years the people have derived their subsistence from the soil. With this basis of life come attitudes towards the earth and weather which might be expected, intensified by the mystic tendency of most American Indians. To this may be added the factor of hunting game animals and birds, not only as a sport, serving as a relief from the monotony of agriculture, but to provide an important addition to the food supply of a particularly enjoyable kind. Hunting is also based upon the soil.

Life-sustaining as the land has been and continues to be for the people, it has also been the major source of conflict with newcomers. The rivalry between using the land for commercial agriculture, timber, mining, and grazing, and using it for hunting and religious purposes has triggered immense conflict. While other Indian tribes have experienced continual conflict, Jemez's problems were at a minimum until recently. As this is being written problems are surfacing that we shall examine in later chapters.

The ancient homeland with its shrines is still a major part of Jemez tradition today, although most of it is now administered by the U.S.

Forest Service, with some in private, non-Indian control. The ownership of these former Indian lands by the federal government, and supervision by the Forest Service should be a consolation, since private ownership by non-Indians has often resulted in destructive acts by artifact hunters. Federal dominion has resulted in the enactment of the protective legislation known as the "Archeological Resources Protection Act of 1979," P.L. 96–95, (93 Stat. 721), passed on October 31, 1979.

Concepts of land, its ownership, and its use have always differed between aboriginal Americans and European invaders. While the Europeans' main purpose has been commercial exploitation, Native Americans have always practiced alternative uses of their land; for example, certain areas were mainly of religious significance. Such are the shrines that are scattered throughout the Jemez country today, mostly on non-Indian land. Forest lands in these same areas could not be used for hunting areas, but were restricted to eagle catching exclusively by the Eagle Catching Society. Then there were those areas that grew the sacred fir used during ceremonials. No single area was used for collecting the fir trees, in order to preserve the natural appearance. Deer hunting areas were shared with Zia and Santa Ana pueblos, but each group customarily camped at different spots. The forested areas were also used for grazing horses in the months prior to threshing wheat. The traditional pasture was Valle Grande, the huge, grass-covered bowl on the north side of the magnificent Redondo Peak. The northeast corner of the Jemez boundary was on the east end of this huge pasture, marked by the mountain called Pa-shun ("flower mountain"). The Tewas of Santa Clara, San Ildefonso, and San Juan also recognize this marker, which they call Tsi-ku-mu ("obsidian-covered mountain"). The state map lists it as Chicoma.

Oral history tells us that the herd was left to graze on the pasture while young Jemez men camped on the edges of the grassland to protect the herd from Navajo raiders. The forested areas near the natural bowl were also used by the eagle catchers in late fall, following the harvest. Just south of Pa-shun is the area where flagstones for making paper bread were quarried by both the horse herders and the eagle catchers in spare moments.

A majority of American Indians think of their land as sacred mother earth. This is the reason America looked so new when it was rediscovered by Europeans. But it is not a "new world"; only the conquerors were different, strange, and new to the natives. America, in fact, is as old as any other continent in the world, and has nourished living creatures for many hundreds of thousands of years.

The natives took care of the land, and are proud that it has served and saved thousands of people throughout the world from starvation. When Europeans arrived, America was well cared for, so beautiful, so loved—hence, so plentiful. America had remained new since it had not been made old and scarred by human greed—it had not yet been exploited ruthlessly. Instead, America had been lived on by people who regarded life on their part of the earth as a sacred experience of caring for all life.

To the Pueblo Indian the land is not inanimate. It is a living entity, the mother of all life, the Mother Earth. All her children, everything in nature is alive; the living stone, the great breathing mountains, the rushing rivers and streams, the trees and plants, as well as birds and animals—and, of course, human beings.

All of these the Pueblo Indians, and other Indians, view as united in one harmonious whole. Whatever happens to one affects the others, changing the interlocking relationships between the parts.

For many years, due to misunderstanding and a lack of interpretation, Pueblo Indians have been called nature worshippers. In fact, we worship the Creator of the magnificent, incomparable nature around us; it serves as an awesome reminder of the Creator whom we worship. Likewise, we do not believe in mastery over nature, nor in controlling or destroying it. The Pueblo Indian belief is that in destroying nature, man—who is also part of nature—ruptures his own inner self. We are land-based creatures rooted in nature consciously and unconsciously.

This is not a unique view. Dr. Jack D. Forbes, in the spring, 1974, issue of *The Indian Historian*, said, "It is true that a people who do not recognize the intrinsic rights of other living creatures will destroy them at will."Thoreau said, "A man is rich in proportion to the number of things he can afford to let alone."

Unfortunately, Jemez lands have not been let alone. Today, Jemez owns only 89,622.99 acres, much less than its traditional holdings. Jemez lands, composed of three areas, are located in the north-central part of New Mexico, in Sandoval County. The first official grant of 17,331 acres was made by the Spanish crown through Governor Domingo Jironza Petriz de Cruzate, on September 20, 1689. The boundaries of the grant were measured from the front of the Catholic church; so many *varas* in each main compass direction.

Earlier that year Cruzate had toured the pueblos, prior to his as-signment of land grants to ten Indian pueblos (Bloom and Mitchell 1938). Cruzate's party left Zia Pueblo in ruins and took at least one Zia man back to Guadalupe del Paso. This Zia man, of mixed blood, later testified to the fidelity of the Pueblos; his name was Bartólome de Ojeda (Sando 1976:58).

This granting of land took place nearly a century after Juan de Oñate and the initial Spanish settlers arrived in the general area and asked for permission to settle. And it was nine years after the Spanish had been expelled from the province by the Pueblo Rebellion of 1680 (Sando 1976:53). The logic of the "new generation" Pueblo Indians, then, is that it would be impossible for the King of Spain to *give* the Pueblo people land that they already occupied and had occupied long before the Spaniards came to the Pueblo world; not to mention the absurdity of giving them the same land from a distance of nearly three hundred miles away, after they had been expelled from the area. Others have also recognized this strange situation.

"The Pueblo Indians needed nothing from the King of Spain or his Viceroys; nothing from the Republic of Mexico or the Treaty of Guad-alupe Hidalgo, or Acts of the American Congress to add to the validity of a title to land occupied and cultivated for 300 years" (*U.S. v. Lucero*, 1 N. Mex. 422, 1869).

As they still do, the Pueblos held their lands by the highest evidence of title: peaceable and open possession for centuries of time. The village community had developed by necessity for common protection against raiding tribes; their dwellings were grouped together, as in a fort, and they cultivated their jointly held lands in common, with an armed group to protect them from the enemy. They had a tribal government with specific duties, but this tribal organization constituted no rec-ognized part of the governments of Spain, Mexico, or the United States. It was a pure democracy. Extensive research by other historians of Spanish and Mexican laws has failed to reveal any enactment whereby Indian pueblos were ever invested with the character of corporations, either private or municipal. However, since the Indian Reorganization Act of 1934, Indian tribes, including the Pueblos, have been strongly urged to develop constitutions and bylaws with which to govern them-selves. Many tribes and some pueblos have done this, but most still govern in the traditional way, as they have for centuries.

The administration of the Spanish grants and other lands passed to the United States after Mexico lost the Mexican War, in 1847. The

Treaty of Guadalupe Hidalgo of 1848, in Articles VIII and IX, provided that the United States should recognize and protect the rights to private property established under the Spanish and Mexican regimes. To administer those provisions in the treaty, the United States Congress, by an act of July 22, 1854 (10 Stat. 308), established the office of surveyor general for the Territory of New Mexico. Section VIII of that law provided that the surveyor general, under instructions given by the secretary of the interior, should investigate and make recommendations in order to confirm all bona fide land claims within the newly ceded territory.

Based upon the surveyor general's report of September 30, 1856, Congress confirmed the old grant to the "Pueblo de Jemez" by an act of December 22, 1858 (11 Stat. 374). A patent covering this grant was issued to the pueblo by the United States, and signed by President Abraham Lincoln on November 1, 1864.

The original Spanish land grant papers, as translated by David V. Whiting, followed the surveyor general's report of October 14, 1855, and read as follows (from a copy in the files of the Southern Pueblos Agency, Albuquerque):

"A" *Pueblo de Jemez*[1]

In the town of our Lady of Guadalupe del Paso del Rio del Norte on the twentieth day of the month of September in the year one thousand six hundred and eighty nine, His Excellency Don Domingo Jironza Petroz [*sic*] de Cruzate, Governor and Captain General stated: that whereas in overtaking the Queres Indians, and the apostates and the Thequas and those of the Thanos nation in the Kingdom of New Mexico and after having fought with all the Indians of all the other Pueblos (villages) an Indian of the Pueblo de Zia named Bartolome de Ojeda one of those who were most conspicuous in the battle, lending his aid everywhere, being wounded by a ball and an arrow, surrendered who as formerly stated I ordered to declare under oath the condition of the Pueblo de Jemez who were apostate Indians of that Kingdom having killed their priest Friar Juan de Jesus Morador.

Being interrogated if this Pueblo would rebel again in the future as it was customary for them to do, the deponent answered no—that they were very much intimidated and although they were concerned with those of Zia in what had occurred in the year previous he judged it would be impossible for them to fail in giving in their allegiance. Whereupon His Excellency Dn. Domingo Jironza Petroz de Cruzate granted them the boundaries herein set forth: on the North one league; on the East one league; and on the West one league; and on the South, one league to be measured from the four corners of the Temple which is situated in the centre of the Pueblo (village) His

Excellency so provided, ordered and signed before me the present Secretary of Government and war to which I certify.

Don Domingo Jironza Petroz de Cruzate

Before me
Pedro Ladron de Guitara
Secy. of Governmt. & war.

Surveyor General's Office
Santa Fe, New Mexico
October 14, 1855

The foregoing is a correct translation of the original on file in this office.

David V. Whiting
Translator

The original Spanish land grant began to be whittled away early in the twentieth century. By the decisions of the Pueblo Lands Board, created by an act of June 7, 1924, the pueblo's title to 19.18 acres within the Jemez Pueblo Spanish Grant was extinguished; the pueblo received compensation for the lands and water rights lost. However, the pueblo bought back 4.091 acres of this land from the Bernalillo Mercantile Company, deed dated April 16, 1940; the other 15.089 acres remain as a private claim belonging to the Roman Catholic Church, although it is used for the benefit of the pueblo, since the San Diego Mission School and residences for the priests and nuns are on this acreage. Another 2.06 acres, on which the pueblo day school is located, are now administered by the Bureau of Indian Affairs. Adjacent to it is another 1.92 acres which is leased to the Bureau of Indian Affairs, extending the day school.

Another area, of approximately one acre, is leased to the Presbyterian Church (see Appendix III). Although the first formal classes for Jemez people were started here in March, 1878, the school had a difficult time becoming established. It had only three students in 1925, when it finally closed. Immediately thereafter, the tribe began to negotiate for the return of this tract of land in the heart of the village; it has not succeeded yet.

An executive order of December 19, 1906, signed by President Theodore Roosevelt, set aside the initial reservation, and reads as follows (Kappler, 1904–27 [3]:686):

It is hereby ordered that the following described lands in New Mexico, namely: Township 16 North, Range 1 East, Jemez Meridian, excepting any tract or tracts the title to which has passed out of the United States Government or to which valid legal rights have attached, be, and the same aré, hereby withdrawn from sale and settlement and set apart as a reservation for the use and benefit of the Indians of the Jemez Pueblo.

THEODORE ROOSEVELT
THE WHITE HOUSE, December 19, 1906

The above order was supplemented by another executive order, of September 1, 1911, this time signed by President William H. Taft (Kappler 1904–27 [3]:686):

Executive order of December 19, 1906, withdrawing Township 16 North, Range 1 East, Jemez Meridian, for the benefit of the Indians of the Jemez Pueblo, is hereby amended to read as follows:

It is hereby ordered that the following-described lands in New Mexico, namely, Township 16 North, Range 1 East, New Mexico Principal Meridian, excepting any tract or tracts the title to which has passed out of the United States Government, or to which valid legal rights have attached, be, and the same are, hereby withdrawn from sale and settlement and set apart as a reservation for the use and benefit of the Indians of the Jemez Pueblo.

WM. H. TAFT
THE WHITE HOUSE, September 1, 1911

By this order 14,933.65 acres were set aside. However, it was soon discovered that there was a sliver of unassigned land between the Spanish land grant and the lands specified by the executive orders of 1906 and 1911. Thus another order followed in 1915 (Kappler 1904–27 [4]:1029):

It is hereby ordered that the following-described lands in New Mexico, namely:

That strip of land bounded on the east by the west boundary of the Jemez Pueblo; on the west by the range line between ranges 1 and 2 east of the New Mexico principal meridian, in Township 16 North; on the south by the north boundary of the San Ysidro grant; and on the north by the south boundary of the Canyon de San Diego grant, containing approximately 908.48 acres.

Excepting any tract or tracts the title to which has passed out of the United States, or to which valid legal rights have attached, be, and the same are hereby withdrawn from sale and settlement and set apart as a reservation for the use and benefit of the Indians of the Jemez Pueblo.

WOODROW WILSON
THE WHITE HOUSE, 4 October, 1915

Additional reservation land was purchased after 1924, using compensation funds awarded to the pueblo by the Pueblo Lands Board for the value of lands and water rights within the pueblo grant to which Indian title was held to be extinguished. These appropriations were made by an act of March 4, 1929 (45 Stat. 1569), together with subsequent acts, and were deposited with the United States Treasury.

The west half of the Cañada de Cochiti Grant, consisting of 9,647.94 acres, was purchased in 1942 from the Bonanza Development Company, a Massachusetts corporation. The quit claim deed was dated September 24, 1942, and was recorded in Sandoval County, New Mexico, on October 10, 1942. Mineral rights were reserved by the vendor.

The next parcel of land, 160 acres, was purchased on August 14, 1944, from Jose Mora Toledo and his wife, Esther Chavez Toledo, tribal members who had homesteaded at an earlier date. It was recorded in the Sandoval County Courthouse on August 14, 1944.

By an act of August 13, 1949 (63 Stat. 604), another 1,092.05 acres of land, from the San Ysidro Grant, were placed in trust for the Pueblo de Jemez. The San Ysidro Grant had originally been made to Antonio de Armenta and Salvador Sandoval. Armenta was chief justice at Jemez Pueblo when it was the administrative center of an *alcaldía* during the Spanish era; at this time he signed the San Diego de Jemez Grant to the Garcia brothers and eighteen others, in his role as agent of the governor.

By an act of August 2, 1956 (70 Stat. 941), Jemez received in trust 35,483.00 acres within the Ojo del Espíritu Santo Grant. It also placed in trust for Jemez 869 acres of former public domain land adjoining the grant. This was done to correct irregularities in the exterior boundaries.

The federal government had purchased the entire 113,141.15 acres of the Ojo del Espíritu Santo Grant for $2.50 per acre, under Title II of the National Recovery Act of June 16, 1933 (48 Stat. 200), as part of the submarginal land acquisition program. It was purchased from the Ojo del Espíritu Santo Company, C.C. Catron, president.

Executive Order Number 7792, of January 18, 1938, had transferred jurisdiction of the grant from the secretary of agriculture to the secretary of the interior, for administration by the commissioner of Indian affairs for the benefit of Jemez and Zia pueblo stock growers. On February 28, 1941, the grant was transferred back to the secretary of agriculture, with the requirement that grazing facilities continue to be granted to the two pueblos.

However, in the November 1954 issue of the *New Mexico Stockman*, the following headline appeared: "657,526 Acres of Bankhead-Jones, Title III, 'Land Utilization' Lands in New Mexico May Be Disposed of by U.S. Dept. of Agriculture." Upon reading the article, Jemez governor and cattleman Patricio Toya wrote to the general superintendent of the United Pueblos Agency in Albuquerque, concerning this betrayal. Jemez and Zia would be affected by this sale, as they had permits for a total of 400 cattle per year.

Fortunately, after an introduction to back-room politics, portions of the Espíritu Santo Grant were put in trust for both Jemez and Zia by an act of August 2, 1956 (70 Stat. 941), Jemez getting 35,483 acres. An area of 640 acres, known as the "administrative site" was later included by an act of June 29, 1960 (74 Stat. 256), to be used jointly by both Jemez and Zia.

Another tract, 163.76 acres adjacent to the northeast corner of the Ojo del Espíritu Santo Grant, was purchased from Effie Frederickson Jenks by warranty deed dated October 11, 1960. It is also recorded in the Sandoval County Court House. By an act of September 14, 1961 (75 Stat. 500), 7,819.28 acres of public domain east of the pueblo grant were placed in trust for the Pueblo de Jemez.

A parcel of 479.92 acres formerly leased from the state of New Mexico became Jemez trust land on November 12, 1968, by a Bureau of Land Management–State of New Mexico land exchange, made by authority of the act of September 14, 1961 (75 Stat. 500). This land is located just above Zia Pueblo, adjoining the former public domain placed in trust in 1961.

In addition to lands owned by or held in trust for the Pueblo de Jemez, the pueblo also uses some goverment-owned land. Of the original Spanish land grant, the Bureau of Indian Affairs administers 2.06 acres for day school purposes. The pueblo uses 4.65 acres of government land for a diversion dam site, purchased for the pueblo for $200; the dam is located just north of the reservation, where the main irrigation ditches for the tribe begin. The United States government ment acquired title to the land by condemnation in U.S. District Court, pursuant to the provisions of an act of Congress approved February 26, 1931 (46 Stat. 1421). The land was formerly owned by Estanislado Cabeza de Baca, popularly known by the Jemez people as Stanley.

The latest recovery of former land holdings, authorized by the act of September 14, 1961, took place on September 29, 1978, when a deed was signed by the state to return two parcels, of 116.06 and 640 acres, to Jemez ownership. The pueblo had previously been paying for grazing permits on these lands.

As of 1980, then, tribally owned land, trust land, and government use land total 89,622.99 acres. This total does not include the above-mentioned 640 acres of joint-use trust land donated to Jemez and Zia by the act of June 29, 1960 (74 Stat. 256).

3

Jemez and the Conquerors

Land ownership has been a constant source of conflict between indigenous peoples and conquerors throughout the world; Jemez has not been spared this conflict. As a Pueblo Indian looks at history, the intent of the colonial Spanish administration seems to have been more understanding and tolerant than that of either the Mexican or American governments; but the Spanish were not the best administrators. And a further difference can be seen between the American territorial and modern federal governments; Jemez is fortunate that the days of territorial jurisdiction are over.

The Spanish *Recopilación de Leyes de los Reynos de las Indias*, or Laws of the Indies, is a compilation containing nine books of royal laws and cedulas (ordinances) covering ecclesiastical, military, and civil administration. It was the "Bible" of administration and judicial authority for the Council of the Indies, which was responsible to the viceroy and the governors. Book II, Title I, Laws 1 and 2, provided that only the laws actually set forth in the *Recopilación* would apply in the Indies, although in matters for which no provisions were made, the laws of the Kingdom of Castile were to be observed (Engstrand 1978:321). There were many laws specifically protecting Indian rights to lands, waters, and watering places, as well as against Spanish encroachment upon Indian land and Indian property rights.

Despite the nine books of royal laws and cedulas, the Spaniards who were given the responsibility of governing the Pueblos were all too human, and all too humanly brazen and rapacious. Many had in common a huge appetite for personal gain, and most had a stormy relationship with the Franciscans as a result of competition for Pueblo Indian labor. The era produced governors such as Juan de Eulate (1618–25), who was characterized by Kessel (1979:105) as a "particularly avaricious exploiter of Indians in the friars' eyes," and as a "petulant, tactless, irreverent soldier whose actions were inspired by open contempt for the church and its ministers," by Scholes (1937:136). Francisco de la Mora y Ceballos (1632–35) and Luís de Rosas (1637–41) are especially notorious for their greed for profits. Alonzo Pacheco de Heredia (1642–44) is known for the stern administration of all his subjects; he beheaded eight Spanish soldiers (Kessel 1979:165). Bernardo López de Mendizábel (1659–61) may best be remembered for enraging the Jemez people by killing friendly Navajos while they were trading at Jemez Pueblo. The Navajos consequently became bitter enemies of the Jemez people. Diego Dionisio de Peñalosa Briceño y Berdugo (1661–64), was willing to give away the Spanish colony to England or France, especially after he was expelled from New Mexico by the tribunal of the Inquisition for his unruly and corrupt activities as governor. These are just a few of the more rapacious and sadistic governors; in their fights with the Franciscans the Pueblo Indians were often caught in the crossfire.

Wherever they went, the Spaniards justified their conquest by their laws. Some laws, decreed long before the Spaniards set foot in the Pueblo Indian Southwest, were later used to justify their actions. For instance, in 1535 a cedula was issued, directing that conquerors and well-deserving persons should be compensated for their services in land. Thus, much aboriginal Indian land was given to these "deserving" persons, despite the clear restrictions of the *Recopilación*.

In 1551 a decree was promulgated, later repeated several times,[1]

that Indians should be brought together in settlements and should not continue living separated and apart in the mountains and forests, deprived of every spiritual and temporal benefit, without the aid of a minister and without the help which human needs require and which men should extend to one another.

We shall see presently that this decree was partly responsible for the founding of Walatowa, or Jemez Pueblo.

In 1567 a decree was issued, stating that the viceroy "shall give to the Indians of the Pueblos such land as they may need to live upon and sow," but specifying that at least five hundred varas be given them, and that whatever additional land they might need be added to it. Thus, the original land grants to the pueblos consisted of at least 17,000 acres each. This 1567 decree undoubtedly formed the basis for the decree leading to the Pueblo Indian Land Grants of 1689, since it specifically refers to it.

As wards of the Spanish crown, the Pueblos were theoretically given every protection possible, protections too numerous to list. One that should be pointed out, however, is the decree of 1781, which stipulated that Indians could not sell or alienate their lands without the permission of the government. This law was partly honored by the Mexican government, and still remains in force under the American government.

Adamant as the Spaniards were in trying to maintain their laws during the early years of their control, there is no doubt that later they noticeably neglected the enforcement of these laws. It has been said that this was due to Spanish conflicts with other European powers, so that less thought could be given to the colonies than before. Since they were far from the center of authority, abuses were bound to arise under the circumstances. During the Mexican revolution of 1820 against the Spanish, the Indians of Mexico were active in the overthrow of Spanish control. Consequently, the Indians of New Mexico were regarded under the law as absolutely on a par with the rest of the population. Nevertheless, in the brief quarter of a century that the Mexican government held jurisdiction over the Pueblos, much Pueblo Indian land was lost. Many of the land problems that have haunted the Pueblos ever since date from this period.

Although the individual developments are too numerous and complex to specify here, during the Mexican period many laws were passed to facilitate the acquisition of land through homesteading. In addition, while some authorities contend that there was a certain amount of control exercised by the Mexican government over Indian land sales, Pueblo legends indicate that the Indians were told they were independent and free to do pretty nearly as they cared to regarding their real property. Written sales were the rule, but verbal sales of real estate were often regarded as legally valid.

The period of American territorial government can be recalled as the "years of the tilted scales of justice," as rarely did the Pueblo Indians win a case in court. The situation was similar to the modern one of a visiting ball team and its fans complaining to no avail against a biased, "home-team" referee. The most serious threat came in 1904, when the Supreme Court of New Mexico decided that the Pueblo Indians were citizens of the United States, and therefore subject to taxation. Fortunately, the Indian agent at that time argued that the Pueblos were not ready to accept the burden of taxation, and the matter was dropped. Very likely most Pueblo land would have been sold for taxes; and the people would have ended up on government welfare.

Before the United States took over the Southwest, the federal government had taken steps to protect Native American lands from encroachment by outsiders. Thus, on April 22, 1800, an act was passed to provide for the protection of land in Indian territory. Another, passed on March 30, 1802, provided for a military force to keep out trespassers. These acts led to the Trade and Intercourse Act of June 30, 1834, which provided, among other things, that settlers might be driven off by military force, and set a fine of a thousand dollars for settling on Indian land. It also stipulated that no purchase, grant, lease, or other conveyance from Indian nations or tribes would be valid except by treaty or convention entered into pursuant to the Constitution of the United States under Article I, Section 8. However, the Pueblo Indians did not qualify for protection under this act because they were "too peaceful and civilized." This was determined during the court hearing of an 1876 case (*U.S. v. Joseph*, 94 U.S. 614), in which the court held that a pueblo was not an Indian tribe within the meaning of the Trade and Intercourse Act.

The tribes for whom the act was made were those semi-independent tribes whom our government has always recognized as exempt from our laws. . . . left to their own rules and traditions. The character and history of the Pueblo people are not obscure. . . . For centuries these people have lived in villages, in fixed communities, each having its own local government. They have been a pastoral and agricultural people, raising flocks and cultivating the soil. They have adopted mainly not only the Spanish language, but the religion of a Christian church. They manufacture nearly all of their clothing, agricultural and culinary impliments [*sic*], etc. Integrity and virtue among them is fostered and encouraged. They are as intelligent as most nations or people deprived of means for education. The criminal records of the courts scarcely contain the name of a Pueblo Indian. In short, they are peaceable, industrious, intelligent, honest and virtuous people. They are Indians only in feature and complexion. In all other respects they are superior to all but a few of the civilized Indian tribes of the country, and the equal of the most civilized thereof (Cohen 1942:387).

A year after the American government took possession of New Mexico on August 18, 1846, a Legislative Assembly met under the Kearny Code of 1846, and this body passed an act incorporating the pueblos. This meant that they could sue and be sued, which made them vulnerable to land speculators of all sorts.

In 1849 James S. Calhoun was named Indian agent for New Mexico, and he moved to Santa Fe. He was instructed to advise the American government in Washington with reference to laws necessary to govern the Pueblo Indians and their lands, since it had little knowledge of their condition. On October 4, 1849, he wrote that "the protection of the Pueblo Indian property is of great importance."[2] On October 15, he added:

Few old Spanish villages are to be found in the vicinity of, perhaps, all the Pueblos—and the extent of their grants and privileges is not yet known, and judicial proceedings can reveal the truth in relation to these matters. In this way is the Indian country of the Pueblos checkered, and the difficulties in relation to the disposition of them suggested.

And on November 16:

What the Government may determine to do in reference to the Pueblo Indians should be done without delay. The exact number of the inhabitants of each Pueblo, together with the extent of their territorial grants, should be ascertained and the conflicting claims—and there are several—to a portion of their soil set up by Spanish and Mexican should be adjusted at the earliest possible day.

As a result, on December 4, 1849, President Zachary Taylor recommended to Congress that a commission be appointed to decide upon the validity of land titles in New Mexico. He recommended, furthermore, that the office of Surveyor General in New Mexico be established; this finally came about with the passage of an act of July 22, 1854.

In his quest to find help and protection for the Pueblos, Calhoun in 1850 required authorization to negotiate treaties with ten pueblos. Consequently, Santa Clara, Tesuque, Nambe, Santo Domingo, Jemez, San Felipe, Cochiti, San Ildefonso, Santa Ana, and Zia placed themselves under the exclusive jurisdiction and protection of the United States. One article of the treaty provided that the United States would adjust and set the boundaries of each pueblo in the most practical manner.

The treaty was never ratified, however, and on February 16, 1851, Calhoun reported that "the Pueblos are excessively annoyed by the Mexicans and others. The encroachments are innumerable and we have promised them protection, yet daily outrages are perpetrated."

On March 3, 1851, Indian Agent Calhoun became the first governor of the New Mexico Territory. On October 29 of that year he reported that pueblo boundaries must be established; the same recommendation was repeatedly made by other officials as well. Later he was to say that the complex Pueblo-Mexican land troubles would continue until the end of time unless the federal government of the United States would provide for their adjustment. That statement has been repeated over and over since then.

All in all, relations with the U.S. government appear to have improved, beginning with the appointment of John Collier as Commissioner of Indian Affairs during the administration of President Franklin D. Roosevelt. Although the Navajos did not approve of Collier's stock-reduction program, in retrospect there was much to appreciate about him (see Philp 1977).

In recent years the Pueblos have begun to exercise their right of franchise, that is, their rights to participate in political elections. The late U.S. Senator Joseph M. Montoya was the first elected official trusted by the people to look out for Pueblo interests in Washington. Since his unfortunate defeat for office and subsequent premature death, his helpful position has been filled by Senator Pete Domenici, who grew up in Albuquerque; Senator Domenici now looks after the legislative interests of the Pueblo people as did Montoya before him. Congressman Manuel Lujan plays a similar role in the House of Representatives.

But let us return now to the complexities arising from Spanish rule, the results of which are still with us. Under the Spanish administration, the Pueblos were to be protected by both religious and civil authorities. Governors and judges were commanded, under threat of severe penalties, to protect them and see that justice was given the Indians. As early as the seventeenth century special officers were appointed, solely to assist Indians in difficulties they might have with outsiders. Below are listed some of the more important regulations affecting the Pueblos:[3]

They could not be taken to Spain, but they must be Christians and must be taught the Spanish language.

They could farm, raise livestock, buy, sell, and even dispose of their personal and real property, under certain governmental restrictions.

Spanish people could not locate a cattle ranch within one and one-half leagues of an Indian pueblo, and the Pueblos might lawfully kill any cattle trespassing on their lands.

No Spaniard, mulatto, or Negro could maintain a residence in an Indian Pueblo, nor could any traveler stop overnight at the home of an Indian if an inn was available reasonably nearby.

Only the higher officials—the governor and viceroy—could make Indian grants and validate Indian sales; *alcaldes* were specifically denied the right to do so.

In the case of land grants, since officials used the pueblos as administrative and religious centers, it is understandable that, as at Jemez, many of these officials lived on Indian land in the beginning, and soon started *ranchos* nearby. Under both Spanish and Mexican rule, land passed from the government into private and communal ownership through this mechanism. There were three basic types of land grants: the community, the *sitio*, and the proprietary (Knowlton 1967:5).

The community land grant was the most important in the non-Indian settlement of northern New Mexico. This type of grant was given to a petitioning group of at least ten families, for the purpose of establishing a rural farming community. Naturally all the necessities of a rural community were eventually built into it: church, central plaza, irrigation system, farming plots, etc. The families drew lots for their home sites, and around the village site and the irrigated farm lands stretched the village ejido, the "commons," used communally for grazing, hunting, and collecting firewood or timber. Grant boundaries were rather vague and indefinite, as the American surveyors were later to find out. The sitio, a large grant of land given to a single individual for the establishment of a rancho, was more important in other areas of New Mexico, such as the south and the east, although there were some within the Pueblo area. The proprietary grant was made to a prominent individual who, in exchange for the land and other economic privileges, promised to attract settlers and establish the usual Spanish community.

After centuries of existing side by side with the Pueblo Indians—although it has never been admitted—it is only to be expected that the descendants of the early Spanish settlers eventually took on many fundamental Indian concepts toward land. Thus, both groups believe that land is not a commodity to be bought or sold, and that it should pass down through a family. In sharp contrast, the Anglo-American has tended to regard land as a natural resource, to be exploited for personal gain; land may be abused to the detriment of neighbors and of future generations. In time, a major conflict developed between Anglo-Americans and Spanish-Americans, over these differing methods of defining ownership. Fortunately, the Pueblos relied on their Spanish land grants of 1689 and the Treaty of Guadalupe Hidalgo, in order to be spared inclusion in this particular warfare.

In the 1890s, however, as part of the responsibilities of the Court of Private Land Claims, one Will M. Tipton made a study of the Pueblo land grants issued by the Spanish Crown (Sando 1976:91). Tipton's conclusions were that Governor Cruzate's grants were "spurious," invalid, and fraudulent for several reasons:

First, the grants were countersigned by a Pedro Ladrón de Guitara. No such individual had served as secretary of government and war during the Spanish period; the correct name of Cruzate's secretary was Pedro Ortiz Niño de Guevara.

Second, when the signatures of the grant documents were compared with official documents on file in the Spanish archives of New Mexico and the Museum of New Mexico at Santa Fe, it was found that they were counterfeit.

Third, a supposed grant to Laguna Pueblo was made ten years before the pueblo was even founded.

Fourth, Tipton found that various parts of the documents were taken from a book entitled *Ojeada sobre Nuevo Méjico*, written by Antonio Barreyro (Barriero) in 1832 (reported in Brayer 1938).

Nevertheless, genuine Spanish documents may have existed. While Tipton's investigations may be valid, they were in effect redundant. From a Pueblo Indian point of view, his efforts made a case for non-Indian squatters and claimants, and appear to be a means of discrediting Indian ownership of the pitiful remains of formerly vast holdings of choice lands.

In a review of the Treaty of Guadalupe Hidalgo, Donald Cutter (1978) asked, "Is the treaty a milestone or millstone in the cultural history of the Southwest?" He concluded that "there can be no doubt that the United States Government, either by acts of commission or acts of omission, did not live up to the obligations which it willingly accepted and wrote into the treaty" (1978:314). Dr. Cutter concurs with the Native people when he says, "The treaty was not fully implemented. Justice has been delayed." But again, for the Pueblo Indian people, these documents serve as symbolic recognition of sovereignty over traditional lands; they represent the Indian Magna Carta.

Legal Spanish land titles were those based, in the beginning, upon written deeds that conferred land upon the grantees. Copies of the documents were given to the families and to the villages that received land from the Spanish or the Mexican government; the originals were kept in the government archives in Santa Fe. Unfortunately, however, American territorial governors between 1854 and 1891 partially destroyed those archives (Hallenbeck 1950). Furthermore, in those days a majority of the Spanish-Americans were illiterate, and written documents had little meaning—some were simply misplaced, so that over the course of the years, the written deeds have tended to disappear. Thus, the right of a family or village to use land has actually come to rest more upon the consensus of the inhabitants of the region than upon written documents. The result is that when Spanish land titles and land claims were challenged by Anglos in the American courts, Spanish-Americans were often unable to produce written titles, and were left without legal protection for their lands (Sanchez 1940:18).

Under the American system, a valid title is one based upon a written document carefully filed and protected in a government office that has the legal function of registering land claims and deeds. This document must trace the sequence of land ownership on a specific parcel of land from the first settler down to the present. The document must also specify exactly how the land was transferred from one owner to another. If the sequence is not described in exact detail, the land title may be flawed and insecure, and thus open to litigation.

Under the Treaty of Guadalupe Hidalgo, signed following the Mexican-American War, the United States agreed to recognize the land grants made by Spain and Mexico in the ceded area, which included all the pueblos. In order to determine just what those land grants entailed, the office of U.S. Surveyor General for New Mexico was established in 1854. The surveyor general received the evidence from the pueblos, and in turn recommended confirmation to Congress.

In 1891 this system was discarded, and the U.S. Court of Private Claims was created by Congress. This court, consisting of five judges, had jurisdiction over New Mexico, Colorado, and Arizona. It passed upon petitions seeking confirmation of land claims under titles deriving from Spanish and Mexican grants. Appeals to the U.S. Supreme Court were allowed under this procedure.

Some of these documents, along with the records of the surveyor general of New Mexico and the files of the Court of Pirvate Land Claims, are presently housed in the offices of the United States Bureau of Land Management, in Santa Fe. Others are in the National Archives

(Record Group 49), Records of the General Land Office, in Washington, D.C., and in the National Archive Regional Office, at the Federal Records Center in Denver, Colorado.

Ojo del Espíritu Santo Land Grant

The first land ownership conflict faced by the Pueblo of Jemez surfaced in connection with the Ojo del Espíritu Santo Grant. The grant, originally about 276,480 acres, is located on the western portion of the aboriginal Jemez holdings. It was issued to the three pueblos of Jemez, Zia, and Santa Ana on August 6, 1766, during the second term of Governor Tomás Velez Cachupín, in accordance with the Laws of the Indies, Book IV, Title 12, Law 5 (Engstrand 1978:322).

Following the Pueblo revolt of 1680, it had taken the Pueblos several decades to settle down and become full-fledged farmers and stockmen; as they began to raise cattle, available grazing land was soon used to capacity. Thus, the three pueblos petitioned the Spanish governor for additional grazing land on which to pasture their growing herds of cattle and horses, and the governor commissioned the chief alcalde of the "Queres and Hemes" nations, Bartólome Fernández, to examine the land requested. His investigation resulted in the following report (Spanish Archive document 1141; see Appendix IV):

In the name of his majesty, thereunto authorized by virtue of his office, the edicts, laws, ordinances, and customs, then in force and observance in the said province, made and issued unto the said Indian Pueblos of Zia, Santa Ana, and Jemez, your petitioners, in writing, a formal and final grant, in fee absolute, coupled with no conditions, whatsoever, other than that, in case of necessity the horses of the Royal garrison of Santa Fe might be pastured thereon without let or hindrance upon the part of the said grantees; and in said grant the Governor General directed the Chief Alcalde Bartolome Fernandez, to give unto the said Pueblos the Royal possession of the said tract, to place his proceedings on record following the granting degree. . . . official copies thereof be given to each said Pueblo.

According to this same document, the following Indian officials from the three pueblos were present to receive the grant: the governors Cristóval Naspona, Cristóval Chiguigui [sic], Pedro Chite, Sebastián, Lázaro, and Juan Antonio, the war captains Agustín, Tomás, Juan Domingo, and other Indian magistrates. The document does not further identify the individuals, but it is probable that Cristóval Chiguigui was the Jemez governor, as the same surname is connected with Jemez in 1911 and 1919 (spelled Chihuihui), as well as in 1946 and 1952 (spelled Chewiwi, which is used by the family today).

On September 28, 1766, the alcalde awarded judicial and royal possession to the three pueblos. The papers are available today for review at the University of New Mexico Library's Coronado Room, as well as on film at the State Archives in Santa Fe. The English translation was made by Dav. J. Miller and Sam L. Ellison, and approved before the attorney for the pueblos and James K. Proudfit, surveyor general, on July 25, 1873.

On February 2, 1874, Surveyor General Proudfit issued an opinion on this the grant:[4]

From the language of the granting-decree of Governor Cachupin, it is evident that he intended to extend the boundaries of the pueblo lands so as to include the grant [Baca] now under examination. The grants of the original pueblo lands were made in 1689, and have been confirmed by Congress. A translation of the papers in this case was made in this office, probably in 1856, but for some reason, probably, as I am informed, on account of some fear or disagreement among the Indians, it was withdrawn and not prosecuted, and but for this reason no doubt these lands would have been confirmed when the others were.

I am of opinion that the Indians show an absolute grant and full possession under it, and that Congress ought to confirm the same, which I respectfully recommend.

This recommendation was necessary, since a dispute over ownership had been raging for some time, concerning a junior grant supposedly made to Luís María Cabeza de Baca, sometime in 1815—in direct opposition to Law 23 of Book IV, Title 7 of the Laws of the Indies (Engstrand 1978:322). On May 23, 1815, Baca, of Peña Blanca, supposedly petitioned the governor, Alberto Maynez, for the tract, since it was unused. It was not in fact used by the three pueblos, because of incessant raids by the Navajos, who roamed to the west and northwest. Later testimony shows that Baca stayed there only five years, also due to Navajo raids. He was later shot by a Mexican soldier.

Records show that the junior grant was made on May 24, 1815; however, the original confirmation and patent papers issued by the United States have never been found. During the 1873 hearing, a Spanish resident of Cañon de Jemez testified that an heir of Baca's,

Diego Baca, had lived at the ojo (spring) for three or four years, but under whose authority he did not know. No doubt his length of stay was also decided by the Navajos.

Papers supporting the claims of the three Indian pueblos, on the other hand, had always been available. Thus, in a letter of June 8, 1883 to the governor of Zia Pueblo, Pedro Sanchez, the U.S. Indian Agent at Santa Fe, stated that he found in the general land surveyor's office a valuable grant to the pueblos of Zia, Jemez, and Santa Ana— presumably the Espíritu Santo Grant. He wrote, "I am going to strongly recommend the approval of this grant."

At Court of Private Land Claims hearings in 1892, at which the three pueblos challenged Baca's heirs, the attorney for the defendants, Thomas B. Catron, admitted that Baca had never been given a patent. The hearings nevertheless continued into 1893. At this time Catron

denied there is such a body or person known as the Pueblo of Zia, Santa Ana, or Jemez, or that any such body, either jointly or separately, exists or has any right to exist in proceedings for the confirmation of any grant title whatever, or that any such body is or was an [sic] authorized, empowered or entitled to hold, take, possess or enjoy said real estate, either under the laws of the Kingdom of Spain, Mexico, or the United States. He denied such Indians can sue or bring suit by virtue of designation as Indians.

As a result of these hearings, the petition of the three pueblos was dismissed on August 10, 1893, based on the decision that the 1766 grant was not for ownership, but only for a license to pasture livestock. An appeal to the Supreme Court was decided in October of 1897, upholding the decision of the Court of Private Land Claims; the petition went against the three pueblos since it was judged that the grant was abandoned, forfeited for nonuse. The defending attorney ultimately ended up owning the Espíritu Santo Grant; he paid for surveying and platting the grant, with a certificate of deposit in the amount of $502.68, and a patent was transmitted to him on October 14, 1916.

Of interest to many Jemez people today is that the governor testifying at this 1893 hearing was Jose Rey Yepo, the original Yepa man; we have heard our grandparents talk about Yepo toh-ohler ("Grandpa Yepo") and Yepo vela ("Yepa man"). One of Yepo vela's sons was probably Juan Antonio Yepa, who in turn had two sons, Jose Manuel and Cristino; Jose Manuel is the maternal grandfather of this writer. Two daughters of Juan Antonio were Rita and Francisquita. The first married Pablo Toya and the latter married Pedro Baca; there are today many grandchildren.

Also testifying for Jemez was the Pecos immigrant Jose Miguel Vigil (further discussed in Chapter 9). Whether he was testifying as an ex-governor of Jemez or because of his knowledge of Spanish is not explained; but most men who immigrated from Pecos spoke better Spanish than they did the Jemez language. Jose was known at Jemez as Zer wa-kin ("snow-white eagle down"). The third man from Jemez was also an ex-governor, Ignacio Colaque. Testifying for the Zias was their governor, Lorenzo Lobato.

The attorneys for the three pueblos were George Hill Howard, of Santa Fe, and William Earle, of Washington, D.C. In a letter of February 28, 1892, to the pueblos of Jemez, Zia, and Santa Ana, Howard had agreed to handle the case before the Court of Private Land Claims on the following terms: (1) That the pueblos pay all costs which might arise; (2) that they give Howard one-tenth of the confirmed land; (3) that they give him the exclusive privilege, for twenty-five years, of removing coal and coal oil and to build roads upon the grant for that purpose, with royalty payments of 2½ cents per ton of coal removed. Since the case was lost, Howard's rewards were nil. He later became special counsel to the Pueblo Indians.

Ojo de San José Land Grant

As has been indicated earlier, Jemez Pueblo was the headquarters of the alcaldía for the "Queres and Hemes" Indians. It also served as a rendezvous and marshalling area for troops preparing to pursue Navajo raiders. Many of these resident Spanish officials requested community, sitio, and proprietary land grants in the vicinity of Jemez Pueblo. The first community land grant made of aboriginal Jemez land was given to six Spanish militia men. Although the land was properly an Indian ejido (common area), since it was well utilized for deer hunting, eagle catching, and wood gathering, the Spanish did not take this into account, as they were mainly interested in the land for grazing and farming. Torribio Gonzales, Paulín Montoya, Bárnabe Gallegos, Antonio Gallegos, Féliz Casados, and Antonio José Casados were granted seventy varas each, in a square, in response to their petition for "vacant and unused farmland." The grant was known as the Ojo de San José Grant, subsequently also identified as the Vallecito Grant. The presiding Spanish governor was Captain Pedro Fermín de

Mendinueta, who served from 1767 to 1778; signing for him was the same chief alcalde who signed the Espíritu Santo Grant papers of two years earlier, Bartólome Fernández. The signing was witnessed by the Jemez tribal officials and their padre, Ramón Salas.

American territorial officials later approved and confirmed the grant on September 29, 1894, over the signature of Chief Justice Joseph R. Reed. Controversy over its boundaries was settled by a second survey in August, 1898, which resolved the problems of overlap with other grants and identifying corner markers.

Meanwhile, just a few miles southwest of the Ojo de San José Grant, and east of the pueblo, another piece of aboriginal Jemez land was changing hands. A Diego Gallegos evidently had homesteaded around a spring in the area, which was later named for its next owner, Diego Básquez Borrego. His heirs sold the holdings to Felipe de Sandoval Fernández; until that time there had been no title to the grant, the Ojo de Borrego Grant. In 1765 Nerio Antonio Montoya petitioned Governor Tomás Cachupín to buy or take over the land from the widow of Felipe de Sandoval Fernández; at the time of the petition Montoya was a resident of Peña Blanca. Very likely this is the same man who later became chief justice of Santa Ana (Sandoval) County. On March 7, 1768, Governor Pedro Fermín de Mendinueta granted Montoya the Borrego Grant, and the alcalde of the area gave him title to the grant on March 20. Other records show that on September 5, 1812, Eusebio Rael, husband of Rosa Montoya, daughter of Nerio, sold the entire grant for one yoke of oxen and two bulls.

San Ysidro Land Grant

Antonio de Armenta was the chief justice at Jemez Pueblo in the late 1700s. He petitioned Governor Juan Bautisto de Anza for a sitio grant for his Rancho de San Ysidro. The grant, commonly known as the Town of San Ysidro Grant, was originally made on May 16, 1786, to the chief justice and a fellow petitioner, Salvador Sandoval. The senior justice and *capitán de la guerra* of the jurisdiction of Santa Ana County, Nerio Antonio Montoya, signed the papers. The boundaries of the grant were described as follows:

On the north by the lands of Jemez; on the south the lands of the Pueblo of Zia; on the west the mountains of the Espiritu Santo Spring, at the place commonly called Los Bancos; on the east the lands of the aforementioned senior justice Montoya, (Ojo de Borrego Grant), which is [on] the road leading from Cochiti to Jemez.

Although the private land claim of the town of San Ysidro was recommended for confirmation by the surveyor general for the Territory of New Mexico, in his report dated February 3, 1860, and it was subsequently confirmed (as number 24) by Section III of the act of Congress approved June 21, 1860 (12 Stat. 71), a patent for the grant was not issued until November 14, 1936, to the legal representatives of Antonio Armenta and Salvador Sandoval.

The San Ysidro Grant was purchased by the United States government from the San Ysidro Land Company, by a deed dated April 22, 1936. The purchase involved 10,032.78 acres, after excluding 1,120.78 acres in small-holding claims and 323.12 acres included in the Ojo del Espíritu Santo Grant. It was acquired by the Resettlement Administration, Department of Agriculture, under the authority of Title II of the National Industrial Recovery Act of June 16, 1933, the Emergency Relief Appropriation Act of April 8, 1935, and Section 55 of Title I of the act of August 24, 1935.

By executive order of January 18, 1938, administration of the grant was transferred from the jurisdiction of the secretary of agriculture to that of the secretary of the interior. Under the Bureau of Indian Affairs, it was managed by the United Pueblos Agency; Zia Pueblo was allowed to use the portion of the grant east of the Jemez river. In January 1940 the UPA surveyed the north boundary and proceeded to install fencing; Jemez Governor George Toledo immediately protested to General Superintendent Sophie Aberle, in a letter dated January 23, 1940. He questioned the authorization for the fence, stating that the three pueblos (Jemez, Zia, and Santa Ana) were entitled to use the same grazing land, and that prior to the fencing of the northern boundary, Jemez had had free access to the San Ysidro Grant. Historically the three pueblos had used much of north-central New Mexico in common, from the Rio Puerco to the Rio Grande.

By this time about three miles, or approximately half of the northern boundary, had been fenced. On January 26, 1940, Dan T. O'Neill, acting director of the Land-Use Division of the UPA, attended a meeting at Jemez, at which the councils of Jemez, Zia, and Santa Ana were present. Mr. O'Neill stated that it would be impossible to pull up and move the fencing already in place, and suggested that Jemez

and Zia agree upon some division of the remaining area. In a report
to the files dated January 27, 1940, Mr. O'Neill wrote:

> The Jemez Indians were very urgent that the San Ysidro Grant be fenced in
> their allotment. They gave as their reasons:
>   1. They need the range more than the Zias.
>   2. They need the water which might be on there during the summer
> months.
>   3. It is a sacred area of the Jemez.
>   4. They haul wood from this area.
>   5. They hunt rabbits in this area.
> The Zias had only one reason and that was they had used the San Ysidro
> Grant since the Government purchased it and that the fence had already
> begun being constructed on the north boundary and as far as they were
> concerned they would not allow it to be changed.

According to UPA files, the Jemez officials asked at that meeting
that the grant be divided through the center east and west; Zia officials
demanded that the grant be fenced within their grazing area. They
finally asked O'Neill to decide the location, which he agreed to do if
they would sign a statement accepting his decision. They then went
to the location of the boundary fence, and O'Neill set out the approximate line which he determined the fence would follow. There
was a discussion about gates, since Jemez wanted access to the rest of
the grant, and then the Jemez governor asked to be allowed more time
before signing the agreement. In his report for the files, O'Neill stated
that he told the governor that

> the gates were not a part of the agreement and therefore I believe it should
> be signed before the fence crew approached the contemplated change in
> location, because if we did not come to a decision they probably would fence
> on the original line which was already surveyed.

Thereupon the agreement was signed by both governors.
    O'Neill set the fence line as follows:

> It will begin on the southeast corner of Section 34, T. 16 N., R. 2 E.; thence
> one-quarter (¼) mile south; thence southeast diagonally to the southeast
> corner of the San Ysidro Grant, leaving the Jemez-Santo Domingo road on
> the north side of this fence; thence southeast to a point approximately one-
> third (⅓) mile north of the southwest corner of the Borrego Grant.

The following day Jemez officials phoned UPA to request a meeting. On February 1, 1940, the officials met in Dr. Aberle's office and asked that the boundary fence be placed in a different location; they protested the division as made and agreed upon a meeting in the field. They stated that the governor had signed the agreement under the misapprehension that if he did not sign, the fencing would be completed along the northern line, to the complete exclusion of the Jemez people—which was exactly what O'Neill had stated.

The next day, O'Neill went to Zia to discuss the matter with the council, but with little success. They felt that since the Jemez governor had signed the agreement, it was binding.

The Jemez officials returned to UPA on February 5. They expressed their feeling that as a matter of principle they were entitled to as much land as Zia. Acting Superintendent Alan Laflin told them that they would be issued permits to enter the grant to hunt rabbits, collect firewood, and conduct ceremonies at their sacred areas, but that the agency could do little else, in view of the signed agreement. The fencing was delayed two weeks pending further negotiations, but eventually it was completed in approximately the location outlined in the agreement.

By an act of August 13, 1949 (63 Stat. 604), the portions of the San Ysidro Grant which Jemez and Zia pueblos were using became trust land of those pueblos; this amounted to 1,092.05 acres for Jemez and 4,074.18 acres for Zia. The western portion of the grant was transferred to the Bureau of Land Management for grazing use by non-Indians.

Cañón de San Diego de Jémez Land Grant

Besides officials and volunteer soldiers, there were Navajo interpreters in the service of the Spanish government living at Jemez. In 1798, two of these interpreters, the brothers Francisco García de Noriega and Antonio García de Noriega, along with eighteen Spanish men, petitioned Governor Fernando Chacón, for land north of the Jemez Pueblo land grant. On March 14, 1798, they were given the papers for the Cañón de San Diego de Jémez Land Grant, including the town of Cañón de San Diego. This grant covered most of the Jemez homeland.

The Jemez had been compelled by Spanish officials to abandon the highlands in favor of the flatlands below, mainly following the battle of July, 1694, when Astiolekwa and other highland villages were occupied by the Spaniards for sixteen days. After the battle, Hemish prisoners, mostly women and children, were taken to Santa Fe; only after a promise to move to the lowlands were they released, in September. An additional stipulation for returning the women and children, of more importance to the Spanish, was that the Jemez warriors should assist the Spaniards in fighting the Tewas on Black Mesa, north of San Ildefonso Pueblo. Another uprising, in June, 1696, clinched the abandonment of the many sites in the highlands; those people who did not move to the lowlands fled to the original homeland of Gy'a-wahmu, or Cañón Largo, in northwest New Mexico (Chavez 1967). When the Jemez returned, between 1702 and 1706, they settled at Walatowa. Little did they know that their former homeland would be lost forever.

The Cañón San Diego de Jémez Grant was awarded by Governor Chacón in March of 1798. Although the transaction took place at Jemez Pueblo, the old documents tell us that Chief Justice Antonio de Armenta and two others, Salvador López and José Miguel García, signed in the absence of a pueblo representative or a royal notary, on March 16, 1798.

The grant papers were translated and approved by the American territorial government in June 1859, over the signature of William Pelham, who was then surveyor general. It was confirmed by the U.S. Congress on June 21, 1860, and a patent was issued on October 21, 1881, to the heirs of the original twenty grantees.

Today, portions of the San Diego Grant remain extremely important to the Jemez people. Not only are there important shrines, but other old sites on the grant are still linked spiritually with many religious ceremonies still practiced. For a similar reason, a small piece of land on top of Redondo Peak, four feet by four feet, is actually owned by Jemez.

Cañada de Cochiti Land Grant

Another parcel of land in the ownership of Jemez Pueblo today is the western half of the Cañada de Cochiti Grant, consisting of 9,647.94 acres with an estimated carrying capacity of forty-eight cattle units per year. This is another portion of aboriginal Jemez land that was interpreted as unused by the Spanish, although it was in fact used as an ejido by the Jemez people.

On August 2, 1728, Antonio Lucero of Peña Blanca petitioned

Governor Juan Domingo Bustamente for the grant. Subsequently, the chief alcalde of the pueblos of Cochiti, Santo Domingo, and San Felipe was asked to examine the land, since the eastern half was used by those three pueblos for the same purposes as Jemez used the western half. However, on August 6, 1728, the alcalde, Juan Antonio Cabeza de Baca, reported the land to be unused and available, and signed the papers over to the petitioner. There was the usual struggle for direct ownership by later heirs; some sold their rights while others no doubt lost them to their attorneys. In due time (exactly when is unknown) the grant ended up in the hands of the Bonanza Development Company, a Massachusetts corporation. The pueblo purchased the western half of the grant on February 13, 1943, with $7,500 from its compensation fund, derived from the act of March 4, 1929 (45 Stat. 1569), that awarded monies to the pueblo for the value of lands and water rights within the pueblo grant to which Indian title was held to be extinguished. Mineral rights were reserved by the vendor, and this has caused some problems for Jemez. Although it is fenced, the public often enters from Pena Blanca to haul away firewood and even to chop down—for firewood—valuable dried timber that could be used for vigas.

Livestock and Grazing Rights

After the intrusion on Jemez land by the eighteenth-century equivalent of Thomas B. Catron, Luís María Cabeza de Baca, the pueblo was left with no grazing land. Cabeza de Baca had usurped former Jemez land on the Espíritu Santo Grant, as well as in the Valle Grande; he also laid claim to Cochiti Pueblo land at El Ojo de Santa Cruz. What little grazing land remained for Jemez was poor and badly overgrazed, resulting in serious erosion. This period of the 1700s was one of extreme drought; the problem was finally recognized by the Indian Service in the early 1930s, and a program was begun to purchase submarginal land in order to improve the economic condition of Jemez, to keep the people from becoming a burden on relief organizations.

C.C. Catron, president of the Espiritu Santo Land Company, was approached by the agency superintendent, following approval by the Submarginal Land Board, regarding the purchase of the Ojo del Espíritu Santo Grant. The board of directors of the company authorized Catron to sell, and on August 6, 1934, he signed an offer to sell land to the United States, "to assist in the program of the United States to conserve natural resources and to rehabilitate people living on sub-marginal lands." The 113,141.15 acre grant was appraised at $2.50 per acre, for a total price of $282,852.87.

On July 19, 1934, Robert E. Putney, president of L.B. Putney, Inc., signed an offer to sell the Ojo de San José Grant to the United States government for $1.25 an acre—a total of $4,983.36 for the 3,986.89 acre grant. The Putneys operated a trading post at Jemez in the 1930s.

Ultimately, this program did not result in ownership of the land by the pueblo. However, both grants were purchased by the federal government at the appraised prices, under the authorization of Title II of the National Industrial Recovery Act of June 16, 1933 (48 Stat. 200), as part of the submarginal land acquisition program. The deed for the purchase of the Ojo del Espíritu Santo Grant was dated December 27, 1934, and that for the Ojo de San José Grant was dated July 28, 1936.

No further mention of the Ojo de San José Grant has been located in Southern Pueblos Agency files. Forest Service personnel explain that by order of January 30, 1939, the grant was transferred by the secretary of agriculture from the Soil Conservation Service to the Forest Service. It acquired national forest status by Public Law 87-631, passed on September 5, 1962, and was incorporated into the Santa Fe National Forest.

The Espíritu Santo Grant, however, was destined to be the source of much consternation for the people involved. Early in 1935, the pueblos' attorney, William Brophy, had secured permission from Joseph Doherty of Folsom, New Mexico, who had a grazing lease on this grant, for some of the southern pueblos to run sheep on it, since the grant had been purchased for their use.

Thus Jemez and Zia sheepmen began using the grant in April 1935. In 1936 Laguna grazed 2,511 sheep on the grant, Zia 1,220, and Jemez 682. In 1937 Laguna grazed 2,068, Zia 1,405, and Jemez 845; in 1938 Laguna grazed 2,215, Zia 950, and Jemez 930; and in 1939 Laguna grazed the community ram herd of 700 plus 2,068 sheep, Zia had 1,000, and Jemez had 910 sheep on the grant. The Jemez sheep-men were Juanito Sando and his sons, Jose Manuel Loretto and his sons, Juanito Chinana, his father, Juan Domingo, and his brother Antonio. The Zia sheepmen were Antonio Medina and his brother Rosendo, Torevio Aguilar, and the Galvan brothers, Andres and Emiliano.

Although the grant had been purchased by the Department of Agriculture, Executive Order 7792 of January 18, 1938, transferred custody for administration of the grant from the secretary of agriculture to the secretary of the interior; the Soil Conservation Service was to supervise the management of the land.

Since at that time the Pueblo Indians did not have the right to vote as they do today, they were unable to counter the political pressure that began to build up. Spanish-American neighbors, who also coveted the grant, had petitioned Senators Dennis Chavez and Carl A. Hatch, as well as Representative John Dempsey, requesting that all Indian livestock be removed from the Espíritu Santo Grant, and that the entire grant be made available solely for livestock of non-Indians. Meanwhile, the Rural Rehabilitation Corporation and the Advisory Board of New Mexico Grazing District 2A (established under the Taylor Grazing Act), while recognizing that the Espíritu Santo and other grants had been bought for Indian use, had motivations for favoring exclusive non-Indian use.

The Rural Rehabilitation Corporation, a branch of the Resettlement Administration, had made loans to non-Indians in the Rio Puerco area, with a reported delinquency rate of 90 percent. The Resettlement Administration felt that the only way it could collect on those loans would be to have the debtors engage in commercial livestock raising, for which the use of the Espíritu Santo Grant was seen as essential. Thus, one branch of the federal government sought to oust Indians from a grant bought for Indians, allocated to Indians, occupied by Indians, and pledged to Indians, never before then occupied to any extent by non-Indians of the Rio Puerco area. The Indians could only depend on the hard work of the Indian Service director, John Collier, to progress through official channels to battle the opposing bureaucrats.

Recommendations for use-rights on the various Indian purchase areas were made initially by the Rio Grande Advisory Board, made up of representatives of the Indian Service, Soil Conservation Service, Forest Service, Division of Grazing, State Land Commissioner, State Planning Board, and the University of New Mexico. In January 1937, this board was replaced by the Interdepartmental Rio Grande Board, consisting of one individual each from the Indian Service, Forest Service, Soil Conservation Service, Division of Grazing of the Department of the Interior, and the Resettlement Administration. Members were to devote all their time to the study of problems of the Rio Grande watershed.

In 1938 a memorandum of agreement was drafted to contribute to the stabilization of the agricultural economy of the Indian and non-Indian populations in the watershed of the Rio Puerco in Sandoval, Valencia, and Bernalillo Counties. In effect the agreement recommended to the president of the United States that the Antonio Sedillo Grant be transferred to the jurisdiction of the secretary of the interior for Indian use, and that the Espíritu Santo Grant be transferred to the jurisdiction of the secretary of agriculture, under Title III of the Bankhead-Jones Farm Tenant Act (LU-NM-38-22), for non-Indian use.

The memorandum was signed by the Department of Agriculture on June 29, 1938, and by the Department of the Interior on July 14, 1938. Under this agreement, at the end of the 1939 grazing season the Laguna sheepmen moved their herds to the Sedillo Grant, while Spanish-Americans were permitted to move onto the Espíritu Santo Grant to join the Jemez and Zia sheepmen, until such time as other satisfactory rangeland could be found for the two pueblos.

It was proposed that sheep belonging to my father, Juanito Sando, be transferred from the Espíritu Santo to the Bernabe Montaño Grant; due to the distance from Jemez Pueblo, my father refused to cooperate. He reported the threat to the Tribal Council of Jemez, which then invited the councils of Zia and Santa Ana to raise a strong protest, based on their historic ownership of the use-right to the grant, which they had lost once and were about to lose again.

A petition, signed by seventeen Jemez councilmen and nine officials, and by the governors of Zia and Santa Ana, was directed to the secretaries of agriculture and the interior, with copies to the Indian commissioner and the general superintendent of the Pueblo Agency. The petition made a strong plea that the pueblos to be allowed to continue using the Espíritu Santo Grant; attached to it was a copy of the grant papers whereby the three pueblos were given the grant by Don Tomás Velez Cachupín, governor general of New Mexico, on August 6, 1766. The petition read in part:

Our friends, please look over this matter again and think of all the times that we have wondered why we lost the Espiritu Santo Grant, why we couldn't use it when old Catron had it when in fact we thought it was ours, and think about how helpless we were in any old court proceedings, and when you think about these things, try your very best to let us keep the Espiritu Santo Grant which, no matter what the papers say, actually in spirit belongs to us.

Upon receipt of the petition, Commissioner Collier wrote a memorandum to Secretary of the Interior Ickes on November 30, 1939, recommending that the department seek a revision of the 1938 agreement between Interior and Agriculture, such revision to give Jemez and Zia Pueblos continued use-right to the portion of the Espíritu Santo Grant they then occupied. Collier admitted that he had recommended the removal of all Indian sheep from the Espíritu Santo Grant to the Montaño Grant without clearance from the tribes or the superintenennt.

On that same day, Secretary Ickes wrote to the governors of the three pueblos, saying,

Your recital of the history of the Espiritu Santo Grant is very interesting and persuasive. . . . In the light of the record I am instructing Commissioner Collier to negotiate for a revision of the agreement.

There followed several letters from the secretary of the interior to the secretary of agriculture, requesting reconsideration and revision of the 1938 agreement. In a letter of December 28, 1939, to Secretary of Agriculture Wallace, Ickes wrote:

An important item in this cooperative procedure [the 1938 agreement] was the voluntary surrender by the Pueblos of 269,000 acres which had been bought for their use. The surrender by the Pueblos of these 269,000 acres was not unconditional but was expressly conditioned upon a recommendation made unanimously by the Interdepartmental Rio Grande Committee upon a pledge that the Indians would receive compensatory advantages in the form of range, irrigated land or other economic resources acceptable to the Office of Indian Affairs. The recommendation of the Rio Grande Committee bore the endorsement of the Soil Conservation Service, the Forest Service and the Farm Security Administration.

Following further correspondence between the secretaries, a memorandum of agreement for modification of the 1938 agreement was signed, on April 14, 1941, by Interior, and on May 27, 1941, by Agriculture. One of the four provisions was that Jemez and Zia be given permanent use privileges on the Espíritu Santo Grant, while Laguna sheepmen were to use the Bernabe Montaño and Antonio Sedillo Grants.

The value of the surrendered 269,000 acres was equivalent to year-round grazing resources for two thousand cattle. Granting permanent use privileges on the Espíritu Santo to Jemez and Zia satisfied the pueblos' claim to only 400 cattle units yearlong, leaving a balance of 1,600 units yearlong necessary to satisfy the total claim. No specific evidence has been found as to how this balance might have been satisfied, although additional public domain was subsequently declared to be held in trust for different pueblos by various acts of Congress.

Crisis on the Espíritu Santo Grant

Soon after the government purchased the Ojo del Espíritu Santo Grant, the Civilian Conservation Corps established two work camps on it. However, the spring for which the grant was named was being claimed by Manuel Sanchez, an heir of the junior grantee of 1815, who operated a 160-acre ranch and lived by the spring. In December 1935, Federal Judge Colin Neblett issued a permanent injunction, finding the Sanchez family guilty of trespass, and ordered them to release the use of the spring to the federal government. Gilbert Espinosa, assistant U.S. district attorney, represented the government, and William A. Brophy, attorney for the pueblos, assisted in preparing the case.

Those were the years when America was recovering from the throes of the great economic depression; to prolong the misery, the summers of 1936 and 1937 were very dry. Consequently, grazing and feed for animals were at a high premium. The Spanish communities bordering the Espíritu Santo Grant were in desperate condition.

By New Year's Day, 1938, stockmen from the villages of Cabezon, La Ventana, Guadalupe, San Luis, and Casa Salazar were sitting on a powder keg ready to explode into some dangerous economic and political fireworks. Claiming that feed for their stock would soon be depleted, they threatened to trespass upon Indian grazing land. Communications with the site of the expected explosion were difficult, as there were no telephones, and the road to the grant from Albuquerque was nothing more than an improved wagon trail (even today, New Mexico 44 is still narrow and dangerous due to heavy use by commercial trucks). Telephone calls and telegrams were feverishly exchanged by the interested parties and various bureaucrats in Albuquerque and Washington, D.C.

The New Mexico Sentinel, of Santa Fe, New Mexico, on Wednesday, February 2, 1938, quoted the leaders of the Spanish stockmen as saying, "We are desperate, we are going to enter the grant. There is no use to try to stop us." Before the trespass, the name of each man had been taken by the Soil Conservation Service guards, and warnings were posted at each gate leading to the grant. Quoting parts of the U.S. Criminal Code (18 USC 110), the warnings read:

Whoever shall knowingly and unlawfully break, open, or destroy any gate, fence, hedge, or wall enclosing any lands of the United States . . . set aside for any public use; or whoever shall drive any cattle, horses, pigs, or other livestock upon such land . . . or whoever shall knowingly permit his cattle, horses, pigs, or other livestock to enter . . . shall be fined not more than $500, or imprisoned not more than one year, or both.

The situation was so serious, however, that by February, forty-two men, with 458 cattle and horses and 1,200 sheep, grimly marched through the gates onto the grassy lands of the grant. And grassy it was, since it was under the strict supervision of the Soil Conservation Service; to this I can personally attest, since I spent most of my teenage summers on the grant, herding sheep with my brothers or hired Navajos and Mexicans. I have never since then seen grass that tall—there, or on any part of the reservation. [5]

Another notice of trespass followed, which read:

This will constitute formal notice to you that the following stock in such numbers and brands as indicated below, which have been placed on the government-owned grant by you on this date in defiance of oral warning on the part of the S.C.S. administrative officers are in trespass on lands of the United States; and you are ordered to remove them from such lands without delay.

This warning was ignored, as the previous ones had been, and by 1940 the Spanish stockmen were officially allowed to graze their stock within the grant. This problematic grant is discussed further in a later chapter.

The Valle Grande

After the ancient homeland was granted to the Spaniards in 1798, under a grant known as the Cañón de San Diego de Jémez Land Grant, the Jemez people began to depend on the forested area farther east for religious activities, herb collecting, hunting, eagle catching,

grazing community horse herds, and collecting fir branches for ceremonial dances. They had free access and use, along with neighboring
Pueblo Indian tribes, until 1905.

On October 12, 1905, President Theodore Roosevelt declared
34,900.27 acres of aboriginal land to be the Jemez National Forest
Reserve. This occurred in spite of Article 1, Section 8 of the Constitution of the United States, which states that Indian tribes, like foreign
nations and states, will be consulted on important transactions. No
records have been found to indicate that the United States Indian
Service was consulted on this matter.

Further loss of aboriginal land in Valle Grande, amounting to
16,811.74 acres, took place in the 1920s under the Homestead Act.
This land was listed as Tract B before the Indian Claims Commission
in Docket 137, and is covered in Chapter 6 of the present work. The
rest, Tract C, was taken over by the government under the Taylor
Grazing Act of April 4, 1936. The total losses, as presented before the
Indian Claims Commission, were 282,415.73 acres; this is discussed
at length in Chapter 6.

Problems of the Present

In the summer of 1979 Jemez Pueblo learned that a subsidiary of
the Union Oil Company, known as the Union Geothermal Company
of New Mexico, proposed to build and operate a geothermal power
plant cooperatively with the Department of Energy (DOE) and the
Public Service Company of New Mexico (PNM). This power plant,
to be located in Redondo Canyon, on aboriginal Jemez land and within
the pueblo's watershed, would initially provide fifty megawatts, enough
power for a community of 50,000.

Jemez leaders evaluated the project as another threat to their very
physical and tribal existence at Jemez Pueblo, since the project impact
statement indicated that up to 13 per cent of the base flow of the Jemez
River could be utilized to begin the operation. As the project expanded
from its demonstration stage to an ultimate 400 megawatt capacity,
more water use would be anticipated, with an additional decrease in
the Jemez water supply. Further reduction of the stream flow on the
river would infringe on the prior reserved water rights of Jemez, as
well as those of Zia and Santa Ana Pueblos. This was the very same
fear that Jemez leaders in the 1920s had articulated; they were con-

cerned that their grandchildren would be competing for an ever-diminishing supply of water with newcomers to the Jemez country.

On August 16, 1979, Harold Sando, the great-grandson of Jose Manuel Yepa, who was involved in the struggle of the 1920s, arranged for a meeting with the project proponents. Held at the Indian Pueblo Cultural Center in Albuquerque, the meeting was organized in order for all the Pueblo Indian leaders to express their assessment of the project; the full membership of the Jemez Council and other tribal officials were present at this meeting. The council's appraisal of the project was explained by Councilmen Antonio Sando and Patricio Toya; the present writer explained the historical background of the area and its value to our tribe. Another public meeting was held with the three development organizations on August 30, at the Shalako Inn in Albuquerque. The Jemez Council and officials were again present, and the representatives again explained Jemez's position to the public. On January 23, 1982, the Albuquerque *Journal* announced that at a meeting in Los Angeles four days earlier the decision to "kill the project" had been reached by the Department of Energy, the Public Service Company of New Mexico, and the Union Geothermal Company of New Mexico. Thus the Pueblo Indians won another round and can continue to dance and sing on their land as a way of honoring the Creator and asking for justice and harmony in the world.

It is unfortunate that these threats reappear to prove the cliches that "history repeats itself," and that "we only learn from history that people do not learn." Non-Indians are rarely aware that Indian tribes are in many ways independent nations, and that as a sovereign nation, Jemez Pueblo has prior water rights to the Jemez River that flows through its reservation.

Jemez has had to fight the rapacious conquerors long and hard for its lands and its traditional system of usufruct, because our values and cultures are so different. To paraphrase Dr. Donald Cutter, justice is delayed; the United States government is guilty of malfeasance and nonfeasance, as is evidenced by the Indians' loss of choice farm land, forest land, and grazing land along the Rio Grande and its tributaries.

The future is perplexing: many Indian tribes throughout America are demanding the return of aboriginal land illegally taken over by non-Indians and the supposedly benign federal government. There is no reason to believe that the struggle for what is rightfully ours will cease in the near future.

Tu-va-kwa, the place where the Jemez culture blossomed in the 1300s, as it looks today. (Courtesy E. S. Scholer.)

Two descendants of the ancient Hemish inspect a ceremonial chamber at Tu-va-kwa; the author and Barnabe Romero of the U.S. Forest Service.

Three post-1696 Hemish refugee-fortress homes in or near the rim of Largo Canyon. (Courtesy E. S. Scholer.)

Three views of Jemez Pueblo in the past century. *Opposite above*, in 1887, with a burro corral in the left foreground; today this is the site of the Community Center near the plaza. (Courtesy Smithsonian Institution.) *Opposite below*, in 1935 (courtesy Museum of New Mexico, T. Harmon Parkhurst, photographer). *Above*, in 1980 (courtesy E. S. Scholer).

Augustine Sando, Jemez Councilman and the first Indian member and the
past Chairman of Sandoval County Commissioners. (Courtesy E. S. Scholer.)

Jemez officials on the site of the geothermal project near Redondo Peak. *Left to right*, Pat Toya and Tony Sando, Councilmen; Paul Toya and John R. Yepa, 2nd and 1st Lt. Governors; and Harold Sando, with Jack Maddox of the Public Service Company of New Mexico. (Courtesy 19 Pueblo News photograph.)

Threshing wheat in the 1920s. Machinery eventually replaced horses. (Courtesy Museum of New Mexico.)

Juanito and Augustine Sando branding sheep in June 1950. The Sando family, along with the Chinana and Loretto families, pastured a flock of sheep on the Ojo del Espíritu Santo Grant before the range was turned over to cattle growers.

Chili harvest 1980. (Courtesy E. S. Scholer.)

Spring runoff in 1941, producing a flow in mid-May of 4,000 to 5,000 cubic feet per second on the Rio Jemez, caused the complete destruction of the concrete diversion dam north of the Pueblo. Also washed out were the Santa Fe Northwestern Railroad tracks; nearly one hundred acres of Jemez farmland bordering the Rio Jemez were destroyed. (Courtesy Southern Pueblos Agency photograph.)

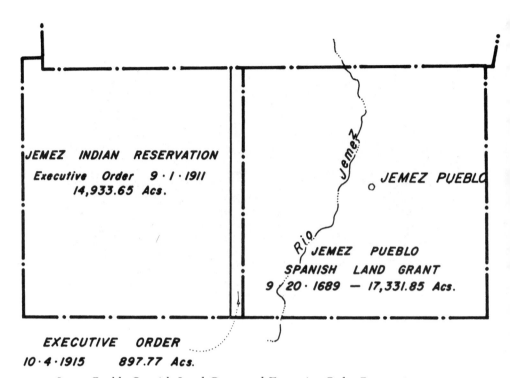

JEMEZ INDIAN RESERVATION
Executive Order 9·1·1911
14,933.65 Acs.

RIO Jemez

o JEMEZ PUEBLO

JEMEZ PUEBLO
SPANISH LAND GRANT
9·20·1689 — 17,331.85 Acs.

EXECUTIVE ORDER
10·4·1915   897.77 Acs.

Jemez Pueblo Spanish Land Grant and Executive Order Reservation.

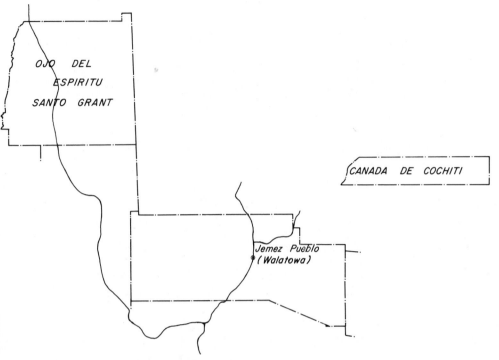

Tribally Owned Land and Trust Land.

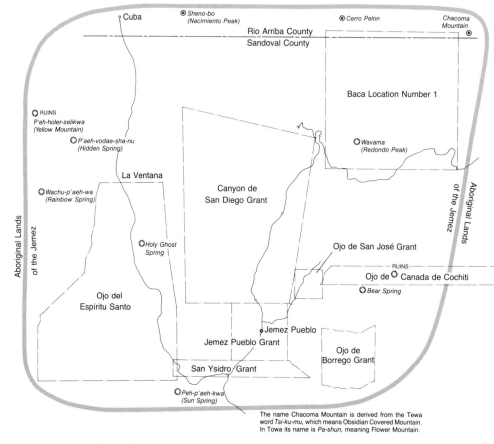

Spanish Land Grants Superimposed on Traditional Jemez Land Base.

4

Government and Leadership

Jemez Pueblo government today is a combination of native and European forms. The native form of government has been with the people since time immemorial. The titular head of the traditional government is the *cacique*, who serves with a staff and members. The term "cacique" is from the Caribbean Arawak Indians; this was the first tribe that Columbus discovered and demoralized by enslaving them to hunt gold, as well as seizing them to take to Spain. The Spaniards introduced their term to describe the head of each Indian pueblo. The Pueblos quickly became comfortable in using the term when dealing with outsiders, since it provdied a good way to avoid having to explain what their own term for the theocratic village leaders meant. The cacique and members serve for a lifetime.

The *opng-soma* ("war chief") and his two aides form the executive arm of the leadership, under the cacique; they enforce the rules, regulations, and ordinances of the theocratic system. These three men are selected by the religious council, and they also serve for a lifetime in their positions.

Another branch of government, under the war chief, includes the positions of war captains and their aides. War captains were known by the Spaniards as *capitanes de la guerra* in colonial days. These positions are filled annually by appointment of the caciques, society leaders, and the opng-soma. A war captain and his five aides are selected from one of the two moieties (kivas) of the pueblo, alternating years. There is also a lieutenant, with five aides. These men are responsible for policing the pueblo, and for supervising the traditional social activities of the people of their moieties—Turquoise or Pumpkin. These activities range from ceremonial and social dances to recreational rabbit hunts, competitive foot races, and hunting game animals. The war captain is also responsible for the reservation land, as well as domestic and wild game animals.

The European form of government was introduced by the Spaniards in colonial times, in three stages. The very first was introduced in 1590 by the slave trader, Gaspar Castaño de Sosa, who was the lieutenant governor of the state of Nuevo León. When the governor, Luís de Carvajal de la Cueva, was arrested, in order to break up the illegal slave traffic on the northern frontier, Castaño continued to deal in Indian slaves. And because of his reputation a petition for permission to go to New Mexico had been explicitly forbidden by Viceroy Luís de Velasco.[1] Castaño defied the viceroy, however, and traveled throughout Pueblo country, prospecting for minerals and seizing Indians to take back, supporting his ill-organized, undisciplined group of men, women, and children by extorting provisions from local people (John 1975:34).

Through gestures, Castaño explained his "peaceful" purpose as he went from village to village, pledging the people to be vassals of his own king. The people were to be under a three-man local government consisting of an *alcalde* and two *alguaciles*. Amidst the sounding of trumpets and gunfire, the Spaniards would erect a large cross in the main plaza of each pueblo, to serve as the symbol of their new status. Of those original crosses, perhaps only the one at Zia Pueblo remains (although Antonio de Espejo's expedition evidently erected a cross there in 1582). Zia Pueblo is also the spot where traditional legend tells us that the Jemez, Zia, and Santa Ana people were first christened by the early missionaries. All things considered, Castaño's ceremony must have been impressive to the pageant-loving Pueblo people, but beyond that the event probably had little significance.

And Castaño's days were numbered. When Viceroy Velasco learned that Castaño had defied his orders, he sent Captain Juan Morlete, in October 1590, with forty soldiers to search for the defiant one traveling with "all the riffraff left over from the war against the Chichimecas" (John 1975:35). Castaño's camp was finally found at Santo Domingo

Pueblo; he surrendered meekly and rode back to Mexico in irons. In 1593 he was found guilty of charges including the invasion of lands inhabited by peaceful Indians, raising troops, and unlawful entry into New Mexico. He was sentenced to six years of exile from New Spain, serving the king without salary in the Philippine Islands, under penalty of death for any default. There he died, when Chinese galley slaves revolted on the vessel under his command.

The second form of Spanish government, the governor system, was introduced when the first legal colonizer, Juan de Oñate, met with Pueblo leaders at Santo Domingo Pueblo on July 7, 1598, to lay the groundwork for the Spanish settlement of Pueblo country. Oñate probably had two reasons for creating this form of government: it was a form that the Spaniards understood; and with this kind of government, he probably saw a way of making village officials conform to his way of doing things.

The third stage of introducing a Spanish style of government came with a royal decree in approximately 1620 during the reign of Governor Juan de Eulate. At the beginning of Spanish rule over the Pueblos, the royal governors of the territory considered it their prerogative to appoint officials, "governors" of the pueblos, to handle local government. As symbols of authority, under royal decree, they gave those appointed officials *varas*, or canes. While there were crosses inscribed on these canes, they were symbols of secular authority. They soon came into conflict with the aims and ambitions of the church, which felt that it had not only the obligation to spread Christianity among the natives, but also the right to govern them.

In 1620 His Most Catholic Majesty—King Phillip III of Spain— moved to resolve this conflict of interest by requiring each of the pueblos to vote into office a governor, a lieutenant governor, and such other officers as would be necessary to administer their affairs. He specifically stipulated that these elections be held without interference from either the crown or the church.

As a symbol of authority the king ordered that a vara, or silver-headed rod, be given to each pueblo for its governor, to serve as his commission and legal authority; it would be passed down from each governor to his successor. King Phillip further ordered that the individual pueblos should hold their elections within a week of the end of each calendar year, and that they might incorporate into these ceremonies such of their own as they might desire; some essentially religious rituals have been included over the years. The king's system of self-government was thus superimposed upon the ancient tradition of selecting war captains and their aides to govern the civil aspects of pueblo life.

And why canes or rods? Ever since the time of the Spanish, it has been said that the king was thinking of the passage in the Bible,

And the Lord spake unto Moses saying, 'Speak unto the children of Israel, and take every one of them a rod according to the houses of their fathers . . . and it shall come to pass that man's rod which I shall choose, shall blossom . . .'

Although it is unknown exactly when and under what circumstances the pueblo governors received their canes from the Spanish, they still serve as their symbol of office. The tradition today is to have all the canes of higher civil officials, plus the war captains in recent years, blessed on January 6—the Feast Day of The Three Kings. The Catholic priest impresses upon the leaders the lessons of leadership in Exodus 4 and Numbers 17: the cane is to be their comfort and strength, and their token against all enemies.

A second cane in the possession of the governor is the Abraham Lincoln cane. During the Civil War, in October 1863, Lincoln sent his private secretary, John Nicolay, to accompany the governor of Colorado Territory in making a treaty of friendship with the Utes, at Conejos in the upper Rio Grande Valley. This was done to keep the Utes from entering the conflict between the North and the South, as the Apaches and Navajos had done.

The acting superintendent of Indian Territory from Santa Fe, Dr. Michael Steck, was also present at the treaty signing. Steck no doubt spoke of the peaceful pueblos to Nicolay, but the secretary was not able to meet with them. A month later, in early November, Steck was called to Washington, ostensibly for Senate confirmation. Steck undoubtedly told the president about the Pueblos, and the recognition extended to them by the Spanish government in the form of canes, or rods, as symbols of authority.

Lincoln thereupon ordered nineteen silver-headed canes, one for each pueblo in the Territory, to be engraved for presentation to their governors. Steck purchased the nineteen ebony canes from John Dold of Philadelphia, each with silver head and ferule. The heads were engraved with the name Lincoln, and the date, 1863; they cost $5.50 each.

Steck was confirmed as superintendent of Indian affairs of the territory by the Senate on January 22, 1864. The next day he wrote to his deputy in Santa Fe that he was returning, bringing with him several pueblo land patents and an official staff for each of the pueblo governors. These Lincoln canes were distributed to the eight northern pueblo governors during the months of October and November of 1864; the southern pueblo governors had sent delegations to the Indian Agency at Pena Blanca, New Mexico, and were given their canes in September of 1864 (Kubicek 1968).

Today the Pueblo Spanish and Lincoln canes are symbols to the people that authority exists in their own form of government; that their government is responsible to the people; and that they owe allegiance to the United States of America. On the other hand, the canes are also symbols of the United States government's responsibilities and trusteeship toward the Pueblo Indians.

Thus, the government introduced by Spain is today the civil government of Jemez, in contrast to the religious government. Under the cacique, the civil governor is responsible for tribal affairs in the modern world; he is the liaison with the outside, business world. Since Indians in the past have had little effect on the wider society, most Americans have been taught that our "federal system" is made up exclusively of local, state, and federal governments. But that is not true. From the beginning, Indian tribes have been recognized as separate governmental units, distinct from the states in which their reservations may lie. In fact, the United States Constitution, Article I, Section 8, gives the federal government exclusive authority to regulate commerce (1) with foreign nations, (2) with Indian tribes, and (3) among the states. Both before and after the adoption of the Constitution, more than three hundred and fifty treaties were entered into with the tribes, ratified with all the solemnity and formality of any other treaty. Indians, then, are different from other ethnic groups in that their tribal organizations are legal units of government.

The governor of the pueblo has an official staff, composed of a first lieutenant governor, a second lieutenant governor, and a sheriff, who in turn has a complement of five aides, who serve as messengers and chauffeurs.

Other members of the governor's official staff are the "fiscale" and his lieutenant and five aides, who are church officers. They are responsible for activities involving the Catholic church, such as burials, janitorial duties, and maintenance of church property.

All these officials at Jemez are selected annually by the cacique and his staff, rather than by popular vote, as the Spaniards had envisioned. All pueblo officials served without salary in the past, considering the year's service as a duty to their people and their community. Since about 1968, the governor has been offered a token salary, and in the 1970s, many of the other officers received C.E.T.A. (Comprehensive Employment and Training Act) positions and worked in the village under Manpower Program funds.

Known Jemez Leaders

When Juan de Oñate met with Pueblo leaders at Santo Domingo in 1598, present also was the first Jemez leader to be mentioned by the Spaniards—Pe-stiassa ("sun-god"), who was said to represent the eight Jemez villages which then comprised the Jemez nation (John 1975:42). He might have been an alcalde, if Jemez had by then accepted Castaño's suggestion; if not, he was probably a war captain. (See Appendix I for a chronological listing of Jemez leaders.)

The next Jemez leader mentioned is Governor Francisco, in 1681 (John 1975:104). After the revolt of 1680, this governor, with seven other Jemez men, accompanied the recently expelled governor of New Mexico, Antonio de Otermín, back to the territory. He was returning to the scene of his expulsion to determine the cause of the revolt, and to learn the identities of the leaders. His army of 146 soldiers, Mexican Indian aides, and the eight Jemez men, however, merely succeeded in sacking and burning both Tamaya (Santa Ana) and Tsia (Zia), at which time the people fled to Mesa Colorado, directly west of Walatowa (Jemez). Our Sun Clan patriarchs have long told us the legend of a Sun Clan man journeying south to assist the Spaniards returning to Pueblo country to restore harmony; harmony between which parties is never explained, however. It has been assumed that he accompanied the Zia man, Bartólome de Ojeda, and other Pueblo men, in a similar expedition with Diego de Vargas, a few years later. Since no names of Jemez men have been recorded in connection with the de Vargas *entrada*, the Sun Clan man of Jemez legends may be the governor Francisco, who accompanied the Otermín party.

The third Jemez leader reported is Governor Luís Cunixu, or Cuniju (Conejo?). It was the habit of early writers to indiscriminately apply the titles of governor or captain to Pueblo leaders. The nature of the early conflicts, however, gives us a clue that governors were more apt to cooperate with the Spanish authorities, while war captains and war chiefs were usually opposed to them. Applying this line of reasoning, one would conclude that Cunixu was a war captain. It had been his unfortunate task to club to death the priest, Fray Francisco de Jesús María Casanos, during the short-lived revolt of June 4, 1696. Following this episode, Luís escaped to Pecos, where he was received at the home of the cacique, Diego Umbiro (Espinosa 1942:250). A meeting of the Pecos traditional leaders was held, at which the governor of Pecos was also present; no doubt a revolt against the Spanish was the subject. Suddenly the governor, Spanish cane in hand, rose up and said, "Here we are loyal to the King!" (Espinosa 1942:250). The governor's aides overpowered the cacique and his men, and he immediately petitioned Governor de Vargas for permission to kill the rebels; thus the cacique, Diego, and the war captain, Cachina, were hanged, along with two other men. Cunixu and a Nambe man by the name of Diego Xenome were taken to Santa Fe for trial, where they were joined by the governor of Santo Domingo Pueblo, Alonso Guiqui (Waquiu?), a native of Jemez (Astiolekwa; Espinosa 1942:253). These three men

were sentenced to be shot and were given three hours to prepare themselves and confess to the priest. The priest prepared the prisoners for a happy death; and they were then marched in military formation to the front of the old church of the villa, where three arquebus shots ended their early lives (Espinosa 1942:254).

The focus of much interest and speculation is the governor of Jemez listed in the year 1706 as Luís Conitzu; could he possibly be the son of Luís Cunixu? (see Bloom and Mitchell 1938).

According to the Spanish Archives of New Mexico, Document 1141, in 1766, when the pueblos of Jemez, Zia, and Santa Ana were granted the Espíritu Santo Grant, the governor of Jemez was Cristóval Chiguigui. We have no further information about this man.

Spanish records only infrequently mention Jemez leaders, and records of Pueblo Indian activities during the Mexican administration, 1821–46, are also quite limited. In 1849, however, with the coming of the Americans, Lieutenant J.H. Simpson camped with his troops at Jemez during a military reconnaissance of the Navajo country, and he reported meeting the governor, Francisco Hosta. The governor indicated to Simpson that "Hosta" came from his Indian name, Hos-tyi—"lightning." A shield that Hos-tyi presented to the lieutenant is in the Smithsonian Institution in Washington, D.C.

On April 7, 1849, James S. Calhoun was appointed as the first Indian agent west of the Mississippi, and set up office in Santa Fe. In July 1850, he drew up a treaty between the Pueblo tribes and the United States, which, however was never ratified by the U.S. Senate. Perhaps this was because only ten pueblos signed the treaty: Cochiti, Jemez, Nambe, San Ildefonso, Santa Clara, Santa Ana, San Felipe, Santo Domingo, Tesuque, and Zia. Signing as governor of Jemez was Blanco Nostez; a Juan Domingo also affixed his "X" as war captain of Jemez.

When land was leased to Presbyterian missionaries in 1878, Juan Lucero signed as governor. In 1888 the governor was the Pecos immigrant Augustin Pecos. My father was raised by Augustin's son, Jose Antonio Pecos (Soma-kin), and he had heard that Grandpa Augustin, or Whiya-toh-oler, was the village governor when the San Diego de Jemez church was rebuilt, after giving way to the vicissitudes of nature around 1881. Patricio Toya, another grandson, also testifies to the family account.

Other Pecos immigrants who may have served as governors at Jemez were Juan Antonio Toya, the governor of Pecos when he brought his people to Jemez, and Jose Miguel Vigil. Both of these men were listed as *principales* when the Presbyterian missionaries were leased their acre plot in 1878. No dates have been found to indicate when and how many times they might have served as governors of Jemez, however.

The next governor mentioned in the document is Jose Rey Yepo, in 1893, in connection with the court trial over the Espíritu Santo Grant.

In 1899 another Jemez governor made the headlines. That fall, during a ceremonial dance, the guards (her-le-yoush) stopped the U.S. mail carrier from delivering mail to the pueblo post office. At that time the main road and mail route came through the village and passed by the northernmost street of the village, on which are located the halls of the Turquoise and Pumpkin moieties, often off limits for nonresidents and non-Indians. This street served as a short cut from the village post office to Vallecito (today Ponderosa) and Canon, before returning to San Ysidro.

A few days later, following a quick government investigation, the governor, Jose Romero, was bound over to await trial when the U.S. grand jury met again in March, six months later (Reagan 1914). Although the war chief and the war captain were the ones responsible for the actions of the guards, the governor was arrested, since he was seen from outside the pueblo as the paramount leader. The outcome of the case is unknown.

In 1911 the Southern Pueblos Agency was opened in Albuquerque; records of that first year show that a water rights hearing was held on March 13. Delegates to that meeting were headed by Governor Juan Lopez Chinana, First Lieutenant Governor Jose Reyes Chihuihui (Chewiwi), Second Lieutenant Governor George Toledo, and Councilmen (called principales until very recently) Jose Romero, Jose Guadalupe Toledo (grandfather of Frank Toledo), and Jose Reyes Toya (which one is uncertain, as there were several by this name).

The governor in 1918 was Jose Manuel Yepa. Our Aunt Juanita used to tell us that Grandpa was the governor when the present village church was remodeled, and that she danced on that occasion. The festival took two days; November 12 was the annual feast day of San Diego, and the next day the statues, remodeled church, and new chapel were blessed. Father Albertus Daeger was the parish priest; he became a bishop the following year.

Jose Reyes Chihuihui is listed as governor in 1919, in the files of the Southern Pueblos Agency. In 1922 all the Pueblo tribes legally reorganized as the All-Pueblo Council; at this important conference the Jemez delegates were led by Jose Felipe Yepa. He also signed an appeal from the Pueblo Indians of New Mexico to the people of the United States, against the threatening bill introduced by Senator Holm Bursum of New Mexico (for details, see Sando 1976:95). The other delegates were the principales Jose Manuel Yepa and Jose Romero, as well as Paul Toya, Pablo Toya, and Jose Reyes Loretto, with Jesus M. Baca as interpreter.

The official name, All-Pueblo Council, was changed to its present form, All Indian Pueblo Council, in the 1960s, because of court cases involving the water rights of "pueblos," or towns, particularly the "pueblo" of Los Angeles, California, so termed in early Spanish records. Pueblo water rights in this case meant the rights of the city of Los Angeles, in California. Thus the name was changed to clarify and better identify the All Indian Pueblo Council.

Although, as we have seen, the records do not preserve the names of many Jemez governors, tradition indicates that many of them ruled with an iron hand in the early days. Perhaps this is the reason our governors appear to possess absolute authority, as compared to the chairmen of other tribes.

In the 1930s two Jemez men, Juan Gachupin and Jose Maria Toya, were ostracized from the pueblo for taking dance troops to places like Gallup and Flagstaff, Arizona; they were told that they could not help with community ditch work, which meant they would not be allowed to plant corn, wheat, and other crops. Other men who had ventured beyond Jemez invested in the new horse-drawn cultivators they saw, eager to avoid the old time-consuming and back-breaking system of hoeing by hand. But that was not acceptable to Jemez authorities, who quickly hauled these men into tribal court, where they denounced them for disgracing the sacred corn and mother earth.

Today, of course, dance teams perform in many places outside of Jemez. The dance team of the Fragua brothers—Vivian, Clemente, Valentino, Tony, and Phillip—was known as the White Cloud Dance Troop. They sold war bonds during World War II, traveling all over the United States and Europe. In the 1970s they were replaced by another Fragua team, led by the singers Frank and Jerry Fragua, and their dancers. This latter group has been very popular at the annual New Mexico state fairs and at the Pueblo Indian Cultural Center in Albuquerque during the tourist season. In the same vein, hand hoeing was in fact replaced by horse-drawn cultivators; in the 1960s the horses were replaced by tractors.

When I was a child, my peers, as well as adults, used to remark that my grandfather, Jose Manuel Yepa, had sold all our land. Later I began to inquire why there was so much talk about Mr. Yepa; a quick answer was that "he carried the *muleta*"—the briefcase that contained the official tribal papers and any funds in the care of tribal officials. Because of this position he testified during the Pueblo Lands Board hearings in 1925, at which time he gave his age as sixty-five; he had previously served the pueblo as interpreter, treasurer, governor, first principale, and head of the Clown Society. In 1932 the governor was Daniel Mora, and his sheriff was Louis Loretto. These two men came to see Grandpa Yepa, then old and barely able to walk with a cane, and forced him to take them to where he stored his records, in his son's home. In front of his grandchildren he was threatened and cursed, and accused of selling Jemez land. They wanted to know where he was hiding all the money that he was hoarding. The two men took two little boxes, not muletas, in which he no doubt had official papers. Grandpa Yepa was better off financially than the average Jemez head of a household; but he built his fortune on hard work and his wife's inheritance of cattle and land from her father. Later he opened and operated the first general mercantile store at Jemez (Sando 1976:141).

And now, finally, we learn that Jemez really lost a good part of its aboriginal homeland through federal legislation; it was not sold by Jose Manuel Yepa. Perhaps he was accused of selling the land because he testified before the Pueblo Lands Board in 1925, when he was first principale of Jemez.

Jemez Leadership and Federal Legislation

In 1935 Jemez Pueblo voted against participating in the provisions of the Indian Reorganization Act (IRA) of 1934, a part of the New Deal of President Franklin D. Roosevelt and Indian Commissioner John Collier, aimed at reforming federal Indian policy. In retrospect, this seems to have been another case of misinterpretation.

The IRA was an amended version of the "Wheeler-Howard Bill," which the Jemez council had studied. They particularly objected to Title IV of that bill, which had to do with the judicial structure of tribes (Philp 1977:142). No doubt other provisions of the bill, as well, gave the council reason to believe that the bill encroached upon the powers of the pueblo government; but no distinction was made between this and the IRA. Indian Service Superintendent Lem A. Towers wrote to Commissioner Collier on June 24, 1935, explaining that John Shamon and Jesus Baca had interpreted the provisions of the IRA incorrectly, leading the tribe to believe that their government would be turned over to the United States.

The central issue of the IRA, in fact, was constitutions and charters that would allow tribes to borrow money from a revolving credit fund; thus, the principle of self-government was its major goal. But for thousands of years the Pueblos had practiced self-government, and the bill would interfere with it, imposing rigid white political and economic concepts in a situation where flexibility would have been the better choice. To confuse the issue even more, the act was naturally full of specialized legal terms, and most pueblo members at that time lacked even a high-school education.

In the end, an amendment by Edgar Howard of Nebraska became the most controversial to many Indian tribes; its Section 18 made the act inapplicable where a majority of adult Indians on a reservation voted against it in a special election. Collier had contacted most of the tribes throughout the country, and the subject of voting in favor or against became a national Indian issue. It was so significant that for many years, in many reservations, people were identified as "yes" or "no" individuals, according to how their parents or grandparents had voted on the IRA.

Jemez held a referendum on June 17, 1935, and turned the IRA down. Following this show of independence the council sensed that there was a feeling on the part of the Indian Service that Jemez had taken a stand against the expressed wishes of Commissioner Collier. On June 24 Ferdinando Baca of Jemez called on Superintendent Towers, with a message from the cacique, Andres Loretto, requesting another opportunity to vote on the IRA, because he thought the people had been misinformed. Baca also said that Governor Jose Fragua had not allowed other Jemez men, who had heard Collier speak at Santo Domingo on May 9, to explain the act to the Jemez people, although they had assured Collier that they would.

As the New Deal progressed, the people of Jemez reconsidered their opposition to the IRA, and on November 9, 1944, the council drew up a petition to the president of the United States, requesting that the IRA be amended so that Jemez might be permitted to take part in its provisions. The petition was signed by Governor Juanito Chinana, First Lieutenant Governor Cristino Panana, and Second Lieutenant Governor Ambrosio Toya, along with the minor officials Vivian Fragua, Santiago Romero, Jose A. Loretto, Guadalupe Fragua, Jose L. Loretto, and Jack Toya. The president, however, failed to act on the petition.

This change of attitude toward the IRA came about after it was learned that, complicated and controversial as the bill was, there are indeed some merits contained in the legislation. For instance, two sections of the IRA concern the acquisition of land for Indian tribes; Section 5 stipulates that:

The Secretary of the Interior is hereby authorized in his discretion, to acquire through purchase, relinquishment, gift, exchange, or assignment, any interest in lands, water rights, or surface rights to lands, within or without existing reservations . . . for the purpose of providing land for Indians . . . Title to any lands or rights acquired pursuant to this Act shall be taken in the name of the United States in trust for the Indian tribe or individual Indian for which the land is acquired.

Section 7 authorizes the secretary of the interior "to proclaim new Indian reservations on lands acquired pursuant to any authority conferred by this Act, or to add such lands to existing reservations." However, the act of May 25, 1918 (40 Stat. 561 *et seq.*), which provided appropriations for the Bureau of Indian Affairs for fiscal year 1919, included in the last paragraph of Section 2 the following: "That hereafter no Indian reservation shall be created nor shall any additions be made to one heretofore created, within the limits of the States of New Mexico and Arizona, except by Act of Congress." For many years it was the policy of the secretary of the interior to accept lands in New Mexico and Arizona in trust, pursuant to Section 5 of the 1934 act, but not to declare those lands a reservation under Section 7 of that act, because of the 1918 act.

In order for the Pueblos to be in the same position with respect to the addition of land to their reservations as the majority of other Indian tribes are, Pueblo officials requested legislation to remove these obstacles. In response, the acting deputy commissioner of the Bureau of Indian Affairs testified before the November 20, 1979, hearing of the Select Committee on Indian Affairs, U.S. Senate, on Senate Bill 1832, "A Bill to Extend the Authority of the Secretary of the Interior to Declare and Proclaim Lands to be Indian Reservation Land." He recommended that the last paragraph of Section 2 of the 1918 Act be repealed, and that a section be added to S. 1832 that would extend the authorizations of Sections 5 and 7 of the IRA to Jemez Pueblo. With the passage of this bill, Jemez will now be able to benefit from specific sections of the Indian Reorganization Act, which otherwise would be denied to the pueblo.

Two programs should be mentioned at this point, to explain the mistrust of the Jemez people regarding government innovations. In the early 1930s, in the midst of the Depression, a few railroad carloads of milk cows were delivered to Jemez, and brought into the community corral, today the parking lot of the civic center. All the families in Jemez were to get a cow, but it could not leave the corral on its feet; as the families came to claim their "beef," the cow was shot in front of the gate, and then the carcass was dragged home by a team of horses, or behind a wagon. A few people offered to slaughter their own heifers in order to keep the milk cow, but Indian Service officials ruled that the cows that arrived at Jemez were for beef and could not be utilized for other purposes.

Later, toward the end of the Depression, another trainload of cattle arrived at Jemez, all white-faced Herefords. No doubt the Interior Department had purchased them from American cattlemen as part of the program to assist the cattle industry. The cattle all bore a fresh

Interior Department brand, "ID," on the hip. The Indians quickly dubbed them "I Die" cattle, since even as they were coming off the ramps some of them fell on the slope, never to rise again. Others were able to walk from the railroad to the community corral, where they then succumbed to exhaustion; a hardy few were able to reach their new owners' corrals before they also dropped. A handful survived to be fed by the new cowboys, who then drove them to the irrigation ditch for a drink of water. With the combination of too much food and water in their stomachs, however, these cattle fell at the ditch and never took another step. Only two families or so had these "repayment cattle" for any length of time. Others, who were the legal owners of record, were hounded by the Indian Service to repay for the nonexisting stock. In fact, a meeting was held on November 29, 1940, to which representatives from the Indian Agency came in order to collect from the owners, only to learn that most of the cattle had died.

These examples of unsolicited government help, combined with past court decisions, have conditioned the tribal leaders to suspect any offer of help, at least at first.

On December 30, 1940, Superintendent Sophie Aberle wrote to Governor George Toledo to explain the benefits, purposes, and procedures of the Agriculture Adjustment Administration, offered to American farmers under the New Deal. Referring to the tribe's earlier reaction to the IRA, she assured the governor that the program was not designed to steal Indian land, nor would payment received have to be reimbursed, since the plan was only to withdraw land from production as a soil conservation effort. Other goals of the AAA were the planting of alfalfa, green manure plowing, and land renovation. The tribe showed little interest in these plans, but did consider technical assistance with the grazing range.[2]

Jemez Pueblo and Modern Politics

Traditionally the alguacil, or sheriff, served as the tribal interpreter, but on many occasions officials have used other Jemez members as interpreters. Jose Manuel Yepa served as interpreter during the early territorial days, when both Spanish and English were used. He was succeeded by Jesus M. Baca, in the late 1920s and early 1930s, and then John Shamon, Juan Pedro Colaque, Ferdinando (Ferd) Baca, and Emiliano Yepa. Since the 1950s the pueblo government has made use of assistance on special cases from paid general counsel, as well as the field solicitor of the Department of the Interior, and BIA co-ordinators.

The first official bonded tribal treasurer, from 1948 to 1968, was Jack Toya. In 1969 he was replaced by Joe Louis Pecos, followed from 1976 to 1980 by Ciriaco Toya. The current tribal treasurer is Antonia Fragua Toledo. This office is a very important one, but its true value is apparently not recognized, since the incumbents must work as treasurers in their spare time or after their regular work hours. They were not paid until recently.

In 1978 the Jemez Tribe contracted with the Bureau of Indian Affairs, under P.L. 93-638 of that year (the Self-Determination Act) for a formulate share grant (that is, a grant that varies with population). Under this contract the governing officials employed James Roger Magdalena as its tribal administrator, to assist in the day-to-day management of tribal affairs. His importance and contribution to the governing staff is immeasurable.

Since 1975, another form of leadership by Jemez personalities has developed: that of Sandoval County Commissioner of District Two. The pueblo residents began to vote following the 1948 decision that all New Mexico Indians had the right to vote in public elections. They cast their votes in precincts located in nearby Spanish communities.

In 1967 Augustine Sando, then pueblo governor, realized the power of the vote and petitioned for a precinct at Jemez, which was granted. Where the Jemez vote had formerly been split, it was now united in a single precinct, making it a noticeable force in the county, with approximately six hundred votes. Augustine became the first precinct chairman, and soon his charisma was recognized by Sandoval County politicians; consequently, he was persuaded to run for county commissioner in 1974, as a Democrat. He won a two-year term, as the first Indian county commissioner in a county which had previously excluded Indians from political office. When he ran for reelection he won again. In recognition of his earnest efforts, in the last year of his second term his colleagues voted him chairman of the commission, an office he held through 1978. On October 11, 1979, Augustine was one of two hundred state business and political leaders to be invited to a breakfast with President Jimmy Carter in Albuquerque. Five other New Mexico Indian tribal leaders were among the two hundred.

By law Augustine could not be a candidate to succeed himself a second time. However, his devotion to duty as an Indian leader was recognized by the public that he served. And his typical Pueblo Indian knowledge of the three languages of the state was a great asset: he could address his own people in their native Towa, and others either in Spanish or English. The example of this political pioneer made the general public aware of the potential of Indian leadership, and encouraged a young Jemez man, James R. Magdalena, to become a candidate for county commissioner. He campaigned hard against his Republican opponent and won. Thus, another Jemez man is serving a two-year term as a county commissioner beginning in 1979; he was eligible to run for reelection in 1981 and won. From this beginning, as their experience increases, other Pueblo Indian men and women will be running as candidates for other county, state, and national offices.

Jemez is a nation within a nation—a sovereign Indian nation under the American nation. The tribe gains strength from its membership in the All Indian Pueblo Council, a kind of Pueblo United Nations. During the latter half of the 1970s the nineteen pueblos have been working more closely together than at any time since the 1920s. This unity may well be due to the leadership of a young man of Santo Domingo and San Juan extraction, Delfin J. Lovato. When the twenty-nine-year-old Lovato became chairman in March of 1974, things began to change. Pueblo tribes began to work together more closely, as a Pueblo nation; any special problems faced by individual pueblos became a subject of concern for all nineteen pueblos, and any opponents were faced with united fervor and eloquence. For the first time the council began to lobby at the state capital, as well as making itself heard in Washington, D.C. Under Lovato's leadership the pueblos have made great efforts to register their people for state and national elections. Pueblo governors and councils have begun to notice the trend, and at the council election in 1979, the chairman (and the secretary-treasurer, Frank Tenorio, of San Felipe), was elected enthusiastically to a third term. Thus, the Pueblos have begun to develop the tools with which to combat old legislation aimed at reducing Pueblo land holdings and increasing public rights-of-way, and to promote the general welfare of the Pueblo people by political means on all fronts.

5

Farming and Irrigation

In 1894 the Department of the Interior issued a report subtitled *Conditions of Sixteen New Mexico Indian Pueblos, 1890*, which included Jemez Pueblo (Poore 1894). The author reported that about fourteen hundred acres were farmed at Jemez at that time, mostly on the west side of the river, served by the west ditch. The report mentions that the east ditch terminated at Rio Chiquito, which Poore called "Viaceta Creek" (Vallecito), to the north of the village. The part of the ditch which passed through the village was out of use at that time, since its banks were frequently broken by flash floods on the creek. There were said to be two ancient irrigation ditches serving Jemez at that time, which dated from the founding of the pueblo in the seventeenth century.

According to the report,

The pueblo, inclosed [*sic*] on the northwest by numerous little orchards of apple, plum, and apricot trees, emerges from beneath this deep tangle of green. . . . their dried peaches are excellent and command higher prices at Santa Fe than eastern fruit.

Although in later years Jemez farmers were said to be mainly "silt

81

farmers," the report mentions that "an immense bank of manure, 9 feet deep and covering an acre, has been discovered at the site of a former corral. This the storekeeper has prevailed upon some of them to use." In addition to forty barrels of wine made per year, the report states that "this year Jemez will have 10,000 bushels of wheat and nearly as much corn."

Jemez oldtimers still talk about using oxen, but no definite date of their first use has ever materialized. Poore did report, however, that ten years before the report was made, plowing was done with wooden plows and oxen; since that time Jemez farmers had broken many horses to harness, and had discarded oxen. The report states that according to some authorities they owned 3,000 head of horses, according to others, only 750. These were kept on an immense range of unconfined pasture land, fifty miles long and twelve miles wide, owned jointly by Jemez, Santa Ana, and Zia. Here he seems to be talking about the Espíritu Santo Grant, which he called "Spirito Santo." The report goes on to say that it was impossible to get the correct number of either horses or cattle. The Indians did not know how many they owned, and the possession of horses was doubtful wealth, since the Navajos had broken the market by stealing Pueblo horses. Also, the Indians were said to be as willing to take a journey on foot as on horseback, and were able to cover as much ground by one means as the other.

According to Poore, the "Spirito Santo Grant" was given under Spanish authority for pasturage, with the government reserving the right of pasture for its cavalry. Around the time of the report, valuable mineral deposits had been discovered on the grant, especially on the Rio Puerco and near Salisaro (Rio Salado?); he mentions a fifteen-foot vein of lignite coal, copper, gold, and silver. The report states that the Indians threatened all comers to the valley who carried picks and shovels, although they showed no inclination to mine it themselves.

The report also mentions numerous complaints by Jemez farmers that immense flocks of sheep ranged on the land, and that stock from the adjoining village of San Ysidro frequently invaded their corn and grain fields. The fence that protected the fields on that side had been broken, and there was much irritation in consequence. Some years later settlers from San Ysidro built a community of six houses on the pueblo's land. Negotiations were entered into, whereby an exchange was made for an equivalent portion of land on the southern side of the grant, but the settlers still held onto their houses and some of the land around them. A writ of ejection was served, but the Indians seemed timid about using the land until their agent had the vacated houses destroyed. Exactly who was timid is not explained by the report, but Jemez oral history says that it was the governor at that time who was timid; he was therefore impeached. Immediately afterward, Jemez men fell upon the vacated houses, tore down everything in the settlement, and reclaimed the land.

In general the report is revealing and complimentary. Poore describes Jemez people as having a wide reputation for industry, when compared to the other fourteen Pueblo tribes on which he reported. He also included mention of the time a hundred Jemez men aided the Zia Indians—"out of good fellowship"—in the construction of an *acequia* (irrigation ditch), after their brethren, the Santa Ana Indians, had refused them aid following the dry year which touched off near starvation in 1876.

The forty barrels of wine made per year no doubt decreased gradually over the years, as wine and other alcoholic beverages became more readily available for purchase. Although little, if any, wine is made at Jemez today, the pueblo is still well known among other Indians for the quality of its grapes. Brought from Europe by missionaries to provide wine for the Catholic priests, the vines flourished in the sandy loam at Jemez, and eventually most Jemez families had their own little vineyards. The grapes are small in size, a very deep blue, and when allowed to remain on the vines until fully ripe they are exceptionally sweet. In the fall Jemez grapes are a popular item to trade or sell to other tribes, especially during the Jicarilla Apache feast on September 15 and the Taos feast on September 30. They are also taken to the Navajo country to trade for sheep and rugs, along with chili, whole-wheat flour, and bread.

Of great interest and importance is Poore's statement that the fields between the river and the village were surrounded by high adobe walls: "A door, with padlock and key, protects little plots of vegetables, fruit, and grapes." This was said to be the case during the heyday of the Navajo raiders, before they were subdued by the American military in the early 1860s. This was also the reason for the community corral (which left the nine-foot-deep bank of manure). The corral was known as the "burro corral," and was located where the Tribal Community Center is today; the parking area of the Civic Center was the site of a later community corral. In the community corral, the burros and horses could be guarded against Navajo raiders by the war captains and their aides. Chickens and turkeys were also kept close to the family quarters.[1]

In 1931 a study of Jemez water use was made by Paul V. Hodges, a hydrographic engineer; it was mimeographed in March 1938, by the BIA. His report indicates that Jemez farmed 2,100 acres in 1896; in 1917 the figure was 2,090 acres; and in 1923, the area farmed had declined to 1,500 acres. In 1924 the Irrigation Branch of the United Pueblos Agency began making yearly irrigation crop reports; that year only 1,378 acres were reported as being farmed. The reports were yearly, but I shall list only a few to show the gradual decline in farming. One thousand acres were farmed in 1934; 1,353 acres in 1944; 1,356 acres in 1950; 935 acres in 1960; 699 acres in 1970; and 424 acres in 1978, the year of the last report available.

One cause of the decline of agriculture is simply a shortage of water, aggravated by increased population upstream. Along with the limitations on available water, a feeling of insecurity grew, as more and more people from other parts of the country settled upstream, demanding a share of the dwindling water supply so easily promised by the land developers. But there are also other reasons for the decline in farming. Veterans returning from World War II, Korea, and Vietnam, had learned new trades in the service, or took advantage of the GI bill to become skilled workmen and professionals. In addition, the soil bank program, brought on by the strange workings of the federal government, advised Pueblo farmers not to farm—that they would be compensated for idle lands. The availability of this kind of welfare has created a new kind of person in the pueblo.

Another variable that perhaps contributed to the decline of farming was the establishment of crews to fight forest fires. There are twenty men to a crew, including three straw bosses and a leader. They have often been used as night crews—the hardest work. The hard-hatted crews from Jemez, known as "The Eagles," have been flown all over the western United States, wherever fires have burned out of control. Although it is income well earned, and more than could be gained by farming or in average jobs, this work has taken the men away from their farms for weeks at a time.

Thus, considering all the variables, farming on a large scale is no longer practicable. Today the chili and other vegetable gardens remain, but only a few farmers persist in growing alfalfa, corn, and some wheat. The time-honored vocation of stock raising to supplement farming has also passed its peak, since the population is steadily increasing, while there is only limited grazing land. The number of cattle has remained fairly constant, but there are no sheep or goats at Jemez, and the horse population has decreased; horses have generally been replaced by the tractor and the pickup truck.

Hodges mentioned only the west and east ditches as present in 1931, but there were two others in existence at that time. The west ditch branched off, northwest of the village, to become the "upper" west ditch, and ran along the foothills for approximately two miles before it reentered the "lower" west ditch, near the cacique's field. From there it continued on south to the reservation boundary line, and emptied into the river on the north side of the bridge.

The other ditch not mentioned is to the east of the Jemez River; it was called the "Antonio Pecos" ditch. Its diversion dam is just below where the Rio Chiquito (Vallecito) empties into the Jemez River. As it curves along parallel to the river and the old Santa Fe Northwestern Railroad bed, it is approximately four miles long.

The main east ditch reported by Hodges passes through the village proper, and at that time ended north of the government day school. Sometime in the early 1920s my father, Juanito Sando, extended the ditch farther to the south, past the present day school. From there other men extended it even farther south and developed more gardens, so that by now the east ditch is approximately ten miles long. This added from eight hundred to a thousand additional acres for cultivation as compared to the one thousand acres served by the six miles of ditch reported by Poore in 1890. While the new acreage is irrigable land, it is not necessarily farmed, due to a shortage of water and the other factors mentioned earlier.

On March 25, 1911, Governor Juan Lopez Chinana, his lieutenants, and the councilmen, appeared before Superintendent of Irrigation Robinson, to present an affidavit making their prior water rights a matter of record in the Office of the Territorial Engineer in Santa Fe; they had done the same thing at the Sandoval County Courthouse in Bernalillo, on March 13.[2] To each authority the officials stated that the east ditch was about six miles long, and irrigated one thousand acres of land; the west ditch was seven and a half miles long, and irrigated about two thousand acres of land. Since their ancestors had built the two ditches, only a few outsiders were entitled to use them. A Mexican, Francisco Montoya, was still using and maintaining the first mile of the east ditch to irrigate some land outside the reservation and 2.8 acres inside it. At this time he also owned and operated the only water-powered flour mill in the Jemez Valley, which he ran with Jemez irrigation water. He must have sold his property to Seferino Cabeza de Baca, probably a relative of Estanislado Cabeza de Baca, from whom the federal government bought the land where the diversion dam site is today.

On the west ditch there were three unnamed Mexican families, living outside the reservation, who could use the ditch, providing they performed a specified amount of work on it each year, as agreed with Jemez officials. To each authority the Jemez officials also indicated that their water rights originated prior to the enactment of Chapter 49, Laws of 1907.

Long before the Spaniards arrived, in the early sixteenth century, there was already an ancient irrigation system. While the other ditches that have been discussed may well have been built with the guidance of Fray Martín de Arvide, this ancient ditch no doubt served farmland of the early Jemez people in the eastern highlands of the San Juan Mesa and surrounding areas, people whom Arvide encouraged to move to the present site of Jemez Pueblo. This ditch, supported for long distances by rock walls, was fed by the Rio Chiquito, and irrigated approximately eighty acres. This area is approximately three miles northeast of Jemez today. After the Spaniards settled on the Ojo de San José Grant, later called Vallecito, they began to divert all the water for their own use. With additional white settlement, the old Vallecito began to be known as Ponderosa. The area is mentioned in a report by John G. Bourke, who visited Jemez Pueblo on November 5, 1881 (Bloom 1938):

John W. Miller served for a number of years as government farmer. Jemez Indians still remember him with gratitude for showing them how to siphon their ditch under the stream bed by Vallecito Creek, as previously every year it had been washed away in the spring freshets.

A few families still farm this ancient land, depending mostly on water from this stream. Farther upstream, on the northeast boundary line near Vallecito, there is another area that has long been used as farmland. On file at the Southern Pueblos Agency is a mutual agreement drawn up in 1947, between the commissioner of the lower Vallecito ditch and the Pueblo of Jemez. By this agreement Jemez landowners in that area were allowed to use water stored in a reservoir at the north end of the community of Vallecito. The pueblo members were to clean and maintain that part of the ditch that ran through their 16.24 acres of irrigable land.

To this day, the irrigation ditches remain at the center of the pueblo's social life. Each spring, as soon as the ground has thawed out and dried, all the able-bodied men of the pueblo clear the ditches of excess silt and other debris which has collected during the winter months. Young men return home from outside jobs to assist in this annual, ageless celebration of community work. It is often joked that while non-Indian men save up their annual leave so that they can go on vacation, Pueblo Indian men save their annual leave so that they can return home to work on the ditches.

The men are glad to return home to work and visit with the men of their extended family. For centuries, families had worked together, hoeing the corn fields and cutting wheat by hand; today, with the change of lifestyles, ditch cleaning is the last remaining traditional group work. Ditch work today is more fun than hardship, as relatives socialize, sharing jokes and hilarious stories of their experiences; and it now takes only three days to do all four of the pueblo ditches. This reduction in labor is possible because 14.3 miles of the total network have been lined with concrete over the last few years. Furthermore, the population has increased, so that there are many more men in the assigned work groups, traditionally organized by family surnames. Yet another reason behind the quicker completion is that much of the irrigation system has been straightened, where once there were large bends in the ditches, and the high banks, that used to make throwing sand out of the ditches so strenuous, have been removed by heavy equipment.

In the old days the hard work was accompanied by kick-stick races between the two moieties—at the end of a day's work, the two groups would race home, kicking the stick while carrying their shovels in one hand. The following morning, before breakfast and before going to work, the race would be repeated; by the fourth morning the ditch cleaning would have been completed, and the activity was culminated by the *ser-way* dance in the two kivas. This involved each moiety group visiting and dancing in the other's kiva. In the last few years, the stick-race and dance have been performed only sparingly. The life-style has changed, and many men and women have to get up early to go to work in the nearby towns.

Farmland, Floods, and Dams

The amount of irrigable farmland at Jemez has not remained constant, due to numerous, devastating floods on the Jemez River. To provide some idea of the catastrophic nature of these floods, the following table has been prepared from U.S. Geological Survey records, obtained from the gauging station three and a half miles north of Jemez.[3]

Year	Minimum Flow	Maximum Flow
1936	14 cfs*	3,000 cfs on September 26
1941	15 cfs	2,570 cfs on May 6
1941	?	6,000 cfs (est.) on May 15
1955	9.4 cfs	2,570 cfs on August 19
1957	9.8 cfs	3,160 cfs on August 24
1958	15 cfs	5,900 cfs on April 21
1967	?	2,640 cfs on August 9
1971	?	4,330 cfs on August 5
1973	?	3,210 cfs on May 13

*cubic feet per second

According to these same records, the flood of May 15, 1941, went on a rampage. Not only did it destroy the U.S.G.S. gauging station, but BIA records also show the loss of 93.22 acres of the best farmland in the Red Rock area. The flood affected fifty-five individuals, who owned anywhere from six acres to small garden plots along the river. It also destroyed all the flood-control measures constructed along the river banks. Following the loss of the guaging station, the local residents estimated the flow for the U.S.G.S. as over six thousand cubic feet per second.

The flood also put an end to one flour mill located on the banks of the river. There were two flour mills at Jemez at this time. One was owned and operated by Daniel Mora and his nephew, Juanito Mora; the Mora family dug their own ditch to provide the current of water to run the mill. It was located on the west bank, just north of the bridge to the west of the village. The second mill was owned and operated by Manuel Loretto and his sons; it was located on the east bank of the river, next to the road coming from the post office and mission school. This mill was powered by the stream from the "Antonio Pecos" ditch. The flood did not affect it, but eventually it closed due to shortage of manpower during World War II. In recent years a flour mill has been operated by Manuel's son, Christobal, at another site, powered by a tractor; a second flour mill is operated by my brother, Augustine Sando, also powered by a tractor.

Following the 1958 flood, Governor Antonio Sando wrote to Congressman Joseph Montoya in Washington, explaining the great loss and requesting assistance in obtaining permanent flood-control works along the Jemez River. This same request had been communicated in vain by Governor Florencio Armijo in 1955.

As early as 1911 the idea of a water-storage, flood-control dam at the present diversion site had been discussed by the Jemez Council. This discussion was reported by Assistant Engineer E.D. Kinney, in a letter to Herbert F. Robinson, superintendent of irrigation in the United States Indian Service in Albuquerque, on December 26, 1911. The following day Robinson wrote to the commissioner of Indian affairs in Washington, D.C., relaying the wishes of Jemez officials. Nothing came of these efforts. Forty years later, in July 1952, at a conference held at Zia Pueblo, the Indian and non-Indian water users along the Jemez River jointly agreed to make a concerted effort to get the necessary storage project initiated.

Eighteen years later, however, the Bureau of Reclamation, still justifying the construction of a dam, in a 1969 report indicated that, historically, there was a shortage of water on the Jemez River during the irrigation season. This shortage was marked by many days, and even months, of no flow at the river mouth. And this was despite the fact that of the average yearly flow of 48,000 acre-feet, only 9,900 acre-feet per year was consumed by all uses—including nonproductive losses—before about 38,000 acre-feet per year passed into the Rio Grande, below Jemez Dam, near Bernalillo. The Jemez Council believed that the lack of storage facilities for retaining large snowmelt flows for later irrigation-season use accounted for the small fraction of the annual flow utilized within the river valley. The report further stated that streamflow records showed that the natural flow at Jemez in the peak irrigation month of June was adequate to serve the present Indian acreage only once every thirty years. The average midsummer flow was said to support irrigation on only about 1,700 acres of Indian and non-Indian lands, although 6,920 acres of irrigable land had been identified.

The City of Albuquerque, in 1936, had also shown interest in damming the Jemez River. In June 1935 a report was made for Albuquerque by the consulting engineer W.R. Holway, proposing that a domestic water system be developed by constructing a 27,000 acre-foot storage reservoir on the Jemez River. In an exchange of correspondence between Mayor Charles H. Lembke and the United Pueblos Agency, the mayor indicated that the city was willing to deliver to the stream an amount of water equal to that diverted by the reservoir.

The city was also willing to allow the Indians of Jemez and Zia a maximum of thirty gallons per capita per day for domestic use. At this time the population of Jemez was listed as 673; Zia's was 203. On paper the two tribes appeared to benefit, although they feared a rumored additional charge of ten cents per thousand gallons above the thirty gallons per capita per day; this seemed high to them.

In the final analysis, the Indians considered that whether the project would be detrimental or beneficial to them depended upon how much water Albuquerque would actually deliver. They feared that with the city's growth, its request of a year's supply in advance could deplete the Indians' supply. The dam did not materialize, however.

During those years Jemez was supplied with domestic water from three wells pumped by windmills, constructed around 1921, and which served the community until the 1960s. On December 2, 1962, the tribe signed an agreement to have the Indian Health Service construct and install a domestic water supply and waste disposal facility; these were finally completed and turned over to the tribe on December 14, 1966.

In 1942 an event took place which pueblo officials were evidently totally unaware of; if the Indian Bureau knew about it they did not inform the pueblo. On January 16, 1942, the New Mexico State Game Commission filed an application with the Office of the State Engineer for a permit to maintain a year-round storage reservoir of 335.35 acre-feet of water for fish and wildlife propagation; these storage works are Fenton Reservoir, located on Cebolla Creek, a tributary of the Jemez River. According to a resolution drafted by the state engineer, no protests were filed by anyone after publication of its intention in the *Bernalillo Times* on March 3, 1942. An earth-fill dam with spillway was subsequently completed in December 1951.

Filling the new dam with water must have taken quite some time. And a restriction of the natural flow from any of the tributaries to the Jemez river affects the water supply on Indian farms, especially during the irrigation season in dry years. One year in the early 1950s, Governor Juan L. Pecos had to take some men and walk the length of the tributaries, as far as the present location of the San Gregorio reservoir, to open up man-made and beaver dams on Clear Creek, Rio Las Vacas, and Cebolla Creek, in order to save Jemez crops. Whether the new dam contributed to the problem is not known.

About this same time, another water problem engaged Jemez and Zia people. At a joint meeting of the two pueblos' officials, it was reported that the New Mexico Timber Company was diverting water to a pond for its operations at the Gilman mill, on Guadalupe Creek, another tributary of the Jemez River. Logs were soaked at this pond, which the Indians claimed affected the water quality for irrigation purposes; it was destructive to some crops, especially chili.

On April 5, 1951, Governor Juanito Chinana wrote a letter to Eric T. Hagberg, superintendent of the United Pueblos Agency in Albuquerque, asking that he write to the state water engineer in Santa Fe to limit the diversion of water into the pond during the irrigation season. The Gilman pond had been constructed in 1948–49, for the wet storage of logs; it had a 48.5 acre-foot capacity, with 10 acre-feet for the production of steam power. It was approved by the state engineer, with the provision that the license not be exercised to the detriment of any other persons having prior valid and existing water rights to the stream. It was a permit only for unappropriated, or surplus water, which could not be taken during periods of low flow and before the summer rains started. According to the Indians, however, the timber company was not observing the rules of its permit.

At a meeting held on July 19, 1951, attended by officials from Jemez, Zia, and five other pueblos who were members of the Rio Grande Conservancy District, a resolution was adopted to request that BIA irrigation engineers reinvestigate the long-term problem of diversion of water from the Jemez watershed for use by the Nacimiento Community Ditch Association, first addressed in 1925. This resolution also called for a feasibility study for a storage dam on the Jemez to store water for Jemez and Zia. The Indians had been told many times that real relief could come only from the construction of increased storage facilities to hold some of the heavy spring runoff, for use during the low flow season. For a short-term solution of the problem, the resolution requested funds from the commissioner of Indian affairs for drilling wells to provide water for irrigation, stock, and domestic purposes.

On October 10, 1947, the state engineer approved an application for 2,280 acre-feet of water from Clear Creek to irrigate 1,180 acres of land near Cuba from the Nacimiento Community Irrigation System. They claimed rights to the water from around 1885, as compared to Jemez claims dating from 1300. The application was approved in spite of the fact that Pueblo Indian water rights are legally under the exclusive jurisdiction of the United States Congress. The San Gregorio dam, constructed to store 154 acre-feet of water for irrigation and 100 acre-feet for recreation and fish propagation, was completed in October 1958.

As mentioned in Chapter 3, as of 1980 a proposed fifty-megawatt geothermal demonstration project was planned for the Redondo Peak area, principal watershed for the Jemez River. This undertaking, a joint project of the Union Geothermal Company, Public Service Company of New Mexico, and the U.S. Department of Energy, proposed to withdraw 2,640 acre-feet of water per year to provide steam for the electric power plant. On May 5, 1980, the Department of Energy approved the project, despite Pueblo opposition; by January of 1982, however, the project was canceled, due to a variety of factors.

Throughout their written history, the Jemez people have shown a consistent concern for their water and water rights. Considering the premium placed on water in the region, perhaps one day a small dam will be built to accommodate the needs of Jemez, Zia, Santa Ana, and San Ysidro. It does not seem to be too much to ask.

6

The Indian Claims Commission

Many of the land problems that arose under the Spanish and Mexican governments were inherited by the Americans. This chapter will examine one phase of American treatment of this complex topic, the purpose of which was to put an end to the hundreds of unresolved land claims involving Indians throughout the country.

The Indian Claims Commission was established by act of August 13, 1946, to hear claims, arising in or before August 1946, against the United States, on behalf of any Indian tribe, band, or other identifiable group of American Indians residing in the United States or Alaska. The act stipulated that any claim existing before the passage of the act and not presented by August 13, 1951, would be forever barred by Congress; the commission itself was to terminate ten years after the date of its first meeting. The act further provided for tribes to retain attorneys of their own selection, with fees not to exceed 10 percent of the amount recovered, plus reimbursement of actual expenses. The commission was required to make deductions or offsets for property given to the Indians, or funds expended for their benefit.

The term of the commission was later extended by the acts of July 24, 1956 (70 Stat. 624) and June 16, 1961 (75 Stat. 92); and a further amendment on April 10, 1967 (81 Stat. 11), increased its membership from three to five, with an increase in staff, since the claims had grown to more than six hundred cases. The five members were Jerome K. Kuykendall (chairman), John T. Vance, Richard W. Yarborough, Margaret H. Pierce, and Brantley Blue (a Lumbee Indian from North Carolina). When the commission terminated, on September 30, 1978, cases still pending were transferred to the United States Court of Claims.

The Pueblos had felt the loss of their lands in the Territorial Courts as a most devastating and humiliating blow, and subsequent generations grew up hearing the story of how the courts had taken advantage of the Indians. As more Indians learned to speak English, they began to discuss these losses with federal officials. Thus, beginning in the 1940s the agency staff began to interview tribal members at Jemez, Santa Ana, and Zia, to determine the bases for possible claims. Meetings continued for several years, and material was gathered expressing the feelings of the older men.

In 1950 the three pueblos employed the attorneys Dudley Cornell and Claud S. Mann to represent them in their claim to the Ojo del Espíritu Santo Grant. It had come before the Court of Private Land Claims earlier, but was denied on the basis that the grant was supposedly for "grazing purposes only," and did not convey title to the land. This decision was upheld by the Supreme Court.

Official spokesmen for the three pueblos were appointed to meet with the claims attorneys: Patricio Toya for Jemez, Andres Pino and Juanito Medina for Zia, and Porfirio Montoya for Santa Ana. The following is their joint statement:[1]

This has always been our land. We know these matters not merely because our grandparents told us vague stories when we were children, but because our parents and grandparents, and their parents and grandparents before them, made sure to tell us so exactly and so often that we could not forget. We were told again and again in meetings, we were taken out onto the ground to see the exact locations, we were impressed with the importance so that we could protect our land and water rights and maintain the traditions of our people. Those older among us who never learned to read or remember by eye, have an ability to remember by ear greater than that of any non-Indians we know. We have lived in the same area for unknown hundreds of years; seeing constantly the landmarks of our history, we naturally remember the history.

We know that our forefathers were cheated in the Territorial Courts by the Americans. The American Territorial Courts were no better than the Mexican courts where our forefathers were more often denied the right to be heard.

Take for instance the 1890 case before the Court of Private Land Claims; a Councilman and interpreter for Jemez was Jose Miguel Pecos. The opposing attorney asked where he was from and Jose answered that he was from Jemez but was a Pecos by blood. The attorney told him that if he was not a member of one of the three pueblos he could not have any interest and should not be involved in the proceedings. Because he was one of those who came from Pecos to Jemez he spoke Spanish very fluently and because of his ability the attorney kept stopping Jose Miguel from talking. So after some discussion with the other Jemez delegate, Ignacio Toledo, Jose said that he would not do any more interpreting.

But worst of all, our people never really had any idea of what was settled there in the court. We didn't have any help except our lawyer, George Hill Howard. The Indian Service never came out and talked to us about the land, the trial, or gave us any advice. We never saw any papers of any kind about the case. In 1907 Pablo Abeita of Isleta and Jesus Medina of Zia were in Washington, D.C., and they saw some papers. "Here's your paper for Zia, Jemez, and Santa Ana on the Espiritu Santo," Pablo told Jesus, but Jesus could not read and of course we are not sure what papers they saw.

We can tell one story to show just how badly the whole court action was misunderstood. During the trial, near the end, the judge took a piece of paper and colored it dark on one side and light on the other. He asked the Indians which side of the paper they wanted. After the Indians chose, he called on the non-Indian. Then the judge tossed this paper in the air and it came floating down and landed with the non-Indian side up.

The Zia delegates came home and reported that this was how the judge decided on the case against our three pueblos. Anyway, whatever happened, this trial was so completely beyond the understanding of our delegations that this was all the sense Andrecito Galvan and Lorenzo Lovato of Zia could make of the whole thing. If the Indians did not understand what was going on any better than that, we cannot think that the judge understood the Indians very well either.

Based on this and much other information gathered by the team, on July 9, 1951, the attorneys filed a petition entitled *Pueblo de Zia, Pueblo de Jemez and Pueblo de Santa Ana, Claimants, v. United States of America, Defendant*. It covered a tract of land amounting to 382,849 acres (later revised to 410,000 acres), the Ojo del Espíritu Santo Grant, defined by these definite boundaries:

On the North by the Ventana; on the South by the stone ford of the Puerco River, eight leagues, more or less, in distance; on the East by Zia Pueblo; and on the West by the Puerco River, being six leagues, more or less, from East to West; and better shown and designated by actual survey made in 1877 by a United States Deputy Surveyor.

The petition was accepted by the commission and received docket number 137.

After the filing of the original petition, it was determined that the government's translation of the original grant papers was incorrect; this was the same translation used by the government in 1890, which resulted in the Supreme Court decision against the pueblos. The tribal attorneys therefore amended the petition, including a proper translation by Dr. Miguel Jorrin, of the University of New Mexico. The amended petition, filed March 17, 1952, extended the eastern boundary of the claim, increasing alleged aboriginal title to 520,000 acres.

The case began to be heard in December of 1956. In 1957 Mark Clayburg entered the case as a law partner of Dudley Cornell. Finally, in January of 1959, the pueblos' attorneys appeared in Washington to argue the claim before the Indian Claims Commission.

On September 11, 1962, the commission issued its "Findings of Fact," "Opinion of the Commission," and its "Final Order," which read in part:

Upon the findings of fact this day filed herein and which are hereby made a part of this order, the Commission concludes as a matter of law that Petitioners are not entitled to recover and therefore that the Petition should be dismissed.

It is therefore ordered, adjudged, and decreed, that the Petition in the above-entitled action be, and the same is, hereby dismissed.

The claim was denied for the following reasons:

1. That the governments of Spain and Mexico did not recognize any aboriginal title;

2. That the grant of June 16, 1766, for the Ojo del Espíritu Santo area to the three pueblos gave the Indians no right, because of the action of the Court of Private Land Claims, and because of the decision in the Supreme Court of the United States upholding that decision;

3. That the three pueblos had no rights within the boundaries of any conflicting grants approved by the Court of Private Land Claims or patents, as follows: Ojo del San José Grant, Ojo de Borrego Grant, Cañada de Cochiti Grant, Ojo del Espíritu Santo Grant to the heirs of Luís María Cabeza de Baca, and the San Ysidro Grant;

4. That the decision by the Supreme Court was *res judicata* ("decided issue") and could not be reopened;

5. That of the 520,000 acres claimed by the petitioners by virtue of aboriginal title, only 298,634 acres became part of the public domain of the United States under the Treaty of Guadalupe Hidalgo

in 1848, and that the petitioners failed to present the proof required to establish aboriginal title to any of those 298,634 acres.

By letter of November 8, 1962, addressed to the governors of Jemez, Santa Ana, and Zia, their attorneys (Clayburg and Cornell) wrote:

We would like to have an expression from the Pueblos in connection with this case, and, if you are in agreement, your concurrence that we do not appeal. Your attorneys have spent many years of effort and substantial sums of money in expenses in conducting this litigation on your behalf. It has always been our considered opinion that you were entitled to compensation for the loss of the lands described in the claim filed before the Commission, and the action of the Commission came as both a surprise and a disappointment to all of us. In not recommending an appeal, we do not mean to say that we will not willingly conduct an appeal if the Pueblos request it and are willing to advance the necessary costs and expenses.

The pueblos not only requested, but demanded of their attorneys that they appeal the claim, to the highest court of appeals; thus, on December 6, 1962, the attorneys filed a notice of appeal with the U.S. Court of Claims, and submitted their brief on April 3, 1963. The appeal was argued in December of 1963. Before the court rendered its opinion, Dudley Cornell suddenly passed away, on February 24, 1964. Claud Mann and Mark Clayburgh then continued the case.

On April 17, 1964, the U.S. Court of Claims reversed the decision of the Indian Claims Commission, rendering an opinion in favor of the pueblos, to the effect that they had established aboriginal title as of the date of the Treaty of Guadalupe Hidalgo in 1848, to 298,634 acres of land in Sandoval County. The court remanded the case to the Indian Claims Commission, solely for a determination of the value the land had had in 1848. On January 22, 1965, at the request of the pueblos' attorneys, the Court of Claims issued to the Indian Claims Commission a new order for it to receive evidence as to the time of taking of the land in question by the United States, as well as determining the value of the lands as of that time of taking.

This led to a great deal of research in the files of the Bureau of Indian Affairs, especially those of the United Pueblos Agency, concerning land purchases throughout New Mexico by the United States, appraisals of the land, and land holdings of the three pueblos. Hazel Carrick, realty specialist with the bureau, undoubtedly had her hands full with this land research for the pueblos; this has been a familiar situation to her, throughout her working life.

Meanwhile, the three pueblos reaffirmed their claim to their aboriginal land, in a letter to their attorneys:

We had used the land in the mountains long before the Spanish came. Where we grazed and herded our horses we can tell which corrals our people built in our way because we had no axes. The Spanish had axes and you can tell which tree was chopped with an axe. We can show which corrals were Jemez, or Zia, or Santa Ana because of the pictures drawn nearby to show ownership. Where non-Indians would have drawn letters and numbers we drew eagles, lions, the rising sun and so on. [Jemez still uses the eagle as its symbol, or logo.]

The corrals we built are still there, some in use and others in ruin—Valle Grande, Vallecitos de los Indios, and Paliza, the traces of our herding can still be seen. No one else was claiming the land of ours; we lived as we pleased for we were the native people.

We can show land marks where our people drew turkey feet and road runners to point to secret springs. There is a stand of oak trees in a special place where hunters from our three Pueblos traditionally cut off small straight branches or sticks to serve as benefactors during the hunt. We can show you the cave where the collection of years of leaving of the sticks ceremonially were left after a successful hunt. Nearby is a shrine related to our tribal game hunts that we used in the early 1900s. We can show you the worn footsteps that led to one particular hidden spring.

The last time some of us went to see the land that we have lost, we saw prayer sticks, beads of seashells, and turquoise offerings of our grandfathers. We can still tell which Pueblo made these prayer sticks.

The United States should be fully aware that our Indian people have not always known how to protect our land and rights in the white man's way. And if we lost some land it was not because we felt it was not ours. We believe this land is ours, period. It is our mother, it nourishes us.

This material was furnished to the claims attorneys and to the Indian Claims Section of the Department of Justice, in Washington. There was also complicated negotiation between the claims attorneys and the attorneys in the Justice Department to determine the dates for the taking of the lands, and other matters.

On March 7, 1968, the Indian Claims Commission issued an interlocutory order, setting the dates for the taking of the land: October 12, 1905, for Tract A, when President Theodore Roosevelt included 34,900.27 acres in the Jemez Forest Reserve; 1920 for Tract B (agreed upon as an average date to determine fair market value), totaling 16,811.74 acres of land settled as homestead entries during the period from 1887 to 1934; and April 4, 1936, for Tract C, when the order creating District No. 2 under the Taylor Grazing Act became effective, taking a total of 282,415.73 acres. The case then proceeded to the remaining issues: the value of the lands taken at the time of taking, and the offsets to be allowed against the total amount to be awarded.

The initial award to the three pueblos by the commission was $938,000. Tract A was valued at $125,000, Tract B at $63,000, and Tract C at $750,000, subject to deductions for allowable offsets.

In May of 1968, the claims attorneys spent an entire week in Washington, negotiating with the government attorneys in an attempt to settle these matters. On June 24, 1968, however, the Justice Department entered into a contract with the firm of R.H. Sears & Company, of Oklahoma City, Oklahoma, to prepare an appraisal of the land in the claim, at considerable expense to the government; the document ran to 201 pages! It set a value of only $600,000 on the land involved.

The government attorneys then filed a lengthy "Amended Answer," containing nearly one hundred paragraphs, listing what they considered proper offsets. The pueblos' attorneys, in a twenty-one-page "Reply to Amended Answer Claiming Set-Offs," filed December 18, 1968, denied that any of the claimed offsets were legitimate.

Some of the offsets claimed by the government were for such things as distribution of seeds, fruit trees, and fertilizer between 1912 and 1933; another presented a voucher for the payment of $239.69 to Studebaker Corporation of America for five wagons and accessories—the claims commission reasoned that there was no basis for dividing five wagons among nineteen separate pueblos, and therefore denied the claim. Another claim was for $600, spent on a tractor purchased by the federal government for eight pueblos in 1928. Although the federal government had been responsible for the education of Indian children during the whole period, under a trust agreement, government attorneys tried to claim offsets for the pueblos' use of Albuquerque and Santa Fe Indian Schools and the pueblo day schools. In the opinion of these same attorneys, the pueblos were responsible for paying the government back for the services of the Southern Pueblos Agency. As has happened so many times before and after this case, these government attorneys had probably never heard of the legal trust relationship which exists between the Indians and the government these attorneys represented.

The case was set for trial in Albuquerque on April 22, 1969, to settle the remaining issues. In February of 1969, the pueblos' attorneys were advised that the attorney for the United States, Walter Rochow, who had handled the case from the time it was filed, had suddenly retired or resigned. The commission then postponed the trial until July 21, 1969; in the meantime, the pueblos' attorneys filed a twenty-six-page "Pre-Trial Statement," covering valuation of the lands and replies to claimed offsets. The case was finally heard before Commissioner Richard Yarborough, on August 19 and 20, 1969. The Pueblo people could only sit in the courtroom and squirm as they heard the government attorneys present their views, knowing, however, that their own attorneys had heard the truth and knew better.

Commissioner Yarborough reported his findings to the commission in September; he had determined that the value of the lands taken from the three pueblos was $938,000. By January of 1970, attorneys for both sides had filed their findings on "values" and "offsets," and the case was referred to the full commission membership for a final decision.

On December 17, 1970, the Indian Claims Commission issued an "Opinion and Interlocutory Order," which decreed that the pueblos were to recover from the United States the amount of $938,000, less offsets allowable under the Indian Claims Commission Act.

The following offsets were allowed:

Agricultural aid	$ 1,487.67
Flood Control and Relief	1,375.43
Irrigation and water	49,223.57
Livestock	381.25
Land	118,596.00
Total Offsets	$171,063.92

The agricultural aid was for digging wells and providing well equipment in 1915 in the amount of $1,265.90; $221.77 was for clearing, breaking, and fencing land in 1928. The flood control and relief was provided to Santa Ana, going back as far as 1910, for such things as care and protection of ranges, labor, transportation, and lumber and other supplies connected with flood control and irrigation. The irrigation and water offsets were for improvement of irrigation systems and domestic water at the three pueblos. The livestock bill was for feed and care of Pueblo stock during the dry years of 1934 and 1935. The large offset for land represented the return of former land grants purchased by the federal government and placed in trust under different acts; the basis for arriving at the total amount was $2.50 per acre placed in trust by the government. Zia was awarded 20,163.41 acres, totaling $50,408 in offset; Santa Ana was awarded 19,455.87 acres—$48,640 in offset; and Jemez was awarded 7,819.28 acres—$19,548.

On September 15, 1971, the commission awarded $766,936.08 to the three pueblos of Jemez, Santa Ana, and Zia, for lands lost during the period 1887 to 1936; the federal government was granted the offsets of $171,063.92 listed above. Before the judgment could become final (on December 15, 1971), however, attorneys for the United States filed a notice of appeal, claiming that the commission had committed an error in not allowing offsets of over one million dollars—which of course would have wiped out any net award to the three pueblos. Additional offsets were allowed, but they turned out to be $252.33 in grazing fees, plus an allowance for 3,520 acres of land placed in trust for Santa Ana, valued at $5.00 per acre, or a total of $17,600. Thus, the revised judgment read as follows:

Gross Amount of Award	$938,000.00
Less Offsets Allowed	171,063.92
Net Award	766,936.08
Additional Offsets	17,852.33
Final Award	$749,083.75

The attorneys for both parties finally reached a compromise settlement, agreed to by resolutions adopted by the three pueblos during meetings in October of 1973, and signed by Governor Abel Sando, for Jemez Pueblo, Governor Miguel Armijo, for Santa Ana Pueblo, and Governor Gilbert Lucero, for Zia Pueblo.

On January 10, 1974, the commission entered its "Order Amending Opinion and Findings of Fact," and "Amended Final Award," which stated in part, "that the plaintiff shall jointly have and recover in Docket 137 from the defendant the sum of $749,083.75." Funds to pay the award were appropriated by act of June 8, 1974 (88 Stat. 195).

This, of course, was not the end of the matter. The three pueblos had agreed informally from the beginning that any award obtained from their claim against the government would be divided equally among them. This was formalized by an agreement signed in May of 1974.

Before the final award could be made, moreover, the pueblos' attorneys had to petition the commission for attorneys' fees, plus costs and expenses. Their expenses amounted to $6,450.08, over and above what the pueblos had paid out for actual expenses throughout the long, drawn-out case, and their 10 percent of the award (as attorneys' fees) amounted to $74,908.37.

The three pueblos then had to hold hearings with their respective tribal members to consider the use and distribution of the judgment funds awarded by the commission. The hearings were held on November 21 and 22, 1974. The resulting plan for each pueblo provided for the investment of the judgment funds, with the annual income therefrom to be used for purposes such as developing the economic, community, industrial, commercial, social, cultural, and land resources of each of the pueblos.

The plan was submitted to Congress and became effective on June 17, 1975; it was published in the *Federal Register* on August 5, 1975 (pp. 32847–48). The funds, including accrued interest, were then finally divided among the three pueblos; more than twenty-five years after undertaking the pursuit of their land claims, with their attorneys having had to fight the Department of Justice of our benevolent government every step of the way, the pueblos of Jemez, Santa Ana, and Zia received their monetary award. Most of the old people considered this to be infinitesimal compensation for a revered homeland, where the spirits of our ancestors and our religious shrines remain.

In contrast to the fierce struggle put up by the government attorneys against the three pueblos, some of the land within their aboriginal homelands has since become trust land of the individual pueblos by various acts of Congress. Santa Ana regained some of its land by act of October 21, 1978 (92 Stat. 1678), as did Zia Pueblo by act of October 21, 1978 (92 Stat. 1679). It is hoped that Jemez Pueblo, also, may soon be able to regain its aboriginal lands, especially those areas where its shrines are still preserved.

7

Santa Fe Northwestern Railroad
and the Pueblo Land
Condemnation Act

In the history of the Indian and the outsiders, land is a never-ending topic. The sixty-four-year long, epic struggle for Blue Lake, fought by Taos Pueblo between 1906 and 1971, is well known as a symbol of the plight of the American Indians in the nuclear age. Hardly known to the other eighteen pueblos, much less to the world outside Sandoval County, is Jemez Pueblo's struggle against the Santa Fe Northwestern Railroad and the White Pine Lumber Company of Bernalillo, New Mexico, of which Frank H. Porter was the president. In the end this struggle by Jemez against a right-of-way for the railroad, from 1921 to 1926, strongly affected all nineteen pueblos of New Mexico. As a result of Jemez's resistance, an act was passed on May 10, 1926, regulating the condemnation of Pueblo Indian land for public purposes.

Much of the story is scattered through the Jemez files, in the records of the Southern Pueblos Agency. In the summer of 1921 a survey party arrived to make a preliminary survey for a railroad through the pueblos of Santa Ana, Zia, and Jemez. The Jemez Indians, seeing the survey party on cultivated land, protested immediately. Thereafter, Sidney

Weil, vice-president of Santa Fe Northwestern, was advised by the
Indian Service of regulations for acquiring rights-of-way over Indian
land. On September 16 Superintendent Leo Crane of the Indian Agency
met with the Jemez Council, who protested that the survey was cutting
through the best agricultural land the pueblo possessed. The council
members indicated that they would prefer for the railroad to be built
east of the village. All promises of monetary reimbursement for damages fell on deaf ears, as the council wanted only to retain its cultivable
land.

Following the meeting First Principal Jose Manuel Yepa wrote to
the President of the United States, concerning what Jemez leaders
considered an outrage. Leo Crane also wrote a letter, to the commissioner of Indian affairs, C.H. Burke, in which he reported that Jemez
and Zia did not approve of the proposed route of the railroad; then he
added:[1]

It should be understood, however, that no one of the three Pueblos concerned
have any reason to desire a railroad because they wish to live in a sixteenth
century fashion (as Coronado found them) and I have yet to find among any
of the Pueblo Indians as a class, any desire for improvement along twentieth
century lines.

Crane later requested that Indian Agency engineers work with the
railroad engineers on a rerouting, and permission was granted in November of that same year. After seeing more surveyors working on
alternate routes, Councilman Yepa requested information from the
agency on the status of the rail line. At this time Crane wrote to the
government farmer (extension agent) at Jemez, Louis R. McDonald,
asking him to explain to the Jemez Council the status of the proposed
right-of-way, again adding: "I might say that the Jemez Indians will
not likely be permitted to remain in the sixteenth century and completely block progress."

After more meetings in the spring of 1922, Yepa wrote to Commissioner Burke again, expressing the Jemez people's fear of being
cheated by the railroad, and of the tribe's desire to keep the line out
of agricultural land, as well as away from shrines along the way.

As requested by Crane the year before, two land appraisers arrived
at Jemez on August 28, 1922. After inspecting the land along the route,
the two men concluded that the value of the lands to be taken was
only nominal, and should not be assessed at more than the price of

similar government land—$2.50 per acre. They reported that the route was taking a strip seventy-five feet in width through unimproved lands, and fifty feet in width through improved lands, including through and around the village proper. The government farmer, McDonald, then calculated the figure of $569.17 for the community, or open tribal lands, and $2,548.70 to be paid for rights-of-way to individual land-owners. In September, Crane wrote to Vice-president Weil of the railroad that the tribal council had given its consent to the routing, provided that they receive the aforementioned amounts for the damages; in fact, of course, the Jemez people had rejected that offer.

When work started at the southern end of the reservation, Lt. Governor Jesus M. Baca asked if Jemez people would be employed in the construction of the line; Weil confirmed that the Jemez people had been promised a share in the work. But even as the work began, tribal officials were still worried about accepting payment for the right-of-way; McDonald told the new agency superintendent, H.P. Marble, that the individual land owners had approved, but that the tribal council and religious leaders were opposed. He also stated that they wanted to wait until after a meeting, following Jesus Baca's return from a trip to Washington, before making any further decisions. At this time Jemez Governor Francisco Madalena wrote to the superintendent, describing the officials' feelings about the matter. Councilman Yepa also wrote, expressing the fears of the combined council. Later the tribe met with C.C. Coffey, the engineer in charge of construction of the railroad; he assured them that the second survey showed that less cultivated land would be taken, and that the cost of construction would be less.

Still the tribe was not convinced. On February 28, 1923, Jack Toya, writing for his father-in-law, Governor Madalena, wrote to the secretary of the interior, Albert B. Fall, expressing the tribe's concern over the loss of cultivated land and shrines. As a result of this expression of concern, Indian Commissioner Charles H. Burke sent a telegram to Superintendent Marble on March 7, asking for a full report of facts and recommendations for permitting the company to proceed with construction work. The very next day the superintendent received another telegram from the commissioner, informing him that Washington had granted the railroad company permission to proceed with construction across Jemez land, according to the act of March 2, 1899, as amended (30 Stat. 990; 25 U.S.C. 312–18). This act provided for railroad companies to acquire rights-of-way through Indian reservations, Indian agency reserves, and lands allotted in severalty to individual Indians, with full power of alienation. Formal approval for the Jemez right-of-way was given by E.C. Finney, first assistant secretary of the interior, on July 11, 1924.

A few days later, Jesus Baca received a letter from Commissioner Burke, informing the council that permission had been granted for the railroad, and ordering the Jemez people to withdraw their objections to the location of the line. Jemez officials still stood by their decision to allow the railroad to be built only on the east side of the pueblo, where there was no cultivated land.

The council was overruled, and construction began. This brought back memories of the court decision regarding the Ojo del Espíritu Santo Grant a few years earlier, which had first made the Indians distrustful of the white man's courts. They could envision the invasion of the Jemez country, leading to a fight for the limited supply of water, if the upper Jemez area was settled by more non-Indians.

As railroad construction crews approached the village, it was learned that some Indians had allowed the irrigation ditch to overflow, causing a washout on a section of the railroad grade. Superintendent Marble then directed the government farmer, McDonald, to advise the Indians that they were not only liable to be punished, but also to be sued for a large damage claim. Other delays sprang up, due to individual claims of former community land, necessitating separate processing of the claims. November 13, the day following the Jemez feast, was set aside to discuss all damages and final payment; this meeting resulted in a report that sixty-three parcels of individual land, in addition to the community land, had been taken, with values ranging from $2.50 to $150 per acre. The landowners finally met again, on December 3, to accept the amount of the awards for damages. After this meeting, letters were exchanged between Washington and Albuquerque concerning the Jemez right-of-way, but it was not until March 10, 1924, that the landowners signed a document indicating that payments (of from $.38 to $198.30) had been received. This acknowledgment of payments was not yet a formal agreement granting the right-of-way. In fact, after damage payments had been agreed upon, it still took so much time for them to be delivered to Jemez that Charles E. Faris, special supervisor for the southern pueblos, wrote to the Indian commissioner asking that they be speeded up so that the Indians could purchase seeds for spring planting with the money.

It was not long before other legal obstacles were discovered. On March 1, 1926, Herbert J. Hagerman, representing the secretary of the interior on the Pueblo Lands Board, wrote to the secretary, Hubert Work, reporting that the board found that the title to Jemez lands included in the railroad had not been extinguished—the right-of-way had not been legally granted. On the same date, Walter C. Cochrane, special attorney for the Pueblo Indians, wrote to Commissioner Burke, indicating that the Pueblo Lands Board doubted the legal validity of the right-of-way. He reported that George Fraser, special assistant to the attorney general, had already filed suit in district court to determine what rights the railroad company had secured on July 11, 1924. The case was entitled *The United States of America, as Guardian of the Pueblo of Jemez in the State of New Mexico v. The Santa Fe Northwestern Railway Co.*, No. 1629 in equity.

The Santa Fe Northwestern was encountering trouble in raising a bond issue of $1.25 million, since the underwriters could not approve it with the inadequate title held by the company. The real question became that of whether the act of March 2, 1899, applied to the pueblo lands, where the title was one of fee simple in the community; if it did not, then the proceedings were invalid. The next question was how to interpret Section 17 of the Pueblo Lands Act of June 7, 1924:

No right, title, or interest in or to the lands of the Pueblo Indians of New Mexico to which their title has not been extinguished, or hereinbefore determined, shall hereafter be acquired or initiated by virtue of the laws of the State of New Mexico, or in any other manner except as may hereafter be provided by Congress, and no sale, grant, lease of any character, or other conveyance of lands, or any title or claim thereto, made by any pueblo as a community . . . shall be of any validity in law or in equity unless the same be first approved by the Secretary of the Interior.

The court did not set a date for trial, as the railroad company agreed to attempt again to obtain a right-of-way from the pueblo. By this time, however, Jemez officials would only reply that the issue would be decided by the court. Apparently they felt that the United States, acting as the pueblo's "guardian," would really protect their interests and eject the railroad; in fact the suit was just a formality to comply with the terms of the Pueblo Lands Board Act in clearing up the legality of the right-of-way as granted.

Several meetings were held with Jemez officials in March of 1926, but they continued to refuse to sign a deed for the right-of-way. On April 18, 1926, the attorney general of New Mexico forwarded to New

Mexico's senator a proposed bill that provided for the condemnation of lands of the Pueblo Indians of New Mexico. The bill was passed by Congress and signed by President Coolidge on May 10, 1926 (44 Stat. 498).

In a report to H.J. Hagerman, dated May 24, 1926, Walter Cochrane, now special commissioner to negotiate with Indians, wrote:

I am convinced that the attitude of the Jemez Council and their refusal to listen to the advice of anyone in this matter was the prime cause for the introduction of this bill at the time, and that had the Jemez people seen fit to come to some agreement amicable to the railroad company, the passage of this bill might have been deferred to some time in the future. I have so advised the Council and have urged them, even now, to sign the agreement, because the railroad company has offered them $500 in cash or a car load of lumber if they will give them a deed for an easement rather than force them to condemnation proceedings in the Federal Court.

The Santa Fe Northwestern Railroad Company was then forced to file suit for condemnation of the proposed right-of-way. However, the judge dismissed the case on the grounds that the United States was a necessary party defendant, but could not be sued because no consent was given in the 1926 act. In commenting on the act in a letter dated November 16, 1927, to the attorney general, his special assistant, George Fraser, commented: "The statute of May 10, 1926, was obviously a bad one . . . in general because it exposed the Pueblo Indians to a wider liability for condemnation than that of whites in New Mexico."

Fraser, at the attorney general's request, then drafted another bill. This was ultimately approved on April 21, 1928, and provided that the statutes of the United States governing the acquisition of rights-of-way through Indian lands be made applicable to the Pueblo Indians of New Mexico and their lands. With the passage of this act, the railroad company was again advised to submit its application for the right-of-way across Jemez land. John Edwards, assistant secretary of the interior, reapproved the right-of-way to the Santa Fe Northwestern Railroad Company on July 10, 1928.

Now that the company had finally obtained the right-of-way, the case before the district court, filed by the attorney general, was dismissed; the pueblo had received no assistance from its "guardian."

Despite the difficulties and anxiety experienced by the pueblo and the railroad company, the track soon became a part of the daily life of the Jemez people. Besides being used as a pedestrian thoroughfare by working adults, it also became the social meeting place for the younger generation. On Sunday afternoons young friends would walk up and down the tracks, passing the time courting or just enjoying the outdoors.

A few families complained that the railroad crews stopped off to take fresh corn and ripe watermelons on their way home; predictably, they retaliated. It was reported that the brothers Augustine and Guadalupe Toya were so annoyed by raids from their family garden that they placed logs on the tracks. After the railroad men had stopped as usual for a watermelon, they would start their car again, enjoying their stolen melon, and fail to see the log; the log would then jolt the car off the tracks, melon eaters and all. These practices must have continued on both sides, because later a representative of the railroad complained to the superintendent of the Indian Agency, who in turn wrote to Nobel O. Guthrie, principal of the Jemez Day School, to relay the message to the governor so that the dangerous pranks would stop.

Although it survived the depression of the 1930s, within a few years the railroad fell upon hard times. Finally, what Jemez people could not accomplish, nature could: heavy flooding occurred on the Guadalupe and Jemez rivers in May of 1941, and according to Myrick (1970), three miles of track were washed out and several bridges damaged. The cost of rehabilitating the railroad was more than could be justified, and the Interstate Commerce Commission gave its approval for abandonment of the line.

Even prior to the floods, in 1939, W.A. Keleher, attorney for the railroad, had inquired as to whether the cmmpany could retain its right-of-way if it surrendered to the ICC its certificate of convenience and necessity, and likewise abandoned to the state its right to transact as a common carrier. "The primary reason is that there is no present business and no prospect for business which would justify any common carrier position." It was admitted that the Santa Fe Northwestern had become nothing more than a logging road, carrying logs from a point called Porter, in the Jemez Canyon, to Bernalillo, where the sawmill was located. When the secretary of the interior, by letter to General Superintendent Sophie D. Aberle, dated August 8, 1939, advised that changing the status of the railroad from common carrier to logging road would cause the right-of-way to revert to the pueblo, the company dropped the matter.

But when the railroad abandoned its track, in 1941, the question of the right-of-way reverting to Jemez Pueblo did arise, and was resolved in favor of the pueblo. In this connection, William A. Brophy, special attorney for the Pueblo Indians, wrote to Aberle on September 15, 1942:

Because of the confusion there appears to be no express provision that upon abandonment of the railroad, the title to the land free and clear of the easement would revert to the Pueblo of Jemez. However, in view of all the proceedings in the matter, it is my opinion that the intention of the parties, the Santa Fe Northwestern Railway Company, the Secretary of the Interior, and the Pueblo of Jemez, was that the right-of-way was granted upon condition that the easement would be used exclusively for railroad purposes and that by abandonment of the railroad the easement was extinguished, and the title vested in the Pueblo of Jemez.

The Pueblo Land Condemnation Act

The Santa Fe Northwestern Railroad was now dead, but it left a legacy of problems, in the Pueblo Land Condemnation Act of May 10, 1926. Because of it many pueblos lost valuable lands in low-cost rights-of-way to governments and public utilities.

For Jemez the problem first seriously appeared in 1940, when employees of the State Highway Department came to Jemez to consult about rerouting through the pueblo the state road from San Ysidro to Jemez Springs. They had two possible rights-of-way in mind: the first was to follow the railroad tracks along the river, after leaving the San Ysidro bridge, to a point seven miles north of the village; the second plan was to cut out across the flat, keeping to the east of the pueblo and as close as possible to the adjacent foothills.

Jemez officials refused to permit the road to follow the old railroad line, but did agree to the second plan. A meeting to consider the issues was held on December 23, 1940, between Jemez officials and members of the Board of County Commissioners of Sandoval County; representatives of the United Pueblos Agency and the State Highway Commission were also present.

The sum of $3,134 was agreed upon as payment for the private tribal assignments to be taken. It later turned out that the contract for the highway had been made without determining whether state funds were in fact available to purchase the right-of-way from the pueblo; advocates of the project evidently thought that they could generate enough support to force the Indians to give the right-of-way free of charge.

It soon became apparent that building the highway adjacent to the hills east of the village would cost a great deal more for construction. This resulted in an editorial in the *Bernalillo Times*, on March 6, 1941—"Don't Blame the Highway Department if You Get Your Neck Broken Riding Through the Jemez Pueblo.."

Five miles of gravel road will cost $217,000. That's more than the damn reservation is worth. Yes, that is what it would cost the Highway Department, $43,400 for each mile to put the much-needed five miles of new road through the Jemez Indian Pueblo by using the right-of-way that the Indians and the Indian Service Bureau are willing to allow the state to use.

That the Indian can show so little consideration for his neighbors, the rancher, farmer and worker of the Jemez country is hard to conceive . . .

If the Indians like Garbo want to be alone, all right, let them. But let it work both ways. No Indian living in a Pueblo which will not cooperate with the state in securing a decent inexpensive right-of-way for a road should be allowed to buy an auto license in order to use other highways.

Let's stop being sentimentalists. The advice of this newspaper to the Highway Department is to accept the offer of Mr. Tom Gallagher of the New Mexico Timber Company to move the railroad tracks over to the edge of the right-of-way (granted by an act of Congress) and use the balance of the right-of-way for a road. "Then let them howl!"

On March 11, Governor Manuel Yepa replied to the editorial with an explanation of the tribe's stand, published in the *Albuquerque Journal*. He explained that the people of Jemez were perfectly willing for the Highway Department to use the right-of-way that was first agreed upon in 1940, with the slight changes that the surveyor said could easily be made. One of the changes was the proposal to bypass the ruins of Seto-kwa, below Jemez. The Indians had the backing of their general superintendent and Oscar Love, of the Albuquerque National Trust and Savings Bank.

Nevertheless, the Board of County Commissioners of Sandoval County did file suit to condemn the right-of-way without the changes that Jemez asked for, and the defendants were ordered to appear at the U.S. Courthouse in Santa Fe on August 14, 1941. Judgment was declared on December 11, 1941, by U.S. Circuit Judge Sam Bratton, condemning the right-of-way on Jemez land—the second plan—with payment to be made to the defendants in the amount of $3,134, as recommended by land appraisers.

Thereafter, condemnation became a standard operating procedure in dealing with the Pueblo Indians. During the fifty years of the act's existence, it was used nineteen times, against eight pueblos. It was particularly hard on Laguna and Santa Clara Pueblos, each of which suffered from it on five different occasions. The other pueblos against whom the act was used were Isleta, Jemez, Sandia, San Ildefonso, Santa Ana, and Taos.

The 1926 act was obviously unfair, in that it subjected the Pueblo Indians of New Mexico to a type of action from which other tribes in the United States were immune. The act was passed with the intent of solving a unique problem at a specific time, and should have been repealed after it had served that purpose. In addition to the actual condemnation actions, the Pueblos were subjected to intimidation in negotiating rights-of-way, since the threat of condemnation always hung over them.

The Pueblos had for years discussed ways of repealing the act; finally in 1957, William Brophy, field solicitor of the Department of the Interior, persuaded the U.S. attorney to present a legal argument against the act in one of Laguna's cases. At this time District Court Judge Waldo Rogers ruled against Mr. Brophy's arguments, and the Department of Justice determined that an appeal would not be successful. Nevertheless, the All Indian Pueblo Council persisted, determined to right a harmful wrong. On October 20, 1973, the council passed a resolution to request Congress to repeal the 1926 act. A few days later, the National Congress of American Indians, at their annual meeting in Tulsa, passed a similar resolution, at the request of the Pueblos.

During this same period, the National Tribal Chairmen's Association passed a similar resolution for the Pueblos. As time went by, the Pueblos enlisted the aid of Governor Bruce King of New Mexico, during his first term, as well as that of his successor, Governor Jerry Apodaca.

With all this important backing, the All Indian Pueblo Council then approached the New Mexico congressional delegates in Washington, D.C. On July 15, 1974, Senator Domenici, for himself and the senior senator of New Mexico, Joseph M. Montoya, introduced bill S. 3763, during the 93rd Congress, second session; however, the bill did not pass. Consequently, the following year, during the first session of the 94th Congress, Senators Domenici and Montoya again introduced the bill, as Senate Bill 217 (*Congressional Record*, January 17, 1975). This time the bill was passed by the Senate, on May 21, and by the House of Representatives on May 22, 1975.

A hearing before the Subcommittee on Indian Affairs of the Committee on Interior and Insular Affairs of the House of Representatives was held on July 24, 1975, regarding S. 217. Following this, a conference committee met to reconcile differences in amendments to the bill as passed in the two houses; their final report (H. 9145) was published in the *Congressional Record*, August 26, 1976. On September 10, 1976, the assistant secretary of the interior, in a letter to the director of the Office of Management and Budget, recommended that President Ford approve S. 217, which he did, on September 17, 1976 (90 Stat. 1275).

Justice was served, through the efforts of many friends of the Pueblo Indians, but with the opposition of many public utilities in the state. Thus ended another chapter in the continuing struggle of the Pueblos to preserve their land and fight against bureaucracy. However, this is not the end of the matter of condemnation of Pueblo Indian land.

At times throughout the years it has been contended that the act of April 28, 1928, repealed the 1926 act by implication. The federal district court for New Mexico rejected this argument in a decision in 1957. Again in *Plains Electric Generation and Transmission Cooperative, Inc. v. Pueblo of Laguna*, it concluded that the 1926 act was valid. However, this decision was reversed by the 10th Circuit Court of Appeals, which held in 1976 that the 1926 act was inconsistent with the 1928 rights-of-way act and was, therefore, repealed by implication. This meant that the 1926 act had never validly allowed for the acquisition of property rights to Pueblo lands, so that all condemnors under that act appear to have been in trespass since the date of the condemnations.

In 1979, during an investigation of trespass claims involving Indian land, legal proceedings were prepared against all entities that had acquired Pueblo land by condemnation. However, on March 27, 1980, Congress passed a bill extending the time for commencement of actions by the United States on behalf of Indians pursuant to 28 U.S.C. 2415. Section 2 of this amendment provides that the secretary of the interior shall submit to Congress legislative proposals to resolve Indian claims which are not appropriate for resolution by litigation. The Solicitor's Office of the Department of the Interior, in Washington, declined to initiate litigation on these claims on the ground that no demonstrable damage existed. Still under consideration was whether legislation should be prepared covering these claims, and it was proposed that Congress appropriate funds for the payment of current fair market value for the rights-of-way, less the amount originally paid to the Pueblos. That "the wheels of justice grind slowly" was never truer than in this matter of the condemnation of Pueblo Indian land. It is possible that some tribes may file suit on their own against condemners.

8

Catholic Missionaries at Jemez

In 1541, Castañeda, chronicler of the Coronado expedition, mentioned seven pueblos in the province of Jemez, in addition to three others in the province of Agua Caliente—that is, Jemez Hot Springs. He was perhaps talking about Patokwa ("Turquoise Moiety place"), Pebulekwa ("shell place"), Wahangkwa ("pumpkin place"), Kole-wa-hang-anu ("small pumpkin place"), and Guisewa ("boiling place," or "where water boils out of the ground"), plus the three north of the latter—Hanakwa ("horned toad place"), Unshagi ("cedar-growing place"), and Nonyi-shagi ("aspen-growing place"); the number of places does not correspond, due to Spanish confusion. An excavation of Unshagi by the University of New Mexico and the School of American Research places its settlement at from A.D. 1375 to 1604.[1]

The other Hemish were on the east side of the province during initial European contact; their settlements were Bule-tse-kwa ("shell-eye place"), also known as Wahang-chanu-kwa ("Pumpkin Moiety place"), Tien-shun-kwa ("cactus hill place"), Seshokwa ("eagle living place"), and Nokyun-tse-le-ta ("light, or white place"). W.S. Stallings, of the Laboratory of American Anthropology, has set the time of occupancy as A.D. 1657 for Bule-tse-kwa. It was probably for these more numerous eastern people that the church of San Diego de la Congregación was originally established at Walatowa (Jemez Pueblo), in accordance with the decree of 1551 (discussed in Chapter 3).

Juan de Oñate, the first colonizer of Pueblo Indian country, visited the Jemez region from August 3 to August 5, 1598. He had evidently heard of eleven Hemish towns, but reported having seen only eight. A month after his visit to the Pueblo areas, he assigned Franciscan friars to each of them; Fray Alonzo de Lugo was assigned to the "Hemis," as well as to the Apaches to the north and the Navajos to the west (Franciscan Provincial Chronicle). Fray Alonzo began his missionary work by founding San José Church at Guisewa, for the Hemish living in the western part of the province. Following his departure in 1601, a Franciscan lay brother continued to minister to the Hemish for the next few years.

Fray Gerónimo de Zarate-Salmerón was soon assigned as the next missionary; his name appears on the list of six friars who came north to New Mexico with the supply caravan of 1621 (Zarate-Salmerón 1966). That he continued work on the San José de Guisewa mission in the winter of 1621 is verified by Adams and Chavez (1976); they add that soon afterward he started the church of San Diego de la Congregación at Walatowa, named after St. Didacus of Alcala. However, both Walatowa and the church, located in the spacious and open valley, were abandoned because of heavy raids by the Navajos, and the Hemish returned to their mountain homes, where access was more difficult. Struggling daily against the two formidable adversaries of the civil government and the raiding tribes, Father Zarate-Salmerón left in 1626.

This was a very difficult time in New Mexico history. In addition to the raiders, the friars had Juan de Eulate, the fifth Spanish governor, to contend with between 1618 and 1625. Bad feelings between church and state had grown to a stage of open hostility, and there seemed to be no way of coming to any agreement. According to Spanish law, state authority was to predominate; this interpretation conflicted, however, with the ideas of the head of the Franciscans in New Mexico, Fray Isidro Ordóñez (Kessel 1979). The two basic areas of conflict were the problem of ecclesiastical jurisdiction and authority, and the problem of Indian relations, much of which involved *encomiendas* (tributes) paid by the Pueblo Indians to either church or state officials. Despite all the trouble between the Franciscans and the government, the mission program continued to grow; and the supply caravans with provisions and men for the missions continued to arrive regularly (Scholes 1936–37).

In 1623 San Diego de la Congregación was burned in a disastrous fire, instigated by Governor Eulate. According to Fray Alonzo de Benavides, in his Memorial of 1634, this even caused the pueblo to be "entirely depopulated and all the Indians returned to their ancient mountain [homes] and many of them scattered to other parts."

Besides the Spaniards' own internal problems, the Hemish nation was one of the most belligerent of the area; they were probably aware of the intruders' conflicts when they rose in revolt that same year. The tribe was not subdued by soldiers, as there were none to protect the padres; however, Navajo raids and famine weakened the Hemish during the following years.   .

According to his own account, Fray Gerónimo "sacrificed himself to the Lord among the pagans," toiling chiefly among the Hemish, of whom he baptized 6,566, and in whose language he wrote a *doctrina*, or theological treatise. According to Benavides, Fray Gerónimo was a good priest and linguist, and founded a very beautiful convent and a magnificent chapel dedicated to Saint Joseph at the principal pueblo of the Hemish (Guisewa). In spite of the utmost perils and difficulties, then, Fray Gerónimo built churches and monasteries, and wrote a document which, while inaccurate in some details, since he wrote it after he returned to New Spain, is indeed a most important source of information about New Mexico and the Jemez people. Today the ruins of San José Church at Guisewa are preserved as a state monument.

The magnitude of the construction problems faced by the early mission builders was immense—consider the extremely limited numbers of primitive tools available to them, and the frustrations of trying to supervise helpers whose language was entirely foreign. A sample of the tools issued to the padres when they went out to the mission fields would be ten axes, three adzes, three spades, ten hoes, one medium-size saw, one chisel, two augers, one plane, a latch for the church door, two small locks, twelve hinges, and about 6,000 nails of various sizes.

During the initial Spanish colonization of Mexico and South America, professional architects and engineers were among the colonists, and brought knowledge of European methods to the new provinces. This was not the case in seventeenth-century New Mexico, and yet between 1609 and 1628 almost fifty churches had been built in the province, twelve of them in 1625 alone (Scholes 1937:20).

In addition to their construction projects, including a home for the padre, the Franciscans fed and took care of the sick and the poor. They reorganized tribal economies by introducing livestock, new crops, and

European methods of cultivation. They brought scattered extended families together to live in new settlements. And they gave instruction in reading, writing, and the singing of hymns (Scholes 1930).

In 1628, two years after Fray Gerónimo had left, Benavides assigned Fray Martín de Arvide to the Hemish mission field, with orders to revive the two churches, and to bring the scattered communities into one area. Fray Martín had served at Picuris Pueblo for many years. In his new assignment he cultivated land for the Hemish, introducing many new plants. Four years later, after watching the pueblo grow to three hundred houses, however, Fray Martín was transferred to Zuni, early in 1632; there, most unfortunately, he was killed by the Zunis on February 22, only five days after they had killed Fray Francisco de Letrado. Soon after his departure the church of San José was abandoned, and the church of San Diego became the principal mission, with Walatowa the principal pueblo.

Although the Spaniards, with their religion, intended to stay, the Hemish clung tenaciously to their native religion, rejecting Spanish demands to give it up in favor of the strange, foreign religion. During the period of the Spanish Governor Fernando de Arguello Caravajal, 1644–47, they allied with the Navajos and killed a Spaniard, Diego Martínez Naranjo. For this deed and "with just severity," Caravajal hanged twenty-nine Hemish leaders (Bandelier 1890–92). Conditions were developing toward the future "Great Rebellion" of 1680.

Early records of Jemez history are very spotty, and concern mission activities and military expeditions. Even so, such details as the ranks or titles of missionaries have been distorted through the years by interpreters and minor chroniclers. For instance, Diego de San Lucas, to whom the present church at Jemez Pueblo was dedicated, is mentioned in numerous sources both as a padre and as a lay brother. He was serving at San Diego de la Congregación in 1639, when an arrow from a Navajo bow killed him during a raid upon the pueblo.

Diego was succeeded by Fray Juan del Campo, in 1640, who was listed as "Padre Guardián de los Hemis" (Scholes 1938). Fray Nicolás de Chaves may have succeeded Fray Juan in 1660; in that year Fray Nicolás of Jemez was sent to Mexico City with reports for the civil and ecclesiastical authorities in the capital.

In 1661 Fray Miguel Sacristán hanged himself on the day before the Feast of Corpus Christi while stationed at San Diego de la Congregación. His assistant, a lay brother, then journeyed to the convent at Santo Domingo Pueblo to inform other religious leaders of the tragedy.

Walatowa, after its refounding in 1628, became an important center of missionary activity among the Hemish and the Keresans; by 1672, it was the residence of the "padre custodio," head of the Franciscans in New Mexico. Missionaries from all over New Mexico gathered there for chapter elections and appointments on August 13, 1672, with Fray Nicolás López presiding (Scholes 1938). At this time Fray Tomás de Torres was assigned to San Diego de la Congregación, where he served until 1675.

His immediate successor is unknown, but it may have been Fray Juan de Jesús Morador, who had the misfortune of serving there at the outbreak of the Great Rebellion of 1680, when he was killed; he was buried close to the wall of one of the kivas. His arrow-pierced body was recovered and taken to Santa Fe in 1694, by de Vargas. At the time Fray Juan was killed, Fray Francisco Muñoz escaped to Zia with the "Alcalde Mayor y Capitán de la Guerra, de la Jurisdicción de Indios Hemes y Queres," Luís de Granillo. At Zia they picked up Fray Nicolás Hurtado and continued on to Sandia Pueblo, thence to Isleta, and eventually to safety at Guadalupe del Paso del Rio del Norte, in the vicinity of today's Ciudad Juárez, Mexico.

How soon after the revolt of 1680 Walatowa was vacated is unknown. But it is recorded that the following year, in 1681, the Jemez civil governor and seven men went to Mexico and accompanied Governor Otermín back to the Pueblo country (John 1975:104). This fact is supported by Jemez legends, as mentioned in Chapter 3.

For the period immediately following the revolt, there are of course no written records available of any kind. It is suspected, however, that the mission of San Diego de la Congregación was completely destroyed, and that the people moved back to the mountains; it was there that de Vargas found them during his reconquest. At that time, two churches were again built. In the summer of 1694 Fray Miguel Tirzio built one at Astiolekwa, at the northern edge of the village, on San Diego Mesa; the church was called San Juan de los Jémez, and tribal legends concerning it are verified by Bloom and Mitchell (1938). Another church was built at Patokwa, below the mesa; this church was called San Diego de al Monte y Nuestra Señora de los Remedios.

These two churches were not destined to last long. The Hemish religious leaders had a continuing feud with the Keresans of Zia and Santa Ana, due to the two tribes' friendship with the Spaniards. After a raid by the Hemish, the Keresan leaders went to Santa Fe to report to the governor; de Vargas visited the Hemish again in 1693, at which time they promised him that they would live at peace with their neighbors. But as soon as de Vargas left, the Hemish fell upon the pro-Spanish Keresans and killed four Zia men, losing one of their own in the fight. De Vargas then ordered a punitive expedition to Jemez—on July 21, 1694, one hundred and twenty Spaniards, with San Felipe, Santa Ana, and Zia auxiliaries, arrived in Hemish country and camped at the confluence of San Diego and Guadalupe canyons, below Patokwa.

On July 24 Brother Eusebio de Vargas, in charge of twenty Spanish soldiers and some of the Keresan warriors, stormed San Diego Mesa. They planned to go up the San Diego Gorge and climb the mesa by the steep trail at the rear of the highest plateau, to reach Astiolekwa from the east. Meanwhile, Governor de Vargas, with a similar number of men, was to ascend from the southwest, the Guadalupe Canyon side, south of Pebulikwa.

After a desperate engagement this strategy, plus their firearms, eventually succeeded. Three hundred sixty-one women and children were captured, eighty-four Hemish men were killed (of whom five were burned to death) and seven were lost down the cliffs.

According to Jemez legend, it was probably during the course of this battle that some people jumped over the cliffs to avoid capture; at that moment a likeness of San Diego appeared on the cliff, and the people who had jumped simply landed on their feet and did not die. The likeness of San Diego is visible today on the red rock cliffs of San Diego Mesa, facing east at the midpoint between Jemez Springs and the southern end of the mesa. It is especially visible from mid-morning until about noon.

The conquerors camped at Astiolekwa, remaining for sixteen days to remove the booty and the captured women and children. After destroying Astiolekwa, de Vargas and his troops descended to Patokwa, and returned to Santa Fe by way of Walatowa.

The booty collected at Astiolekwa, mainly about five hundred bushels of corn, was given to the friendly Keresans as their spoils. Of the 175 cattle captured, 106 were given to Fray Juan de Alpuente, for use at the Zia mission. Loaded mule trains of additional booty went to San Felipe and Santa Ana, to be relayed in ox carts to Santa Fe.

On August 8 the prisoners were taken to Santa Fe. Six days later a few Hemish leaders came to Santa Fe to plead for their families' lives. They were asked to prove their good faith by helping the Spaniards and their Keresan allies to fight the Tewas; after taking part in the defeat of the Tewas in September at Black Mesa, north of San Ildefonso, the prisoners were pardoned.

On September 11, 1694, the former prisoners and their leaders returned to their homes at Astiolekwa. Before leaving Santa Fe, however, the Hemish were told to return to their abandoned home of Walatowa, and to rebuild their church; by 1695 the residents of Astiolekwa may have completed their move (Bloom and Mitchell 1938). Fray Francisco de Jesús María Casanos was assigned to the pueblo, but on June 4, 1696, he was clubbed to death at Walatowa. Anticipating another punitive expedition by the Spaniards, the people returned to the mountains, from which they sent to the west for help from Acoma, Zuni, and the Navajos. A few days later Luís Cunixu arrived at Pecos, carrying an eight-sided gilded brass container for religious relics, the property of the slain Fray Francisco. The Pecos governor, Felipe Chisto, immediately took Luís to Santa Fe, where he confessed the killing and was shot.

On June 29 Captain Miguel de Lara, stationed at Zia, together with the alcalde mayor of Bernalillo, attacked the Jemez, Acoma, Zuni, and Navajo warriors. Thirty-two Indians were killed; among them were eight Acomas, but no Zunis or Navajos. At this time the invaders destroyed Patokwa, and the defeated Hemish and their allies scattered into the mountains. No doubt their allies returned home, but the Hemish fled with their families to their ancestral homeland in the northwest, Cañón Largo, or Gy'a-wahmu ("stone canyon"). Others went to Anyu-kwi-nu ("lion standing place") to the west, in Navajo country. Many also fled to the Hopi country (Chavez 1967:108). When Captain de Lara reconnoitered the area in August, he found it deserted.

Many of the people who fled evidently lived among the Navajos for many years before they returned; others never returned, but became a part of the Dineh, with Hemish traditions. These descendants are identifiable today as being of the "Maii Deesh-giiz-nii" clan; this and the Navajo name for Jemez today come from the name of the Coyote Clan, whose members remained in Navajo country. Those who fled to Hopi country (the "Moquinos") were returned by the individual efforts of dedicated missionaries, who wanted the Hemish to be nearer the missions. Others were returned by the efforts of troops from other pueblos sent out by Acting Governor Felipe Martínez, in 1716 (see Chapter 9). Upon their return from exile, these Hemish joined those at Walatowa, since both Astiolekwa and Patokwa had been sacked and abandoned by that time.

A completely new church was built after the years of turmoil and bad experiences with San Diego de la Congregación. The new church, San Diego de San Lucas, or San Diego de Jémez, located one hundred and fifty yards east of the original church, was first referred to in a written report of January 12, 1706, by Fray Juan Álvarez, head of the Franciscan Order in New Mexico (Adams and Chavez 1976):

In the mission of San Diego, composed of Xemes . . . Indians and distant from Santa Fe thirty-four leagues, is Fray Augustin de Colina. There is no bell, and only one old ornament and an old missal; there are no vials. The church is being built. There are about three hundred Christian Indians . . . and others keep coming down from the mountains, where they are still in insurrection.

The records of the Franciscan order show that this church was completed in 1710, and that it was visited in 1760 by the bishop of Durango, Pedro Tamarón. Sixteen years later, in 1776, Fray Francisco Atanasio Domínguez made his visits to the New Mexico missions, and described the church as follows (Adams and Chavez 1976):

The church is adobe with thick walls, single-naved facing south. From the door to the ascent to the sanctuary it is 40 varas long, 8 high and 9 wide . . . The nave has forty-six wrought beams without corbels in its roof and the clerestory rises along the length of the one facing the sanctuary . . . there is a small adobe belfry containing two small cracked bells and these came from the King . . . on the wall a middle-sized painting on buffalo skin . . . of the Lady of Guadalupe, and it is now old.

And of the pueblo itself, Domínguez wrote:

It all stands behind the church . . . extending to the north. It consists of five blocks, or tenements, all of adobe, and two of them stand at the ends, one on the east and the other on the west, because the other three run across between them, one behind the other . . . and there are very good streets between them.

During this visit the famous padre also witnessed the rigid regime that Fray Joaquín de Jesús Ruiz had imposed upon the Jemez people; he marched them around like a military drill instructor. Before mass, the bell was rung at sunrise, and, as Domínguez wrote (Adams and Chavez 1976:308):

The married men entered, each one with his wife, and they knelt together in a row on each side of the nave of the church. Each couple has its own place designated in accordance with the census list. When there are many, the married couples make two rows on each side, the two men in the middle and the women at the sides. This may seem a superficial matter, but it is not—for experience has taught me that when these women are together they spend all the time dedicated to prayer and mass in gossip, showing one another their glass beads, ribbons, medals, etc., telling who gave them to them or how they obtained them, and other mischief. Therefore, the religious who has charge of the administration must have a care in this regard. After all, it is a house of prayer, not of chitchat.

Six years after Mexico won its independence from Spain, a rumor appeared in late 1827 that the Spaniards planned to invade and re-conquer Mexico and take over its territories. Thus the Mexican national congress decreed the expulsion of all Spaniards from the republic. As a result several Spanish Franciscans left New Mexico, and the Jemez mission was probably abandoned at this time. It was visited occasionally by priests from other towns, and a padre may have been assigned now and then, depending on their availability in the territory.

Three years after the arrival of the Americans, in 1849 Lieutenant James H. Simpson, commissioned by the U.S. Army Corps of Top-ographical Engineers to survey the Navajo country, observed that the church at Jemez "appeared to be very old and was evidently wasting away under the combined influence of neglect and moisture" (Simpson 1964).

Evidently the elements continued to take their toll, for in 1881 another United States military observer, Lieutenant John G. Bourke, on special assignment to study the Indians of the Southwest, stated (Bloom 1938):

There is no church; the church fell down about ten days ago—the great amount of rain this summer falling upon the earth roof proved too much for the resisting power of the old beams which gave way . . . but leaving the facade intact with the steeple in which are hanging two bells of small size.

Written records concerning the church of San Diego de Jémez disappear here again; but oral history comes to the rescue as the de-scendants of a Pecos immigrant, Agustin Pecos, keep alive the story that their grandfather revived the church when he was governor of Jemez in 1888. Church records show that Father Juan Bautista Mariller was the pastor at this time; he served at Jemez from 1880 to 1892.

In due time the building began to need repairs again, and Father Barnabas Meyer began to work with the tribal leaders on the old church at the same time as construction of a chapel by the San Diego Mission School was going on. In 1918 both the renovation and the new structure were ready; my grandfather Jose Manuel Yepa was the governor that year. On the day after the Jemez feast, on November 13, the two buildings were dedicated. Since then the old San Diego de Jémez church has not undergone any changes other than minor repairs.

The files of the Pueblo Lands Board produce more detailed information on Jemez church history after 1918.[1] On October 29, 1925, the board held a hearing at Albuquerque, concerning the land in Jemez currently occupied by the Catholic church. The pastor at that time was Father Lawrence Rossman, who testified that:

To my knowledge it traces back to the time of Father Barnabas; he was the first Franciscan who was sent to succeed the secular Fathers under charge of the Archbishop, and when he came there he found the territory . . . the same as it is at present, and in the course of these years he added several buildings. He built the school and enlarged the home . . . and continued until Father Albert Daeger, the present Archbishop of Santa Fe, succeeded him.

Father Barnabas Meyer was pastor of a church in Gallup, New Mexico, at the time he was called to testify on the fifteen-acre church holdings to the west of the pueblo at the 1925 hearing. In answer to questions from the chairman of the board, Robert Walker, Father Barnabas replied:

I came to New Mexico in February 1902 and was assigned to Jemez in March 1902. I put up almost all the buildings there with the exception of one . . . a one-story adobe residence built by Reverend Antonine Celerier . . . the present (village) church is about four or five feet from the location of the old church. In 1849, or thereabouts, when the Mexican Revolt broke out, Mexico enacted a law that all foreigners were either to become citizens of Mexico or relinquish their property rights. For that reason the old Spanish padres were obliged to leave the Pueblos, and Jemez, also. Then, at intervals, one would come to look after their charges, but it seems they were not permanently settled for a few years. The last frey to my knowledge was Frey Jesus de Comacho.

I succeeded Reverend Antonine Celerier, the present pastor at Belen, New Mexico, who was there for at least two years since 1900. His predecessors were Fathers Beland, Deshores and Juliard. Prior to them Father Mariller was there for 12 years. His predecessor was Father Manuel Chavez before 1880.

Before 1900 there was a little adobe room in the rear of the [village] church that was used as a residence by the priest. The Indians use that land now. As for the land that you call the 15-acre tract it has been occupied since 1870, not as a school, but it was a ranch. And around 1900 a secular priest established a residence there. With the buildings there today at the former ranch, I could state the approximate value of the buildings on the church property based on the cost of reproduction at this time as $8,000 for the school; $10,000 on the residence; $5,000 on the chapel; $3,500 on the hall; $2,000 for stables and barns; $1,000 for the sewerage system and tank; and $200 for fences. That would be minimum value for a total of $29,700 or $30,000 at least.

The length of Father Barnabas's original stay at Jemez is uncertain, but after being transferred to Gallup he was reassigned to Jemez, when my generation knew him; he is one of the most respected priests ever to serve at Jemez. He was the first Franciscan to return to Jemez after the order had been gone for almost a century, to take over missionary activity at the more than three-hundred-year-old parish of San Diego de Jémez, when Archbishop Pierre Bourgade of Santa Fe invited the Franciscan Order back to New Mexico. He, Fray Zarate-Salmerón, and Father Raphael Weisenback, were the church builders at Jemez.

Father Barnabas wasted no time in building his empire. The Franciscans had moved to an area approximately one-quarter of a mile west of the San Diego church to establish their new living quarters on fifteen acres of land. This land was patented to the Catholic church on October 19, 1931, according to the Pueblo Lands Act of June 7, 1924, after the Pueblo Lands Board had determined that the pueblo's title to the land had been extinguished. The patent was signed by President Herbert Hoover and a secretary, Leafie E. Dietz.

By 1904 a school building had been constructed, and classes were moved there from the front of the pueblo church. A chapel was started, next to the original convent, and was completed in 1918, to be blessed on November 13, 1918, by Father Albert T. Daeger and his special guest, Father Barnabas Meyer. This chapel lasted only until 1937, when it was destroyed by fire on Ash Wednesday.

I was an eighth grader at the mission school that year. On that day all of the students were anointed with ashes at the mass before regular classes started. We had no sooner entered our classrooms, about seventy-five yards from the chapel, when thick black smoke erupted from it. A defective flue on an old, pot-bellied stove must have started the soot in the chimney smoldering, and the fire soon reached the well-dried timbers. By the time the blaze was noticed, it was too far advanced for anything to be done to save the building.

As soon as the smoke had cleared away, Father Raphael and Brother Elzear Pail, O.F.M., set about building another; the Jemez people quickly forget the former chapel, since the new building was apparently more beautiful and fitting than its predecessor.

It is said that Brother Elzear, who had spent some thirty years in the missions of the Southwest, laid the thousands of adobes that went into the new chapel, with help from Juanito Shendo and John Shamon. Helping Father Raphael in supervising the construction was his father, Frank X. Weisenback, who had left his farm in Morris, Indiana, to assist his son; a sad memory hovering over the new church was the loss of Mr. Weisenback, who died of a stroke during the construction. Other prominent contributors to the construction were Father Eugene Rousseau, O.F.M., an assistant at Jemez, and Father Agnellus Lammert, O.F.M., the builder of several outstanding chapels in New Mexico, who gave much expert advice while on visits from Laguna Pueblo.

Of special interest in the new chapel is the wood carving; John Shamon of Jemez, who was trained at Haskell Institute in Lawrence, Kansas, designed the Indian and Franciscan symbols that appear on the square vigas and corbels, and Brother Eugene Stendeback, O.F.M., carved the altar.

Much planning went into the carving of the altar and the timber adornments. As Brother Eugene explains, behind the altar there are four uprights, twelve by sixteen inches. Two have large representations of grains of corn, and the other two of grains of wheat, running from top to bottom. These pillars are crowned by a turban-shaped carving, to register the fact that there is no face that can represent the God Who rules over all. The grains of corn and wheat tell us—Indian fashion—that He, the Great Spirit, gives growth and fertility to all living things. For the space between the uprights, Father Giles Hukenback made three paintings in oil. They represent the apparition of San Diego, sculptured by nature in the rocks some seven miles up the canyon from the pueblo; St. Joseph, the patron of the Franciscan Sisters, who have been laboring in the mission since 1904; and the image of Our Lady of Guadalupe, as it appears in the white cliffs of Guadalupe Canyon, north of Jemez.

The altar was also constructed at the pueblo. One single, four-inch-thick plank of sugar pine, forty-two inches wide, was secured through Mr. Luke Caldwell to serve as the face of the altar. Brother Eugene carved the Last Supper on it, spending endless hours to arrive at the perfection that everyone who visits the chapel today can admire. He carved the tabernacle as well.

The communion rail depicts what John Shamon has described as "all good things, because we receive the God of Goodness at this rail." At the top there is a rainbow from which a "sunray" rises between Indian cloud signs ("thunderheads"). At the bottom the "sunray" appears again, with clouds of the type that send down moisture to produce our food. These indicate that at the communion rail we receive the spiritual food that sustains the spiritual life in us.

The corbels show the "ups and downs of life," with its crosses to bear; the curve is "the span of life," and then we "go to heaven through the clouds," and the moon signifies "in peace." Mr. Shamon explains that the bullet-like carvings on the vigas "represent our prayers going to heaven with the speed of a bullet, and graces returning with like speed." That is the reason for the opposing directions of these symbols. A "Zia sun symbol," the official state symbol of New Mexico, was added more as decoration on the corbels; however, we cannot overlook the fact that we consider the sun as the most benevolent element in life.

Father Agnellus Lammert obtained the carved Stations of the Cross. A circular stair, such as is found in many old Spanish missions, leads to the choir loft. The portal in front of the chapel has uprights with "thunderbird" carvings representing the Holy Spirit. The ceilings are done in a herringbone pattern of aspen logs laid at a forty-five-degree angle.

Usually there were two bells from the reigning authorities in Spain above the entrances of the old missions. One was called the "king" and the other the "queen" bell; under United States government rule, however, this custom is no longer in vogue. The present chapel has only one four-hundred-pound bell, the gift of the wife of Tom Gallagher.[2]

This magnificent chapel was the result of the pooling of ideas of the Franciscans and the Jemez people who helped build it. Fathers Raphael and Agnellus drew the basic plans, and John Shamon was allowed free reign to express his soul through his carvings. If my eighth grader's memory serves me, I recall that three other Jemez men who helped were Juanito Shendo, Jose M. Toya, and Trancito Vigil. Today parishioners see only the beauty of the chapel and the seriousness of its purpose. The long, turbulent past is the farthest thing from their minds as they worship in this shrine steeped in history.

The image of San Diego appeared on the canyon wall in 1696 during the encounter with Diego de Vargas.

San Diego Mission Chapel. (Courtesy E. S. Scholer.)

San Diego de Jemez. (Photograph by Adam Clark Vroman.)

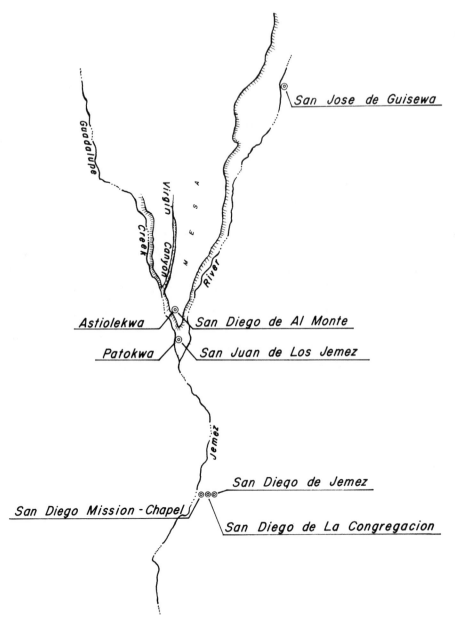

Map of the Churches of the Jemez People.

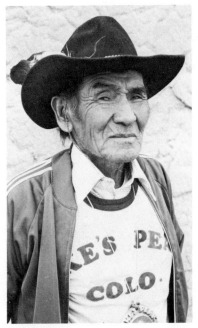

The "Over 65 Champion" of the Pikes Peak run, Lucas Toledo. (Courtesy E. S. Scholer.)

Juanito Sando, 1920.

133

Three of the running Waquius at home—Robert and Stanley with their grandfather, Felipe, Sr. (Courtesy E. S. Scholer.)

Al Waquie as he finishes the La Luz Trail run in 1979. (Courtesy *Albuquerque Journal*, Richard Pipes, photographer.)

Coach Joe Cajero and his New Mexico state AAU cross-country champions from Jemez Pueblo representing the Jemez Valley High School in 1965. *First row:* Frank Armijo, Freddie Sabaquie, Paul Tosa, Coach Joe Cajero, Robert Waquiu, John C. Waquiu, Al Waquie; *second row:* Raymond Loretto, Ernest Tafoya, James Gachupin, Walter Waquiu; *third row:* Matthew Gachupin, Harold Sando, Juan Rey Madelena.

Stephania Toya, the first college graduate of Jemez Pueblo in 1948. (Courtesy E. S. Scholer.)

Facing page, above: Lupe M. Romero learned the basics of pottery making from her Keresan mother. She kept the art alive when it was not popular in the 1930s and 1940s. Here she stands by three of her works. (Courtesy E. S. Scholer.)

Facing page, below: The Institute of American Indian Arts in Santa Fe has also contributed to art as a career at Jemez. This is a stone sculpture by Clifford Fragua. Cliff has taught one other Jemez young man the art of stone sculpting. (Courtesy E. S. Scholer.)

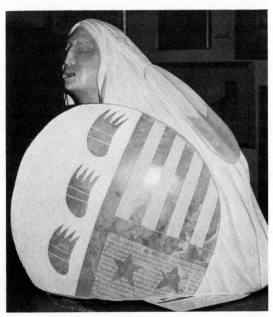

137

Stella Loretto with her clay sculpture. (Courtesy E. S. Scholer.)

Evelyn Mora Vigil with Pecos pottery. (Courtesy E. S. Scholer.)

Lucy Y. Lowden, the creator of "little people." Note the three "little people" on the fireplace mantel depicting traditional dances. (Courtesy E. S. Scholer.)

Jose Rey Toledo, with assistance from his wife Amelia Toya Toledo, working on a mural at the Indian Pueblo Cultural Center. (Courtesy E. S. Scholer.)

Traditional Jemez nativity scene. (Courtesy E. S. Scholer.)

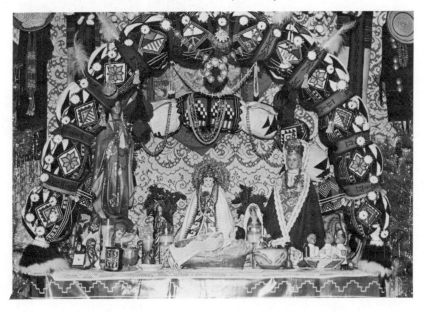

A rare photo of two ancient Jemez ceremonial dances as captured by an unknown tourist sometime in the 1930s. The far one is a Tree Dance and the near one is similar to an American "Virginia reel."

The children of Jemez begin to learn the intricate Dance of the Buffalo very early in life. (Courtesy E. S. Scholer.)

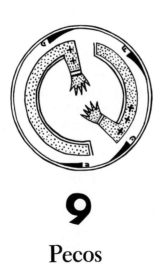

9

Pecos

In 1838 the remnants of the once-powerful Pueblo nation of Pecos arrived at Jemez Pueblo.[1] The ancestors of these people played an important role in the history of New Mexico, since the time when the Spanish conquistadores, new to the Southwest, found them friendly and helpful, and their location advantageous during the Spaniards' search for the mirage of El Dorado.

There are many reports of these events, some of them legendary, some documentary, the latter mainly provided by early researchers who came to Jemez to interview either surviving Pecos immigrants or their first-generation descendants. Pecos Pueblo was described by the conquistadores as the largest in New Mexico at the time of the conquest, and even at the beginning of the eighteenth century it was second only to Zuni Pueblo. Pecos lost nearly 75 percent of its population in three generations; however, among the reasons for its fast decline is its location over the mountains from the Rio Grande, at the gateway of the passage from the eastern plains to Santa Fe. Pecos bore the brunt of raiding by Apaches and Comanches, and later American traders and military men.

We shall not detail all the contacts of the Spanish with Pecos; most of their expeditions used Pecos Pueblo and its people to improve their situation in a distant and uninviting area. Like other Pueblo peoples, the people of Pecos shared their food and lodgings with the ignorant newcomers, until soon the encomienda system (a policy of taking materials from the people as tribute) became unbearable.

From the very beginning Spanish governors used Pecos warriors to bolster their weary troops. Many times they were captured and forced to accompany the Spanish expeditions, as when Coronado's lieutenants met two Pecos men at Hawikuh in 1540 and named them Cacique and Bigotes. Espejo's party used Pecos men to lead them to the eastern plains in 1583. In 1590 the renegades of Castaño de Sosa seized both men and provisions, which the Pecos could ill afford to lose.

The Espejo expedition returned to Mexico with a captive Pecos boy, who was left at the College of Tlaltelco under the tutelage of the famed Franciscan educator Fray Pedro Oroz, to learn Spanish and languages of the Mexican Indians; in return he was to teach his language to other students. Fray Oroz hoped that some day these students would serve as valuable interpreters and catechists. After the lad was baptized he took the name of his teacher (Chavez 1971:29). Pedro died before the next Spanish expedition to his homeland, but he returned in spirit with one of his students, Juan de Dios. Juan was half Indian, offered by his parents into the service of the Christian cause; he was neither a priest nor a lay brother.

Upon his arrival in the Pueblo country with the Oñate colonizers, Juan was assigned in the fall of 1598 to assist an early missionary to Pecos, Fray Francisco de San Miguel (Fray Luís de Ubeda, the first missionary, stayed after Coronado's luckless troops returned to New Spain in 1542). After six months Fray San Miguel was reassigned to the provincial headquarters at San Gabriel del Yunque. In 1601 he returned to New Spain with other deserters, who were disgusted with Oñate's harsh policies and his practice of leaving the friars unprotected while he took his troops on explorations.

The fate of Juan is unrecorded, but he probably remained permanently at Pecos, assisting the friars who came to serve for a few years at a time. It is believed that he was there to help the famous architect and builder, Fray Andrés Juárez, in the construction of the great church in the early 1620s, dedicated to Nuestra Señora de los Ángeles de Porciúncula, as is the mother church of the Franciscans in Assisi, Italy. After visiting New Mexico from 1625 to 1629, Fray Alonso de Benavides praised Fray Juárez for building a "church of unique construction and beauty, very spacious with room for all the people of the pueblo" (Chavez 1971). Pecos men probably learned carpentry from him at that time.

On August 8, 1680, the Pecos governor informed Fray Fernando de Velasco, who in turn informed Governor Otermín, that two young runners from Tesuque had visited to advise the pueblos of the date for the beginning of the revolt of 1680, urging their participation in the effort to expel the Spaniards (John 1975:100). The pueblos of Galisteo and Taos also warned the Spanish.

Twelve years after the revolt there was an aggressive and rebellious faction in Pecos; as the returning Governor de Vargas reached Pecos on October 17, 1692, he and his sixty soldiers were met by four hundred armed Pecos warriors. Pecos Governor Juan de Ye was able to contain his troops, however, and they surrendered peacefully (Hayes 1974:8). De Vargas began to rely on de Ye, calling on Pecos warriors for aid in subduing other tribes and for a show of force against other pueblos.

In the late summer of 1693 Juan de Ye, leading an army of Pecos warriors, accompanied de Vargas to Taos and Picuris in search of food for the additional Spanish families in Santa Fe who had arrived that June. There de Ye risked talking to the Taos people, who had taken refuge in their mountain canyon. Although de Vargas objected, de Ye entered the canyon when the Taos announced that they would speak only to him; he entered unarmed, never to be seen again.

Governor de Ye was succeeded by Diego Marcos, but at the time of the last revolt, in 1696, Don Felipe Chisto was governor. By accident he once attended a meeting of traditional leaders in his pueblo; a Tewa delegation from Nambe had come to discuss the expulsion of the ruthless intruders. Upon learning of the plan, and that his cacique, Diego Umbiro, and war captain, Cachina, were apparently deeply involved, Felipe jumped up, clutching his governor's cane, and exclaimed, "Here we are loyal to the King!" The governor and his men were able to overpower the cacique, who was taken out of the meeting. Subsequently, de Vargas granted Felipe permission to hang the cacique. By the end of the summer four more men were hanged and a fifth was beheaded (Espinosa 1942:250; John 1975:143). It was at this time, also, that Felipe ordered the Jemez man Luís Cunixu to be taken before de Vargas in Santa Fe for trial, where he was shot.

Thereafter Pecos was seriously split into factions. Relatives and friends of the executed cacique plotted vengeance; legends tell of much sorcery having developed between the factions. In 1700 the people of the former cacique were carted off to jail in Santa Fe, but they escaped and fled into the mountains, where they lived with Jicarilla Apache friends. Hostility between the factions continued, and it was only with much difficulty that Governor Felipe, with Spanish backing, prevented open clashes. It was at this time that the anti-Spanish petitioned Governor Pedro Rodríguez Cubero for permission to move to Pojoaque. While there is no record of this having been granted, members of the Pecos family at Cochiti today tell of their ancestors coming to Cochiti from Pojoaque.

In 1704 Felipe was still governor of Pecos; in the spring of that year he supplied de Vargas with four war captains and forty-two warriors, as the Spanish governor campaigned against the Apaches in the Sandia mountains. It was during this campaign that de Vargas became ill and died on April 8, 1704, in Bernalillo (Espinosa 1942:358).

Felipe must have monopolized the power of governing Pecos; in 1715 he was still listed as governor. At this time the Taos and Picuris were being raided by the Faraones Apaches, later known as the Mescaleros. Spanish Governor Juan Flores Mogollón organized a retaliatory expedition including thirty Pecos warriors with Felipe as leader. However, Gerónimo, a Taos war captain, objected to the presence of the Pecos men because they had been friendly with the Faraones ever since they fled the vicinity of Pecos at the time of the reconquest in 1692–93 (Jones 1966:91). And yet Gerónimo's people were also allied with the Jicarilla Apaches.

In 1716 the faithful Don Felipe again submitted to Acting Governor Martínez, when an army was organized to battle the Hopis during the Spanish campaign to return the Rio Grande Pueblo refugees of 1680 and 1696 to their respective pueblos (see Chapter 8). Besides Spanish militia volunteers, Pueblo warriors were recruited from each village, depending on its size. Pecos and Zuni each contributed thirty warriors; Zia and Acoma twenty-five each; Cochiti, Jemez, and San Felipe twenty each; Taos fifteen; Santa Ana twelve; Picuris, San Juan, San Ildefonso, Tesuque, Santo Domingo, and Laguna ten; Santa Clara and Pojoaque six; and Isleta five. Although some Pueblo people were returned to their Rio Grande homes, the Tanogeh Tewas refused to return, remaining at Hano on First Mesa. As for the Hopis, they absolutely refused all Spanish overtures and rejected Christianity, which resulted in the burning of Walpi (Bloom 1931).

These are just examples of the availability of the Pecos people. It may also explain the rapid attrition of the people, as well as the serious split of the factions—those under the traditional leadership, and those under Felipe, who were usually friendly with the Spaniards.

In addition to sorcery and violence, Pecos was hit by smallpox epidemics in 1738 and 1748 (Chavez 1957). When Padre Francisco

Atanasio Domínguez visited in 1776, he counted 269 people at Pecos, in a pitiable condition (Adams and Chavez 1976). Formerly irrigated fields to the north and east were useless, "because this pueblo is so much besieged by the enemy." They had to rely on dry-farming fields closer to the protective walls of the community; they had produced little, due to several years of drought. "As a result, what few crops there usually are do not last even to the beginning of a new year from the previous October, and hence these miserable wretches are tossed about like a ball in the hands of fortune" (Domínguez, in Adams and Chavez 1976:213).

Another, more interesting reason for the decline of the Pecos population is offered by Angelico Chavez (1971):

During the long Mission period, the men of Pecos were distinctly noted for their skill in carpentry. No doubt this penchant for learning the carpenter's trade from the padres was inherited from ancient forebears who had built their pueblo with only the crudest tools of flint and stone. . . . The men may have taken their families to other Pueblos while they did the work, then remained after the job was finished.

He even speculates that Pecos carpenters may have done the ceilings and other woodwork of many eighteenth-century churches and chapels in New Mexico.

Pecos had long been a principal trade center for Apaches from the eastern plains, and by the 1800s it had become important to Santa Fe businessmen seeking the Apache trade. Pueblo hunting groups and Spanish military parties to the plains also stopped at Pecos; according to legends we heard as youngsters, the next big rest stop was at a lake near Tucumcari, where buffalo meat was processed and partially dried before packing it home to Jemez on the sides of burros, with another stop at Pecos. Much later American traders and army men from Missouri, known as volunteers and "los goddames," stopped at the ruins of Pecos on their way to Santa Fe.

As the reader may have realized by now, the Pueblos and the Apaches were not always at war. There were many years of peace, during which they traded crops for buffalo hides and dried meat. It is said that on occasion the Apaches left their women and children at Pecos while the men went to hunt buffalo or scout for the Spaniards against the Comanches. A problem arose from this practice, however, as friendly Apaches were often attacked by the military, which created dissension between the Apaches and the Pueblos; the Apaches suspected the Pueblos of being totally and forever allied with the Spaniards.

In 1746 there was a Comanche raid on Pecos in which twelve people were killed. And again during a winter attack on the pueblo in 1748, thirteen more were killed before the raiders were driven off. In 1749 Governor Tomás Vélez Cachupín erected a fortress with entrenchments and towers at the gates; at least thirty soldiers were stationed at Pecos to defend against the Comanches. These soldiers soon brought their families, and began to move onto the fields abandoned by the Indians, three miles to the north of the pueblo. In a short time there were homes near these irrigated farm lands.

The Comanches were such a problem that several Spanish governors forbade any trading with them; they also put restrictions on hunting buffalo in the eastern plains. Despite the hazards, people had to hunt, because of the usefulness of buffalo meat for food, as well of the hide and horns for household articles. Thus, in 1749 Pecos leaders asked Governor Joaquín Codalles y Rabal for permission to hunt in Comanche country; only after Pecos men did some carpentry work at the palace of the governor, in Santa Fe, were they granted this permission (Chavez 1971). During this venture around one hundred and fifty Pecos men were killed by the Comanches, who then followed the hunters home and killed eight more people at the pueblo.

As the population continued to decline, the Comanche raids abated, until by 1794 they were no longer a threat. At about this time, however, *genízaros* from Analco, in Santa Fe, arrived in the area, and established the settlement of San Miguel del Vado, approximately eighteen miles east of the pueblo. This community was much like Abiquiu in the north, and Belén and Tomé in the south. Genízaros were Christianized Indians of various tribes, most of whom were ex-captives of the Apache, Comanche, and Navajo, who had later been traded or sold at trade fairs to the Spanish. Thus, most were raised by Spanish families carrying out a Christian duty. When these people married, they were assigned land to settle on, usually areas at the limit of safe settlement. As residents of buffer zones, they were the first to encounter any raiders, before they reached the more populated Rio Grande villages. Today there are many people in the area who claim genízaro ancestry, and are searching to discover their roots.

In this same period, Spanish people began to move onto the Pecos land grant, from Santa Fe and from San Antonio de Jacona, north of Santa Fe. They founded the village of San Antonio de Pecos, at the mouth of Pecos Canyon, sometime in 1825. According to Kessell (1979), during the latter part of his term the Mexican Governor Bartólome Baca, and the Diputación Provincial, New Mexico's legislature under the Mexican constitution of 1824, opened the Pecos grant to settlers. They concluded that since the lands had not been cultivated by the Pecos Indians for many years, the new government could issue a Mexican land grant; this was done in early 1825. Rafael Benavides and several companions took possession, and the landless began to pour in, with or without grants. Almost overnight dozens of the destitute families settled the Cañón de Pecos. From then on the Pecos Indians were subjected to plundering and violent harassment by their neighbors, as well as to every form of coercion and compulsion on the part of the local Mexican authorities.

Despite this treatment, the Pecos Indians persevered for a while. Their leaders complained without result to the local alcaldes, who were often related to the troublemakers, if not troublemakers themselves.

In 1826 the alcalde (governor) of Pecos Pueblo, Rafael Águilar, his lieutenant, Juan Domingo Vigil, and José Manuel Armenta, appealed to the Diputación to halt the unlawful alienation of their lands, questioning if in fact they had any rights as citizens under the Mexican government. "Well we know that since the conquest we have earned more merits than all the pueblos of this province" (Kessell 1979: 446).

In March of 1829 Águilar and José Cota approached the new governor, Manuel Armijo; his predecessor, Narbona, had merely suggested that the Pecos Pueblo commons be broken up and each Indian given individual property rights. That way the Indians would progress toward civilization, and lands that lay barren would be brought under cultivation. The Pecos representatives made the following request of Armijo (Kessell 1979):

How great must be the pain in our hearts on seeing ourselves violently despoiled of our rightful ownership, all the more when this violent despoilment was executed while they threatened us with illegal pretext of removing us from our pueblo and distributing us among the others of the Territory. Please, Your Excellency, see if by chance the natives of our pueblo for whom we speak are denied property and the shelter of the laws of our liberal system. Indeed, Sir, has the right of ownership and security that every citizen enjoys in his possession been abolished?

Temporarily, at least, their plea was heeded; a commission was appointed to consider the Pecos question. The commission arrived at a surprisingly unequivocal two-point answer, which the Diputación then enacted into law (Kessell 1979: 448):

1) That all the lands of which they have been despoiled be returned to the natives of the Pueblo of Pecos.

2) That the settlers who have possession of them be advised by the alcalde of that district that they have acquired no right of possession because said grant was given to lands that have owners.

This seems to have solved nothing, however, as there are no records to show that the settlers left Pecos lands.

The only recourse left for some Indians was undoubtedly to move away in search of peace and perhaps prosperity; carpenters could thus have been encouraged to remain wherever they had gone. Some probably left for other reasons; as John (1975) has written, "The quarrels within and among Pueblos, the stresses of enemy raids and warfare, the realities of hunger, and the shadowy apprehensions of Spanish vengeance led many to flee." Those unable to do so built up a high level of tension, ready to explode at any time. But as a tribal group they hung on until 1838, when they moved to Jemez.

Adolph Bandelier, who first came to New Mexico in the summer of 1880 and spent a week at Pecos, wrote that feelers must have been sent out to Jemez; about 1836 a few Jemez leaders had visited Pecos, and Bandelier surmised that the visitors had appraised the Pecos situation and may have extended an invitation to the remnants to come to Jemez. This proposal was not acted upon, however, for reasons not documented. But the following year "mountain fever" broke out at Pecos, killing many people. Hence five men, led by Governor Juan Antonio Toya (Se-h'ng-pae), journeyed to Santa Fe to appear before Governor Manuel Armijo and declare their intention of migrating to Jemez. According to Parsons (1925:4), Jemez officials, led by their cacique, war chief, governor, and a few aides, soon went to Pecos to discuss the situation and extend their welcome.

Aside from the documentation of early researchers, based on information supplied by Pecos descendants, Jemez legends state that the Pecos people said that "they would journey toward the direction in which a greater part of their crumbling pueblo remained"—to the west. Other pueblos were located on the Rio Grande that they would have to pass before they could reach Jemez, however, so they must have decided beforehand. Social scientists have speculated that the

Pecos came to Jemez because they spoke a similar language, Towa, a classification first proposed by John P. Harrington (Hewitt and Bandelier 1937:96; in the Jemez language today *towa* means "home"). But the linguistic similarity is debatable. Was it that they were closer to the Tewas in the Largo-Jicarilla area, and thus settled closer again after the move from the northwest? During the last migration, from the Cuba-Lindrith area, did the Pecos stop with the Hemish in the Las Vacas-Cebolla area, or did they keep going east? The Pecos were neighbors to the Tewas of Tanogeh until close to the end of their existence as tribes; could the linguistic similarity arise from this? What few words are known of the Pecos language sound more like Tewa than Towa; Pecos surnames such as Sidepovi, Pousoi, and Quanima (Kessell 1979:494–95) also sound more Tewa than Towa. The difference is also indicated by the old saying that someone was "just like a Pecos, fumbling for words."

What the pathetic remnants of the once-numerous and powerful tribe brought with them is not clear. They did bring their eagle catcher's society, and later they joined other religious organizations at Jemez. One custom they brought was the Pecos Bull Ceremony, performed at Jemez on August 1 and 2 of each year.

Oral history reports that the immigrants buried all their native religious artifacts in the ground before they vacated their village; since then many of the artifacts have been dug up, especially by Kidder (1932; see Kessell 1979). Chavez (1971) notes that before the Pecos left, they also took down the old painting of Our Lady of the Angels from the wall above the main altar, and left it with the Spanish community of San Antonio de Pecos, on the condition that they celebrate her feast on August 2. While the villagers partly kept their promise, they celebrate her feast along with that of their San Antonio, or St. Anthony of Padua, on June 13. Today Jemez people often go to the village of Pecos to join in the services there on the Sunday following August 2.

Parsons (1925) was told by Pecos descendants that two men, Juan Antonio Toya and José Miguel Vigil, later returned to Pecos to bring the portable church articles to their new home. The story is that only the *niño* was found; the statue they referred to is Nuestra Señora de los Ángeles de Porciúncula (Our Lady of the Angels of Porciuncula), or "Percingula" as the Jemez people call her now. In my childhood, Percingula was kept in the home of the widow of Pablo Toya, the youngest son of Juan Antonio Toya. Sometime during World War II the statue was taken to the village church, where it remains; she is carried out to the plaza to reign on her feast day, August 2, each year.

The Immigrants

It is often assumed that seventeen survivors came to Jemez from Pecos Pueblo. But research by F.W. Hodge in 1895 and 1899, and by E.L. Hewitt in 1902, has produced at least twenty names (see Parsons 1925). By talking to their descendants, Indian names and full Christian names, in some cases, have come to light; we now have twenty-one names of Pecos immigrants.

1) Juan Antonio Toya, or Se-h'ng-pae ("eagle tail mountain"). He was the leader and governor of Pecos when they came to Jemez; a few years later he served as governor of Jemez. Records of Pecos show that he was married to Maria de los Angeles (Kessell 1979:459). Parsons listed his wife as María San Juan, but she was also listed as Juana Maria in a deed signed over to John Ward in 1872.[2] Se-h'ng-pae had two sons and four daughters. From his oldest son, San Juanito Toya, who had four sons, come the many Toyas at Jemez today. The youngest child, and second son, of the couple was Pablo Toya, or Stia-ber. He had two sons, Jose Reyes, the sacristan, also named Se-kuo-se ("eagle shield") and Benito, or Ellr-kuo-se ("elk shield"). His daughters were Rosita T. Nasle, Rosita T. Romero, Lupi T. Sabaquie, and one whose name is unknown, but who was married to a Jose Reyes Chinana. This man must be the one who first used the Chinana surname. In the past he was referred to as Giana-vela ("wealth man") or Giana-toh-oler ("wealth grandpa"). *Giana* means wealth.

Lupi T. Sabaquie was my mother's grandmother. Antonio got the name Toya when he was captured by raiding Comanches as a youngster; in the Comanche language *toya* means "hill," an interpretation verified by Jim Cox, chairman of the Comanche tribe in the 1970s.

2) Shi-to-ne must have been of Pecos origin, since the name has no meaning in Jemez. His son was Agustin Kota.

3) Agustin Kota (often listed as Cota) Pecos, or Sesa-whi-ya, was governor of Jemez in 1888, when Bandelier visited. He was one of four children who came; he died at Jemez on July 20, 1919. A note of interest is that the fishing hole, or earth dam, Dragon Fly, was named after him; it is located just south of La Ventana, on the Espíritu Santo Grant. He grazed his stock in this area, which was commonly

known as Whiya Vega. His wife's name is unknown, but they had two children; one daughter, Juana Pecos Toya, or Hopeh-wa-tai ("Hopi prayer stick"), married the grandson of Se-h'ng-pae, and they had three sons.

One of these sons was Jose Antonio Pecos, known to us as Soma-kin and Wa-chu-aku ("rainbow boy"). Soma-kin's wife was Reyes Fragua; we know of four of their children. Lupe P. Yepa was the oldest, the mother and grandmother of many today. Jose Antonio was hard working, and accumulated much wealth; he built a great mansion in Spanish colonial style, which stood until the 1950s. In addition there was a two-car garage and a large barn; the ruins of the mansion still stand across from my childhood home. This large building was constructed by cousins who came from Las Vegas, New Mexico, according to my father, Juanito Sando. One of Jose Antonio's grandsons, Felix Yepa, was named Cachina, probably after the Pecos leader beheaded by the governor in 1696.

4) Rosa Vigil Pecos, or Hobe-wagi ("kick-stick altar") was the wife of Hopeh (Number 15), and the older sister of Jose Miguel Vigil (Number 5). They had one daughter, Juanita. Juanita was first married to Jose Antonio Waquiu; they had two daughters and one stepson. Their daughters were Isidora W. Sando and Catalina W. Armijo, and the step-son was Magula, or Felipe Waquiu, the great runner featured in Chapter 11, on Jemez runners. Isidora was my father's mother.

Later Juanita lived out her years with Miguel Mora (Pa-her), with whom she had three more children—two sons and a dauughter who died. From this second union come some of the Moras of today.

5) Jose Miguel Vigil, or Zer-wakin ("snow-white eagle down"), brother of Rosa Vigil Pecos (Number 4). That he served as governor of Jemez is verified by the fact that he is listed as a principal during 1887 and 1893; he died in 1902. Zer-wakin was married to Rosita Chavez, who was also listed as Chama. Their two children, Guadalupe and Juan Pedro, like many Pecos refugees, adopted the surname of Pecos. Guadalupe was married to Luis Colaque; they had one son, Jose Guadalupe Pecos, who married Guadalupe Armijo. They had three daughters. Juan Pedro Pecos married Maria Antonia Chihuihui; they had two sons and two daughters. Many of their descendants are alive today, some with the Pecos surname. My uncle, Juan E. Sando, a grandson of Rosa Vigil (Number 4), married the second daughter of Juan Pedro Pecos, so my cousins are also descended from this man, as well as from his sister.

6) Wayu, according to records, was married to an unknown Pecos woman, who probably died before the trek to Jemez. The Parsons genealogical records indicate that their daughter was probably Maria Encarnacion Armenta, Number 7. Many of today's Romeros and some Lorettos are Wayu's descendants.

7) Maria Encarnacion Armenta, or Sntyu-wagi ("turquoise altar"). She married an unknown man; their daughter was Guadalupe, who married Manuel Romero. Their son, Jose Romero, was governor in 1899, and was punished for Jemez officials having stopped the government mail carrier in that year.

8) Mata (possibly a loanword from Spanish *manta*, or shawl). Parsons lists her as the mother of three daughters, Numbers 9, 10, and 11 here.

9) Simona Toya, also listed as Toribio, known at Jemez as Shyn-dyu-kinu ("mountain lion young corn").

10) Daloh, reportedly a Pecos dancer, no descendants.

11) Haiashi—probably another Pecos name. Of the three daughters of Mata, Simona is listed as the wife of Juan de Jesus Madalena. They had two daughters, one whose name was unknown and married to an also unknown person. But the couples' three children are known. They are Francisco or Gameh-yon ("hornet"), Ramon or Stia-shun ("arrow hill"), and Lupe M. Loretto or Oh-stia-pa ("sunflower"). The second daughter was Reyes Madalena; she was married to the Jose Antonio Pecos who was a grandson of Zer-wakin (Number 5), not the one known as Soma-kin.

12) Pove (a popular Tewa girl's name meaning "blossom," or "flower"). She was the mother of Francisco Kota (Number 13), and possibly Jose Kota (Number 14).

13) Francisco Kota (or Cota), or Wa-kin ("eagle down"). The 1872 warranty deed signed by many Pecos descendants shows Francisco to be married to a Lupe Chama. This union produced two daughters, both named Juanita. The first, Toh-wagi ("decorated altar," or "decorated altar lines") was married to Juan Reyes Fragua, an albino, whom we knew as Aher-ye. They had two sons, Francisco E. Fragua and Polito Fragua. The second Juanita was married to a Eusebio Colaque; one of her grandchildren who died fairly recently was Mary Celo Reed.

14) Jose Kota, or K'ela ("Navajo"). He is listed as married to Wapah (?-"blossom"), in the Parsons records, and the 1872 warranty deed shows his wife to be Rosalia Machuela. Their daughter was Hobe-wachu ("kick-stick rainbow"). This daughter married a Santiago Ar-

mijo, and they had two daughters and one son, was also named Santiago, or Haw-shun ("roasted-corn pile"). Haw-shun was married to
Catalina Waquiu, or La-vey, the granddaughter of Hobe-wagi (Number
4); no descendants are listed. His sister, the oldest in the family, produced the Armijos of today through three sons—Jose Reyes, Pablo,
and Florencio; her name, as well as that of her husband, is unknown.

15) Miguel Pecos, or Hopeh ("Hopi"). He was the husband of Rosa
Vigil Pecos (Number 4).

16) Toon-kanu ("fox") and wife (Number 17), whose name was
never listed; no descendants were identified.

17) Wife of Toon-kanu (Number 16).

18) Tyi-koon wachu ("flint society rainbow"). No further information listed.

19) Tsa-aku ("piñon boy"). It is said that when American soldiers
occupied the village, date unspecified, he left with Mexican soldiers,
and was presumed killed by the Americans.

20) Tabu-taa ("clown tea," a corn drink served during the clown
society's retreat). No further information.

21) Juanita Kota Fragua, or Toh-wagi, the last immigrant from
Pecos to die at Jemez. Toh-wagi outlived all the others of direct Pecos
lineage, and many of us knew her; she told her children that she was
brought to Jemez as an infant.

The People and Their Land

Although the Pecos people had physically left their aboriginal homeland, spiritually they remained. Since that time a religious society of
Pecos descendants returns in certain years to pay homage to the deities
and shrines that were left behind; until the 1950s they traveled on
horseback, but since then they have driven in trucks. The shrine in a
cave near Tererro is still recognized, even by New Mexico state officials,
as the private property of the Pecos Society from Jemez. On occasions
the Pecos people have stated their rights to the land; as uneducated
people in today's world of legal sophistication, they may have been
taken in by questionable advice, but more than likely, their requests
for action have simply been ignored.

The first Indian agent of the Indian Territory of the West, James S.
Calhoun, came to Santa Fe in 1849. Mr. Calhoun subsequently be-
came the first American territorial governor of the Territory of New
Mexico, on March 3, 1851, when one company of artillery and one

company of infantry escorted him to the Government House in Santa
Fe. As territorial governor, the office of Superintendent of Indian Affairs
also devolved upon him. Calhoun had served with Zachary Taylor in
the Mexican War, 1846–48, and later, as president, Taylor appointed
him to be the first Indian agent of New Mexico. Calhoun was dignified,
sharp spoken, and succeeded in winning the respect and confidence
of the Pueblo Indians. Furthermore, it is said that he served his nation
well and gave his life to the job in the West. Broken in health, he
died somewhere on the plains of Kansas, on the way back to Washington. According to Horn (1963), "He lies in an unmarked grave in
a pauper's plot in Kansas City."

In a report on November 20, 1849, Calhoun wrote that within two
days of the time he took office as Indian agent, certain Pueblo delegations came to him at Santa Fe to confer with him in reference to
their land titles and ownership, but the Pecos people were not named
as complainants until later.

Various representations have been made to me by the Pueblo Indians of
Mexican and Spanish encroachment upon their grants, and it may be many
of them will be difficult of adjustment. I do not hesitate to say that many of
the present possessors, deeming that lapse of time had perfected their titles,
are taunting the Indians with that fact.

Indian Agent John Greinger, in fact, wrote to Governor Calhoun on
March 25, 1852, reporting that, "annoyed beyond endurance by the
encroachment, the Pecos people, have removed to Jemez." Calhoun
also reported that the situation was acute, but no action was ever taken.

Nevertheless, this problem, along with that of other non-Indian land
grants, did finally lead to the establishment of the office of Surveyor
General of New Mexico, by act of July 22, 1854 (10 Stats. at L., 308).
Section 87 provided that the surveyor general should ascertain the
number, extent, and validity of all Spanish and Mexican grants and
report their origins, nature, character, and extent. While there was
much correspondence between the surveyor general and the Department of the Interior office in Washington, the main problems mentioned were the inadequate staff and the lack of money to carry out
the requirements of the act.

In 1855 the surveyor general made an examination of the title to
the Pecos Pueblo Grant, and approved it in his report recommending
confirmation:

PECOS 155

The Pueblo Indians are constantly encroached upon by Mexican citizens, and in many instances the Indians are despoiled of their best lands; I therefore respectfully recommend that these claims be confirmed by Congress as speedily as possible, and that an appropriation be made to survey their lands, in order that their boundaries may be permanently fixed.

Consequently Congress confirmed the grant by act of December 22, 1858; a patent was then issued to Pecos Pueblo on November 1, 1864, even though the remnants were living at Jemez Pueblo. However, throughout the period that New Mexico was a territory of the United States, territorial courts held that the Pueblo Indians were "citizens" and could dispose of their land, although they could not vote. Congress had passed a Non-intercourse Act in 1834, providing that settlers could not enter or settle on Indian land, and by an 1851 act this protective measure was extended to the "Indian tribes" of New Mexico—but that only meant the Apaches, the Navajos, and the Utes. The territorial courts continued to hold that these laws applied to Indians who were wards of the government, not to Indians who were "citizens."[3]

In the files of the Southern Pueblos Agency there is a request by Pecos Pueblo to the Indian agent in Santa Fe, dated 1859, that their lands be restored to them, that they be sold or leased for their account, or that additional land be purchased for them in the Jemez area. It is obvious, therefore, that there was never any intentional abandonment of their rights by the few surviving Pecos Indians; it was the unbearable Mexican harassment, coupled with government disregard of their desperate situation, that caused them to move to Jemez. Later records also show that similar requests, even before they actually signed a power of attorney and a deed of conveyance to one John Ward in 1868, were presented to the local alcalde and officials in Santa Fe.

On August 24, 1868, eleven survivors executed their power of attorney to Ward.[4] He had been an Indian Agent in Santa Fe, and while he was reputed to be a drunkard, the survivors relied on his friendship and integrity in acting on their behalf—representing them legally and defending their rights and interests to obtain some relief in connection with their land, confirmed by the United States Congress on December 22, 1858, and secured by patent on November 1, 1864. The reason for this action is clear, for a report at the time concluded that "the many hardships which they now suffer make them urge of their said attorney that he do all possible to help them in their cause."

At the same time they executed the power of attorney, the eleven survivors executed a deed of conveyance, by which for $10 they conveyed to Ward one-fourth of their grant, namely, the northern quarter, that part already encroached upon by the residents of San Antonio de Pecos. Both the power of attorney and the deed were recorded on September 22, 1868, in Deed Record 5 (pp. 21 and 24), Santa Ana County (later San Miguel County), New Mexico. The signatures that can be read are those of Jose Miguel Vigil, Francisco Kota, Jose Kota, Simona Toribio Toya Madalena, Maria Encarnacion Armenta, Juan Antonio Toya, Agustin Kota, Reyes Chama, and Juana Vigil. Francisco Kota was listed twice; it is unclear whether there was a younger Francisco. The eleventh name is lost to history.

By 1872 Ward had found a buyer in the Las Vegas merchant and speculator, Frank Chapman. Thus on April 12, 1872, the Pecos people signed a new deed, in which many more people joined (including minors); this deed states the area of the grant as 18,763.33 acres, to be sold for a fee of $4,000. The deed was executed by the following people:

Juan Antonio Toya and wife, Juana Maria;
Jose Miguel Vigil and wife, Rosita Chama;
Francisco Kota and wife, Lupe Chama;
Jose Kota and wife, Rosalia Machuela;
Antonio Kota and wife, Encarnacion Jetoma;
Agustin Kota and wife, Juana Maria Yepa;
Simona Toribio and husband, Juan de Jesus Ma[g]dalena;
Maria Encarnacion Armenta;
Reyes Chama and husband, Jose Reyes Gallina;
Maria Andreita Kota and husband, Jose Armijo;
Jose San Juan Toya and wife, Rita Toledo;
Lupe Toya and husband, Juan Isidro Sabaquie;[5]
Lupe Kota and husband, Jose Antonio Paulin;
Juan Pedro Vigil and wife, Maria A. Rita;
Rosa Toya and husband, Juan de Jesus;
Reyes Aragon and husband, Santiago Juan Ignacio.

This deed was recorded on March 17, 1873, Deed Record 7 (p. 146), by the Santa Ana County probate clerk.

On March 10, 1873, John Ward and his wife deeded all their interest in the Pecos Grant to Frank Chapman, for $1,300 (a profit of $1,290). In February of 1879, Chapman entered into a partnership with Andres Dold to operate the Pecos Grant; they were already involved in the mercantile wholesale and retail business in Las Vegas. When Chapman died in 1880, his heirs and the administrator of his estate, Marcus Brunswick, sold Chapman's interest to Dold. On July 6, 1881, Dold conveyed the entire grant to J. Whittaker Wright; it was then sold to George D. Roberts on March 31, 1883. Roberts in turn sold it to James M. Seymour on June 3, 1884. On January 20, 1887, Seymour brought suit to quiet (that is, secure) title against all unknown owners, including the Pecos Indians. This had to be done because of the many Mexicans who had moved in earlier and who were squatting in many sections of the land. A decree in favor of Seymour was entered in this case, but on December 19, 1887, it was set aside and declared null and void.

On May 6, 1889, Seymour and his wife conveyed their interest to James W. Fox by quitclaim deed. On May 7, Fox and his wife conveyed the holdings to the Flushing Bank, of Flushing, New York. However, on July 21, 1889, Lorenzo Lopez, sheriff of San Miguel County, entered a suit in Territorial Court against the Pecos Grant for non-payment of taxes. As a result of this action, on July 25, 1889, James L. Bridge bid for and won the grant by paying the $253.56 in taxes due. The legality of the sheriff's action was later questioned, since the grant was Indian land; but the tax sale established a second line of ownership.

On December 17, 1889, Bridge sold to W.M. Mahin, by quitclaim deed, a one-fourth interest in the land. Mahin, on the same day, by special warranty deed, sold an undivided one-eighth interest in the grant to J. A. Bell and another undivided one-eighth interest to F. W. Blair. On June 17, 1895, Blair and his wife, by quitclaim deed, sold their undivided one-eighth interest in the land to John L. Laub. On January 14, 1895, Bridge and his wife, by quitclaim deed, conveyed another undivided one-fourth interest in the entire tract to Frank L. Keeler. On March 2, 1896, Keeler and his wife, by quitclaim deed, conveyed their one-fourth interest in the grant to John L. Laub.

Meanwhile, following the original line of ownership, on December 14, 1895, the Flushing Bank, by quitclaim deed, conveyed the entire grant to Mattie G. Smith. On December 26, 1895, Mattie Smith and her husband conveyed their interest in the tract to John L. Laub, who now definitely appeared to have majority ownership of the Pecos Grant.

In the meantime, a third line of title, based on a Mexican grant of 1825 and subsequent transactions, developed among the settlers who occupied the more favorable areas of the grant. Records make reference to a proceeding in 1841–42, before the Mexican governor, Armijo, seeking a ruling of abandonment of the pueblo by the Pecos Indians, following their departure to Jemez Pueblo. There is no record of his approval, but even if he gave it, it would not have been in accord with existing Mexican laws of the time; otherwise, it would hardly have been reasonable that Congress should confirm the grant and authorize the issue of a patent to the Pecos people.

Nonetheless, on February 25, 1896, Balentin Flores and nine other Mexican settlers filed a petition for incorporation in San Miguel County District Court, stating that they and others named were inhabitants, owners, and proprietors of the Pecos Grant. The attempt failed since, in the election ordered by the court, the majority of the fifty-six persons listed in the petition voted against incorporation.

On October 30, 1897, John Laub and his wife, by quitclaim deed conveyed their entire interest in the grant to H. W. Kelly. In 1911 Kelly and his wife, Ellis T. Kelly, sold out to Gross, Kelly and Company, of which Kelly was a partner; the company had used the land, probably for grazing cattle, since its incorporation in 1908.

On June 5, 1914, Gross, Kelly and Company filed suit in the 4th Judicial District (Case Number 7631), to quiet (secure) title to the Pecos Grant. The final decree was filed on October 9, 1915, and the plaintiffs were declared owners in fee simple, with eleven exceptions listed. The exceptions were the New Mexico Archeological Society (the area of the pueblo ruins, twenty acres), the Atchison, Topeka and Santa Fe Railway (a right-of-way), eight individuals, and The Valle Ranch, a corporation. The latter land represented an overlap of the "Alexander Valle Grant" on the Pecos Indian Grant, so the corporation was awarded forty acres. The Pueblo Lands Board also recognized this claim (in the 1920s, described as Private Claim Number 184), which the board awarded to the Forked Lightning Ranch, lately operated by Mr. and Mrs. Fogelson; the latter is also known as Greer Garson.

Prior to the sale of their share of the Pecos Grant, H. W. Kelly, his wife, and the company in 1920 deeded an eighty-acre tract, including the mission church and the pueblo ruins, to Roman Catholic Archbishop Albert T. Daeger, who was the pastor of Jemez two years before. It was stipulated in the deed that in turn the archbishop would deed the historic area to the Board of Regents of the Museum of New Mexico and the Board of Managers of the School of American Research, in Santa Fe.

Following the above transaction, on May 15, 1920, Gross, Kelly and Company sold the entire tract to which it had quieted title to the Western Investment Company, of San Diego, California. From then on there were further conveyances to various parties.

On April 25, 1921, three descendants of Pecos, Pablo Toya, Jose
Antonio Pecos, and Jose Romero, wrote to Southern Pueblos Superintendent Leo Crane, asking him to inquire from the commissioner
of Indian affairs as to the possibility of reacquiring their lost land. Mr.
Crane then wrote a long history of the Pecos people and their land to
the Indian commissioner. On November 5, 1922, when representatives
of all the pueblos gathered at Santo Domingo to go on record officially
as an All Indian Pueblo Council, two second-generation Pecos members of the Jemez delegation signed the document representing Pecos
Pueblo; the two were Jose Romero and Pablo Toya. The document
was an appeal to the people of the United States in the Pueblo Indian
nation's fight against the proposed Holm Bursum Bill of 1922. This
was probably the last official act by Pecos descendants until eleven
years later, when they signed a joint Jemez and Pecos tribal resolution
of December 21, 1933, asking for consolidation of the pueblos.

This was the vastly complicated situation that faced the Pueblo Lands
Board when it considered the Pueblo of Pecos in the late 1920s. After
studying all the transactions, the board concluded that it did not seem
reasonable that the Pecos Indians had any interest remaining in the
land that could be recovered in a court proceeding. In a report to the
board, its chairman, Louis H. Warner, wrote:

This seems to be a case where if the very early recommendations of the Indian
officials, as for instance Calhoun, who was sent out here to look into the
situation, had been followed, that this grant would definitely have been
recovered to the Pueblo and held in their interest. Such suggestion was not
followed although he recommended that a board similar to ours be created
because of the various encroachments on pueblo areas which then existed.

In view of the action of Congress in confirming this grant, at least by
implication if not actually, to the few remaining [Pecos] Indians who then
were residing at Jemez, the Government undertook to assume a position that
it did not seem to protect insofar as the Indians were concerned. It would
seem, therefore, that there was a liability there for their neglect so to do and
that liability should be the basis for an award.

The Pueblo Lands Board, among other things, recommended that
if possible suitable lands be purchased near Jemez, and that such lands
be assigned for the specific use of Pecos descendants living in the
Pueblo of Jemez; or if such lands could not be segregated for the
specific use of Pecos descendants, that they be added to those of Jemez
Pueblo generally. The board was informed that according to church

records there were then about two hundred and fifty people at Jemez
with Pecos blood, and that it would be difficult to divide lands between
Indians of the two backgrounds. Most of the land surrounding Jemez,
however, was already claimed by non-Indians. In 1930 Lem Towers,
superintendent of the Southern Pueblos Agency, discussed with the
owners of the San Diego Grant the possibility of purchasing the grazing
land in that grant. The owners stated their willingness to consider any
proposition that the government might offer, but apparently their main
idea was to turn over the grazing lands in the San Diego Grant to the
Forest Service, in exchange for additional timber in the Santa Fe
National Forest. The owners of the grant also asked more for the land
than Congress had authorized to be expended.

In its report of August 4, 1930, the Pueblo Lands Board determined
that the numerous adverse claims to Pecos lands had legally and utterly
extinguished all Indian title to the entire Pecos Pueblo Grant in accordance with the provisions of the Pueblo Lands Act of June 7, 1924.
None of the 18,814.559 acres was recoverable (the survey and patent
had indicated 18,763.73 acres as the total area).

The board recommended instead the payment of $1.50 per acre,
based upon "approximate average value from the occupancy of this
territory in 1846 to the present time," which amounted to an award
of $28,145. The money was appropriated by Congress by act of Feb-
ruary 14, 1931 (46 Stat. L. 1122). The Pecos descendants later spread
rumors that it would be divided among them, but the only concrete
result was that a roll of all 305 Pecos descendants was made by Jesus
M. Baca in 1933.

On December 21, 1933, resolutions were passed by the Pecos Pueblo
heirs and by the officials of Jemez Pueblo, requesting that Pecos and
Jemez Pueblos be consolidated into one pueblo, to be known as Jemez
Pueblo. Signing for Jemez was San Juanito Loretto, governor, Juan
E. Sando, lieutenant, and Ferdinando Baca, secretary. Signing for Pecos
was Juan Luis Pecos, governor, Benito Toya, lieutenant, and Jesus M.
Baca, secretary. Both resolutions specified that money awarded by the
Pueblo Lands Board must be spent for the purchase of land and water
rights of benefit to the entire tribe, or for permanent improvements
on lands already held by the tribe. A bill to this effect was introduced
in Congress by Senator Dennis Chavez and it was approved in 1936.

Following the 1936 act, the sum of $28,145, together with a payment
of $2,385 for Jemez land held by non-Indians, was transferred to the
Jemez Pueblo trust fund account in Washington, D.C., in 1937; of

course, 10 percent of the total amount was immediately paid as attorneys' fee (Towers to Governor Jose Fragua, 1935). Land was later purchased for the pueblo with some of the compensation funds, such as the west half of the Cañada de Cochiti Grant, and other small parcels near the northern boundary of the Jemez Grant.

Thus, after all these years, the Pecos descendants, by the acts of their ancestors, court actions, and decision of the Pueblo Lands Board, have apparently lost all possible recovery rights to their original homeland. By their consolidation with Jemez Pueblo, the Pecos as a pueblo joined the legends of Quivira, El Dorado, and the Seven Cities of Cibola.

Today, the historic eighty-acre tract deeded by the Kellys in 1920 (including the ruins of the pueblo itself) has been enlarged several times over by the donation of portions of the Fogelsons' Forked Lightning Ranch. In 1935 the land was declared a New Mexico State Monument; in 1965 it became a national monument.

10

Education

In 1744, after the Treaty of Lancaster in Pennsylvania, between the government of Virginia and the Six Nations of the Iroquois, the Virginia commissioners offered to educate six of the chiefs' sons at a college in Williamsburg, Virginia. The chiefs replied as follows (Benjamin Franklin, *Two Tracts*, . . ., 2nd ed., 1794, pp. 28–29):

Several of our young people were formerly brought up at the colleges of the Northern Provinces; they were instructed in all your science; but when they came back to us they were bad runners; ignorant of every means of living in the woods; unable to bear either cold or hunger; knew neither how to build a cabin, take a deer, or kill an enemy; spoke our language imperfectly; were therefore neither fit for hunters, warriors, or counselors; they were totally good for nothing. We are, however, not the less obliged by your kind offer, though we decline accepting it: And to show our greatful sense of it, if the gentlemen of Virginia will send us a dozen of their sons, we will take great care of their education, instruct them in all we know, and make men of them.

A similar educational philosophy was expressed by a number of older Pueblo people as late as World War II, but the war made it possible for a few veterans to go on to higher education. Many others saw the importance of higher education for their children in a rapidly changing world, and have encouraged them to go on. Thus, while the government began with forced education to "civilize the savage" and save the soul, Indians now feel that the education of Indian children should be under the control of Indian people. Services and courses being offered should benefit from direction provided by Indians, and should meet the needs of Indian people—that is, strengthen their identity by providing a more positive and meaningful image of themselves, and ultimately allow them to participate in the larger society, while maintaining their dignity and individuality as members of a great race identified as American Indians (see Appendixes V and VI).

As it is today, many Indian childen are lost even during the first twelve years of their education, due to what Dr. John Aragon, president of New Mexico Highlands University, describes in workshops as "the devastating success of the American education system in confusing the children of the subcultures." Indian children and others are bewildered by the contrasting lifestyles and values of the dominant society, and by pressure from educators to emulate that society; this confusion leads to a rejection of their culture and heritage. Fortunately, upon reaching adulthood many Indians, after having compared the values of their heritage with the values of the dominant society, return to their culture. This stage is reached, according to Aragon, after a "pseudo" reacceptance of their culture, followed by a fourth stage, multiculturalism. In this stage the individual understands both the Indian culture and that of the dominant society.

Young Indian adults may often return to the culture of their heritage because of cultural insecurity in the dominant society. Edward Sapir describes cultural insecurity as one of "bewildered vacuity," the tragic confusion that results when one "has slipped out of the warm embrace of a culture into the cold air of fragmentary existence."

Fortunately, a great majority of Jemez students and young adults appear to be culturally secure; most participate in the social and ceremonial activities of the pueblo. Although there was initial suspicion that formally educated students would reject their heritage, this has not happened. Today there are many men and women who have had a formal higher education; a list of Jemez university graduates as of the date of writing can be found in Appendix II. This is not to say that the lives of young men and women who have chosen other alternatives are not as rewarding, either economically or otherwise.

   The first member of Jemez Pueblo to enroll at a university was Jose Rey Toledo. He entered the University of New Mexico in 1937, but dropped out after two years, because he could not afford the expense; there were no scholarships of any kind available at that time. The next person to enroll, and the first to graduate, was Stephania Toya (the daughter of Jack Toya); she graduated from Eastern New Mexico University at Portales, in the spring of 1948. In 1949 two more students graduated from ENMU: Mary Loretta Toya Dodge (Stephania's sister), and myself; Jose Rey Toledo had meanwhile enrolled again, and was graduated from the University of New Mexico in 1951. Once these four had become models, many more began to enroll in universities. A good start toward professional education was made in the summer of 1978, when two young Jemez men were graduated from the University of New Mexico Law School; they were T. Parker Sando (my son), and Allen Rey Toledo (the son of Jose Rey). Parker passed his bar examination soon after graduation, so he is Jemez Pueblo's first attorney.

   No doubt there are a few Jemez men and women who have married away and rarely return to Jemez, so that the educational achievements of their children may be unknown. A niece of Jose Rey Toledo, Juana Toledo Mangold, who lived in Jemez at a very early age and returns to visit from Pennsylvania, has a son who was a cadet at the Air Force Academy in Colorado Springs.

   The old problem of financing a university education is no longer insurmountable, as the All Indian Pueblo Council scholarship program assists scores of Pueblo Indian students in colleges throughout the country. For help in financing graduate and professional study there is American Indian Scholarship, Inc., located at Taos Pueblo, which serves Indian graduate students nationwide. The American Indian Law Program at the University of New Mexico allows Indian students to attend a summer introduction to the study of law as preparation for going on to law school. There are also a few other professional programs leading to medicine, school administration, and guidance and counseling.

   But problems do exist for Indian students in the nation's universities, problems that contribute to a high attrition rate among Indian students: poor study habits; lack of discipline to settle down and study; lack of experience in reading for enjoyment; the language problem (since traditionally Indian students have not read much, and have had little practice in speaking English in the public schools); lastly, there is the problem of cultural interference, including such things as going home to participate in dances during feast days, or attending a feast day at some other pueblo. Often it is difficult to return to class assignments after participating in a tribal dance the day before.

As students struggle through the first year, those who survive learn to take university life seriously. With their language handicap, Indian students may have to try harder and read texts a second and third time in order to comprehend the text. Because thinking in the English language, especially in the variety required in college, is not yet a part of the Indian gestalt, writing compositions comes harder at the beginning. After living entirely in the English-speaking world for a few years, however, students begin to actively use what their grammar and English teachers had tried to teach them a few years before. Examinations may also improve as students no longer have to translate their thoughts.

Management of finances can also be a problem. Most children in the Indian pueblos do not grow up with a weekly allowance. As freshmen, Indian students may often have more money in their pockets than they ever had before. Accountability then becomes a problem. Should I get a university T-shirt to wear home, or should the few extra dollars left after tuition, room and board, and books be saved for laundry, paper, and pencils? Many Indian students have succumbed to the temptations presented by suddenly having extra money.

The relatively high attrition rate of Indian university students is of concern, but a greater problem is that of students who drop out of high school. A dropout study was conducted by the New Mexico State Department of Education during the school year 1976–77, which grouped students in New Mexico as Anglo, Spanish, Indian, Black, and Oriental, in order of size of enrollment. Indian students, comprising the third largest enrollment, were also third in dropout rate; major concern was with the Spanish-speaking students, since they had the second highest enrollment, but were first in percentage of dropouts. The top-ranking reason for dropping out was nonattendance (44.1 percent), followed by lack of interest (8.0 percent), marriage (7.3 percent), employment (6.6 percent), and disciplinary difficulties (6.6 percent). Nine other reasons were also listed, mostly under 6 percent of the total. Of these, poor academic achievement may be a greater contributing factor for Indian students, due to language and reading problems, although statewide this particular problem was eighth, with 2.9 percent of the total.

Nonattendance is certainly an Indian problem, due to a number of factors. Lack of personal interest can be a problem, since historically the American education system has been a European-based system, teaching primarily the culture and history of non-Indians; Indian children get the impression that they are nonentities, described as "savages" in many textbooks as late as 1960 (Szasz 1974). The social sciences, especially history, could easily attract and arouse the interest of Indian children, but not when it is seen exclusively from the European-American viewpoint. This makes sense if the curriculum is being used to indoctrinate all students into the American way of life. It is not surprising that Indians, as well as members of other ethnic cultures, want a curriculum that will reflect the contributions made by all ethnic groups to human culture.

In the few years that educators have been aware of the minority students in the public schools who see the world through a different language and culture, they have found it difficult to respond effectively to the needs and demands of these students. For while these students may possess high levels of intelligence, they are mired down by a lack of identity with the curriculum fostered by years of neglect and indifference and, often, racial prejudice as well.

These students differ from middle-class children mainly in their ability to take advantage of the typical American school curriculum, which is cognitively oriented and attuned to a middle-class background. The values, concepts, and processes of middle-class life may well be foreign to the Indian student's environment and everyday experiences. Until very recently little has been published that would relate to the Indian students. Very few American Indian heroes have been recognized, but popular literature abounds with non-Indian figures, characterized in the classroom as heroes and statesmen. Indian students often want to know which president was responsible for the loss of Indian lands, or which legislator was responsible for pieces of anti-Indian legislation. Now, however, non-Indian students are also interested in the history and viewpoints of Indians in many fields.

Marriage as a reason for dropping out is not so much an Indian problem; a related problem probably contributes more—pregnancy of Indian girls. Statewide, pregnancy came in eleventh, accounting for only 2.4 percent of the total. Employment as a reason for dropping out is hardly an Indian problem, as even adults have a high unemployment rate in the pueblos. Disciplinary difficulties could be a symptom of lack of academic achievement, lack of interest, and nonattendance.

Lack of academic achievement can be very frustrating to non-Eng-

lish speakers. Pueblo Indian children who attend local day schools
compete with local peers who also speak the native language. While
some may be influenced at home by the educational background of
their parents and do better, achievement is really not an elusive phe-
nomenon until they reach high school and beyond. In high school
Indian children begin to compete with peers who have spoken only
English from their first words. When these children begin school they
have a strong English speaking vocabulary, and an even larger listening
vocabulary. With this experience of listening, speaking, reacting, eval-
uating, and making judgments in the English language, the English
speaker enters school. As this student remains in school, progress along
the national norm is maintained more easily and the vocabulary also
increases.

For the Indian child, the home language is totally different. It is
not a European-based language like Spanish or the Black dialect of
English. English is heard only for about six hours a day, if that much.
There is little reinforcement outside of television when they return
home, where the native language is spoken. Vocabularies do not increase if the words learned are not practiced and reinforced and reinforced again; so Indian children often have limited vocabularies.

With these different backgrounds the students are all supposed to
compete equally in the classroom. The teacher has been taught to
grade according to test results, verbal responses, and degree of participation. Unfamiliar with the vocabulary and aware of defective artic-
ulation due to faulty learning from poor models of speech, the Indian
student will more than likely be shy and not volunteer responses. Indian
children do, however, perform normally in spelling, rote memory
work, physical education, music, and art, in which they often excel.
But after a few years of poor grades and poor achievement, Indian
students drop out or may even be pushed out of high school.

One broad objective of education is to help people function con-
structively as citizens within their society. If this is a goal, then the
schools have failed the students who are different in language and
culture. Why has our education system not reached these students?
Because education is irrelevant. Why is education irrelevant? Because
these students have usually learned English words from texts that describe or discuss events that are foreign to them and their culture.

As one of the numerous federal study and research reports states,
"after over 100 years of federal civilizing policy . . . only a handful
of teachers and administrators speak any of the Indian languages."

Some Indian languages are taught in the universities, such as Dakota or Navajo, but Pueblo leaders do not want their languages taught to non-Indians, so that non-Indians will not be able to listen and probe into our religion. And even where language itself is not a barrier, very few teachers fully understand, let alone share, the values of their Indian students, nor accept their religious commitments.

As a general rule the American education system is designed to instill dominant-society values, such as competitiveness and even self-aggrandizement, in students. These values are alien to most American Indian cultures. Some of the main value differences and comparisons are listed in Appendix V.

Education at Jemez

Jemez has had a long involvement with non-Indian forms of education. The very first school was purportedly run by the second missionary to the Jemez people, Fray Gerónimo de Zarate-Salmerón, who came to Jemez in 1618. After building the church and a convent at Guisewa, he established a school there. Having learned the Towa language himself, he composed a catechism in that language, which he used to teach the people to read and write; he also taught them to sing, and to play the organ, the violin, and the guitar. We must not think that those first classes were anything like our present schools. Supplies were brought from Spain, thousands of miles distant; it took months to cross the ocean, and after unloading the ship in Mexico, it took another thousand miles and several months to deliver them by oxcart to the province. For writing material, the padre would cover a wooden frame with sheepskin, let it dry, and afterwards rule the parchment with a leaden bullet, sharpened to a point. Ink was made from pulverized charcoal diluted with water, and the inkstand from deer antler or cow horn. Turkey, crow, and eagle quills were used for pens.[1] It is very likely that succeeding missionaries continued this basic instruction.

A report on American education at Jemez Pueblo in 1871 was made by the Indian agent at the time, Ben M. Thomas. In his annual report he stated that "this village contains 344 inhabitants, of which only four persons can read and write; 138 are children. . . . These Indians desire a school, and I have employed Jose Ma. Garcia, at $40 a month to teach the children."

In 1877, after the devastating smallpox epidemic of 1876, two Pres-

byterian missionaries, Henry Kendall and Sheldon Jackson, conferred
with the trader in the Jemez Valley, John W. Miller, about the situation
at Jemez before deciding on locating a mission there. The following
year, on February 18, 1878, John M. Shields, a medical doctor and
an elder in the Presbyterian Church of Mount Pleasant, Cavode, Pennsylvania arrived. After a two-day wagon ride from Santa Fe, coming
over the mountains via Pena Blanca, the Shields family settled at
Jemez.

The first session of the mission school began on March 18, 1878,
with fourteen scholars, in rented rooms in one of the old buildings at
the pueblo, and stayed in session until August 1 of that year. A Sunday
school was also organized during this time.

A meeting with the Presbytery of Santa Fe followed; a committee
was appointed to visit Jemez and organize a church, if a way could
be found to do so. Following this meeting Reverend Jackson and Dr.
Shields met with Jemez officials on September 28, 1878; both the
governor's civil council and the cacique's religious council were present. The federal government was represented by Agent Thomas (see
Appendix III). The acquisition of land for the mission was discussed
and an area was granted—"devoted to school purposes for the benefit
of Jemez Pueblo so long as the parties building the house shall maintain
a school upon said premises for the benefit of said Pueblo"(*Jemez
Mountain Views*, 1976). The land, defined as a loan for as long as it
should be needed for mission purposes, was seventy-five yards square,
and located in the northeast part of the village plaza.

Reverend Jackson then made arrangements for the erection of a
mission building; the doors and window frames were shipped from
Denver. By October 12, 1878, the walls of the building were up, and
it was completed on December 7.

The following year two additional mission teachers arrived at Jemez
from Pennsylvania: Lora B. Shields, of Bennet, Pennsylvania (the niece
of Dr. Shields), and Belle R. Leech, of New Lebanon, Pennsylvania.
During the Pueblo Lands Board hearings in the 1920s, it was revealed
that the Presbyterian Board of Home Missions operated the school
continuously from 1887 to 1893. During those years it was also supported by the Federal Government. No reports are available of classes
from 1893 to 1897. Various individuals testified that a minister was
present but no teacher served the school.

One of the former teachers, Mrs. Mary L. Miller, testified that after
six years at Jemez Pueblo she married the local trader, Mr. Miller, in

1894, and they moved to Jemez Springs, where she spent another twenty-seven years.

There was a constant struggle for enrollment, however, since the Catholic Jemez did not want to send their children to a Protestant school. It is interesting to note that the school gave out blankets and clothing, as part of the mission. In 1897 the school buildings were rented by the Federal Government and Miss Emma Dawson began to teach in the government school. She had arrived at Jemez Pueblo in 1896. In 1909 the government school merged with the Catholic Mission school, and moved to the buildings owned by the Church, located in front of the Pueblo church, and Miss Dawson retired.

The impetus for the Presbyterian invasion came from a congressional act of 1870, which made army officers ineligible for service as Indian superintendents. Consequently, President U.S. Grant called upon the churches of the country to nominate members of their organizations as agents. Tribes under federal administration were thus placed under the management of churchmen nominated and endorsed by the Protestant churches. Presbyterians were assigned nine agencies in Arizona, New Mexico, and Utah. Thus, following Grant's Peace Policy, Presbyterians became interested in Jemez (Indian Agent's Report from Santa Fe, dated October 10, 1872). The Joseph Case of 1876 was still six years away, so the Pueblo Indians were being considered under the terms "Indian" and "Indian country."

It is very likely that the establishment of this mission school is the reason Jemez people were not recruited to attend the famous Carlisle Indian School in Pennsylvania, which opened in the fall of 1879. Carlisle was the first Indian boarding school established by the federal government, and was under the direction of Captain Richard H. Pratt, of the Tenth Cavalry, U.S. Army. Opening with 147 students, two years later the school boasted an enrollment of 196 students, 57 of whom were girls; many of the students were the children of chiefs or headmen.

In 1882, in tribal areas throughout the country, vacant army posts and barracks were authorized by Congress to be used for establishing a system of normal (i.e., teacher) and industrial training schools for Indian youth from nomadic tribes which had educational treaty claims upon the United States.

This does not imply that American Indians began the white man's education only at this time, however, since the first Indian school in the New World was founded in 1568 in Havana, Cuba. And as early as 1791, the Seneca Nation of New York requested from President George Washington that teachers be sent to their land to teach tribal Senecas the white man's system of education.

In 1819 the Choctaw Nation of the Southeast began its own schools for tribal members in their communities (Foreman 1934). They were so successful that many future tribal leaders were sent to "Ivy League" schools to receive a higher education. Unfortunately, the removal process of the 1830s, known by the Choctaw as the "Trail of Death," interrupted their education system; it never regained its former level. By 1841 the Cherokee Nation in Oklahoma had established a school, supported by the interest on its school fund—money paid to the Cherokees by the federal government as part of the removal. This school, although very successful, was closed by the Civil War.

In 1891 Indian education experienced a great positive change: the president of the United States declared that all teachers appointed to Indian schools from that time should pass an examination and be certified by the Civil Service Commission. As the army cooks and ex-privates who had been teaching left, the Indians began to notice the difference in the quality of teaching in many schools, and even began to attend classes voluntarily and to stay for the entire school year; previously students had stayed for no more than six months.

In 1896 Congress passed further legislation, making it unlawful to spend public moneys to support sectarian schools. The Protestant churches, therefore, released their schools to the federal government after passage of this act, and in many cases sold their equipment and buildings to the government. As early as 1883, however, the Indian agent at the time, Pedro Sanchez, reported that the school at Jemez was supported partly by the government and partly by the Presbyterian Board of Home Missions.

With the passage of the nonsupport legislation in 1896, the mission school at Jemez was abandoned and the federal government rented the misson buildings to use as a school, until 1909. Miss Emma Dawson was the first government teacher, and remained for the next thirteen years. For years the old people said that their teacher had been "Me Dasa" or "Misa Mila." Their English names remained unknown until a chance discussion with the late Guadalupe Fragua, a veteran of World War I, revealed that the two teachers were "Miss Dawson" and "Mrs. Miller." The latter taught at Jemez for thirty years, as her husband was a trader in the Jemez Valley.

Upon the retirement of Miss Dawson in 1909, two Catholic nuns came to Jemez, employed by the federal government; their classrooms were in rooms adjoining the village church, which later became the San Diego Mission School. The first two nuns who came to Jemez were Sister Mary M. Boyle and Sister Stephanie Schramme. Sister Stephanie became known as Sister Stephania, and later became a symbol for the Jemez people of cleanliness, high principles, and high standards of virtue. When I was a youngster, we would go to play in the ditches when water was let into them in the spring; our hands would become rough and even bleed. Anyone with clean hands would evoke the remark, "Gee, your hands are just like Sister Stephania's." She remained at Jemez for many years and taught three to four generations of Jemez families. She was finally retired, to the order's retirement home in Denver. One year Sister Stephania made a surprise visit at the same time as the Archbishop of Santa Fe came for his official call. It was a bad time for the archbishop, to say the least, as all the Jemez people were more interested in the sister. Two additional nuns who taught during that early period were Sister Matias and Sister Joseph; they were not paid by the government.

A report to the Indian Agency by the government farmer (extension agent), Louis R. McDonald, in 1925, shows that the Presbyterian Mission School had reopened that year to serve three students. He also reported that there were three members of the church, a Zuni man married to a Jemez woman, and their son. Previously the church had had five members, but since then the field matron, Ellen Lawrence, had moved to San Felipe Pueblo, and the farmer himself had moved to Zia Pueblo. However, he added that during church services there were sometimes as many as a dozen people present, since a few Indian children came out of idle curiosity.

The San Diego Mission School, on the other hand, has prospered; in 1979 there were 136 children from kindergarten through the eighth grade enrolled there, in 1980/81 the enrollment was 120, and in 1981/82 it was 118. The parochial school has been of immeasurable service to the Jemez people and the neighboring Spanish communities. During the depression of the 1930s many Spanish students were brought to Jemez and boarded with a Spanish lady, Viviana Atencio, while they attended the mission school.

The federal school, known as the day school, opened new facilities in 1929, at the same time as similar facilities were opened in other pueblos. Although its enrollment has been smaller through the years, it is also increasing; in 1979/80 the enrollment was 125 from kindergarten through the sixth grade. In 1980 the school opened a new facility, which replaced a portable row of classrooms that were rushed in following a destructive fire in late 1972; the old building that burned was the original day school which began operating in 1929. In 1981/82, 177 students were enrolled.

Many Jemez students also attend St. Catherine's School in Santa Fe, usually after finishing the eighth grade at the San Diego Mission School. Others have gone to mission schools in Arizona, such as St. John and St. Michael. And in recent years the Albuquerque Indian School opened under the auspices of the All Indian Pueblo Council; the major part of the student body now attends the Santa Fe Indian School. A few Jemez students have attended AIS and the Santa Fe Indian School since that time. The Institute of American Indian Arts in Santa Fe has also been a popular place for Jemez students after they complete high school.

Since the creation of the Jemez Valley School District in 1957, Jemez students have attended the Jemez Valley Schools in increasing numbers each year. During the school year 1978/79 there were 33 in the elementary school, 62 in the middle school, and 148 in the high school, for a total of 243 students from Jemez Pueblo; for 1981/82 the figures were 16, 40, and 97, respectively.

Since the pueblo has a greater population than the other communities in the school district, Jemez people have been able to elect the school board members of their choice. Some of the residents from Jemez who have served on the board are Jack Toya, Antonio Sando, Mike Romero, Jose Rey Toledo, and Ciriaco Toya.

A point of interest is that in many school districts where Indian minorities are unable to elect an Indian school board member, the feeling appears to be that the school, its curriculum, facilities, and daily attendance would improve if an Indian were on the board. This has not happened and does not happen. The American school system is a gigantic institution and changes slowly, like any large bureaucracy. Regardless of the ethnic composition of the school board, the curriculum and other traditional aspects remain bound to middle-class Anglo values. Indian parents may, however, exert pressure through the various federal title programs to have special courses added that may be relevant to their children.

When a community makes a great change in schools, as Jemez did in changing from a BIA school to a public school, there naturally arise many arguments regarding the advantages and disadvantages of the change. But after all the dust has settled, what stands out for Jemez is the accessibility of the local school board and the state department of education in Santa Fe; previously, Indian people had had to deal with the huge bureaucracy of the Bureau of Indian Affairs, mainly in Washington, D.C.

Another advantage in dealing with a public school district is that it is less likely to become involved in tribal politics, since it is a subdivision of state government, totally independent of the tribe. Thus school board members can devote more attention to educational than political problems. Dealing with the state public school system has also given the people some assurance of continuing financial support. Under the BIA school of the past, the Indians generally suspected that educational funds were being detoured to other facets of the bureau's programs. Now, besides financial support from the state, federal government support has also provided financial assistance to the public school districts. Finally, public school graduates are more easily accepted in state universities than are graduates from bureau schools.

On the other hand, Indians have had fears that integration into the state educational system would constitute a threat to the special status that Indians have long enjoyed in their relationship with the federal government, and that most have wanted to retain. Still further, a "let sleeping dogs lie" attitude comes into play, due to fears that as Indians begin to draw upon services provided by the state government, the Indian people's rights to freedom from state regulation, taxation, and control will become vulnerable. Consequently, there has been an undercurrent of mistrust and suspicion between Indian people and state officials. State officials are unaccustomed to dealing with Indian people, and are suspected of being less appreciative of Indian culture, traditions, and values than are BIA personnel. This mistrust applies to all levels of state government; one branch is suspected of being interested in taking over the control of Indian water rights.

Prior to the Citizenship Act of 1924, responsibility for the education of Indian children rested with the federal government, since most Indians were not officially citizens of the United States and therefore did not possess the right to attend state-supported, public schools. Citizenship had, however, been conferred on some tribes through treaty and on others through the General Allotment Act of 1887.

Today the federal government has no legal obligation to provide educational services for Indian children. Congress has authorized the Bureau of Indian Affairs to provide educational services, and has regularly appropriated funds for that purpose, but no statute requires the continuation of educational programs. Thus the Bureau of Indian Affairs, which operates over two hundred schools for Indians, could presumably close them all at any time. Federal policy concerning this legal relationship was described by a representative of the BIA as follows:[2]

The Federal Government takes the position that legal responsibility for Indian education rests with the states. . . . When public schools are not accessible because of geographical isolation, non-taxable status of Indian lands, or for other reasons, the Federal Government recognizes its responsibility to continue to meet the educational needs of Indian children until such time as the states are able to assume full educational responsibility for all of their children.

After the act of 1924, however, public school systems did not accept large numbers of Indian students, until financial subsidies from the federal government became available through the Johnson-O'Malley Act of 1934. For many years, although with many deficiencies, the Johnson-O'Malley Act was the only federal education program in public schools that uniquely benefited Indians.

Later in the 1950s, two impact aid laws were passed, PL 81–815 and 81–874. For all practical purposes these laws providing federal assistance to state schools played an important role in facilitating the integration of Indians into the dominant society. They were enacted to assist public school districts that were burdened by the impact of federal installations, primarily military bases; but these statutes were later made applicable to districts with large Indian populations living on tax-exempt land, to compensate school systems for the loss of part of their tax base from this tax-free land.

Public Law 81–815, known as the School Facilities Construction Act, authorized grants for the construction of public schools attended by Indians. When the initial act was passed, it provided that a district had to have an enrollment increase in order to qualify for funds. School districts where Indian children were already enrolled did not qualify, since the problem in those districts was that many Indian children were not in public schools because there were no facilities for them, and the local districts could not afford to construct schools.

The law was amended in 1953 to include such districts; Section 14 of the act was expressly designed to finance the construction of facilities at schools attended by large numbers of Indians, where the immunity of Indian land from taxation would impair the ability of the public school districts to finance necessary construction. Funding under this act was generous in the 1950s and 1960s; New Mexico received at least $47 million. In the 1970s appropriations decreased dramatically, as appropriated funds have been earmarked for disaster relief or for other temporary federal activities.

Thus there was no new construction of school facilities in districts with large Indian enrollment. This is not to suggest failure or non-support of federal Indian policy; instead, the freeze on building construction appears primarily to be part of an overall attempt to combat inflation on a nationwide basis.

Public Law 81–874 provided public school districts with funds for general operating expenses. These funds are again appropriated in lieu of the taxes that local governments could collect if it were not for the presence of large tracts of nontaxable, federal property. According to a report by the U.S. Office of Education, in fiscal year 1972, appropriations under this law totaled $26,390,000, making it the single largest program of federal support for Indian education in public schools at that time (U.S. Office of Education 1971).

As usual, Indians were not originally included in P.L. 81–874, due to the fear of "dual funding." But in 1958 Congress decided to permit school districts to receive payments from both impact aid and the Johnson-O'Malley Act, under the rationale that impact aid would provide general operating funds, while J.O.M. would support special programs for Indians.

Title I of the Elementary and Secondary Education Act of 1965 (P.L. 89–10) is designed to provide aid for economically and educationally deprived Indian students. It was perhaps the first federal aid program that recognized that deprived children might need compensatory educational services in order to perform satisfactorily in school. This program provides financial assistance to local school districts for supplemental educational services to qualified students. Natually there are those observers who have said that this program provides benefits to one category of children and denies them to others. But discriminatory as the program may be, in favoring the poor and undereducated, it does enable these students to reach the same levels of educational attainment as their middle-class peers.

Title IV of the Indian Education Act (Public Law 92–318) was signed by President Richard M. Nixon on June 23, 1972, in recognition of the special problems and unique educational needs of Indians as revealed by numerous national surveys. This act opened the way for public school districts to develop a positive relationship with Indian communities, which was something new in the lives of American Indians. Historically, Indians have been shut out of planning programs, developing budgets, and sharing in the decision-making process, which is so common and taken for granted in the non-Indian communities; the BIA has been responsible for most of this. P.L. 92–318 authorized funding for a series of new education programs for Indian children and adults; some of them may be supplemental to the regular school program, designed to meet the special education needs of Indian children—others may be innovative and experimental.

An outstanding feature of this program is that it stresses Indian parental and community involvement in writing funding proposals for planned activity. While this provision does not guarantee responsiveness to parental and community wishes, it at least makes applicants more aware of the philosophy of the projects, and they are thus more likely to adhere to the regulations of the act.

Title IV was amended in 1974; new programs were added to existing provisions, under five parts. For instance, Part A amends P.L. 81–874 (impact aid), and gives further clarification and assistance.

Part B provides for special programs and projects to improve educational opportunities for Indian children; it amends P.L. 89–10. Part C provides for special programs relating to adult education for Indians. Part D establishes the Office of Indian Education, its staff, and a fifteen-member National Advisory Council on Indian Education. Part E allows for miscellaneous provisions, including the provision of funds for the training of personnel to teach in BIA-operated or supported schools.

Title VII, the Bilingual Education Act, has been very helpful in the education of children whose dominant language is other than English. This act was passed to provide equal educational opportunity for all children, as well as to encourage the establishment and operation of educational programs using bilingual educational practices, techniques, and methods, and to demonstrate effective ways of providing for children with limited English proficiency, so that the children, while using their native, or dominant, language, could achieve competence in the English language.

This kind of program is suitable where only one non-English language is involved, such as at the San Diego Mission School and the federal day school. At a school such as the Jemez Valley Elementary

School, however, the difficulty is that the children also speak Keresan (Zia) and Spanish, besides Towa (Jemez). To make the program effective in this kind of situation, there would have to be a multilingual teacher, or a monolingual teacher with three bilingual aides, each speaking one of the three languages of the children.

The Head Start Program made possible more actual experiences in dealing with school programs; parents realized that the education of their children was also their responsibility. Parents also began to take an active part in the planning and operation of the Head Start class, and gradually moved to the other schools under the Title IV and VII programs. During this time the importance of education became increasingly apparent to more parents who were eager to help their children escape poverty by learning a skill or profession. Overall, the encouragement, understanding, and assistance of the parents have been an invaluable contribution to their children's educational success.

The formerly distrusted and even hated "white man's school" has become the last chance for the salvation of the Pueblo Indian people and their culture. Through the years we have been aware of who we were and why we were here; with this new insight we should also know where we are going and how we are going to get there: through education to learn the ways of the dominant society so as to be able to compete in the widest possible job market, while culturally remaining Pueblo Indians.

11

Track Town U.S.A.

"Track Town USA, Jemez Pueblo, New Mexico," reads the license plate proudly displayed on many vehicles driven by citizens of the pueblo—and rightly so. Jemez Pueblo has been a track town since it was founded in the seventeenth century. Jemez athletes in recent years have participated in every form of running spectacle—from the Boston Marathon, the La Luz Trail run (near Albuquerque), the Pikes Peak run (in Colorado Springs), to every marathon and little week-end community run in the southwest.

Before the advent of television, tales of running were a major form of entertainment during the long winter evenings. Grandfathers, fathers, and uncles used to tell their families exciting stories of the running which they had witnessed or in which they had taken part. Favorite topics were the victories and heroics of the outstanding runners of their day.

While there are many stories of individual exploits and family heroes, the classic tale concerns a chance meeting between two outstanding Hemish runners sometime around the end of the last century. This is the story of Paawhasaiyu of the Fragua family and Tyi-la ("sand"), also known as Pablo Gachupin.

Paawhasaiyu started out at dawn and proceeded north, toward Jemez Springs, twelve miles away. Running on dirt wagon trails, he passed through the tiny community while the inhabitants were still asleep. He continued on to Soda Dam, Battleship Rock, LaCueva, Deer Canyon, and finally to Valle Grande, on the north side of 11,254-foot-high Redondo Peak. From there he turned south toward Rabbit Mountain, then on to Ruiz Peak and Tres Cerros, and out along the east ridge of Paliza Canyon until he reached Hondo Canyon. He had traveled a total of approximately forty miles along wagon trails and over rugged, roadless terrain that morning. From Hondo Canyon it is only about twelve miles to the pueblo, as the crow flies, ending with a quick descent from the 8,000-foot-high ridge of Mesa Prieta, on the east side of the pueblo.

Tyila also started at dawn, but he went south, toward San Ysidro, past White Mesa (where a gypsum mine is today), and on to Eagle Butte or Eagle Peak, to a point about twelve miles from Jemez. From here he turned east, passing Zia Pueblo about a mile to the south and east, before turning north to cross Jemez Creek. Soon he was parallel with the south end of Mesa Prieta, the black range visible a few miles to the east of Jemez. He continued on past Borrego Dome and Loma Canovas.

All morning he had run on the sparsely wooded flat before crossing Jemez Creek. Now he began to run on sandy soil, sinking in at some places, until he approached the vicinity of Borrego Canyon, which rises gradually in elevation from Jemez Creek, east of Zia Pueblo. After a run of approximately thirty-five miles, Tyila arrived at Hondo Canyon, where he met Paawhasaiyu.

At this chance meeting they stopped to chat and agreed to race home over the ten to twelve miles of rugged, narrow burro trail. Jemez people in those years would climb to the top of Mesa Prieta to gather wood, tie it on both sides of a burro, and leave it to the sure-footed animal to carry the wood down the steep, narrow, boulder-strewn trail.

Tyila immediately took the lead, bounding gracefully as they started down Hondo Canyon and headed toward Borrego Canyon. As they came stumbling down the steep burro trail, each concentrated on maintaining his balance and keeping up a fast trot, hoping to conserve some energy for the sprint once they had descended to relatively flat land. Tyila was still leading, but this gave Paawhasaiyu a good chance to pace himself. He could also watch to see if Tyila was running relaxed, flat-footed, and on his heels, or if he was lifting his knees and landing on his toes. The well-conditioned runner runs on his toes, but may use his heels to relax or rest before the final effort.

As they approached within five miles of the pueblo they were springing like deer, their feet only lightly touching the ground. They raced along the Rio Chiquito, their effortless movement cutting through the still, early morning air. The village was but three miles away, over the hills. The creek at this point is contained by mesas on both sides within a valley about four hundred yards wide; they would have to climb the south mesa to approach the pueblo. The pace was quickening, and both were attempting to control their panting, in order to keep the effects of the killing pace to themselves. There was no more time to plan strategy; the crucial second had arrived. They crossed the Rio Chiquito and headed toward the short climb on the south side. Paawhasaiyu acted first—with his last remaining energy he sprinted past Tyila, just before the climb. Seeing this figure pass him, after he had led the way, seemed to break Tyila's concentration. In one last surge of effort, Paawhasaiyu raced up the hill and saw the village before him; he had won. Traditionally all Jemez runners drink water from a special *olla* (earthen jar) when they return home, and regurgitate it to cleanse their systems. Paawhasaiyu and Tyila followed this tradition loyally.

Tyila outlived his historic competitor by several years. During that time, as the story was retold countless numbers of times, some say that Tyila began to tell it as if the race had been a draw. Later, some said that he even won the race in his stories.

As teenagers, my peers and I were brought up under a similar system of training; a few still are today. We would be awakened at dawn, usually on Sunday mornings, and a destination was suggested, depending on age. Stronger runners traditionally ran to Bird Peak (Saeyu-shun), approximately nine miles to the northwest, in the Nacimiento Range. The going was mostly uphill on a well-worn wagon road for at least six miles, followed by three more miles of a hard-surfaced riding trail and running path, leading through a valley to the spring at the base of the peak. Customarily we would wash our faces at this spring, legendary for its cool freshness. Jemez men will often say, as they stop to rest from their work in the fields during the hot summer days, leaning on their hoe handles, "I wish I could drink the cool, fresh water at Bird Peak spring." The return home was mostly downhill, maybe a little quicker, and we would arrive just in time for breakfast with the family before Sunday mass.

Some of the runners best remembered today were active in the first decade of this century. One of them, Felipe Waquiu, Sr., died August 26, 1979, at the age of 89. Felipe was known well enough that he was invited by the University of New Mexico to run in exhibition race on an oval track against two Hopis. Felipe said that since he had never run on an oval, he did not know how to pace himself, and one of the Hopis beat him. He did not recall the year this event took place, but he said he was in his early twenties; that would put the year around 1909 or 1910. Louis Tewanima, a Hopi, was in his prime during these years; he participated in the Olympiads of 1908, in London, and 1912, in Stockholm. He was running for Carlisle Institute, the Indian school in Pennsylvania. He placed ninth and second, respectively, in the marathon in those years.

Felipe's chief competitor was Ciriaco Toya, who died at age 70, in 1959; these two men were the outstanding runners in the village between 1910 and 1917. Felipe was the five-time winner of the ceremonial long-distance races from the north and south of Jemez until Ciriaco beat him on his sixth try. In 1962, during the Fourth Annual Jemez All-Indian Track and Field Meet, Mr. Waquiu was honored as an outstanding Indian athlete. His children have also satisfactorily filled his "moccasins," as we shall see.

Two other runners who blossomed at the time Jemez people began to attend the Indian boarding schools at Albuquerque and Santa Fe were Maximilliano Shendo (10/12/1900–6/30/66) and Pilar Armijo (11/12/1903–3/16/51). These two became stars at the Indian schools, where many Indians from other pueblos knew them; even today old acquaintances occasionally ask if they are still alive. Upon returning to the pueblo, each was recognized as an outstanding runner; they competed against each other in winning the ceremonial long-distance races at different times.

A phenomenal athlete of the 1930s was Jose Tosa (died October 1981). Jose won ceremonial races for several years, but the most striking example of his greatness is the unbelievable feat of running down wild horses. He would run after the wild ponies through rugged, boulder-strewn canyons, as well as over flat plains, often thick with scrub oak, piñon, and pine trees. This was during the stock-reduction days of John Collier in the 1930s, so that it was entirely legal. Jose worked with his father and a brother, Abel, who was also a runner of note at the time. Sometimes they would build traps in deep canyons, into which Jose would chase the unsuspecting wild animals; his assistants would then spring from hiding to shut the gates. Jose said that they captured at least ten wild horses, which they sold to ready customers during the difficult days of the depression. Some of the places he ran mustangs down were the rugged east side of the Espíritu Santo Grant, the Ojo San Jose Grant, north of Jemez, and the wild Mesa Prieta, northeast of the village. Jose related that in some instances the mustangs would just stop dead in their tracks, unable to run another step, whereupon his dad would place a rope around their necks and drag them to a corral to mix with domesticated horses.

Following Jose Tosa was Cristino Waquiu (1913–3/26/65), who also won a few of the ceremonial long-distance races. He was followed by Felix Waquiu, the son of Felipe, Sr. Felix was at the apex of his running career when he was called into the armed forces, like many other American athletes at the beginning of World War II; before entering the army he had won several of the ceremonial races. Among his competitors was Pablo Fragua, who was also a great runner; sadly, he died in a Japanese prison camp in the Philippines during World War II. But for Felix, life continued long after his army "hitch"; he has many sons, who we shall discuss below.

Another athlete famous at Jemez was my father, Juanito Sando (11/13/1890–4/5/1973). Juanito was famous as a dashman, or speedster, for an unusual number of years. Besides participating in the races at Jemez, he also ran for many years in the feast-day races of the Jicarilla Apaches, held annually at Stone Lake, on September 15. There he would run on the side of his friends Lindo and Frank Vigil, Sr. Following the races he would be given presents of beadwork, tanned buckskin, or dried venison. Runners from San Juan and Taos Pueblos would also compete for their Apache friends. The Jicarillas are the only non-Pueblo tribe in the area whose culture has a moiety system similar to that of many Pueblo tribes. Instead of turquoise and pumpkin moieties, however, the Jicarillas have Olleros ("pottery makers") and Llaneros ("plains people") moieties. These have very likely developed as a result of influences from Taos and Picuris, from the time when the Jicarillas lived in the Cimarron area, east of Taos. Both Taos and Picuris also have similar foot races on their feast days of September 30 and August 10, respectively; the runners race back and forth, about three hundred yards each. Many runners take part, racing individually against an opposing runner. The race continues until one side is far enough ahead that the other side has no chance of overtaking their runner.

Juanito was always ready for a race. One year in the early 1930s, his friend, Coach Jim Jones of the Albuquerque Indian School, brought his champion 440-yard runner, Bernard Little, of Mescalero, New

Mexico, to Jemez to run against Juanito. They ran from a point just south of the day school, where the ground is very sandy so that it is difficult to get good footing. Being used to running on all kinds of ground other than prepared tracks, Juanito got a good start on his competitor and was able to beat the student champion. Even when he was nearing age 40, he was still very active and competitive. For this reason he was honored as an outstanding Indian athlete during the annual Jemez All-Indian Track and Field Meet in 1963, as his uncle had been the year before.

The next Jemez athlete of note is Lucas Toledo. He was never a winner at Jemez, but when he was over 65 years old, he was still challenging young men in the two-mile run during the annual Jemez track meets. He has been a winner away from Jemez, however, proudly representing the pueblo at marathons and mountain-climbing runs. He has participated twice in running to the top of 14,110-foot Pikes Peak in Colorado; in 1969, on his first attempt, he won first place in the over-65 category by beating the former champion from California. In his next attempt, the following year, he led his age group until he was beaten at the finish line by a few seconds. At age 75 he still runs, and is often seen participating in the grueling harvest dances and corn dance on feast days.

Another example of his love for running is his participation in the 1980 tricentennial commemorating the feat of the two Tesuque boys who in 1680 took the knotted strip of deerskin to the various pueblos, informing them of the beginning of the Pueblo Revolt against Spanish domination. The Pueblo people reenacted this event in August of 1980, and Lucas joined the young Jemez boys who brought the knotted message the thirty miles from Santa Ana to Jemez Pueblo. As a special honor, Lucas was appointed to bring the knotted message to the tribal leaders who were awaiting the runners at the center of the village. Lucas loves running and competition; consequently, Jemez will remember him.

During this tricentennial run, the Jemez runners met the other Pueblo runners at Santa Ana, as they arrived from the Tewa country, north of Santa Fe. Other runners proceeded to Sandia, Isleta, Laguna, Acoma, and finally to Zuni. But the Hopi and Jemez runners traveled westward from Santa Ana, making their first stop at Zia. There the Zia people awaited them at the plaza; women with water-filled ollas sprinkled water on the runners on this hot August afternoon. From Zia the runners continued on to Jemez, where hundreds of people awaited them; the original run was known only to a few religious leaders.

Jemez women donated food for the runners that evening. Early the next morning, before sunrise, the Hopi runners, accompanied by Jemez runners for the first ten to twenty miles, started out for their home, over a hundred miles to the west.

Jemez Runners After the War

After World War II many changes came in the societal and cultural structure of Jemez, including the creation of a new school district in the Jemez Valley, to accommodate the rapidly increasing population of Jemez and surrounding areas. Today young Jemez men and women excel in running for Jemez Valley High School, as well as in basketball and baseball. Every year Jemez young people run the 880, the one and two-mile runs, as well as cross-country, at the New Mexico state high school championships; their greatest competition has come from Acoma, Laguna, and Zuni Pueblo youngsters. A review of records indicates that I started off the parade of state high-school track championship participants, when I ran the mile as a fifteen-year old in 1939, representing the Santa Fe Indian School. The next two years I was able to qualify in both the 880 and mile run. Today a young Jemez man, Anthony Armijo, still holds the Class AA record for the mile, established in 1977 with a time of 4:22.4.

In 1965, Joe Cajero started coaching the Jemez Valley High School cross-country team, which won the state AAU championship for the three consecutive years from 1965 to 1967. In 1979 and 1980 they were again state champions in their division. In 1981 they came in third, but Victor Chinana of Jemez had the best time of anyone in all divisions. And on November 20, 1977, the Jemez boys won the national Indian cross-country championship in Stewart, Nevada.

Because of the several high schools Jemez students have a choice of attending, more boys and girls have had a chance to excel at their particular school (e.g., Jemez Valley, St. Catherine in Santa Fe, and the Albuquerque Indian School). With more athletes and much competition in recent years, different young men have tended to win the ceremonial races each year. Even so, a few athletes from this post-war group still stand out.

Steven Gachupin won the Jemez ceremonial races every year from 1963 to 1967. He began running for Jemez Valley High in his junior year, when he competed in the mile run, as he did during his senior year, also. The Jemez All-Indian Track and Field Meet was organized at the right time for Steven. From successes against local competition, he went on to numerous other challenges. When Jemez boys started competing outside the pueblo in 1965, Steven ran the six-mile race and placed third in the state AAU championship. This prompted him to enter a meet in Denver, Colorado, in June 1966, where he placed second against tougher competition. The following month he entered the Denver Marathon for the first time, and again placed second. In August he participated in the Pike's Peak Marathon, which he won; he subsequently won every year until 1972. His best performance was in 1968, when he set the record for ascent to the top in 2 hours, 14 minutes, 56 seconds. His best time for the round trip to the top and back to the starting point was 3 hours, 39 minutes, 47 seconds.

He also took part in the grueling La Luz Trail run, in Albuquerque, from 1966 to 1971, and won four years in a row, 1966 to 1969; his best time was 1 hour, 4 minutes. In 1967 he took part in the Boston Marathon and in the World Masters Marathon, in Las Vegas, Nevada. In 1967 and 1968 he was included in the Western Hemisphere Marathon in Culver City, California. He ran the Artesia, New Mexico, marathon from 1967 to 1969, and the Golden Gate Marathon, in San Francisco, in 1970. He also participated in the Alamosa, Colorado, marathon from 1966 to 1968; he placed second the first year, third the second year, and fifteenth during the Olympic trials in 1968. At this race he ran with Billy Mills, the Sioux Indian who later won the 10,000-meter run at the Tokyo Olympics. He has participated in the Albuquerque Marathon four times, the Portales Marathon twice, and is still looking forward to competing for a few more years. Steven's participation and victories in marathons alongside world-class athletes give one an idea of how well Jemez runners can hold their own against the stiffest competition.

Robert Eugene Waquiu, the oldest son of Felix, was a track star at both St. Catherine and Jemez Valley High; it almost seems that the two-mile run was created just for him. In 1964, when Robert was a freshman at St. Catherine, the New Mexico Activities Association added the two-mile run to its schedule of track and field events. Robert won the two-mile run in every meet he entered that year, including the Class AA state track meet. From 1965 to 1967 Robert was enrolled at Jemez Valley High; during this period he continued to win every two-mile run he entered, including the Class AA state track meets.

Robert probably has the distinction of being the only track man who won his event four years in a row at the state high-school championships.

During his Jemez Valley years Robert participated in other special meets with his team. He was on the team that won the New Mexico AAU cross-country championship in 1965, 1966, and 1967. He also competed in the Albuquerque Jaycee Indoor High School Meet, where he ran the mile and the 880. In 1968 he received a track scholarship to attend Artesia College, where he ran in that city's marathon. That year he also ran in and won the ten-mile "Run for the M" at Socorro. Robert was able to participate in the Jemez all-Indian meets only in 1965 and 1966, at which times he won the two-mile run. He also ran in relay events at the Jemez meets.

Harold Sando, the grandson of Juanito, also started as a high-school star at Jemez Valley, as well as in the Jemez meets. From there he became a "walk-on" All-American at Eastern New Mexico University, at Portales. After being on the Jemez state AAU cross-country championship team in 1966 and 1967, he also ran cross-country for the ENMU Greyhounds from 1969 to 1971. In 1969 Harold was honored with "All-American" status by virtue of his top performance in the cross-country championship of the National Association of Intercollegiate Athletes. His team placed second in 1969 and third in 1970. He was also on the Greyhound track team in 1970 and 1971, and placed fourth in the six-mile event during the NAIA championships. In 1969 Harold won the La Luz Trail run in Albuquerque, breaking the four-year winning streak of Steven Gachupin.

Following Harold as an outstanding performer is the current star of the running Waquius, Aloysius Waquie (this spelling was originally given by the newspapers, who also call him "king of the mountains"). Al is the second son of Felix. Beginning as a high-school star at Jemez Valley, he went on the Haskell Indian Junior College in Lawrence, Kansas, where he became a second-team Junior College All-American in 1971. As running has become more popular, there are now many week-end meets and other special runs. Al has not missed many of these locally, nor have there been many he has not won. At 5'5", this small athlete continues to amaze spectators as he appears to run at top speed even after a grueling, long-distance race. People have been heard to remark that it seems inhuman to maintain such a fast pace mile after mile. A bachelor, Al spends many hours training, reviewing invitations to meets, and reading publications for runners. He is employed by the U.S. Forest Service in the Jemez Mountains, a few miles from his home.

On August 20, 1978, Al startled the running world when he ran the Fourteenth Annual La Luz Trail Run, 7.6 miles long, up the west side of the 10,678-foot Sandia Mountains, to the east of Albuquerque, in the unheard-of time of 57 minutes, 40 seconds. He ran away from well-known collegiate and AAU runners who had starred at such schools as Harvard and the University of New Mexico; he left them to finish two to three minutes behind him. For this achievement Waquie was cited by the national sports magazine *Sports Illustrated*, September 11, 1978, in that publication's "Faces in the Crowd" section. He also received a trophy by mail from the magazine.

On September 10, 1978, Al won the long-distance ceremonial race at Jemez. A few days later, on September 18, he ran the Governor's Cup Annual Scholarship Run in Albuquerque. He won this race over four hundred other participants, including the governor of the state, Jerry Apodaca. Al covered the 6.2-mile course in 30 minutes, 50.7 seconds. The race was followed by the second ceremonial long-distance race at Jemez, on October 4, which he also won. On October 15 Al ran his first marathon, the "Tour of Albuquerque," which he enjoyed; again he set a record, running the 26.2-mile course in 2 hours, 26 minutes, 59 seconds.

The Fifteenth Annual La Luz Trail Run was lengthened by two miles, in order to accommodate the nearly four hundred athletes expected to enter. On Sunday, August 26, 1979, as the sun emerged from the morning clouds, Al conquered his mountain again, with a time of 1 hour, 14 minutes, 8 seconds. A member of the United States marathon team came in second, four minutes later.

Unlike his brother Robert, who was unable to participate in the sport won by their grandfather, Felipe, Sr., at the beginning of this century, and by their father, Felix, in the late 1930s and early 1940s, Al is fortunate to be able to run in the Jemez ceremonial races. Including the two races in 1978 and one in 1979, Al has won the long-distance races at Jemez six times, thereby surpassing the records of his grandfather and Steve Gachupin. Al ran only the second race in 1979, because he was too stiff from running the Olympic trial Nike Marathon in Eugene, Oregon, to compete in the first one. One record that continues to lurk in Al's mind is the one still held by his cousin, Steve Gachupin: four consecutive wins in the La Luz Trail Run.[1]

Al has three younger brothers; the one most likely to succeed him as a runner is Stanley. After following his two brothers to Jemez Valley and then to Haskell Indian Junior College, Stan enrolled at the University of New Mexico, where he has been on the cross-country team. His teammates have included world-class, foreign runners with Olympic experience. But until his brother Al slows down, Stanley is in for second best, and will have to "try harder." By doing just that he won the first "Popay Run" at San Ildefonso Pueblo, on July 15, 1979.[2]

The Younger Generation

As we look into the future, there is much hope. The young men and women, boys and girls, of Jemez continue to enjoy the ancient sport of running. Not only are the youngsters participating at Jemez, but they are beginning to compete nationally. As a result of the success of the boys' team, a girls' team, known as the Towan Track Club, was formed a few years ago; it sponsors its own annual meet on Mother's Day, in May; the coaches have been Frankie Armijo and Jerry Fragua. The boys have held their annual meet on Father's Day, in June.

Two performers have stood out in the short life of the girls' team: Erna Chosa and Amalia Sando. A younger athlete with exceptional ability is Joetta Cajero, the daughter of Mr. and Mrs. Joe Cajero. In 1977 she participated in the National Cross-Country Championship, in San Mateo, California; in 1978 she went to Miami, Florida, to participate in the Girls' National Track and Field Championship.

The younger boys are led by Joetta's younger brother, Aaron Cajero. Besides being a finalist in his age group at the "pass and kick" championship in 1977—held during a Dallas Cowboys football game half time—Aaron went to the National Junior Track and Field Championship, in Memphis, Tennessee, in June of 1978. He took second place in the half-mile race, with a time of 2 minutes, 15 seconds, and third place in the 440-yard sprint, with a time of 57 seconds.

On October 14, 1978, Aaron took part in the Junior Cross-Country Championship, in Walnut Creek, California, where he captured first place in the 10–11 age group. On November 11 he and other Jemez youngsters traveled to Denver, under the auspices of the Duke City Dashers, to participate in the Region 10 AAU Cross-Country meet. Again Aaron was the winner in the 10–11 age group. In the AAU national age-group cross-country meet held in Albuquerque on November 25, 1978, Aaron took second place for his age group with a time of 11:08.

On July 14, 1979, young Cajero established a national record of 2:03.6 for the 12–13 year-old age group in the 800-meter run at the International Classic, in Eugene, Oregon; the previous national record was 2:05.2. The next day Cajero also ran, finishing sixth in the 1500-meter run with a time of 4:24, beating the meet record for his age of 4:28. As a result of his showing, the New Mexico Amateur Athletic Union honored him as "Athlete of the Month" in July of 1979.

Other younger boys who have taken part in national competition are Francis Sarracino, son of Mr. and Mrs. Ralph Sarracino; Ward Yepa, son of Mr. and Mrs. Alonzo Yepa; and Henry Tosa, son of Mrs. Mary T. Madalena. In 1978 at Walnut Creek, California, Sarracino and Yepa ran in the 12–13 year-old age group; Sarracino took fourth place and Yepa eighth in the Junior Cross-Country Championships. At the Denver Region-10 meet, later that year, Sarracino was second and Yepa tenth. And at the National AAU age-group meet in Albuquerque, Sarracino was second again with a time of 10 minutes, 31 seconds. (Joe Cajero, Jr., Aaron's brother, also participated at the national meet in Albuquerque; he took fourth place in the seven-and-under age group.)

Because of his showing in cross-country competition and the two-mile run in the school year 1978/79, Henry Tosa was one of three track performers selected from New Mexico to go to a meet in Florida in June 1979, where he made a good showing.

On November 10, 1979, three Jemez boys participated in the Pacific Cross-Country Championships, held in Vancouver, British Columbia, Canada. In the 13-year-old group, Aaron Cajero took second, with a time of 10 minutes, 20 seconds. Francis Sarracino took first place in the age-14 group, with a time of 9 minutes, 48 seconds. In the 15-year-old group Ward Yepa placed eleventh, with a time of 13 minutes, 3 seconds.

During the 1980 track season, Aaron made the track team at Jemez Valley High School as an eighth grader; he was eligible to participate due to the small size of the school. He placed in the district meet, and was thus able to run in the 800-meter run at the prestigious state track meet. During the summer, with other Jemez boys, he ran for the Duke City Dashers; he was the sole qualifier to participate in the International Meet with Canadian youngsters at Eugene, Oregon. Later that summer he qualified to participate at the Athletic Congress Boys' Nationals, at Pleasant Hill, California. At this meet he won first place in the 12–13 age group's 800-meter run, in the record time of 2:02.5, won second place in the javelin throw, and ran anchor for his team in the 800-meter medley relay. In 1980/81 fourteen-year-old Aaron was enrolled at Sandia High School, in Albuquerque. At the state track meet that year, in Hobbs, he placed third in the 800-meter run, with a fine time of 1:56.8.

The Organized Promotion of Running at Jemez

For untold generations Jemez young people have competed in two annual ceremonial races. Although they have religious significance, the races are also eagerly awaited sporting events.

In these ceremonial races the contestant who first reaches the designated runner with the trophy has to be able to reach top speed within fifty to four hundred yards. Following this sprint, other runners, who excel at different distances, may overtake the runner with the trophy, and carry it as a sign of superiority in running at that distance. Eventually, at a point approaching the village, the leading long-distance runner takes the trophy and brings it to his house, as a sign of victory. In the eyes of the people, the winner is endowed with much prestige, which is seen as coming directly from the spirits. So the people will greet the winner that day to congratulate him and to share in his grace, by touching him and following the traditional Indian custom of breathing into his hands.

The trophy for long-distance races is a stalk of green corn. The corn stalk can be extremely cumbersome when one is trying to generate speed, maintain balance, and see where one is running. It takes skill to carry the trophy under these conditions, but still the weight never diminishes. For short-distance races of between one and one and a half miles, an ear of corn wrapped in fir branches is used. The ear of corn is much lighter and easier to run with, as one can swing his arms as he holds the ear of corn in either hand.

Besides this traditional interest in and motivation for running, a new focus of interest has sprung up at the pueblo, beginning in the summer of 1959, with the first annual Jemez All-Indian Track and Field Meet.

In the spring of 1958, Jimmy Yepa, a miler who was then a senior at Santa Fe Indian School, approached me about the possibility of staging an all-Indian track meet at Jemez that summer; I sent a letter to Joe Cajero immediately. He was at that time a student at New Mexico Highlands University, where he was a physical education major and track star. His response was enthusiastic, but financial problems prevented further action that summer.

Meanwhile, Jimmy asked his mother, Mrs. Lupe S. Yepa, to consult with the Jemez Community Woman's Club concerning assistance in financing the proposed track meet. Additional positive response through the year encouraged me to speak to the governor, Guadalupe Fragua, during Easter vacation of 1959, about permission to plan the meet. That summer I took a volunteer crew from my guidance and counseling staff to Jemez where, together with volunteers assembled by Joe Cajero, we laid out a quarter-mile track. Donations of time and materials made everything possible. Wooden stakes were used as edge markers, and someone donated powdered milk from his grandparent's cupboard to mark the lanes. Lumber for the all-important sale stand was also donated. The Women's Club sold food they had prepared and donated the proceeds. Through bake sales, bingo games, and raffles they were able to purchase four trophies, as well as ribbons for the first three finishers. A large trophy was purchased, to be kept for a year by the team winning the meet. Second and third-place team trophies were also provided, as well as one for the highest individual scorer in the meet. With more successful fund raising, ribbons were extended to the first five finishers beginning the following year.

To support the Track Town title, the traveling meet trophy was won by Jemez seven times in the first ten years; and from 1974 to 1979 the string of victories was not broken. The Jicarilla Apaches from Dulce, New Mexico, won the meet the third year, Taos Pueblo won the fourth year, and the Albuquerque Indian Track Club won the tenth year.

The summer of 1980 was extremely dry; a number of young Jemez men who work for the Forest Service during the summer months could not be spared to come home for the annual Indian track meet because of the high fire risk. Others were actually out fighting forest fires. But the younger boys who comprised the Jemez team made a surprisingly strong showing, coming in second to a seasoned team of Kiowas from Carnegie, Oklahoma.

Joe Cajero of Jemez was the individual high-point man for the first two years. Since then other high-point men have been Ronnie Lente of Isleta Pueblo, Bennie Romero of Taos Pueblo, Larry Echohawk, a Pawnee, from Farmington, New Mexico, and Bob Williams, a Creek, from Albuquerque.

Since the meet's inception, numerous tribes, pueblos, and intertribal groups have sent teams to compete: Taos Pueblo, San Felipe Pueblo, Santo Domingo Pueblo, Isleta Pueblo, Laguna Pueblo, Acoma

Pueblo, Zia Pueblo, Jicarilla Apaches, Mescalero Apaches, Canoncito Navajos, Shiprock Navajos, Torreon Navajos, Hopis from Arizona, the Totah Track Club from Farmington, and the Albuquerque Indian Track Club. The Totah Track Club has consisted mainly of the Echohawk brothers, managed and coached by their father, Ernest "Crip" Echohawk, along with a few Navajos from the area. The Albuquerque Indian Track Club has had many tribes represented, including Cherokee, Creek, Kiowa, Blackfeet, Gros Ventre, Paiute, and Sioux. These boys have been managed by one of the originators of the meet, Jimmy Yepa. Besides the many other stars, the Pawnee Echohawk brothers, John, Larry, and Tom, have been some of the more colorful performers. All three subsequently went on to further stardom at Brigham Young University, in Provo, Utah, and later became attorneys. John, especially, has been active in cases of pan-Indian importance, in his position as director of the Native American Rights Fund, an organization that has helped many.

As a result of the annual track meet, the Jemez Athletic Club was officially organized in 1961. This partially relieved the three originators from the planning and fund raising. Frank I. Sando was the first club president, and later was replaced by Joe Cajero. Among the men largely responsible for the success of the annual meet at the beginning were Juanico (John) Cajero, a former bruising All-State fullback for AIS during the successful era of Coach Jim Jones in the 1930s, and the former track stars Felix Yepa, Bennie Shendo, Barnabe Romero, Candido Armijo, and Christobal Loretto. Others were Frank Sando, Freddie Toya, Jerry Fragua, Maurice Armijo, and Ciriaco Toya (namesake of his famous uncle).

Some of the most involved Women's Club members were Carry R. Loretto, Lupe S. Chosa, Juanita Y. Armijo, and Lupe S. Yepa; many others held no offices, but were eager volunteers who assisted during critical times of need.

Today the Jemez Track Club continues primarily under the guidance of Bennie Shendo and Joe Cajero. During the summer months the team participates in any meet to which it is invited, and continues to bring home more than its share of trophies. The team has been as far away as Colorado, California, and Indiana.

Running as a ceremonial sport continues at Jemez Pueblo, and as Americans in general discover running as a part of healthful living, the young men and women from Jemez are finding plenty of fine athletes to compete against. But still, more than any other community in the country, Jemez Pueblo is "Track Town, U.S.A."

12

Art and Artists at Jemez

In the eyes of non-Indians, almost all Pueblo Indians are artists in the creation of such practical necessities as ceremonial paraphernalia, baskets, and pots. From early childhood many Pueblo Indian children are taught to do things with their hands, not by an instructor who explains how and why, but through observation and practice. Their "art" is learned by sons from fathers, by daughters from mothers; children learn the skills of their parents almost by osmosis.

The Jemez people have no word for "art," and I doubt if other tribes have one, either. Non-Indians use the word art in many ways, but for its use here it may be more related to crafts or craftsmanship—a skill in making an object. For Indians the art involved in creating objects cannot be isolated from features of practical necessity. The original idea is to create for functional use; since the object is to be used, it should be pleasing to the eye and bring satisfaction to its creator. Its creation also serves as a form of mental recreation, providing pure, esthetic pleasure. This is one of the reasons that Indians have regarded time so leisurely; time is secondary to the enjoyment the Indian experiences while creating a soul-satisfying object.

Besides items made for functional, household use, artifacts that are a by-product of religion have accounted for the demand for craftsmanship and artistic expression, and for their growth. Natural, earth colors have been used in these spiritual and religious expressions; they come from ground roots, bark, leaves, minerals, hulls, berries, and cancerous growths on corn stalks, and produce the basic Indian colors of black, red, yellow, blue, turquoise, and brown.

Indian artists have drawn on a multitude of symbolic designs to embellish their art. The colors are used to depict rainbows, and different shapes and colors are used for the morning star, the evening star, the moon, and the sun. Other motifs are corn, squash, melons, tobacco, and chili, as well as lightning, thunder, swelling rain clouds, rising fog, rays of light, falling rain, and the stepped earth-altar outline of hills and mountains, used on the walls of ceremonial chambers. Also included in these chambers are hunting scenes, as well as pictures of all the useful animals which furnished food to the people—buffalo, elk, deer, antelope, and rabbit—as well as birds—eagle, turkey, humming bird, hawk, bluebird, parrot, and wild canary. Feathers from these birds have been the favorite decorations for themselves or their art objects.

The idea is to give all artistic creations and chambers a joyous form, to heighten people's sense of their importance, and above all, to remind us mortals of the Great Creator for whom every ceremonial is invariably offered. For this same reason the pueblo Catholic church also contains murals of agricultural scenes, chili, corn, melons, squash, and wheat.

Pottery has traditionally provided the main creative outlet for Pueblo artists. Their expression has progressed from woven baskets and simple pots to pottery decorated with simple marks followed by simple sculpturing of society symbols and the addition of color.

The Jemez, like their Pueblo Indian relatives in New Mexico and Arizona, traditionally made pottery for functional use, rather than as an art. In retrospect, it would appear that after a time the Jemez stopped making fine, artistically decorated pottery in favor of functional culinary pots. These pots were used to bake pudding in the outdoor ovens, in cooperation with neighbors and fellow clan members, before a ceremonial or festival. Similar pots were made for cooking over open fires, indoors as well as outdoors. Outdoor fires were also used to heat water for washing and other special purposes requiring large amounts of hot water. Pots were also used for storing bread, and extra large pots were used for storing crops over the winter months.

Jemez pottery making, after its temporary lapse, may have been revived by women marrying in from the neighboring, Keresan-speaking pueblo of Zia. The person most often credited for the revival is Benigna

Medina Madalena, or Sai-you pa ("bird blossom," or "flower"), of the Young Corn Clan. Benigna was married to Ramon Madalena, or Stia-shun ("arrow hill"), around the turn of the century.

Having learned to make pottery as a youngster from her female relatives, she continued the craft after moving to Jemez as a young bride. At Jemez she would invite another Zia bride, Refugia Moquino Toledo, to join her in gathering the materials needed to make pottery, as well as in making it. When Benigna's daughters were old enough, they began to help their mother, and thereby learned the process from her. These women soon branched into another Jemez functional art, that of making yucca ring baskets, which their mother had learned at Jemez and then taught to her children.

Benigna's daughters are Rita M. Casiquito, Lupe M. Romero, Percingula M. Gachupin, Elcira M. Chavez, and Josephine M. Sando. Of these sisters, Lupe Romero may have been the most outstanding potter, personifying the return of pottery to Jemez. Although pottery was not popular or of much economic benefit in the 1930s and 1940s, Lupe made decorated ashtrays, miniature two-story, Pueblo-type houses, and small pots to be used for cornmeal containers and other useful and decorative purposes. Jemez people knew her as "the one who makes pottery."

Her next younger sister, Percingula Gachupin, was also an outstanding potter. As pottery making became more popular and profitable, the other sisters also became involved, but raising families prevented them from spending as much time at it as did their sister Lupe.

When the sisters first started showing their pottery outside of Jemez, the Zia people accused them of copying Zia pottery; of course, the girls were using Zia designs, taught them by their Zia mother. To avoid further misunderstanding, the sisters began to use Jemez designs, relying on natural colors derived from native dyes. They talked of going after the clay as "tyi-la pela-a," sometimes on foot and sometimes in a horse-drawn wagon, driven by their father. They also collected dried bones, driftwood, and cow dung for use in firing the pottery. The girls learned to split yucca, with which they drew the thin, straight, black lines that outline the designs on the pottery. They were taught the different kinds of clay and where each kind was located, as well as which color of clay produced which colors after firing.

When pottery became popular as a tourist trade item, Jemez potters were unfortunately introduced to the use of readily available "artista" colors and acrylic paint, by the day school teacher, Noble Guthrie.

The paints, bright and attractive if used well, were not permanent, and were subject to smearing. Luckily for tourists, the potters soon went back to the natural earth colors, which they still use today. Jemez pottery is recognizable by its reddish finish, decorated with gray and white designs highlighted with straight black lines; sometimes a touch of turquoise is added in appropriate spots. Today, pottery is definitely more of an art form than a necessity, since Jemez people use all the modern cookware and containers available to any American.

Benigna Medina has been followed by her descendants, some several generations removed. Her oldest daughter, Rita, had six daughters, of whom two are engaged in pottery making; they are Geronima C. Shendo and Juanita C. Fragua. Geronima also markets gourds handsomely decorated by her husband, Frank Shendo. Juanita Fragua often displays her work in craft shows throughout the Southwest. Her ambition may be reinforced by that of three of her children—Glendora F. Daubs, Betty Jean Fragua, and Clifford Fragua; these three all exhibit the artistic talent inherited from their great-grandmother. Although the two girls both learned the basics from their mother, their pottery styles are distinctly individual. Glendora and her husband, Dennis Daubs (great-grandson of the runner Tyi-la), create exclusively small art pieces, elaborately etched, of beautiful birds and animals on trees, flowers, and mountains. Betty Jean, or BJ, produces pots and miniatures close to her mother's style, but with her own variations.

Clifford Fragua, who recently burst upon the art world, works with the rugged silence of stone sculpting—primarily Apache and Colorado alabaster. He began to learn at the Institute of American Indian Arts, in Santa Fe, and then studied further at the San Francisco Art Institute, in California. His work can be seen throughout the Southwest, as well as in other parts of the country.

Lupe M. Romero had four daughters, two of whom married away from the pueblo, and one of whom died. But the eldest one, Percingula R. Tosa, has carried on the trade taught her by her mother. She is well known for her production of colorfully decorated owls of all sizes; and her daughter, Mary T. Madalena, currently appears to be one of the most popular Jemez potters. The shapes and smoothly flowing straight lines of her pottery identify her fine artistic expression.

Benigna's third daughter, Percingula M. Gachupin, also taught her two daughters, Marie G. Romero and Lenora G. Fragua, the fine points of pottery making. Marie is especially noted for her outstanding interpretation of the ever-popular "story teller" figure, with the many children hanging onto her. Marie's daughter, Maxine G. Toya, has combined her traditional training with a university training in art; she expresses her ideas flexibly through her pottery. Marie's other daughter, Laura, and Laura's cousin, Bertha, daughter of Lenora Fragua, are also seriously involved in pottery making.

Benigna's fourth daughter, Elcira, is the mother of another outstanding potter whose work is in demand these days, Mary Rose Toya.

Benigna's fifth daughter, Josephine M. Sando, was a young girl when her mother died. Consequently, she had to learn the greater part of her art from her older sisters. Three of Josephine's own daughters are employed in other areas, while the fourth one is still in school; although they all make some pottery occasionally, they are not as seriously involved with it as their cousins are.

In two or three instances, the wives of the original pottery maker's grandsons have also learned to make pottery, from their mothers-in-law, and in turn are teaching their own daughters.

Today, then, there are many outstanding potters at Jemez. Some are especially gifted in shaping or sculpting clay, while others are masters with a paint brush or the traditional yucca fiber. These Jemez women now make many forms of pottery: bowls and candle holders, canoes and tipis for ashtrays, miniature birds and animals, and miniature Pueblo houses, with small figures engaged in grinding corn with metate and mano, or making paper bread on a flagstone heated by fire. Although these forms of clay sculpture are small masterpieces, the outstanding, characteristic Jemez pottery art appears to be wedding vases, large and small—single vases with two spouts, symbolizing the transformation through marriage of two persons into one.

Nowadays, other forms of art are also emerging at Jemez, practiced by the individuals described below.

Lucy Yepa Lowden

The creator of "tiny little people" is Pb'ong-kin ("little trail"), also known as Lucy Yepa Lowden. She was an accomplished weaver before she began her successful and highly honored recent career as a doll artist. Her little figures, she says, are her way of preserving her own Jemez heritage, as well as other Indian cultures.

Some people have said that her creations look like people seen through the wrong end of a telescope. Others have found her little people more than sculpture, more than lessons in art, anthropology, or sociology. These famous miniatures are about a foot high, and authentic in every detail. Each is a product of her childhood memories of dances she saw and participated in. From her secret clay compound, which took years of experimenting to perfect, Lucy is able to reproduce the faces of the family members that influenced her life, such as the one of Tuvahey toholer ("grandfather"), who was her constant companion when she was very young. Then there are the representations of Navajo friends who came to Jemez feasts year after year; the male corn dancer with his fierce determination after several hours of dancing; the serene and graceful rainbow-dancer maiden; the deer dancer; the eagle dancer; the fluteplayer; Pueblo women from different villages— all give off a strong sense of movement, as if they had been stopped in the midst of their activities. She also collects furs, feathers, and jewelry for her miniature friends to wear. She makes miniature heishi out of turquoise and coral, trims feathers to size, weaves tiny rain sashes and kilts for the dancers, makes moccasins, and generally spares no detail for the figures. It is no wonder that they are valued by collectors and museums all over the world.

As a teenager at the Albuquerque Indian School in the early 1930s, Lucy was introduced to weaving and embroidery by Mrs. Ellen Lawrence, who had learned the Pueblo's ancient art at Jemez when she was a field nurse, living at the old Presbyterian Mission grounds. At first Lucy did not really enjoy crafts, but Mrs. Lawrence almost literally pushed her into them; they later proved to be a stepping stone to greater things for Lucy. In her crafts work she made plain, white handwoven cloth, plain mantas, ceremonial mantas, dance kilts, embroidered men's shirts, belts, shawls, rain sashes, leggings, colonial-type rugs and coverlets, yucca-ring baskets, pottery, beadwork, and even attempted oil painting. This, then, was the unconscious beginning of her amazing miniature people.

Pb'ong-kin was born at Jemez Pueblo, on February 16, 1916. Her parents were Jose Reyes Yepa, of the Sun Clan, and Margarita Colaque Yepa, of the Charcoal Clan (this clan came with a woman from San Felipe Pueblo; her descendants soon formed a large clan group at Jemez). Lucy was the middle child in a family of nine siblings; only five daughters are alive today, of whom Lucy is the second oldest. Three of the sisters, Andrea Y. Fragua, Sefora Y. Tosa, and Corina Y. Waquiu, are well-known ring-basket makers, and also do some pottery for the tourist trade. Growing up in an all-girl family, Lucy was a tomboy in her early years; she irrigated and hoed with her father and grandfather, as well as rounding up cattle with her father.

While in high school, as a result of her aptitude in crafts, she went to a summer camp in Honesdale, near Scranton, Pennsylvania, to teach crafts and archery. This was at a time when her peers had hardly traveled beyond Albuquerque, a full day's wagon ride from Jemez. Her inspiration was tremendous, and she began to draw on her heritage in her own weaving. She taught crafts at both the Albuquerque and Santa Fe Indian schools, and later at the Institute of American Indian Arts, in Santa Fe. At one time she also taught Navajo tuberculosis patients at the old Presbyterian Hospital Center, in Albuquerque.

Later, when a bout of rheumatoid arthritis took her out of circulation for a while, she used the time to plan future projects and to write poetry. One poem, addressed to her numerous non-Indian friends, explains her philosophy of life:

> I will come to you
> And take you by the hand,
> Let you walk with me in my paths,
> The paths of moccasin footprints,
> in search of things,
> of my people I love.
> We will call on the stars to guide us.
> We will follow the music
> of the Fluteplayer in the air we breathe.
> When we have reached these places of worship,
> these humble places
> where my ancestors once stood in silent prayer
> I will try to explain the meaning
> of our beautiful prayers from the Old Ones.
> And why my people are the way your eyes see them
> And you sometimes cannot understand.
>
> I would teach you names
> of Mother Earth's creatures and all her gifts.
> I would share my moccasins with you
> And let you walk my paths,
> my corn meal paths,
> my yellow pollen paths,
> That you may know
> And hear the echoes of the past as I do.
> Then you will know why it is not easy
> sometimes to be Indian
> And live as you do, my non-Indian friends.
>
> You are also great people
> with much to learn,

much to give.
Together we will walk
on this, Mother Earth's land,
in peace with love
and respect for each other
As only Mother Earth intended.

Lucy was married to Joseph E. Lowden, originally from Acoma
Pueblo, on January 14, 1937, at Acomita; they met at the Albuquerque
Indian School, where they were classmates. The Lowdens have three
children—Bernadette L. Cheromiah, of Paquate, New Mexico, and
Renee and Anthony Lowden. They also have three grandchildren and
one great-grandson.

It is sad to see so many of our old customs dying out. My little people are
my way of preserving some of our traditions. I want to share with others what
I have loved and respected all my life. I especially want to have my children
and grandchildren and other Jemez children see through my work what they
have missed.

Jose Rey Toledo

Classroom teachers often say that drawing and painting appear to
be a natural for the average American Indian child. This may be so,
as drawing is learned naturally, through observation and trial and error.
There are also those who excel in a given field, however, especially if
they have been motivated by observing an inspiring model.

This was the case for the man commonly known at Jemez as Stia-
na, short for Ha-stia-na. He was named by his grandfather after a song
(perhaps from Tampiro Pueblo, to the east of the Manzano Mountains)
sung by a men's society to which Stia-na belongs. He is also known
as Jose Rey Toledo.

When he was about five or six years old, his brother-in-law, John
Shamon, painted water-color scenes of Jemez, including animals. At
the same time his uncle, Juanito Moquino, of Zia Pueblo, used to
drop by on his early morning runs. Sometimes Uncle Moquino would
stay for breakfast, and while it was being prepared for him, he would
sketch along the walls of the Toledo home. Moquino also painted
scenes of deer and forests, according to Jose Rey. "This is where I got
my earliest inspiration."

Later, while Jose Rey was in junior high school, a cousin from Zia

Pueblo, Velino Shije, became a nationally known artist. Velino sold his work to art collectors, and Toledo was tremendously inspired; when Velino moved to Santa Fe in 1932, Jose Rey went along. He imitated his cousin's work, "in a humble way." But there was enough ability showing through that Frank Patania, of the Thunderbird Shop in Santa Fe, hired him to demonstrate Indian painting to tourists.

When Jose was in the tenth grade at the Albuquerque Indian School, an art department was started as part of the vocational course; he enrolled in the first art course. When he graduated from high school he enrolled in the College of Fine Arts at the University of New Mexico, but dropped out after two years, for lack of funds. When he reentered he enrolled in art education, from which department he received his bachelor's degree in 1951. He continued doing graduate work while teaching, and in 1955 earned his Master of Arts in Art Education.

But his salary as a teacher was not enough to feed and clothe a family of four girls and three boys, so he went to the University of California, at Berkeley, to work on another master's degree, this time in comprehensive health planning, which he finished in 1972.

With this added educational security he returned to New Mexico, where he was employed by the Indian Health Service at Laguna Pueblo, as a community health educator. From there he transferred to the Albuquerque Service Unit as a tribal liaison officer in health, in which position he was able to live at Jemez. During his employment he continued to paint, and also spoke before conventions and workshops on the meaning of art to Indian people. He finally retired from the Indian Health Service in 1976, to devote more time to art and related activities.

Of such teachers as Mela Sedillo Brewster, Edward Del Dosso, and Kenneth Adams, Jose Rey remarks that,

I seemed to discourage my professors because I really was not conscious of perspectives. I appreciated perspective, but I could not make myself draw angles and foreshortened areas of the human body as they would have desired me to. But I worked on it because that made for good grades.

He believes that he first became a professional artist in the 1930s, after he received recognition and prizes for his work at the Gallup Indian Ceremonial art show and the Philbrook Art Center in Tulsa, Oklahoma. Since that time his work has been exhibited and purchased by permanent collections in many art centers and museums throughout the world.

Stia-na was born at Jemez Pueblo, on June 28, 1915. His father was Jose Ortiz Toledo, of the Sun Clan; his mother was Refugia Moquino, from Zia Pueblo, of the Tobacco Clan. He had two older sisters, Andrea T. Fragua and Angelita T. Shamon, and a younger brother, Jose Ignacio Toledo; only Stia-na and his sister Andrea are still living.

Because of his involvement in Jemez dances, Jose Rey vividly remembers the details of costumes, and tries to portray accurately the dance figures he draws. As an Indian artist he believes he has a commitment to communicate a message to the younger generation, as well as to the non-Indian world, through the Indian life he portrays in his paintings. The solemn expressions of his dancers convey the seriousness of the "prayer, or thanksgiving" dance—prayers for rainfall in a desert environment, and thanksgiving for rain and harvests granted by nature.

Jose Rey sells some prints of his work by mail order; and like many of the early Indian artists, his style is often copied by the younger generation and even by non-Indian artists. Of all the murals that he has done, one of the most popular ones is on the east wall of the patio at the Indian Pueblo Cultural Center in Albuquerque, depicting a Tewa basket dance.

Because of his knowledge of the Pueblo Indian lifestyle, the meanings of dances and songs, as well as his articulateness in the English language, Mr. Toledo serves as a master of ceremonies for the Indian Pueblo Cultural Center and as announcer at the Indian Village at the New Mexico State Fair. He describes the dances that are performed for tourists on holidays and weekends during the center's tourist season.

Estella C. Loretto

Another example of the merging of traditional crafts with a variety of experiences, including a college degree, is the blossoming young Jemez potter Stella Loretto. She was born at Jemez on January 26, 1954, the daughter of Albenita Toya, of the Oak Canyon Clan, and Joe D. Loretto, of the Sun Clan. Her American education began in the village day school, which went to the sixth grade. Fortunately for Stella, the principal of the school, and her teacher during her elementary school years, was Al Momaday, well-known artist of Kiowa Indian descent. Along with the basic courses, art was high on the list of subjects taught at the school. Of course, during those years she also watched her mother and other relatives making the style of pottery made at Jemez at the time. After the day school, Stella went to the local San Diego Mission School, through the eighth grade. From there she went to Jemez Valley High School for two more years, before transferring to the Institute of American Indian Arts, in Santa Fe, "for a change from the regular home life." At the Santa Fe school she widened her experience in the art world as she was introduced to oil painting, watercolor, ceramics, and wood-block printing. When not in class, Stella worked as a waitress near the campus.

After graduating from high school she went to Belgium on an American Field Service scholarship; it was here that she experienced homesickness for the first time. She lived with a Flemish family of thirteen, none of whom spoke English, and this did not help her situation. She spoke to herself, however, and soon convinced herself that she was here to learn about other people and another world. She quickly learned some Flemish, and taught the family some English and a few words of Towa, her native language. "This experience really broke me in; I knew I could do anything after that."

Upon her return home a year later, she went to Ft. Lewis College, in Durango, Colorado, not sure of her major. At first she was intrigued by Spanish, but the Spanish in college was quite different from the speech her parents used around Jemez in communicating with neighboring Spanish-speaking friends. So in the manner that was to become characteristic of her, she took her sophomore year of college in Oaxaca, Mexico, and became familiar with Spanish as taught in classes there and reinforced by speaking to the local people. Returning home she enrolled in another program that made it possible for her to visit Nepal and India in the summer of 1974.

In 1976 Stella graduated from Ft. Lewis with a degree in social sciences; at that point she decided to stop traveling to paint and relax for a year on a ranch near Durango. A college friend who had visited Japan talked a lot to her about the country and its culture. Stella became interested herself, especially in their art; she read that wood-block printing, formerly important, is dying out today. So she decided to study wood-block printing in Japan. She sold all of the paintings that she had finished at the ranch, and with her sister, Arlene, was soon off to Japan. To supplement their income, Stella got a job teaching English to the Japanese for Encyclopaedia Britannica. "It was a great opportunity to meet the Japanese, and to be classed in the same category as a *sensei*, a teacher, who enjoys high status." She immersed herself in the new experience with her typical fervor. After nine months in Japan, the two sisters returned home.

In Japan, as she visited shows and galleries, she had thought of returning home and making pottery in the old way. "After rushing around during the day and viewing native art, at night I would dream of shapes and colors." On returning home she was still excited by the idea of making pottery as her ancestors had, with native clay and vegetable dyes. "I would sacrifice all side attractions, like further travel and dating." She had previously helped her mother mold pottery and sand it to shape, and had used acrylic paint on it, but this was not getting her anywhere. Now she was going to experiment with native dyes.

She knew where her mother had always gone to dig clay, but she wanted to experiment with different colors, from different areas of the reservation.

Watching the different colors come out, which I collected from different areas, was exciting; it was a feeling I never had before. It was beautiful; I felt I was doing something worthwhile. I was finally discovering my own artistic expression using my traditional background and the experiences from my travels. Just think—I had just discovered my latent talent when another culture invited me to share theirs.

This invitation to share another culture came soon afterwards, through the influence of a friend, Jay Gluck, publisher of a twenty-volume work on Persian art, who had lived in Iran for thirty years. Mr. Gluck had known of Stella's interest in pottery, and so suggested a second visit to Japan, to attend the Oomoto School of Traditional Japanese Arts, and a trip to Iran to evaluate their lost technique of pottery making, and to meet the royal family. "Mr. Gluck thought I might look at the Iranian clay and learn some of their old ways and help them get started again." However, exciting as this all appeared to be, there was one catch: Stella could not afford the trip. She wrote her thanks and explained her situation; in due time a letter arrived, informing Stella that the royal family would sponsor her scholarship to the art school, and her plane fare as well.

With this new and exciting development Stella called on her mother for help; the invitation to the Japanese art school had been issued on the assumption that she would bring some pottery. So she stepped up her experiments with dyes, digging clay in different areas, first designing on paper, then shaping and firing the pots with her mother's help. Stella even made representative copies of other Pueblo pottery to take along for exhibit.

After arriving in Japan she had a one-woman show in the Osaki-Imabashi Gallery for one week; she showed forty-four pieces, including the thirty-two that she had brought from Jemez. The others were made while she studied Japanese pottery. She said the Japanese were very impressed and honored to have an American Indian artist presenting her work in person. They appreciated sharing ideas for making pottery and identifying some cultural similarities. All her pieces were later sold, with the help of Mr. Gluck in setting prices.

With a rare serious expression on her face, Stella remarked about this experience:

The whole five-month trip was one of the best things that has ever happened to me. It brought reality to me; I could picture everything falling into place. The experience was so stimulating I could hardly wait to return home to resume my experiments with my newly found ideas and the influence of my fellow students.

Among these people she met in Japan were a ballet dancer from New York City, a weaver from San Francisco, two or three writers from London, and a physicist, as well as a Tibetan *rinpeche,* or "holy man."

She spent five weeks at school in the town of Kameoka, "way out in the sticks by itself."

We were totally immersed in Japanese tradition. We removed all our jewelry and eye glasses, and washed to purify ourselves before we put on the proper kimonos. Everyone was quiet and there was time to concentrate and observe everything—patterns, a scroll, the bamboo, the floors, the flowers. When it was your turn to make tea, you didn't look at the people; there was total concentration on what you were doing, for this might be the only time you would make tea for that particular person or those people. You were doing this thing for them so you transferred all thoughts to them.

It was indeed a moving experience for Stella to respond to such a different culture, but it was also similar in some ways to her own. For one thing, there was the same intense concentration on everything she was doing. She also learned to control her mind and body together, in her martial arts classes in *buddo* and *kendo*. "I think I got the spirit of it."

When Stella returned home it was with a purpose—to work with clay and put all her energy into it.

I give it everything I've got so when I finish a piece of art I set it down to admire it, and it looks at me to thank me for the way I handled, talked to it, and finished it. All my art pieces are entities and I cannot make two alike. One Japanese man wanted to mass-produce one of my pots, but I had to explain to him that they are separate entities and cannot be mass-produced.

Stella also began to sculpt clay in earnest, and by February 1979 she had finished seven pieces; she took the new creations to the Great Western Fine Art Show, in Los Angeles; it was the first juried show that she had ever entered. Her work was well received; she won the award for the "best of show" and two blue ribbons. Following this showing she was invited to another show, in Santa Monica, in June 1979, to which she took twenty pieces. She won the "best craftsman" trophy and ribbon. In her future she sees stoneware as her new project.

Stoneware is mixing of rock and clay to make cooking vessels. There are some people who know how to make these things and they will show me how. And maybe some more travel; I would like to see Greece and Africa, to study their art and cultures—and maybe South America to visit Peru and Guatemala for the same purpose.

During an Indian wedding ceremony held at the Red Rock area of Jemez Pueblo, in June 1980, Stella became Mrs. John Eagle Day. John is from the Shoshone-Bannock reservation in Idaho. During a tour of the South Pacific Island nations, the Eagle Days were called home in June 1982 from Australia upon the death of Stella's mother Albenita.

Evelyn Mora Vigil

The story of Evelyn Mora Vigil is the story of a quest to recapture the pottery technique of the ancient people of Pecos Pueblo. While anthropologists, archeologists, and historians have sought to solve some of the mysteries of Pecos, Evelyn and a few others have been searching for the key to the art of pottery making practiced by the women of Pecos generations ago.

It all began when Lois Wittich, a volunteer worker at the Pecos National Monument, began to search for clays in the Pecos area that might have been traditionally used by Pecos women. Lois, who later married the superintendent of the monument, Tom Giles, had heard of Evelyn in 1973, when she was teaching the women of Sandia Pueblo to recapture their ancestors' pottery techniques.

During a trip to Santa Fe with the Sandia women to observe ancient Pueblo pottery at the Museum of New Mexico and the laboratory of Anthropology, Evelyn had observed the old, glistening, glazed designs of prehistoric Jemez pottery. Then and there she vowed that she would begin a search for the ancient system of glazed designs for Jemez pottery, to replace the use of tempera colors, introduced with the rebirth of pottery making at Jemez in the early 1930s, by the government day school principal, Noble Guthrie.

Evelyn was urged by Lois Giles to consider taking on the project of trying to reincarnate the ancient Pecos pottery. Evelyn was already experimenting with glazes and finishes, so this provided a good opportunity to continue in cooperation with someone else. In 1975 she started by making two trips a week to Pecos, mainly to search for clay in the local area. Lois had already located some clay, which Evelyn used to begin her Pecos project, but for some reason the pots all cracked during firing.

At first Evelyn used Jemez clay, with excellent results; but since that combination would not be genuine Pecos, she never attempted it again. Finally, she decided to search further for the right clay. She started out one day with Lois, but then went off by herself; she did not respond to periodic calls as they had prearranged. Instead, she meditated and addressed her Pecos ancestors, inquiring about the location of the right clay; she was restricted to searching within the confines of the property of the National Park, as neighboring areas were privately owned. Her prayers to her ancestors brought her blessings, as she located some clay just east of the monument—with this clay the pottery did not break. Her next project was to find the proper temper for the clay. She finally learned that the use of finely ground sandstone would produce the desired results.

As her two-day-a-week trips stretched into five days each week, she had more time to find the other colors represented in the ancient, pre-Spanish Pecos pottery collected by Alfred Kidder during the initial excavations in the 1920s. Lois had already located and worked out the glaze formulas of galena, red iron, and silica, and Evelyn had learned to make guaco, the medium that holds the coloring agents. All Pueblo potters know how to extract guaco from the common plant known variously as quelites, bee plant, or buffalo grass, which is how the Jemez people know it. This plant is also picked in its early stages and eaten as a wild spinach.

To continue her project of making authentic Pecos pottery, she used only broken pottery and gourds to work and smooth her clay, as well as the traditional yucca stem as a brush with which to paint the simple designs. She would make each pot with a distinguishing individual trait, but still carrying the stylistic weight and vibrant concern for design of the ancient, original Pecos ware. After a time, she says that the design called "el capitán" appeared to be the most popular.

The only real problem she had was help—some of the helpers she brought from Jemez became too aware of the abandonment of the ancient pueblo. Like Evelyn, most of them had Pecos blood in the veins, and they could not sleep at night, thinking of the past, as the legends that have been passed down through the generations played in their minds.

Evelyn survived those first years, and each year she looks forward to Labor Day weekend as that is the last weekend she spends at Pecos National Monument, demonstrating to curious tourists the technique of her ancient, ancestral art.

Evelyn was born at Jemez Pueblo, on January 3, 1921, the daughter of Daniel Mora, of the Sun Clan, and Gavina Sandia, of the Oak Canyon Clan. She had two sisters and a brother. Evelyn is married to Joe Vigil, of the Charcoal Clan. They have seven children, fifteen grandchildren, and two great-grandchildren. Evelyn is known at Jemez as Pang-umpe-ke ("young doe"), and her husband is Whoa-der-shun ("hawk hill"). The story is told that when her husband was young, an inquisitive tourist approached Joe and asked him his name. He gave his name, but then the tourist wanted to know what his Indian name was. He replied that it was Whoa-der-shun. Hearing this the tourist replied, "My, what a beautiful name—Four Dishes."

To know Evelyn and her background is to know that she is a great woman. Because she lost her parents at an early age, she has had to struggle to become the person she is as an adult. With little formal education—she had to work to support her younger sisters and brother— she learned the crafts of the tribe from other Jemez women. Besides art pottery, she can also make the heavy, functional cooking pots, willow baskets, and ring baskets. Unlike some others, she is always willing to help other people learn the arts and crafts of the tribe. She has even been called on to teach Head Start classes to sing and dance some of the old, traditional dances no longer performed at Jemez. Among the dances and songs that she teaches is an old, colonial Spanish dance, sung in Spanish to the beat of an Indian drum. The young students like to learn from Evelyn, and they are often seen performing before appreciative, astounded parents and grandparents.

Her involvement with the Pecos pottery project has contributed much to her development as a person. Endowed with a pleasing personality, she meets people and makes friends easily. She likes to joke and usually has a humorous story to tell. She is also a willing volunteer, and, as a result, was on the Day School Board, to which she was elected by the parents of the students. She is also quite fluent in the English language now, very likely as a result of the Pecos experiment. Her long-term efforts to revive the use of Pecos clays, glazes, and firing should stand as a lasting monument to this outstanding crafts person.

And other tribal crafts continue, such as the willow baskets woven by the brothers Rosendo and Pablo Gachupin, who learned the craft from their father, Alcario. These baskets are commonly known as Jicarilla baskets; the brothers make them at Jemez for local use, now that Apache Jicarilla baskets have gone beyond the price range of the average buyer. However, a source of competition are the similarly constructed imports from Africa, which are reasonably priced but not as colorful and sturdy as the Indian-made baskets.

From its beginnings in the construction of functional objects for everyday and ritual uses, art at Jemez has become a matter of economic and personal survival. With the creation of art forms by a few individuals concerned with the survival of the culture, and subsequent acceptance by non-Indian art collectors and tourists, the way has been opened for more large-scale commercial enterprises. Shopkeepers from the cities, as well as tourists, now roam the pueblos looking for new and old art forms alike—old pottery, watercolor paintings by famous and unknown artists, old silver jewelry, heishi, and coral-string necklaces. Realizing the demand, Indians raise their prices, only to learn that shopkeepers still place a 50 to 100 percent markup on items similar to what one might see at a garage sale in another part of the country.

Epilogue

Since the end of World War II, the Jemez way of life has changed in certain areas, beginning with the influence of returning veterans and others who went to metropolitan areas for defense-related work. But the core of the culture—Jemez religion and tribal government—have changed little over the years.

Religion continues to permeate all phases of community life. There is a feeling that to imitate white man's ways too closely would cause Jemez people to lose much of their essential spiritual outlook. The more materialistic standard of the dominant society stands as a definite warning against leaving the pueblo, even for a short time, for places where there is pressure to "keep up with the Joneses." Most people in the village feel that the abandonment of their tribal heritage, including their language and the understanding of tribal traditions by their children, is too high a price to pay. A few families have experienced this kind of loss already, and the children are the ones most aware of it.

But there are fewer reasons to move, as all the material comforts of life are now available at the pueblo: electricity, running water, telephones, a community sewage system, and trash pickup. Butane gas tanks appear in yards beside *hornos*, or outdoor beehive ovens; television antennas rise above dirt roofs to vie for attention with drying strings of red chili and stacked white and blue corn. Pickup trucks, a car, or both, are parked outside most homes. Orderly rows of H.U.D. homes, built in the 1960s, have been naturalized by the addition of Pueblo Indian outdoor ovens and strings of chili hanging from eaves. The old Pueblo habit of taking from the invader that which is useful and combining it with that which is meaningful from the native culture still continues, from the time of the first Spanish contact, centuries ago. And thanks to government funds and construction projects, there is now a large community center, housing the local government and a myriad of programs: the village library, the health clinic, and an all-purpose hall for recreation and large meetings both for the young and the old.

Despite all the sophistication, there is still some fear that someone like Elsie Clews Parson may come to stay in the village again. Parsons came to Jemez in the early 1920s and enjoyed the usual Pueblo Indian hospitality; always friendly and eager to please, the people were unaware that the anthropologist was collecting secret religious data. In 1925, a few years after she left the pueblo, *The Pueblo of Jemez* was published by Yale University Press. Jemez people found that many secrets of their religion had been wrung out of them, to appear in public without their permission. On a more material level, because they believed in the good will, the trust, and the legality of the white man's documents and court systems, the Jemez people realize today that they have lost thousands of acres of land, surrounding Jemez and Pecos, and of course millions of dollars in unearned income from the loss of natural resources. One of the most painful experiences is to lose your land in court because of technicalities and the skill of a clever lawyer, and to face the added insult of having to buy the same land back a few years later. This has happened! And matters are not improved by the reluctance of non-Indian business people to hire Indian workers, who are often less well trained and aggressive than the recent immigrants from other parts of the country.

An example of the fear of non-Indians on Indian land is the 7,266-acre Suquamish Reservation, in Washington state, where 63 percent of the reservation was owned in fee simple by 2,928 non-Indians, compared to 37 percent ownership by the approximately fifty Suquamish Indians. To make the story short, an arrest by tribal authorities of two non-Indian residents eventually reached the Supreme Court (Case No. 76-5729), which ruled on March 6, 1978, that Indian tribal courts do not have criminal jurisdiction to try or to punish non-Indians.

Like its eastern Keresan neighbors, Jemez is very traditional, and continues to observe a full, yearly religious calendar—the tribe has retained most of its culture, including the various religious societies and organizations. Most men and women still belong to different societies. Having Indian blood or claiming Indian ancestry does not make one an Indian, according to Pueblo values; one has to be an active participant in Indian life. There are few traditionally raised Indian youngsters who are searching for an identity today.

The pueblo is known throughout Indian country for its many feast days. Unlike non-Pueblo Indians, who celebrate American holidays such as July 4 with rodeos, followed by round and war dances, the Pueblos celebrate Christian feast days, designated by the Spanish padres of the past. Thus, Jemez begins with the Christmas celebration, which is followed by the New Year's Day celebration, and culminates in the Feast of the Three Kings, on January 6. This is also the day on which the authority of newly selected officials is confirmed, and the canes of authority blessed in the pueblo church. In the beginning the higher officials went on to Santa Fe on this date, to be received and confirmed by the Spanish governor. January 6 also marks the last day of feasting during the winter holiday season.

Prior to the Christmas season, a family volunteers (or is asked to volunteer by the governor) to host the Christ Child, and they represent Joseph and Mary in the manger. The household and their relatives then host the village and people from the outside. Besides much money spent for groceries and many other expenses, the challenge of entertaining thousands of people calls for a tremendous reserve of patience and a sense of cooperation and personal sacrifice. This combination of trying circumstances on any feast day is accepted patiently as a sacrifice to the saint being honored that day, especially by the Pueblo women, since they are the ones who stay at home and feed guests. Often they do not even get to see the dances of the day, so many people come to their homes to eat. Almost nowhere else in the United States is this custom of serving free meals to large numbers of guests observed.

Among the Pueblos this tradition is a reciprocal one. Since the annual feast days are scattered throughout the year, and different pueblos celebrate different ones, each has a chance to visit the others as guests, to be fed, and on occasion, given a place to sleep, also; this was more common before modern transportation. Neighboring Spanish people had a similar tradition of visiting with Pueblo Indian friends on feast days.

Navajos and Jicarilla Apache friends would bring mutton or venison, which the Jemez women would then cook in the traditional way. The friends who had brought the meat were welcome to share at the table. Since the 1960s, non-Indians have discovered the Indian table. Hippies nearly ruined it for the whites during their heyday; but more considerate white friends have begun to visit Indian homes on feast days, also. From these visitors hosts have received fruit, cakes, and cookies to add to the feast.

During the entire Christmas season the figure of the Christ Child remains at the host family's home in a specially decorated area, usually in the living room—it represents the stable in Bethlehem. An animal dance is generally held to coincide with the birth of Christ, and all game animals known and beneficial to the people are represented.

During my childhood, the Jemez people used to roast corn in the fireplace, and while that was going on, other members of the family would draw pictures of wild game animals and birds, as well as farm crops, on the wall next to the fireplace. All this was in hopes that the birth of Christ would also result in the birth of the animals and plants being drawn on the wall.

Skeptics may snicker that this is all superstition and ancient out-moded beliefs. However, the world is full of strange coincidences that are hard to explain sometimes. For example, as an eleven-year old in 1935, I drew a buffalo on the wall next to my brother's corn, wheat, and melons. Naturally nothing was said until sometime that summer (it may have been on July 4) an event took place at the Santa Fe Indian School campus where my father, as lieutenant governor of the village, was among the group representing Jemez. On that particular day all the pueblos represented there were given a butchered buffalo to take home and distribute to the tribe. Lo and behold, the huge, hulking carcass of a young buffalo was placed in front of the fireplace just below my drawing.

Although the roasting of corn and drawing on the walls have been replaced by the exchange of gifts and watching television, pine logs, chopped into smaller pieces, are still stacked in square piles in front of each home. Soon bonfires are lit throughout the village; the children frolic merrily around them. These bonfires are to attract the newborn Infant Jesus.

When the last embers have died out, the children return to their homes to await midnight mass. In my youth, not much time was devoted to Santa Claus, except at the school, where he was drawn in colored chalk on the blackboard; and after a school play he would enter with stockings full of candy, an apple, and an orange for each child.

Following midnight mass many people follow the newborn Infant in a procession to the home of the hosts; there the activities of the exciting night culminate in a huge, traditional dinner. After dinner many people go home to sleep for a few hours. But sleep often does not come easily, as they think of the hours just passed and the new excitement scheduled to take place just before sunrise. Even as the first rays of daylight appear in the east, many children are awake, anxiously waiting for the animal dancers to appear on the hilly skyline to the east and southeast. Before the animals appear, clouds of smoke are visible. Soon the deer and mountain sheep emerge, to the east, nearest the village, and then the buffalos make their appearance, in the hills just south of them. Meanwhile, further south, the antelopes are teasing the children by appearing and disappearing one by one, before they all line up in a row on the hilltop. By the time the sun leaves the eastern horizon, the animals have arrived in the village, to gather in front of the drummers, who are singing welcoming songs. The welcoming is repeated by the Pumpkin and Turquoise moieties. By this time many people are there to welcome the animals, which are then paraded to the plaza, where they will dance all day. As in all dances, the moieties take turns performing for the people.

Since January 6 is the last festival day of the Christmas season, there is much sincere and emotional participation by the tribe. Figuratively speaking, they "let their hair down," and it is customary for women to get up from their seats and perform on the spot, "to assist the dancers," as they say. Again an animal dance is performed, but much larger than the one on Christmas, representing buffalo, deer, antelope, mountain sheep, eagle, hawk, and turkey (the elk has been discontinued because the antlers were too heavy; only the dedicated oldtimers persevered in wearing them).

The next festival is the Easter Sunday observance of the traditional corn dance by members of both moieties, or kivas. This dance is preceded by visits to aunts and clan aunts, and eating at their food-laden tables. Children are told that if they do not visit at least one aunt, they will turn into frogs.

In the period between festivals the community turns to the mundane tasks of everyday living involved in tending the farms or commuting to work in the nearby towns; and soon the mid-summer festivals arrive.

The saints' days of June 24 (St. John), June 29 (St. Peter and St. Paul), and July 25 (St. James), are celebrated not by dancing but by rooster pulls and races around the village on horseback, with a rooster decorated with ribbons as the prize offered for the fastest and cleverest horseman; these observances are of Spanish origin. On June 24, for example, any tribal members whose names may be Juan, John, Juana, Juanita, and Joan, are hosts to the people, inviting them to eat at their homes. The men donate the rooster for the games on the plaza; after it is buried in the ground the horsemen gallop by, reaching down to grab it by the head and pull it out, if they can. Once a rider is successful in pulling the rooster out of the ground, he has a choice of galloping out of the plaza to challenge the speed of the other riders' horses, or he may select to remain in the plaza and challenge the others to a rooster pull, or fight.

While these festivals are mainly for Jemez people and occasional visitors from other tribes, or even tourists, the Pecos feast, on August 2, is a major event in which all the community is involved. Jemez people plan and prepare for weeks to receive the thousands of visitors who come to see the corn dance, the "Pecos bull," and to eat. This celebration is in honor of Our Lady of Percingula.

The back-breaking harvest season which follows is soon enlivened by preparations for yet another feast day—that of the patron saint of Jemez Pueblo, San Diego, on November 12. This feast is the grandest of all in the year. Whereas until the 1960s both kiva groups were able to dance the finale in one plaza, since the 1970s, with the growth of the Jemez population, there have been so many participants in the corn dance that a single kiva group fills the three-hundred-yard-long dance plaza.

Outside the plaza there are cars, pickups, vans, and buses jammed side by side throughout the village. The north and south plazas are filled by traders—Navajos selling rugs and jewelry, Santo Domingos selling turquoise nuggets and heishi, other Pueblo people selling pottery, Spanish villagers and other whites selling apples, chili, pumpkins, and other farm produce. Meanwhile, in nearby lots carnival types are wooing, with amusement rides, the younger children who, for the time being, are unable to find a spot in the long row of corn dancers.

A month later another dance is performed by the tribe, in honor of Our Lady of Guadalupe; hosts on this day are all those named Lupe, Lupita, and Guadalupe. They invite guests to their homes to eat, as on the mid-summer feast days. Prior to World War II, this day was not observed at Jemez, for Our Lady of Guadalupe is the patron saint of the neighboring Spanish community of Cañon, six miles to the north of Jemez. But with more Anglos moving to Cañon, the Spanish tradition was waning; as discussed below the *matachina* dance at Jemez has become associated with this feast day.

Jemez people say the matachina dance was performed on different occasions in the past, usually on New Year's Day; and it was the Spanish version, accompanied by a fiddle and a guitar, as danced by the Turquoise group. But sometime in the early 1900s two brothers from the Pumpkin group, Juan Baptisto Cajero and Santiago San Juan, saw the Indian version, danced to a drum beat and Indian songs at Santo Domingo, and they liked it. The two men introduced this version to Jemez, and the Pumpkin group has been performing this lively dance ever since, alternating with the other kiva group. Although this version was introduced to Jemez from another pueblo, the matachina is now danced by Jemez people in their own high-stepping, spirited style. Tony F. Garcia, of San Juan Pueblo, summed it up when he made the comment that, "Spanish people, my pueblo, as well as other pueblos perform this dance, but once you have seen the Jemez version, the others are nothing and hardly compare."

Following World War II the matachina has been danced on December 12 at Jemez. Because it is one of the most graceful, colorful, and beautiful dances, so that Jemez people, as well as outsiders, began to demand it, Jemez was almost coerced to perform this beautifully choreographed drama, called matachina at Jemez and matachine by the Spanish.

The matachina is not of Pueblo Indian, nor of American origin; and while the Spaniards performed this dance initially at San Gabriel, soon after they arrived to establish their capital there, the dance may not be Spanish, either. According to Kurath (1957), the name of the dance probably comes from the Arabic *mudawajjihin*, meaning "those who put on a face," or "those who face each other." Through the Middle Ages the dance was performed in Spain, where it was called *matachini*, and *matacinio* in Italy, *mattachins* in France, and morris dance in England ("morris" = Moors'). The dancers were masked buffoons, in motley costumes with ribbons and bells, and made passes at each other with swords, dancing in pairs with low kick-steps.

Europe's hinterland evidently abounded in similar dance-dramas, sanctioned by the church as *moriscas*, or unsanctioned, under many local names. There were the *mouriscas* and *bugios* of Portugal, *el cossiers* of Mallorca, the *perchtentong* of the Austrian Alps, the *calusar*, or horse-play of Rumania, and finally the Thracian *kalogheroi*.

The Spaniards in the New World no doubt used the dance-drama as a moralizing influence, by presenting as it does "El Toro," a young bull, to represent evil, and "Malinche," a young girl dressed in white, to represent purity, virginity, innocence, and any other opposition to evil. At the end of the dance, the bull is usually killed. The original symbolism may have been forgotten or changed, but the choreographic features, the paraphernalia, the waving of wands, and the symbolic victory over evil and paganism, remain as the dance is performed to Our Lady of Guadalupe for supernatural blessings connected with Catholic rites.

Of course, alongside the Christian calendar, there remain the traditional Indian ceremonial dates, which are not open to the general public—sometimes not even to non-Pueblo Indians, who do not understand the religion of the Rio Grande people. Because of their private nature, missionaries and government authorities have suspected these ceremonials of being paganistic orgies. However, since the 1950s one can hardly find room to stand at the Shalako ceremony at Zuni, or the snake dance in the Hopi country, which are open to outsiders. So the non-Indian has learned belatedly that Indian ceremonials are not blatant orgies, but well-organized, sacred dramas, dedicated to the Creator in thanksgiving, or pleading for more blessings.

The New and the Old—Names, Food, Tools, and the People

Among the Pueblo Indians certain surnames are peculiar to a given pueblo. Two distinctively Jemez surnames, Chinana and Yepa, have been dealt with in other chapters; other Jemez surnames are Cajero, Casiquito, Celo, Colaque, Fragua, Gachupin, Loretto, Panana, Sandia, Sando, Shendo, Tosa, and Waquiu. Except for Sando, Shendo, and Waquiu, these surnames all appear to be of Spanish origin. Other old Jemez names of Spanish origin are Armijo, Chavez, Romero, Toledo, and Vigil.

As far as we can tell, from what we have been told, the name Sando comes from an ancestor whose Jemez name was Sai-th'r ("game animal"); Sando was the closest the Spanish pronunciation could come. It has often been asked if Sandoval was shortened to Sando, but that was evidently not the case. It was first noted in the census of 1830, as reported in Chavez (1957). Chavez also mentions other Jemez surnames of today, such as Baca, Chaves (Chavez), Madalena, Vigil, Selo (Celo), Xendo (Shendo), and Chihuihui (Chewiwi).

Shendo is of unknown origin, but very likely derives from one of the words for welcome, *deh shendo*. Waquiu might be from the Jemez for "one planted row"; recently the younger generation has adopted the spelling "Waquie," originally a newspaper misprint.

Sandia at Jemez comes from the grandfather of the current generation. His Indian name was Sandaya (from the Spanish Sandia). His surname had been Gallegos. Panana became a Jemez surname sometime in the early 1940s; prior to that time the patriarch, Cristino Panana, was surnamed Casiquito.

No doubt there have been many other Jemez surnames that are no longer in use. Two recent examples are Lado and Shamon. There is, also, only one person remaining with the surname of San Juan.

Pecos Pueblo immigrants brought a number of surnames to Jemez, but it appears that many took on the surname of Pecos. Today Toya and Pecos are the only surnames at Jemez that signify Pecos ancestry, although most people at Jemez have equal amounts of Pecos blood. Some surnames that came from Pecos are Cota (also spelled Kota), Vigil, and Armenta.

In the 1970s and 1980s at Jemez surnames are important in the community ditch work, as most groups participating are identifiable by their surnames. When the village officials for the year are selected, the groups responsible for the ditch work are kept in mind so that not too many officials are taken from any one group, since at the ditch work the officials form one group, in addition to the groups identified by surnames.

Since the 1950s many more surnames have appeared on the Jemez tribal rolls, as Jemez girls have married outside the tribe and then returned with children and different surnames.

The food served at Jemez, especially on feast days, has changed also; some foods have been added and a few dropped. The old people explain that feast-day food was very simple at the beginning of the twentieth century; but it was also more exciting at that time.

After the Depression, the staple continued to be soups and stews with chile. There was chile-mutton soup, thick red chile soup, and green chile soup. To these were added fried chicken, roast mutton ribs, and other meats, such as pork and venison, served with white and blue-corn paper-bread as well as chilied paper bread, outdoor oven bread, fried bread, and sweet bread. Also served were homemade cakes, cookies, fruit pies, bread pudding, rice pudding, canned desserts, and fruit in season.

Through the years turkey, ham, meatloaf, salads, and a variety of gelatin desserts have been added. The old standby, coffee, has been joined by *Kool-ade* and canned pop. Missing today are rice pudding and sweet bread, both introduced by the Spanish in colonial times.

The Indian feast-day table is amply stocked today, and usually there is hardly room to place one's plate and cup. But behind this opulent table is the danger of excessive expenditure on food for the feast day. Naturally, the expenditure results in depleted funds with which to meet the other obligations faced by the people these days—obligations such as bills for domestic water, gas, electricity, new H.U.D. homes, plus those owed merchants at Jemez or in cities and towns nearby. The food prepared is offered to the saint to whom the day is dedicated, but the modern business world does not understand ancient traditions where money is concerned. This is not an isolated Jemez problem, however—all the other eighteen pueblos find themselves in the same situation.

Coming from the Pueblo Indian culture, it is difficult to appreciate American technology. For many years Pueblo Indian men relied on the hoe and shovel to work their fields and gardens. Not to own a hoe was tantamount to being only half a man. The hoe blade was made from a bent shovel, while the handle was selected from scrub oak in the hills; shovels were purchased at the trading post or in town. These two tools are still available today, but are not used much, since tractors and cultivators are used for growing corn, and rototillers are also used in the garden.

Most of the cooking ware used by the women was made by Pueblo potters, although knives, ladles, and large spoons came from town. Most other items were also homemade, such as baskets and pots for storage containers.

There was a time when there were only two sewing machines at Jemez; they were owned by Mrs. Jose Manuel Yepa and Mrs. Jose Antonio Pecos. The people would take their material to these homes to be made into dresses, shirts, and whatever else was needed. You can imagine what it was like just before feast days, with all the material stacked at the seamstresses' homes. Hardly any clothes were purchased at the store, since the people all wore homemade, Indian-style clothes and moccasins.

When television made its appearance at Jemez following World War

II, again there were but two or three sets at first. Interested people would take along a few ears of corn to pay for an evening in front of these wonders. Now every home has a set, in addition to many other appliances. The younger generation would have a hard time even thinking of doing without the conveniences that they now take for granted; but the oldtimers not only worked hard, they may have lived longer, also. A familiar remark by today's senior citizens is that in their younger days there were many more aged people in the community.

Other American Indian groups are better known by the dominant society in the United States and throughout the world than are the Pueblos. This is probably because the dramatic, early conflicts known as "the Indian wars" are obvious focuses of attention. The Jemez people, as we have seen, have done their fighting in an undramatic fashion, mostly in the American courts. Nowadays, however, the little-known Pueblos, including the Jemez, are beginning to attract attention by their tenacity in maintaining their tribal culture.

Their history has done a great deal to shape the character of the Jemez people. Though they were unprepared to face the ways of the white men of the past, especially in the courts, now the people can look forward to improved understanding and justice, since many of their sons and daughters have had a well-rounded white-man's education. And if the hardships of the past do indeed produce "inner strength," then the Jemez people have acquired a fair amount of that quality. By knowing their history, the Jemez people can use that strength to make the future whatever they want.

Appendix I

Chronological List of Jemez Leaders
(Beginning with 1926, the second name listed is the first lieutenant governor and the third name is the second lieutenant governor)

1598	Pe-stiassa	1919	Jose Reyes Chihuihui
1681	Francisco, of the Sun Clan		San Juanito Colaque, 1st Lt.
1696	Luis Cunixu		Victoriano Yepa, 2nd Lt.
1706	Luis Cunitzu		Jose Mora Toledo, Sheriff
1766	Cristóbal Chiguigui		Jose Reyes Loretto, War Capt.
1849	Franscico Hosta		Jose Reyes Gachupin, Lt. W.C.
1850	Blanco Nostez		Santiago Armijo, Fiscale
1878	Juan Lucero		Juan Domingo Chinana, Lt. Fis.
1881	Juan Pedro Culaca (Colaque?)		Jack Toya, Interpreter
1888	Agustin Pecos	1920	Francisco Madalena
1893	Jose Reyes Yepo	1922	Jose Felipe Yepa
1899	Jose Romero	1923	Francisco Madalena
1911	Juan Lopez Chinana	1924	George Toledo
1918	Jose Manuel Yepa	1925	Hilario Baca

1926	Daniel Mora	Manuel Chiwiwi, Fiscale
	Lucas Yepa	Jose Armijo, Lt. Fis.
	Jose Mora Toledo	Jose Antonio Toya, War
1927	Daniel Mora	Capt.
1928	Jose Fragua	Joe G. Bacca, Lt. W.C.
	San Juanito Loretto	1941 Manuel Yepa
	Manuel Yepa	Jack Toya
1929	Jose Reyes Loretto	Juanito Baca
	Jose Reyes Lado	1942 Manuel Yepa
	Emilio Toya	Florencio Armijo
1930	Felipe Yepa	Jose A. Sando
	Jose Guadalupe Pecos	1943 Alcario Gachupin
	Florencio Armijo	Patricio Toya
1931	George Toledo	Manuel Fragua
	Santiago Loretto	1944 Juanito Chinana
	Jose Reyes Toya	Christino Panana
1932	Daniel Mora	Ambrosio Toya
	Jose Manuel Toya	1945 Juan Luis Pecos
	Salvadore Fragua	Manuel Sandia
1933	San Juanito Loretto	Augustine Sando
	Juan E. Sando, Sr.	1946 Manuel Chewiwi
	Juan Luis Pecos	Juanico Cajero
1934	Avelino Casiquito	Vivian Loretto
	Jose Manuel Toya	1947 Juanito Chinana
	Francisco Fragua	Jose Manuel Loretto
1935	Jose Fragua	Rosendo Gachupin
	Juanito Sando	1948 Guadalupe Fragua
	Patricio Toya	Jose A. Sando
1936	Transito Vigil	Jose Lucero
	Alcario Gachupin	1949 Manuel Yepa
	San Juanito Toledo	Patricio Toya
1937	Jose Manuel Toya	Antonio Sando
	Juanito Chinana	1950 Transito Vigil
	Juan Pedro Colaque	Juanico Cajero
1938	Manuel Yepa	Juan R. Colaque
	Juan Luis Pecos	1951 Juanito Chinana
	Guadalupe Fragua	Joe Guadalupe Baca
1939	Juan E. Sando, Sr.	Abel Sando
	Jose Manuel Toya	1952 Manuel Chewiwi
	Benito Yepa	Manuel Sandia
1940	George Toledo	Joe F. Toledo
	San Juanito Shendo	1953 Juan Luis Pecos
	Diego Pecos	Juanico Cajero
	Augustine Sando, Sheriff	Rosendo Gachupin

1954 Patricio Toya
Jose Guadalupe Baca
Juan E. Sando, Jr.

1955 Florencio Armijo
Abel Sando
Jose Rey Panana

1956 Manuel Sandia
Augustine Sando
Max Shendo

1957 Juan Luis Pecos
Maximo Chinana
Frank E. Fragua

1958 Antonio Sando
Jose G. Loretto
Ray San Juan

1959 Guadalupe Fragua
Juan I. Toledo
Pablo Gachupin

1960 Jose Manuel Toya
Abel Sando
Cristobal Loretto

1961 Antonio Sando
Joe Guadalupe Baca
Frank Toledo

1962 Jack Toya
Augustine Sando
Felix Yepa

1963 Juanico Cajero
Manuel Fragua
Henry Mora

1964 Antonio Sando
George Yepa
Ray San Juan
Frank E. Fragua, Fiscale
Michael Toledo, Lt. Fis.
Guadalupe Toya, Sheriff
Jack Toya, Treasurer

1965 Abel Sando
Jose G. Loretto
Ramon Fragua
Joe R. Gachupin, Fiscale
Guadalupe Chosa, Lt. Fis.
Joe G. Baca, War Captain

Louis Casiquito, Lt. W.C.
Joe V. Cajero, Sheriff

1966 Juan Luis Pecos
Rosendo Gachupin
Isidore Chinana

1967 Augustine Sando
Francisco Loretto
Guadalupe Toya

1968 Jose L. Loretto
George Yepa
Arthur Sandia
Jose A. Sando, War Captain
Pablo Gachupin, Lt. W.C.
Michael Toledo, Fiscale
Juan B. Toya, Lt. Fis.
Napoleon Loretto, Sheriff

1969 Abel Sando
Rosendo Gachupin
Celestino Romero

1970 Jose G. Baca
Joe F. Toledo
Julian Tafoya
Juan E. Sando, Jr., War Captain
Henry Mora, Lt. W.C.
Lawrence Chinana, Fiscale
Felix Waquiu, Lt. Fis.
Casimiro Toya, Sheriff
Joe L. Pecos, Treasurer

1971 Jose A. Sando
Jose Mora
Ciriaco Toya

1972 Patricio Toya
Manuel Fragua
Joe L. Pecos

1973 Abel Sando
Henry Mora
David Yepa
Napoleon Loretto, Fiscale
Joe R. Madalena, Lt. Fis.
Frank I. Sando, War Captain
Juan D. Toya, Lt. W.C.

1974   Francisco Loretto
        Joe L. Pecos
        Casimiro Toya
        Celestino Romero, Sheriff
        Joe G. Gachupin, Fiscale
        Felipe Chinana, Lt. Fis.
        Juan E. Sando, Jr., War
            Captain
        Felix Waquiu, Lt. W.C.

1975   Jose A. Sando
        Frank Toledo
        Juan Rey Yepa
        Albert Fragua, Sheriff
        Joe V. Loretto, Fiscale
        Clemente Fragua, Lt. Fis.
        Pablo Gachupin, War
            Captain
        Pete Toya, Lt. W.C.

1976   Henry Mora
        Candido Armijo
        Arthur Sandia
        Tony Romero, Sheriff
        Lazardo Chinana, Fiscale
        Joe R. Madalena, Lt. Fis.
        Louis Casiquito, War
            Captain
        Robert Fragua, Lt. W.C.

1977   Rosendo Gachupin
        Joe V. Cajero
        Paul S. Chinana
        Leonard Loretto, Sheriff
        Felipe Waquiu, Jr., War
            Captain
        Ernest Shendo, Lt. W.C.
        Patrick "Paddy" Toya,
            Fiscale
        Albert Fragua, Lt. Fis.

1978   Louis Casiquito
        Frankie Fragua
        Celestino Romero
        Joe R. Madalena, Fiscale
        James Toya, Lt. Fis.
        Pete Toya, War Captain
        Juan Rey Madalena, Lt.
            W.C.

1979   Frank Loretto—
            impeached April 19,
            replaced by
                Henry Mora
        Juan Rey Yepa
        Paul Toya
        Alonzo Yepa, Sheriff
        Julian Tafoya, Fiscale
        Martin Toya, Lt. Fis.
        Frank I. Sando, War
            Captain
        Lazardo Chinana, Lt.
            W.C.

1980   Jose A. Sando—
            impeached May 14,
            replaced by
                Frank Loretto
        Manuel T. Fragua
        James Roger Madalena
        John D. Yepa, Sheriff
        Napoleon Loretto, Fiscale
        John Baca, Lt. Fis.
        Jose Armijo, War Captain
        Jose Romero Toledo, Lt.
            W.C.

1981   Rosendo Gachupin
        Manuel T. Fragua
        Harold Sando
        Freddie Toya, Sheriff
        Casimiro Toya, Fiscale
        Miguel (Mike) Mora, Lt.
            Fis.
        Candido Armijo, War
            Captain
        James Toya, Lt. W.C.

1982   Joe R. Madalena
        Arthur Sandia
        Paul Tosa
        Jerry Fragua, Sheriff
        Albert Fragua, Fis.
        Patrick Waquiu, Lt. Fis.
        Ernest Shendo, War
            Capt.
        Randolph Padilla, Lt.
            W. C.

Appendix II

Jemez College Graduates and Their Schools

*Bacca, Joseph Ray	University of Albuquerque
Cajero, Eleanor Janice	University of Albuquerque
Cajero, Esther H.	College of Santa Fe
Cajero, Joe V.	N.M. Highlands University
	Master's, University of Minnesota
Casiquito, Sarah Yepa	N.M. Highlands University
Chinana, Samuel	University of Albuquerque
Chinana, Theresa Pecos	University of Albuquerque
Dodge, John	University of New Mexico
Dodge, Mary Loretta Toya	Eastern New Mexico University
Emerson, Frances June Toledo	University of New Mexico
Felipe, Barbara Armijo	Eastern New Mexico University
*Foster, Leonard, Jr.	N.M. Highlands University
*Fragua, Elizabeth	N.M. Highlands University
	Master's, University of California
Fragua, Laura J.	University of Albuquerque
Gachupin, Crecensia Panana	University of Albuquerque
Gachupin, Linda Toya	University of Albuquerque
*Gachupin, Raymond	Western New Mexico University

Levantonio, Eleanor Patricia Toya — Eastern New Mexico University
Loretto, Arlene — University of New Mexico
Loretto, Estella C. — Fort Lewis College
*Loretto, Raymond — New Mexico State University
Master's, Colorado State University

Lowden, Jacquelyn Renee — University of New Mexico
Madalena, James Roger — Eastern New Mexico University
Mitchell, Margie Lou Benally — Brigham Young University
Montoya, Lucy Fragua — University of New Mexico
Mora, Marie Sando — University of New Mexico
Narum, Gertrude Smith — Arizona State University
Panana, Eva Shamon — University of New Mexico
Park, Priscilla Fragua — College of Santa Fe
Sando, Alfred Alex — Eastern New Mexico University
Master's, New Mexico State University

Sando, Harold — Eastern New Mexico University
Sando, Joe Simon — Eastern New Mexico University
Master's, Vanderbilt University

Sando, Rueben — Fort Lewis College
Sando, T. Parker — Dartmouth College
Law degree, University of New Mexico

Shendo, Jennifer — Eastern New Mexico University
*Tang, Mary Toledo — University of New Mexico
Master's, University of New Mexico

Toledo, Allan Rey — University of California, Long Beach
Law degree, University of New Mexico

*Toledo, Cipriana Celo — N.M. Highlands University
Toledo, Jose Rey — University of New Mexico
Master's, University of California, Berkeley

Toledo, Jose Raphael — Kansas State University, Winfield
*Toledo, Rufina Yepa — University of New Mexico
Toledo, Wilma — University of New Mexico
Tosa, Paul — University of New Mexico
Toya, Christino — Eastern New Mexico University
Toya, Mary Ellen — University of New Mexico
Toya, Mary Sando — University of New Mexico
Toya, Maxine Gachupin — University of New Mexico
Toya, Michael S. — Fort Lewis College
Toya, Ronald — Westmont College, California
Toya, Stephania — Eastern New Mexico University
Vallo, Lawrence — University of Albuquerque
Vigil, Bernard Thomas — N.M. Highlands University
Master's, University of Southern California

Vigil, Felix	Maryland Institute College of Art
*Waquiu, Angelo Wayne	Western New Mexico University
Waquiu, William	Fort Lewis College
Yepa, Anthony	Eastern New Mexico University
*Yepa, David Ralph	New Mexico State University
Yepa, Harriet Louise	College of Santa Fe
Yepa, Ramona Toledo	New Mexico State University

*Currently working on graduate degree

Appendix III

Lease Agreement between Jemez and the Presbyterians

It is hereby agreed by and between the Pueblo of Jemez, represented by the Governor and Officers and Principales thereof, on the one part; and B. M. Thomas, U.S. Indian Agent, on the other part; that a certain piece of land situated on the north-east side of the Pueblo of Jemez, extending from the house now being built thereupon for mission and school purposes distances and directions herein described, viz.—To the north, seventy-five yards; to the east, thirty-five yards; to the south, seven yards; to the west, ten yards; be and hereby is devoted to school purposes for the benefit of said Pueblo so long as the parties building the house shall maintain a school upon said premises for the benefit of said Pueblo.

(Signed)

In testimony, thereof, We, the parties of both parts, hereby sign our names at the Pueblo of Jemez this twenty-eighth day of September, one thousand eight hundred and seventy-eight.

Juan Lucero, Governor	Jose Marcus Kolake, Act. Lt. Gov.
Jose Mora, 2nd Lt. Gov.	Miguel Waqui, Cacique
Jose Sauiquiu, Cacique	Jose Miguel Vigil, Principale
Armijo Sando, Principale	Victoriano Martin, Principale
Pedro Jose Chavez, Principale	Mariano Madelino, Principale
Mariano Kalake, Principale	Lorenzo Waquiu, Principale
Francisco Nasle, Principale	Juan Antonio Toya, Principale

Ben. M. Thomas U.S. Indian Agent

A True Copy. (Signed) Ben. M. Thomas

Appendix IV

(From the Spanish Archives of New Mexico, No. 1141)

XEMES, ZIA, and SANTA ANA, 1713.

Receipt of order by Alcalde. Tibursio Ortega, Alcalde. San Geronimo de Taos. Receipt of the same. Miguel de Sandoval Martinez, Alcalde.

In the year 1766 "In compliance with the directions of his excellency, Don Tomas Velez Cachupin, governor and captain-general" Bartolome Fernandez, chief alcalde and war-captain of the pueblos of the Queres, delivered possession to the pueblos of Xemes, Zia, and Santa Ana of a tract of land bounded "from north to south from the place Ventana to the stone ford of the Puerco river, the boundaries also of the citizens of the place San Fernando of Nuestra Senora de la Luz; and from east to west from the pueblo of Zia to the said Puerco river, the eastern edge, the whole valley of the Holy Ghost spring being embraced within the center and within the boundaries of this grant." At the time possession was given there were present the following Indian governors (caciques): Cristoval Naspona, Cristoval Chiquiqui, Pedro Chite, Sebastian, Lazaro, and Juan Antonio, and the war-captains Agustin, Tomas, Juan Domingo, and other Indian magistrates.

Appendix V

Comparison of Cultural Value Systems

Traditional Tribal Cultural Values	Middle Class, Urban Values
group, clan, or tribal emphasis	individual emphasis
present oriented	future oriented
time: always with us	time: use every minute
age	youth
cooperation	competition
harmony with nature	conquest of nature
giving, sharing	saving
pragmatic	theoretical
mythology	science
patience	impatience
mystical	skeptical
shame	guilt
permissiveness	social coercion
extended family and clan	immediate family
nonaggressive	aggressive
modest	over-confident
silence	noise
respect others' religion	convert others to own religion

religion: a way of life
beneficial, reasonable use of
    resources
equality
face-to-face government
low self-value
compact living, close contact
life: adult-centered
children participate in adult
    activities
life is hard and dangerous
children can only hope for much
    clothing and many toys

religion: a segment of life
avaricious, greedy use of
    resources
disparities of wealth
representative democracy
high self-importance
spacious living, privacy
life: child-centered
adults participate in children's
    activities
life is easy, safe, and bland
many toys and much clothing
    are accepted as normal

Appendix VI

Jemez Philosophy of Life and Learning

1. The first and most important element in the human constitution is the soul, or "inner persona." This persona is the means by which a person has life or a personality. Associated and paired with the inner persona is one's breath *('hing)*. This gives life to the heart.

2. The second is a pair of innate elements, the mind *(vae)* and the voice *(toon)*. The mind organizes thought and makes planning possible, while one's voice makes speech and exchange of communication possible.

3. The third and fourth elements in the constitution of a human being are the body *(kwaa)* and the heart *(pe'h)*. The body is divided into inner and outer organs.

4. A fifth set of elements is one's energy *(weh'ng)* and one's means of movement. Energy provides the everyday strength by which one works and lives.

Six Life-Sustaining Elements of the World

1. AIR—an essential element in the soul and the breath;

2. EARTH—provides food and other life-sustaining materials;
3. FIRE—provides heat for warmth and cooking;
4. SUN—provides light and heat, and makes growth possible;
5. WATER—together with the sun, makes growth possible;
6. WIND—circulates the air and provides contact for plant life.

Notes

(SPA = Southern Pueblos Agency, Bureau of Indian Affairs, Department of the Interior, Albuquerque, New Mexico)

Chapter 1

1. Such vicissitudes of life in the early years did not abate, as a new, more aggressive people entered the picture. These were the homesteaders who simply settled on Hemish lands, claiming them according to the rules of their government, based on a philosophy called Manifest Destiny.

Manifest Destiny arrived in the Jemez country disguised as the Stock Raising Homestead Act of 1916 (39 Stat. 862; U.S.C., Title 43, Secs. 291). At this time communications with the Bureau of Indian Affairs were still marginal, and contact with the state government probably did not exist; the first governor of the new state of New Mexico, William C. McDonald, was still in office. Had the Jemez people known of the Stock Raising Homestead Act, it is fairly certain that their tribal officials would have acted to safeguard their aboriginal land.

Chapter 2

1. According to Dr. Myra Ellen Jenkins, who for many years was in charge of the Archives Division of the State Records Center, the depository of the official Spanish Archives of New Mexico, much mystery surrounds the Cruzate Pueblo grant papers as no genuine grant documents have come to light.

She states that they were not in the official Spanish and Mexican archives when the United States occupied New Mexico in 1846. There is also the possibility that they were destroyed by early Territorial American officials as were many similar papers. Apparently officers of various pueblos possessed the Cruzate papers and after the office of surveyor general was created in 1854 pueblo leaders brought the papers to Santa Fe to be registered and approved by the surveyor general.

Regardless of any written grant documents, the Pueblo Indians were entitled to the lands occupied by them. This was recognized by the Spanish conquerors and set forth in cedulas of 1567 and 1687 and incorporated in *Recopilación de Leyes de Los Reynos de las Indias.*

Based on the surveyor general's report and as confirmed by Congress in 1858, the original Jemez Grant included only 17,315 acres, but they used a far greater amount of land.

Chapter 3

1. Translated document, Jemez Pueblo files, SPA.
2. The collected letters of James S. Calhoun can be found in Annie H. Abel, ed., *The Official Correspondence of James S. Calhoun . . .* , Washington, D.C., U.S. Government Printing Office, 1915.
3. From translations of Spanish originals in the *Recopilación*, made at various times, Jemez Pueblo files, SPA.
4. Unless otherwise stated, this and subsequent documents cited in this chapter can be found in the Jemez Pueblo files, SPA.
5. But it was not grassy for very long. Due to extensive timber cutting in the upper watershed of the Rio Puerco, by 1930 the river began to carry excessive silt in the spring floods. The land along the river had historically been able to support only 36,000 head of livestock, yet the area at the time carried at least 80,000 (Rittenhouse 1965). Because of these factors, by the late 1930s the land along the Rio Puerco had declined from a maximum vegetative area of 10,000 acres to only 3,000 acres, and the perennial grasses that fed livestock in the 1800s were replaced by clumpy ring grasses and snake weeds.

Chapter 4

1. The name New Mexico (Nuevo Méjico) first came into use in 1582, as a result of the Rodríguez-Chamuscado expedition (Bloom 1940).
2. In recent years Jemez has participated in a successor program to that of the AAA, called the Agriculture Stabilization and Conservation Program. But, as in the case of many other current programs, it appears to suffer from a lack of funds, and no one at Jemez has benefited from it recently.

Chapter 5

1. While talking about deterrents for raiders, I might add that a certain

emergency yell was reserved for warning of Navajo raids while the men were out in the fields; its use as a prank was subject to severe punishment. And because of the possibility of raids, all the women would go to the river for water only at a certain time of day. These women, with their *ollas* on their heads, were guarded by war captains. The road they used is still called P'aeh-pela-p'owng ("water-getting road"); it is west of the last street to the north of the plaza.

2. The other Jemez officials were Jose Reyes Chihuihui, first lieutenant governor; George Toledo, second lieutenant governor; and Principales Jose Romero, Jose Guadalupe Toledo, and Jose Reyes Toya. Affidavit in Irrigation, Jemez Pueblo, files at SPA.

3. These records (as well as other documents cited in this chapter) can be found in the Irrigation, Jemez Pueblo, files, SPA. The lowest minimum flow recorded was 4.2 cubic feet per second, on January 5, 1972, due to the river freezing. The lowest summer flow was 5.8 cubic feet per second, on July 11 and 12, 1951.

Chapter 6

1. Unless otherwise stated, all information in this chapter comes from the Indian Claims Commission Docket 137 documents, in the Jemez Pueblo files, SPA.

Chapter 7

1. Unless otherwise stated, this and all subsequent documentation in this chapter can be found in the Jemez Pueblo files, SPA.

2. Originally it was the intention of the promoters of the railway lines of which the Santa Fe Northwestern was a part, to extend the railway to Cuba, on to Farmington, and then up into Colorado and possibly Utah. By 1939 the Cuba extension was in receivership; however, that plan did not include the line through Jemez, but rather the line from San Ysidro to La Ventana and Cuba.

Chapter 8

1. These records are now in the Jemez Pueblo files, SPA.

2. *Provincial Chronicle* 38 (Spring 1966).

Chapter 9

1. For a detailed account of the history of Pecos see John L. Kessel, *Kiva, Cross and Crown*, Washington, D.C., National Park Service, 1979.

2. A record of this deed can be found in the Jemez Pueblo files, SPA.

3. Pueblo Indians had been considered citizens since they lived in settled communities, surrounded by their farm lands, had Catholic churches in their communities, and had a recognizable form of government.

4. Documentation concerning the following complex transactions can be found in the Jemez Pueblo files, SPA.

5. These two were my mother's grandparents. Juan was named Baa-taa. From many family stories we learned that he was exceptionally wealthy for his time; it is said that he had from three to five hundred horses and several thousand cattle. Many of the cattle were later taken to the mountains to the west of Jemez, where they became wild. Baa-taa later told the Jemez people that if they ever wanted meat, they should go hunt for some of his wild cattle. For helping him with his cattle, he gave land at Ser-la-be'gu to Hilario Baca and Jose Romero, land which their descendants farm today. Baa-taa also owned most of the land west of the present church, extending to the site of the original church, where his descendants, the Sabaques, Gachupins, and others now live. My grandmother Yepa was an heir to some of the cattle that Grandpa Jose Manuel Yepa managed—along with his many farms and the village grocery store.

Chapter 10

1. *Provincial Chronicle* 25 (1952).
2. Lovett to Rosenfelt, 10 March 1972, Jemez Pueblo files, SPA.

Chapter 11

1. Al broke Steve's record when he won the La Luz Trail Run in 1982. The race wasn't held in 1981. He also set a record of 3 hours, 26 minutes, and 17 seconds for the Pikes Peak Marathon in 1981, a race he won again in 1982. Al likewise made a good showing at the Boston Marathon in 1982 by finishing in the top ten.

2. Popay (or Popé) was one of the leaders of the 1680 Pueblo Revolt.

Bibliography

Abel, Annie H. 1915. *The Official Correspondence of James S. Calhoun While Indian Agent at Santa Fe and Superintendent of Indian Affairs in New Mexico.* Washington, D.C.: U.S. Government Printing Office.

Adams, Eleanor B., and Fray Angelico Chavez, eds. 1976 (first pub. 1956). *The Missions of New Mexico 1776: A Description by Fray Francisco Atanacio Dominguez with Other Contemporary Documents.* Albuquerque: University of New Mexico Press.

Bandelier, Adolph F.A. 1890–92. *Final Report of Investigations Among the Indians of the Southwestern United States, Carried on Mainly in the Years from 1880 to 1885.* 2 vols. (Papers of the Archaeological Institute of America, American Series, 3 and 4). Cambridge, Mass.: AIA.

Bloom, Lansing B. 1931. "A Campaign Against the Moqui Pueblos by Governor Phelix Martinez, 1716." *New Mexico Historical Review* 6(2).

Bloom, Lansing B. 1938. "Bourke in the Southwest." *New Mexico Historical Review* 13(2).

Bloom, Lansing B. 1940. "Who Discovered New Mexico?" *New Mexico Historical Review* 15(2).

Bloom, Lansing B., and Lunn B. Mitchell. 1938. "The Chapter Elections in 1672." *New Mexico Historical Review* 13(1).

Brayer, Herbert O. 1938. "Pueblo Indian Land Grants of the 'Rio Abajo.'" *University of New Mexico Bulletin* 1938.

Chavez, Fray Angelico. 1957. *Archives of the Archdiocese of Santa Fe, 1678–1900.* Washington, D.C.: Academy of American Franciscan History.

Chavez, Fray Angelico. 1967. "Pohe-Yemo's Representatives and the Pueblo Revolt of 1680." *New Mexico Historical Review* 42(2):85–126.

Chavez, Fray Angelico. 1971. "The Carpenter Pueblo." *New Mexico Magazine* 49(Sept.-Oct.).

Cohen, Felix S. 1942. *Handbook of Federal Indian Law.* Washington, D.C.: U.S. Department of the Interior.

Cutter, Donald C. 1978. "The Legacy of the Treaty of Guadalupe Hidalgo." *New Mexico Historical Review* 53(4).

Driver, Harold E. 1969. *Indians of North America.* 2nd ed. Chicago: University of Chicago Press.

Engstrand, Iris Wilson. 1978. "Land Grant Problems in the Southwest: The Spanish and Mexican Heritage." *New Mexico Historial Review* 53(4).

Espinosa, J. Manuel. 1942. *Crusaders of the Rio Grande: The Story of Don Diego de Vargas and the Reconquest and Refounding of New Mexico.* Chicago: Institute of Jesuit History.

Fell, Barry. 1976. *America, B.C.: Ancient Settlers in the New World.* New York: Quadrangle.

Ford, Richard I., Albert H. Schroeder, and Steward L. Peckham. 1972. "Three Perspectives on Puebloan History." In *New Perspectives on the Pueblos,* edited by Alfonso Ortiz, pp. 19–39. Albuquerque: University of New Mexico Press.

Foreman, Grant. 1934. *The Five Civilized Tribes.* Norman: University of Oklahoma Press.

Goodman, Jeffrey. 1981. *American Genesis.* New York: Summit Books.

Hallenbeck, Cleve. 1950. *Land of the Conquistadores.* Caldwell, Idaho: Coxton Printers.

Hayes, Alden C. 1974. *The Four Churches of Pecos.* Albuquerque: University of New Mexico Press.

Hewitt, Edgar L., and Adolph F.A. Bandelier. 1937. *Indians of the Rio Grande Valley.* Albuquerque: University of New Mexico Press.

Heyerdahl, Thor. 1978. "Sails in the Wake of Sumerian Voyagers." *National Geographic* 154(6).

John, Elizabeth A.H. 1975. *Storms Brewed in Other Men's Worlds.* College Station: Texas A and M University Press.

Jones, Oakah L. 1966. *Pueblo Warriors and the Spanish Conquest.* Norman: University of Oklahoma Press.

Kappler, Charles Joseph. 1904–27. *Indian Affairs: Laws and Treaties.* 4 vols. Washington, D.C.: U.S. Government Printing Office.

Kessel, John L. 1979. *Kiva, Cross and Crown.* Washington, D.C.: National Park Service.

Knowlton, Clark S. 1967. "Land Grant Problems Among the State's Spanish-Americans." *New Mexico Business* (June).

Kubicek, Earl C. 1968. "The Cane That Lincoln Gave." *Mankind* 1(10).

Kurath, Gertrude P. 1957. "The Origin of the Pueblo Indian Matachines." *El Palacio* 64(9–10).

Morgan, Lewis H. 1877. *Ancient Society.* Chicago: Charles H. Kerr and Co.

Myrick, David F. 1970. *New Mexico's Railroads: An Historical Survey*. Golden: Colorado Railroad Museum.

Parsons, Elsie Clews. 1925. *The Pueblo of Jemez*. (Papers of the Phillips Academy Southwestern Expedition, 3). New Haven: Yale University Press.

Philp, Kenneth R. 1977. *John Collier's Crusade for Indian Reform, 1920–1954*. Tucson: University of Arizona Press.

Poore, Henry R. 1894. "Report on Indians Taxed and Indians Not Taxed in the United States: Conditions of Sixteen New Mexico Pueblos, 1890." Washington, D.C.: Department of the Interior.

Reagan, Albert B. 1914. *Don Diego, or the Pueblo Indian Uprising of 1680*. New York: Alice Harriman Co.

Rittenhouse, Jack D. 1965. *Cabezon: A New Mexico Ghost Town*. Santa Fe: Stagecoach Press.

Sanchez, George I. 1940. *Forgotten People*. Albuquerque: University of New Mexico Press.

Sando, Joe S. 1976. *The Pueblo Indians*. San Francisco: Indian Historian Press.

Scholes, France V. 1930. "The Supply Service of New Mexico Missions in the Seventeenth Century." *New Mexico Historical Review* 5(1,2,4).

Scholes, France V. 1936–37. "Church and State in New Mexico, 1610–50." *New Mexico Historical Review* 11(1–4), 12(1).

Scholes, France V. 1937–41. "Troubled Times in New Mexico, 1659–70." *New Mexico Historical Review* 12(2,4), 13(1), 15(3,4), 16(1,2).

Scholes, France V. 1938. "Notes on the Jemez Missions in the 17th Century." *El Palacio* 44(1–2):61–102.

Simpson, James Hervey. 1964. *Navajo Expedition: Journal of a Military Reconnaissance from Santa Fe, New Mexico, to the Navajo Country Made in 1849*. Edited by Frank McNitt. Norman: University of Oklahoma Press.

Szasz, Margaret. 1974. *Education and the American Indian*. Albuquerque: University of New Mexico Press.

U.S. Office of Education. 1971. "Office of Education Expenditures in Indian Education." Washington, D.C.: U.S. Office of Education.

Wall, Leon, and William Morgan. 1958. *Navajo-English Dictionary*. Phoenix: U.S. Department of the Interior.

Zarate-Salmerón, Fray Gerónimo de. 1966. *Relaciones*. Trans. by Alicia Ronstadt Milich. Albuquerque: Horn and Wallace Publishers.

Index